Donnchadh Mac Gabhann was raised in a rural part of the northern borderlands of Ireland. He received a Gaelic-speaking education and had an early interest in language, reading, and writing. During his formative years, he was fascinated by the differing patterns of behaviour and belief he observed in people according to their circumstances and dispositions. This interest led him to study history and political science at Trinity College Dublin and has subsequently led to his current education at Uppsala University where he is specialising in Holocaust and Genocide Studies to obtain a greater insight into the nature of humanity.

For all those who inspired me to gaze long and deep into the darkest and most forbidden corners of the human mind.

Donnchadh Mac Gabhann

THE LONG SHADOW

AUSTIN MACAULEY PUBLISHERS™

LONDON • CAMBRIDGE • NEW YORK • SHARJAH

Copyright © Donnchadh Mac Gabhann 2023

The right of Donnchadh Mac Gabhann to be identified as author of this work has been asserted by the author in accordance with sections 77 and 78 of the Copyright, Designs and Patents Act 1988.

All rights reserved. No part of this publication may be reproduced, stored in a retrieval system, or transmitted in any form or by any means, electronic, mechanical, photocopying, recording, or otherwise, without the prior permission of the publishers.

Any person who commits any unauthorised act in relation to this publication may be liable to criminal prosecution and civil claims for damages.

This is a work of fiction. Names, characters, businesses, places, events, locales, and incidents are either the products of the author's imagination or used in a fictitious manner. Any resemblance to actual persons, living or dead, or actual events is purely coincidental.

A CIP catalogue record for this title is available from the British Library.

ISBN 9781398486881 (Paperback)
ISBN 9781398486898 (ePub e-book)

www.austinmacauley.com

First Published 2023
Austin Macauley Publishers Ltd®
1 Canada Square
Canary Wharf
London
E14 5AA

I would like to express my appreciation first to my father, Felim, for his patient reading and critiquing of my work for many a year; to my mother, Dara, for her encouragement and support for my creative writings; and to my sister Aoibhin for her literary insights and her willingness to assess my writings with fresh eyes. I owe an intellectual debt to my good companion and contemporary, Michael Sharry, whose academic intuition and knowledge inspired and compelled me to expand and diversify my own critical understandings of socio-political phenomena. Last but not least, I would be remiss not to acknowledge the counsel and labours of my friend, Pranav Darshan, without whom I would never have been prompted to write or publish this work.

Table of Contents

Chapter I: The Protector — 11
- *Part I: Tolerance* — 11
- *Part II: Deference* — 29
- *Part III: Malevolence* — 35
- *Part IV: Perseverance* — 40
- *Part V: Patience* — 49
- *Part VI: (In)Justice* — 60

Chapter II: The Dissenter — 73
- *Part I: Defiance* — 73
- *Part II: Dissidence* — 90
- *Part III: Resistance* — 100
- *Part IV: Resilience* — 109
- *Part V: Endurance* — 117
- *Part VI: Eminence* — 123
- *Part VII: (Un)Reliance* — 136

Chapter III: The Predator — 144
- *Part I: Prejudice* — 144
- *Part II: Penance* — 156
- *Part III: Silence* — 169
- *Part IV: Negligence* — 181

Part V: Resonance	*191*
Part VI: Deliverance	*200*
Part VII: Transparence	*211*
Part VIII: Vengeance	*231*
Part IX: Reminiscence	*241*
Part X: Virulence	*246*
Part XI: Decadence	*253*
Part XII: Violence	*265*
Part XIII: Convergence	*273*
Part XIV: Governance	*276*
Part XV: (Un)Prescience	*284*

Chapter I: The Protector

Part I: Tolerance

Vaccination is Liberation!
Pandemic Slogan of Doctor Slovenko

Grey rain gusted down on the cracked city. The cobbled streets and baroque buildings wept themselves into the dark slime of wet stone. On the quays, the fluids of the rain sat stagnant and lost on cold tarmac. The smooth flowing face of the Borava River sizzled into a pockmarked sheet of exploding raindrops.

February, thought Vaclav grimly as he sat in his car waiting for the traffic lights to turn. The mere sight of the rain chilled his bones, reminded him of the dark and the snow that had come and gone. The dawn of spring was almost nigh he knew. Yet this miserable shower told him the ghost of winter lingered still, unwilling to let go of the city.

Across the junction, he spied a small group of teenagers scurrying for cover from the downpour. With coats and bags draped over their heads, they huddled together at the bus stop under the Millennium Bridge. Beneath the concrete ruin of this broken megastructure, the adolescents giggled and sniggered at their own misfortune, their spirits undampened by the ill weather. Dressed in their bright and colourful shorts and t-shirts, they were children of summer, born before their time. Out of the corner of his eye though, Vaclav glimpsed the familiar oncoming trouble for these young things.

They came as a pair. Both were clad in the long double-breasted plastic coats and knee-high boots which distinguished their creed. A latex balaclava fitted with binocular goggles tightly embraced their heads so that not a single human feature was visible to the world. From their boots to their masks, every piece of them was an ice-white colour so they appeared like sculptures shorn from a glacier. They marched in robotic unison, their arms tucked behind their backs, their chests thrust out with impunity, the heels of their boots clapping off the wet cobblestones.

As they approached their quarry, they unfurled their arms and unsheathed their white rubber truncheons. With confident authority, they shoved their instruments of coercion between the teenagers, and with a simple flick of the hand, forced them apart till the correct distance was restored.

"Young fools," lamented Vaclav. If they had only left enough space between them, they might have evaded the watching eyes of the White Coats. Their conduct simply would not do. It was out of the question. Too much contact and too little distance. It was impolite, rude, reckless, damnable. One always had to leave room for the virus. It only needed one lucky shot. One moment of deadly fortune to transmit from one human to another and it would return into existence once more.

At least, that's what they said.

It was what they had been saying for years beyond count. Vaclav could even remember when such words were given as mere tokens of advice and recommendation. But those friendly days of care and caution were long since gone. In the present upside-down world, these words were equated to absolute truth, proclaimed not so much as pieces of cautionary advice, but as mandatory sermons demanding servile obedience.

With order restored and catastrophe averted, the two White Coats couched their truncheons under their arms and resumed their vigilant patrol, their heads glancing from side to side on the lookout for yet more lapses of attention. The teenagers glanced at each other with awkward guilt and embarrassment written on their faces and then, without a word, parted ways.

"Nothing better to do than give people grief," remarked Vaclav to himself as he watched the White Coats stride away into the middle distance. The lights went green and he put his foot down on the accelerator. "Poor miserable fuckers," he blasphemed under his breath as he sped under the Millennium Bridge and raced up the quays. At the next junction, he turned right and drove up the one-way route to Ward Five, leaving the River behind him. As he came about the bend of the sloping road, he was faced with the familiar view of five Health Marshals standing at attention next to a road barrier. Above their heads, an electronic sign flashed the same old discriminating words: "V5 ACCESS ONLY."

Vaclav was only a V4. But he had his papers. He had his reasons. He was here on so-called 'essential' duties. Though Vaclav himself hardly recognised this crusty old committee meeting as 'essential', his additional role as liaison officer for the Commission came with its benefits, benefits which allowed him to cross Quarantine Lines, benefits which allowed his wife and daughter to enjoy the comfortable lifestyle they had eased themselves into.

A Health Marshal held up a scanner to Vaclav's vehicle as he approached. The Marshal showed the reading to a security guard. A puzzled frown came upon the guard's brow.

"Fuck," swore Vaclav. The guard was new and didn't know the arrangement. He lowered his window and felt his mind clenching with discomfort as the prospect of the looming conversation.

"Read the sign," instructed the guard, gesturing upwards to the flashing electronic warning. "You're only a V4. If you want to pass through to this ward, you'll need to pay extra premium for a higher vaccine dose."

"I don't want your stronger vaccine dose," bluntly rejected Vaclav. "I'm here to—"

"It's pay or leave, sir," slammed the guard before Vaclav could finish.

"I'm Detective Kovac. I'm the police liaison officer for the Commission. I have Class Six clearance to enter Ward Five." Vaclav handed his badge and papers to the guard. The security man scrutinised the documents with the judging eye of an archivist. "I'm here on essential duties. You can call my boss. He'll tell you everything." The guard remained unconvinced and continued to scan every dot of ink on the paper before him.

"Andor! Andor you fool! Let him through!" came the voice of another guard who came hobbling out from the adjacent facility door trying to close the zipper of his trousers in a hurry. "He has clearance! I told you about him!" Andor at once became quite flustered and sheepishly handed Vaclav's documents back to him.

"Evening Maciej," begrudgingly greeted Vaclav to the older security guard.

"Sorry Vaclav, new meat on the block as you can see," apologised Maciej. "Won't happen again! You have a good day, detective!" The police detective simply smirked in feigned humour and continued into Ward Five.

"Fucking imbeciles," muttered Vaclav under his breath as a bitter afterthought once they were out of earshot. He parked his vehicle under the shadow of the towering Quarantine Wall which divided the prestigious Ward Five from the lesser wards.

Even the rain in Ward Five felt privileged, as though it had been filtered and fragranced before it dazzled down on the beautifully ornate buildings. The people here enjoyed the highest vaccine dosage of all and with it they enjoyed the highest lifestyle. Everything about them screamed luxury. Their appearances were so precisely perfect sometimes that they resembled mannequins more than they did human beings. Nestled upon the heights of Castle Hill, Ward Five was almost a city within a city—a 'Forbidden City' as Vaclav liked to call it. Up here on the heights above the Borava River, they could enjoy their hedonistic orgies, their decadent team sports, their opulent drinking binges, and their care-free shopping habits. Behind their all-powerful Vaccine-Five and their all-imposing Quarantine Walls, they could live their lives in blissful tranquillity, safe from any mutation of the virus which might still fester amongst the 'Lesser Vaccinated'.

Vaclav never dared to loiter on his monthly visits here. He felt self-conscious among the V5s. They always gave him that up-and-down scanning look as he passed them by, judging the imperfections of his appearance. More to the point however, Ward Five had its own special police force and they were not known to be sympathetic to the lower vaccine castes, regardless of what excuses he might have on hand. He was here for one reason and one reason only—to attend a meeting and get the hell out.

The Central Commission held their gatherings within the grand medieval halls of the city castle. The Commissioners had no time for the dusty corridors of the old houses of parliament. Ever since the Doctors' Plot, they had made this museum of a building their residence. Gazing out over the city from the castle ramparts, Vaclav had little doubt that the Commissioners liked to consider themselves feudal lords, the benign members of an intellectually superior aristocracy.

As Vaclav entered the castle grounds, he was confronted with the ugly view of the Martyrs' Pandemic Memorial. Dedicated to the sacrifice of the doctors and nurses who risked their lives in the struggle against the virus, the bronze memorial depicted medical staff dressed in their masks and PPE, a muscular superhuman figure among them wielding up a vaccine syringe as though it were the Olympic torch. It was a jarring sight, one that contrasted angrily against the backdrop of the castle walls, like a spaceship planted amidst mud huts. No matter how many times he passed the damned thing, it still made him cringe. He dared not comment on its modern ugliness though, that would be too much trouble.

Instead, as expected of him, he daubed his hands with the ceremonial sanitiser adjacent to the memorial and thereby paid his compulsory respects.

The detective made his way up to the conference chamber and took his appointed seat at the table. A vast map of the city was sprawled out over the enormous round table, every hospital and medical facility brought into sharp relief with red wooden crosses stacked on top of them. Vaclav casually noted the numbers of crosses at each facility and then relaxed into his leather-bound chair and awaited the arrival of the Commission.

"Late again," he grumbled under his breath. They were always late. They had little appreciation for their own time, let alone his. Typical doctors. They came when they saw fit. The later they arrived the later the meeting would drag on for, the later he would get back home. But he dared not complain out loud. He was meant to be grateful to be here. It was, after all, purely a courtesy that the Commission allowed the police department to even sit on these meetings. Finally though, the commissioners made their entry.

The Commission was a consortium of combined professions deemed essential for the safe governance of the state, each represented by a commissioner. Professor Rakosi was the leader of the most essential of all professions, without which civilisation would have collapsed; the pharmacists. Under his supervision every shade of scientist was mobilised for the sole task of producing and manufacturing the sacred vaccine.

After Rakosi, there was Burgenstein, Director of the Metropole Insurance Company, the firm which had swooped in to take over the financials of the vaccination programme, a move which had left the insurers playing the roles of bankers, taxmen, and auditors ever since.

After the pharmacists and insurers was the upper crust of the Commission: the doctors. To them was entrusted the very vitals of the state. The department for External Hygiene Security, tasked with fending off fresh variants of the virus from the dreaded 'Unvaccinated Zone' beyond the river Borava was in the tried and tested hands of the veteran physician, Doctor Barodnik.

As prestigious as Barodnik's department was, however, it was only ever a shadow of its sister division: Internal Hygiene Security. To this branch of governance was entrusted the conscription of new doctors and nurses, the indoctrination of the subject masses, and the enforcement of the 'Laws of Hygiene' by the Health Marshals or White Coats. The privilege of this hefty portfolio of responsibility belonged to none other than the Pandemic Hero,

Doctor Varga, a fanatical workaholic credited with single-handedly saving three hundred lives and with personally fighting off the virus no less than five times during the height of the pandemic.

Last but not least amongst this assembly of venerable gentlemen was their esteemed leader: Doctor Slovenko, the Supreme Surgeon-General. It was by Slovenko's hand that the Doctor's Plot had come to fruition and the dithering parliamentarians had been shouldered aside. Every man, woman, and child in the city owed him their lives.

And Slovenko made sure it stayed that way.

Slovenko's mission was a simple one: the preservation of human life and the healthy wellbeing of all mankind. The weak were to be protected and the strong were to be their protectors.

That very goal which Slovenko and his Commission so vociferously proclaimed to their patients had always been hard for Vaclav to stomach with any real morsel of seriousness.

For what a fine example the Commissioners made to their 'know-nothing' patients which they ruled over.

Rakosi was a fat balding slob, his belly big enough to serve as his own personal dinner tray. Whatever his skills in chemistry were, he was quite evidently unable to produce a vaccine to cure his own gluttony and slovenliness.

Burgenstein was a thin emaciated creature, his face nothing more than a thin veil of skin stretched over his skull like cling film. For all his millions in insurance revenues, he clearly never had enough to satisfy his body's basic needs.

Barodnik meanwhile was a pimple-faced, greasy-haired, wretch of a man, a permanent drop of mucus hanging from the tip of his nose which never seemed to fall. A fine ambassador indeed for the unvaccinated hordes across the river.

Varga's physical stature on the other hand, in no way matched the vast swathe of responsibilities on his desk. Far from being the heroic superman depicted on the Pandemic Memorial, the Chief of the Health Marshals was a stunted little man with poisonous green eyes and a permanent leering smile of repressed sexual excitement carved onto his face.

As for the mighty Slovenko himself, he in truth was a giant to behold who towered over his contemporaries. Yet even giants grow old, and the revered Surgeon-General now had a slouching belly, a wrinkling face, a greying hairline, and a mouth curled into a permanent scowl.

One and all these exemplary champions of public health, shuffled into the room in their white doctor coats. Even the anorexic insurance man, wore this stark sterile medical attire. Gone were the days of the suit and the tie, those were the garments of the hated *talkers*—the elected fools who had squabbled and gossiped while the world fell to pieces. Only by the swift and decisive actions of the doctor and the scientist had the virus been stopped, it was to them that humanity owed its continued survival. It was their example alone which everyone was to emulate.

With accompanying grunts and grumbles for their aches and ailments, the Commissioners took their seats. Slovenko shimmied on his thick-rimmed glasses and with a low disdainful growl cast his eye over the agenda.

"Well then," he started. "Let's get on with it. Burgenstein! You first, what news from the insurance world?"

"Monthly premiums are in order Herr Slovenko," assured Burgenstein self-assuredly. "Vaccine premiums remain steady. Nothing major to report." Slovenko gave a curt nod of the head and turned to his next commissioner.

"Rakosi!" he boomed with a slap on the table. "Anything to report on vaccine production?" The pharmacist wiped his sweaty brow with the back of his bloated hand.

"Vaccine production remains steady Doctor," said Rakosi, a wobble ripping through the beard of blubber beneath his chin. "Uptake remains consistent amongst the population. Our virologists are preparing an updated vaccine to combat several variants which we believe to be evolving among the refusers on the North Side." Slovenko at once turned to the Commissioner of External Hygiene.

"Have we any intelligence on this variant, Barodnik?" asked Slovenko casually of his old colleague. Barodnik slicked back his oily mop of hair and gulped heavily.

"Not yet Doctor, not yet," admitted the intelligence man. "But we are brainstorming pre-emptive measures. My department has been in cooperation with our pharmacist comrades to develop a 'Vaccine Missile' that we can fire across the river. Once detonated, the vaccine would be expelled into the air and should, theoretically at least, inoculate the unbelievers en masse. By vaccinating them in such a pre-emptive strike, we may thus avoid the prospect of a fresh wave of the virus." Slovenko shook his head disapprovingly.

"No, no, no," he said. "There'll be no attempts to vaccinate the primitives. Let them marinate in their own hell. They're beyond saving. Their lives aren't worth the expense. Keep up the propaganda campaign to coax them into defection. That will do for now. If we bomb them with airborne vaccines, they will most likely retaliate with their own biological weaponry and wreak havoc for us on the Virus Front, the Cancer Front, the Surgery Front, who knows? I'll not have it! Things are steady, let's keep it that way."

"Of course, good Doctor," acquiesced Barodnik with a servile bow of his head. "What do you propose we do then to meet the threat of a new variant from the North Side?" Slovenko raised up his cane, extended it out over the map and shifted the red crosses around, swapping them around to different hospitals.

"We'll concentrate our forces on the riverside facilities," he declared firmly. "Three divisions of doctors and…and about four nurse divisions. That should do it." His twitching eyes flashed across at Varga. "You will be able to make up for these adjustments, yes?"

"I have three conscript units fresh from the academy that can be drafted into Wards One and Two," confidently declared the Chief Health Marshal. "I will instruct the advertisers to begin a new recruitment campaign too."

"Good, good," grunted Slovenko in his deep bearish voice as he moved the last pieces on the map into place. "And. what else do you have to say for yourself, my little Varga? All good and steady too I'm sure. Eh?" The head of internal security adjusted a set of papers before him and cleared his throat.

"Amongst the majority of our patients, yes," confirmed Varga with a touch of nervousness. "But of late, reports have reached me in increasing numbers of that subversive movement again." Slovenko raised one of his bushy eyebrows at this. "Amongst the youth to be precise."

"And what do your reports say of this youth movement my little Varga?"

"Disaffection, Doctor," replied Varga resolutely. "Increasingly my marshals are confronted with packs of youths. Their clothing is noted as unhygienic. Their behaviour is rude. Their attitudes are indifferent to our values and norms. They have a pedigree for dancing, singing, frolicking, and deliberate acts of anti-social distancing. Most urgently of all, esteemed Surgeon-General…they congregate together not only in large flocks…but socialise with youths from other wards. It would appear they wish to skip the waiting queue and simply enjoy our hard-earned vaccine privileges without paying a penny."

"Vaccine cheats…" hissed Burgenstein, his gaunt thin lips quivering with the quiet malice of a miser.

"Hmmm," grumbled Slovenko tiredly before leaning back in his chair to contemplate Varga's report. "This is a problem," he said after collecting his thoughts. "They pose a danger." The entire commission nodded in agreement with his assessment.

"Punitive measures will be arranged Doctor," promised Varga obsequiously. Slovenko gave a nod of approval to this.

Vaclav could barely contain a smirk at this nonsense. For almost two years now, he had seen the number of disenchanted and uncompliant young people grow and grow. His own daughter counted herself among their ranks. But it was no 'movement' which they belonged to. That would imply a degree of skill and organisation. In his own opinion, it was more a fashion trend, an expression of youth in rebellion. But men like Slovenko and Varga could never see it like that. Everything was a battle to them. There always had to be an enemy at the gate.

Even if the enemy didn't exist.

And when victory was attained over the imaginary enemy, they would find a new one to train their efforts on.

"Hmmm, yes," continued Slovenko after giving it further though. "We must crack down on them. Transgression without punishment is a recipe for disaster. If these young virus collaborators run amok with impunity, more will follow, and in time they will make the city ripe for the virus to plunder." He turned directly to Varga and brought his full gaze crushing down on him. *"Sterilise them."*

"It will be done Doctor," said the Chief of the Health Marshals. "Mandatory sterilisation and vaccine penalties will be issued for non-compliance with the regulations. I will inform my advertisers to launch a new campaign to take the wind out of their sails."

"An excellent idea," agreed Barodnik.

"I may have a suggestion, gentlemen," butted in Burgenstein, his bony fingers sprawled out over his financial reports like spider legs. "From what I can discern of your report Herr Varga, these young scoundrels are impatient, frustrated, exasperated, with the way of the world, yes?" Varga curtly nodded in confirmation.

"You are not suggesting we tear down the Quarantine Walls are you?" asked Rakosi in jest with a little laugh, every chuckle sending waves of wobbles across his plump cheeks. The skeletal Burgenstein smiled and emitted his own chilling little laugh.

"When pigs fly, perhaps yes," he replied jokingly. "But I do suggest we throw these dogs a bone. Some dust in the eyes. An illusion. A small act of charity on our part that will make their behaviour seem unreasonable and reckless."

"Go on," encouraged Slovenko.

"I propose that we provide the population with a false icon of hope. In Ward Three, there is a boy of some twelve years of age. His name is Emil Bauer. Little Emil is, how can I put it, a slow learner shall we say. In Ward Three, there are no special needs teachers to accommodate him. And so for the past few months, my fellow insurers have been berated with petitions from his family, requesting a V4 be donated to him so he can attend a school in Ward Four."

"And you believe, this boy fits the bill?" asked Barodnik with a touch of dubiousness.

"I do. Think of it, gentlemen. If this brainless idiot-boy can ascend through the Quarantine Levels without any trouble, then how ridiculous will these ungrateful teenagers appear? We must show them that just as their impatience is punished, so their patience will be rewarded. If they work hard and put their backs into their studies, then they too might enjoy such vaccine privileges as our dear young Bauer."

"Hmmm," acknowledged Slovenko lowly. "An act of mercy."

"For the boy only, of course," clarified Burgenstein. "His family will stay in Ward Three. We're not running a soup kitchen here!" Another trickle of haughty guffaws circled the room.

"Yes," approved Slovenko. "Good work Burgenstein. Make a show of the boy. Give him plenty of publicity. Rub it in everyone's faces how nice and generous we are."

"It will be done Doctor," promised Burgenstein.

"Right," said Slovenko as he raised himself from his seat. "That concludes our business for the day I think unless—"

"Ahem," coughed Barodnik pointing across to Vaclav. Slovenko slouched back down.

"Ah yes our wily policeman. How could I let myself remember?" joked Slovenko to the chuckles of his commissioners. Vaclav gave no reaction. He was well accustomed to the Surgeon-General making the police department the butt of every cheap joke. "How are our little blue-men down in the city?"

Vaclav covered his mouth with his hand as dictated by ceremonial rites, he dared not infect the air for these living gods with his mortal breath.

"All is good," he said curtly. "Nothing to report. I will relay your intentions for collaboration with Varga's men to clamp down on—"

"Pah! No need for that detective! We're here to save lives, not end them! If we need bullets fired at unarmed women and children, we'll know where to find you!" More laughs and belly slaps followed.

"Yes, yes, thank you, thank you, fuck you too," thought Vaclav to himself dryly without giving them the satisfaction.

"Understood," he responded emotionlessly when their laughter had ebbed away finally. Any other policeman might have confronted Slovenko and argued with him. Vaclav knew too well that such a pursuit was futile. It was easier to simply let the Doctor's words pass through one ear and out the other and give it no more consideration.

Such indifference was the best way of getting through life.

"Good, good," asserted Slovenko who then heaved himself to his feet. "We'll leave it there, gentlemen."

"Thank fuck," thought Vaclav as he scrambled out of his seat and rushed for the exit.

"Oh detective!" called a voice after him through the racket of chairs scraping on floorboards. Vaclav pivoted about to find Varga hurrying after him. "A moment please?" asked the green-eyed little man.

"What now?" he cursed to himself silently as he halted in his footsteps to let the dwarf catch up with him.

"I wonder if I might ask a favour of you."

"Of course," retorted Vaclav, knowing there was nothing else he could say.

"My nephew is coming to the city tomorrow from up country. He's a bit of a countryside hick but he's eager to follow in the family business and join the Marshals. Only snag is he failed his medical exams so he's looking now to join by another avenue. I thought perhaps he might earn his spurs with your boys, maybe you'd take him on as your apprentice?"

"Sure, no problem," accepted Vaclav with dulled enthusiasm. Varga slapped him on the shoulder.

"A fine specimen you are Detective!" thanked Varga with that eerie puppet-like smile of his before scurrying off to the nearest hand sanitiser to cleanse his flesh of Vaclav's germs.

"Fucking brilliant," seethed Vaclav behind grated teeth as he returned to his car. It was just his luck to get saddled like this not just with a Commissioner's relative, but with *Varga's* relative. He slammed the car door irritably upon returning to the privacy of his vehicle. "Fuck it anyway," he cursed as a final damning word on the matter and he turned the ignition to head home.

The traffic was bad that night. By the time he had reached the final stretch of his journey, the gloomy neon lights had awoken. The streets were in that tortured condition between night and day, the nocturnal dark mashed together with the buzzing blue, green, and orange of electric lights. On the digital billboards above the streets, he could already see the live news breaking of Emil Bauer's *"BIG LUCKY DAY."* The poor boy resembled a deer caught in the headlights as lights and cameras and reporters crowed around him. The boy's parents were interviewed, tears of joy streaming down their grateful faces. The doctors were there too justifying the act of charity. The doctors were always there.

The bastards moved fast, he had to give them that. Had it been the days of the elected talkers, there would have been meetings scheduled in order to discuss what was going to be discussed at the real meeting. Then they would have given the Bauer household due notice, weeks in advance and had yet more meetings to discuss this. In the world of the Commission though everything was undertaken as though it were life-or-death surgery. Every decision bore instant fruit in the real world.

His stomach was aching for food by the time he was parking his car in the drive. The moment he opened the front door he knew dinner had come and gone. She hadn't waited for him again. Dinner would be in the pot for him, not on the table. It had happened enough times now for him to know the drill. He entered the house without a word and helped himself. His wife, Veronika, and his daughter, Justyna, were already relaxing in the sitting room watching the same report on Emil Bauer's 'vaccine miracle'.

The Kovac household was a cluster of opposites. Like all normal marriages, Vaclav's bond with Veronika had been arranged. They had been brought together purely due to the alignment of vaccine interests. They were what the self-proclaimed cupids at VAXXMATCH.COM liked to call a 'perfect vaccine match'; they were both from families that had the V4. By marrying one another, they ensured that their comfortable livelihoods were secured. With Vaclav's liaison position to the committee, moreover, they were blessed with bonus social credits: allowing them to have more social contacts in their 'bubble'. As far as Vaclav was concerned this was just 'extra floor space for the cage'. There was after all *still* a limit on the amount of people they were permitted to be friends with.

Veronika on the other hand, the quintessential socialite, wallowed in the privileges he had earned for her. She was the type of person's whose primary reading material consisted of waiting room magazines, the type of person who was manufactured into being, not born. Her clothes were those of designer brands. Her blonde Slavic hair was tended to every morning to the point of almost picturesque perfection by the local hairdresser. There was nothing original about her in Vaclav's opinion. Her thoughts and beliefs were simply whatever everyone else thought and believed. She would watch the news and listen to the Commission's PR people and lap up every word they had to say. Though he had never heard her admit it, he was quite certain that in her worldview, independent thought was synonymous with alienation and loneliness. She would do anything, say anything, and think anything, to keep her creature comforts.

He had little time for her in truth. She was not so much his wife as she was the person he happened to coexist with.

Justyna on the other hand was everything her mother was not. Her hair was a purple shock of Mohican spikes. Her clothes were tattered and faded. She had been born into and nurtured in the world constructed by the Commission. All she knew was Vaccine Premiums and Quarantine Walls. And like every teenager, she was adamant on rebelling against it. Unlike in Vaclav's youth when teenagers had voluntarily enslaved themselves to their phones, Justyna and her friends were hell-bent on rejecting the vast digital realm of distraction which the Commission had constructed as a substitute for the stunted material sphere. In Justyna's eyes, devotion to technology was for silly old people too scared to face the real world. She preferred to be brave and free than scared and imprisoned. In an act of extreme defiance, she and her friends had gone so far as to dump all their childhood devices into the Borava River, thereby making themselves untraceable and uncontactable. Like some medieval monk, she now corresponded by pen and paper alone.

Vaclav could respect his daughter's commitment to such principles. Not unlike her mother though he discerned that she was merely a product of her time—a social chameleon blending in with the trends of the day.

Truth be told, Vaclav felt his family to be the most burdensome part of his existence. If he were to come home one day to find both his wife and daughter had vanished into thin air, it wouldn't bother him in the slightest.

Vaclav sat by himself at the dinner table, idly throwing an eye over his two co-habitants lounging on the couches in front of the T.V. Veronika was glued into the report on the Bauer boy, a stupid gullible smile on her face. Justyna meanwhile was reading a book, a thick Tolstoy one by the look of it. Of a sudden then the Bauer story concluded, and the next report hit the headlines: "**Surge in Vaccine Cheat Numbers amongst adolescent population.**"

A montage of teenagers and students not unlike Justyna were paraded across the screen with experts regurgitating lines fed to them by the Commission. As predicted, Veronika's face had now switched to one of abject horror.

"The danger is real," declared one of the Commission's many mouthpieces. "The breach of Quarantine Walls by reckless youths leave us open to attack by fresh strains of the virus. We urge all parents across the city to track the movements of their children. Please make sure they stay at home, both for their safety and yours. Vaccine penalties up to and including mandatory sterilisation will be enforced on those who continue to violate the rules."

"*Fuck,*" swore Vaclav to himself. He instinctively looked away from the sitting room and focused entirely on his dinner. His ears however could not filter out the inevitable conversation he knew would follow.

"That's such bullshit," dismissed Justyna as she slapped her book shut. "The nerve of those old pigs!" Her mother instantly muted the television and snapped at her.

"What did you say?" retorted Veronika sharply.

"It's nonsense," reiterated Justyna. "All of it. We're no danger to anyone. We're just trying to live." Veronika pointed instructively at the television.

"That's not what they're saying!" she rebuked. "It's you and your ungrateful generation whose peddling nonsense. Everything you have, you owe it to the vaccine and the Commission. You owe your very life to them!"

"Yes, we *are* alive," acknowledged Justyna. "But that's all the vaccine offers. Life. And the life it offers is no life worth living. We have about as much life as a lab monkey! Because of *your* generation, I can't fly to Tokyo or Paris or New York. Because of the world *you* made, everyone is stuck in the one place. The poor stay poor and the rich stay rich, forever and ever and ever. If I was to live by your rules, I'd have to marry that ugly Vadim Koresch your matchmaking website allocated to me."

"You *will* marry him!" shrieked Veronika. "If you value the roof over your head, you will marry him. He's a V4. His family may even be a V5 if that business deal goes ahead and you would be able to live up by the castle. It's damn right dangerous for you to even be around those runaways from the lower Wards. They're not insured to even breathe the air around here. And neither would you if something ever happened and a Virus Claim was made!"

"That's my friends you're talking about!" lashed Justyna. "They're just like me. They want out of here! Don't you understand that no one wants to live in this open prison?"

"It's dangerous to mix with people from lower wards. They're not safe to be around."

Justyna shook her head.

"I may as well be talking to a brick wall," she lamented as she put aside her book and rose from the couch. "There is no virus! It's gone! No one's even contracted it in ten years! The vaccine is a con! It's just a way for them to make money off us! Can't you see that? Nobody needs the vaccine! Nobody needs the Quarantine Walls!"

"How can you say that? You yourself are at risk with that asthma of yours! If it weren't for the vaccine, why the virus would have killed my own parents, your dear granny!"

"Yes, granny got vaccinated, and then she died anyway! Because she was almost a hundred years old! People die all the time! All the time! There's no vaccine for death dearest Veronika! It just forces us to live in fear of it. You all live in fear of your own shadows, of things that never even happen! But I suppose that's what happens when you allow a shower of money-grabbing insurance pig-dogs to dictate your life to you!"

"That's it! I've heard enough Justyna! Go to your room!" shouted Veronika in a rare outburst of personal emotion.

"You can't keep me here forever," jibed Justyna as she stomped away mumbling to herself. "You and your cruddy old generation."

"Justyna," called Vaclav to his daughter. She stopped as she reached the stairs, her face a riot of anger. "If you get caught out there, make sure you're caught by the police, not the White Coats. Otherwise I can't help you." His daughter gave her answer to him with a thin smile that calmed her slightly.

Veronika meanwhile was far from finished. She moved to the kitchen table and talked and talked about what they should do about their black sheep daughter.

"I've had it up to hear with her," she continued. "You know she even changed her name? All her friends now call her 'Jane Kelvin'. Such a strange western name! I wonder where we went wrong with her. I think we should have been more…" Vaclav paid no mind to her. He had recognised long ago to stop listening whenever his so-called wife vented her fears and worries on him. His mind focused instead on what Justyna had said.

"*Paris, New York,*" thought Vaclav. It had been a long time since he had seen those places. He wouldn't mind seeing them again himself. But it was probably best he didn't. They were probably no better than his own home city—all locked up and dead to the world. Whatever charm they once had was most likely sterilised out of existence by now. Best not spoil his memory of them.

The next morning, it was still drizzling rain and the sky was still that depressing overcast blanket of grey. He hurried out of the house as swiftly as he could and set out onto the road to pick up Varga's nephew at the station. The young country bumkin was waiting for him with two cups of coffee at the ready. Unlike his stunted uncle, the young Varga stood eye to eye with Vaclav. He had a set of kind blue eyes and a crop of white blonde hair. The sole attribute which he shared with the elder Varga was the grin—thankfully though it lacked the air of perversion which his uncle had.

"Stefan," he greeted as he handed the coffee out to Vaclav. "Stefan Varga!"

"Vaclav Kovac," responded Vaclav after taking a sip, not bothering to thank the boy for the gesture. "Let's go." In a flash, they were back in the car and cruising through city streets. The younger Varga waffled on about his bus journey up to the big city from his family farm and how he had been dazzled by all the old baroque architecture. Vaclav politely zoned out and kept his eye on the road. As they came to the junction at Sanitation Street, a pack of teenagers being harassed by White Coats came into view.

"I saw them on the news last night!" enthused Stefan. "Shouldn't we go and help the Marshals!"

"Nope," curtly rejected Vaclav.

"Well, why not?" queried Stefan confusedly.

"Because it's a matter of public health, not law enforcement. They haven't broken any laws, so it's not our business. Not my problem."

"Well what is our business then?" asked Stefan a little worriedly, no doubt wondering if he had made the right choice to tag along with a police detective.

"Very little," answered Vaclav with a sigh. "Almost everything is counted as a violation of health regulations. That means it's in the jurisdiction of your uncle, not me. Any untoward behaviour can be interpreted as a danger to human health, so, naturally, they take up the lion's share of society's problems. We just fill in the gaps mostly. In fact, most days I just drive around the city aimlessly…just like this."

"But surely even as a concerned citizen you can assist them in—"

"Nope, not my problem. Good things never happen to people who go beyond the call of duty."

"Don't you care about Vaccine Rule? Aren't you a man of law and order?" Vaclav had to laugh at that one. In the privacy of his own car, he felt free to do so, even if the boy was a blood-relation of the mighty Doctor Varga.

"Frankly boy, I don't give a damn," he answered honestly. "If the Commission were to collapse and the Quarantine Walls all came crashing down tomorrow, I wouldn't shed a tear for it. Not one. You seem to be under the illusion that I support the Commission, I don't. Like everything else in this futile life of ours, I just tolerate it."

"Why?" asked the youngster curiously. He pointed over at the teenagers arguing with the Marshals. "If you've no love for any of this, then why not join the troublemakers over there?" Vaclav smirked at that thought. They turned the corner and came around to the quays parallel to the Borava River.

"Because," he answered calmly. "It's better than the alternative." He glanced over at the north bank across the river.

"Wow," gawped Stefan in wonderment, craning his neck around to get a better look. "There it is. The unvaccinated country. I forgot I'd be able to see it here. Gosh, we really are on the front lines." He pointed up at the Millennium Bridge, its arm reaching only halfway across the river before a sudden drop where the infamous 'Quarantine Detonation' had taken place to keep the primitives out. The younger Varga then pointed to the GPS on the dashboard. "Jesus, the street names across the river don't even show up on this. It's like as if it's a desert over there."

"That's because it is," chuckled Vaclav. "It's Land of the Dead over there. They're all dead things walking around waiting for the common cold to brush them over. You know they don't even take the flu jab, right?" Stefan nodded in silence, his attention completely transfixed by the view of the North Side and its ugly concrete apartment blocks. "Life is hard enough and complicated enough without having to deal with unvaccinated morons like them. I'll stick to the Commission till something better comes along."

"It's a wonder we can even see them," continued Stefan, still transfixed by the sight of the North Bank. "You'd think that the Commission would build some kind of Digital Curtain on the river so we couldn't look across at them like this."

"No," laughed Vaclav lightly. "They'd never do that."

"Why not?"

"Because…if we couldn't see the primitives over there, then we might forget who we are. Or more to the point, we might forget why we need the Commission. So, they'd never do something like that."

Before Varga's nephew could make any response to Vaclav's scathing critique, the radio came to life.

"406 do you copy?"

"We copy," answered Vaclav.

"We have a DB on Isolation Avenue. We need you there ASAP."

"Copy that," replied Vaclav and he looked across at the eagerly waiting Stefan.

"What's a DB?" asked the enthusiastic youngster.

"Dead body," curtly expounded the detective. "Looks like I might actually have something to do today…Let's take a peep at a dead thing, shall we?"

Part II: Deference

The great questions over life and death in this century will not be settled by the Talkers and the Electors—that was the great mistake of the 2020s—but by the intellect of the Doctor and the Scientist.

Doctor Varga's welcome address to conscripts at the Medical Academy

END VACCINE PRIVILEGES and *WE ARE NOT YOUR PATIENTS*—the placards read as Vaclav and Stefan cruised by. On the streets to the left and the streets to the right, he could see the crowds of students and teenagers swarming in their masses. In his rear-view mirror, he spied a glimpse of the sparsely deployed line of White Coats ready to meet them with two-metre long staffs in hand. Up on the rooftops their sharpshooters were choosing targets with tranquiliser darts at the ready.

"RETURN TO YOUR HOMES!" boomed the automated voices over the loudspeakers.

"FOR YOUR OWN SAFETY, PLEASE RETURN TO YOUR HOMES! MAINTAIN SOCIAL DISTANCE AND AVERT TRANSMISSION! YOUR HEALTH AND WELLBEING ARE IN DANGER!"

"This is really heating up," commented Stefan with alarm. "The report only came out last night about the disruptive youth culture."

"And evidently, the youth got the message quicker than expected," retorted Vaclav as he cautiously weighed the situation in hand. He had no intention of getting caught up in the middle of a riot. He scanned the road and saw the protestors and authorities closing in around him. Any moment and some young hot head would lead a stampede against the White Coats. He dared not risk it. *Fuck it,* he swore to himself and he slammed his foot down on the accelerator and made a break for the traffic lights.

"Jesus!" exclaimed Stefan, taken off guard by the sudden burst of speed as they rocketed up the street. "Speeding is bad for your life expectancy you know!"

"So is fucking rioting!" fired back Vaclav as he made a sharp turn around a corner, the tyres screeching off the tarmac. With that, they were clear of the mustering kerfuffle. "Now," sighed Vaclav. "Isolation Avenue, wasn't it?" Stefan nodded and wearily peered back at the throngs of protestors. "Don't mind them. They're behind us. Not our job. Not our problem."

"I know, I know," acceded the young Varga. "It's just, I've never seen so many people in one place before, not like that."

"Yeah you and me both boychik. Haven't seen anything like that since I was a tot. But still, not our job, not our problem. That's your uncle's department, not mine."

Not a word was uttered on the matter after that. For the first time in months, the detective had a real job to do. With every fibre of his brain, he endeavoured to focus on what might await him on Isolation Avenue. His mind would not allow it though. The sight of so many people protesting against the Commission kept reverberating through his head. He'd never seen anything like it. All his adult life he had assumed that mere inertia alone would keep any frustration from bubbling over against the status quo. Apparently, this was no longer the case.

He recalled the argument between his wife and daughter the night before. This new generation was clearly a bigger hornet's nest of discontent than either he or the Commission could have estimated. He'd never seen such anger on so many faces before. He had always considered himself closer to the reality on the ground than the Commission but clearly not nearly close enough for him to predict an earthquake of this magnitude.

Not until they turned onto Isolation Avenue, were they greeted with members of law enforcement again. City police in their simple baby blue uniforms stood upon the pavements and waved Vaclav by. The 'Blue Shirts', as they were known, were a dull and simple clump of humanity as far as Vaclav was concerned. Anyone who failed their school exams or dropped out of college usually got fast tracked into the police. It was a well-paid job with little more than a few, fleeting, easy, challenges to handle on a day-to-day basis. Work as a police officer in truth entailed only one simple task to perform every day: put on your uniform to give an air of officialdom and look like you're keeping busy.

In sum, they were a shower of paid simpletons with a brain molecule between them to keep the public distracted while the White Coats did all the real work.

Today was no exception to that rule. As Vaclav parked up his car by on the roadside, he could already see a Health Marshal striding over to take control of the scene. Vaclav recognised the Marshal instantly: Gustaf Schnell. A tall blue-eyed blonde-haired poster boy for the Department of Hygiene Security he was, always ready and eager to 'save the day' from the blunders of the police department.

"Come on boychik," urged Vaclav as he unbuckled his seatbelt. "Let's get a look at this before the scene gets taken off us." The two of them clambered out of the vehicle and ambled over to the sealed-off alleyway where the crime had so obviously been committed. They shouldered past the little gathering of local residents, concerned and curious about the unusual police presence.

Past a line of loitering Blue Shirts and under the line of yellow tape they went, and finally then, into the white forensics tent. No sooner had they entered than both of them nearly stumbled backwards in horror.

The victim was a male. In his mid-forties, perhaps. He had a balding scalp and a clean-shaven face. He was dressed in a shirt and tie. Those facts however only soaked in after recovery from the initial splash of visceral imagery.

At first sight, the victim resembled more a fresh bloody steak than a human being. Dark congealing blood had pooled around him in a little lake. His entire body had been thoroughly gored. There were slashes and stab wounds to his neck, to his wrists, to his stomach, to the insides of his legs. He had been clawed open as though by a wild animal.

Stefan's eyes were wide open, his hand was over his mouth as he tried to steady himself with deep breaths. Vaclav might well have been the same only he knew he had to at least pretend to be the senior figure here. This was not what he had wanted the young Varga to see on his first day.

Of all the things he had expected to be waiting here for them, this was not it.

Ratko, the department's one and only forensics officer came strutting over with camera in hand. Dressed in a chequered shirt and jeans with a thick curly black beard hanging off his face, Ratko was quite the bohemian to look at.

"Ratko," greeted Vaclav. "What do we have here?"

"Vaccine number was VN 7468459, birth name was Oleg Krivokuca," blandly informed Ratko, casually combing his fingers through his curly black beard. "He was a claims adjuster for the Metropole Insurance Company. He must have been here on business. His home address is on Hospital Quay. The cause of death as you can see quite clearly is loss of blood."

Vaclav got down on his hunkers to get a better look at the dripping red cadaver.

"What the fuck happened?" he muttered.

"The answer is simple!" boomed a proclamatory voice behind him. Vaclav privately rolled his eyes to the heavens. He rose to his feet and found the Health Marshal standing behind him dressed in his spotless white uniform, his blonde hair slicked back.

"Morning Gustaf," begrudgingly addressed Vaclav. "Nice to see you again."

"And you Herr Kovacs," returned the Marshal. "Now, what do we have here?" Vaclav slid his hands into his pockets and obsequiously backed away while Gustaf circled the corpse.

"It is clear to me that this is a case of self-murder," declared the Health Marshal. "Evidently, the victim had contracted a viral fungus of some form. This must then have affected his mind. In his unstable mental condition, he must have suffered a lapse of judgement and stabbed himself to death. The fungal disease must have struck him swiftly. Otherwise we can of course be certain that he would have had both the sense and time to avail of medical attention and his life would have been saved."

"You got all that just by walking around the body?" questioned Stefan dubiously.

"Do you have a better explanation young man? How else could a man, an upstanding insurance man no less, reach such an end? There is no other rational means of comprehending this." Gustaf completed his circling of the corpse and came face to face with Vaclav. "As such I'm sure you will agree that this falls within the jurisdiction of Internal Hygiene Security. Your presence is no longer required here detective."

"Thanks for having us," submissively accepted Vaclav. He turned and patted Stefan on the shoulder. "Come on boychik, we're done here."

Vaclav bitterly clenched his knuckles as he made his way back to the car. He was about to unlock the door when Stefan came hurrying up behind him.

"Hey!" the young Varga hollered to him. "We're not seriously leaving, are we?"

"You heard the man, the White Coats are looking after it now."

"Don't tell me you believe the garbage he just spouted out. Self-murder? Have you ever seen anyone capable of doing that kind of damage to themselves? The man was clearly kill—"

"Keep your voice down!" hissed Vaclav suddenly before lowering his tone to a forceful whisper. "We don't use that word around here boychik. No one's used that word in decades. People die for one reason and one reason only: they contract a disease. Life is holier than Christ. To suggest that the man's life was taken by another human being would be heresy. If the vaccines and the science can't cure it, they don't want to know about it. You understand?"

"But that's rubbish. Where's the scientific method? You saw what I saw. That Marshal didn't even do any tests on the body to provide evidence for his theory."

"He doesn't need evidence to support his theory. His theory conjures the evidence."

"But that's ridiculous! That's against everything the Commission stands for. This is clearly a…a homicide. This should be a police case."

"*This* is how the world works boychik. I'm sure you were told all kinds of things in school about the Commission but in the real world this is how it works. *Everything* is a violation of the health code. Drunk driving, domestic abuse, assault, you name it they'll make sure it falls under the health code. The Doctors control everything. And if they say it's not our job, then it's not our job. We move on and we still get paid. You get me? Their word is absolute. You want to be a police officer? A detective? Then learn to do as you're told by the ruling caste."

Stefan appeared almost paralysed before him as the dust settled from his little rant. Eventually though, Vaclav saw a little twitch in the boy's face, a sign that the cogs in his head were moving.

"I am the ruling caste," muttered Stefan and he turned heel and began marching back towards the crime scene.

"Boychik? Boychik? Where are you going?" called Vaclav after him. The boy paid no heed to him. As the distance between them grew greater, Vaclav realised that he was not coming back and he hastily hurried after his protege. "Stefan! Stefan! Listen! Listen to me!" he cried after him, but it was too late.

Stefan burst through the flaps of the forensics tent, startling everyone within.

"Can I help you, young man?" asked Gustaf curiously.

"You will surrender this scene to the city police department!" he bellowed commandingly, taking on a voice that did not appear to be his own.

"Excuse me?"

"Are you deaf? You heard me! You will surrender this scene to the police department!"

"On what grounds? Who do you think you are coming in here and ordering us around—"

"I am Stefan Varga. My uncle is Commissioner Varga, *your* commanding superior. I am here on a summary inspection of your unit Marshal. And I have found you to be overstepping the bounds of your jurisdiction!"

"This is preposterous!" shrieked Gustaf.

"Is it?" snapped Stefan sharply, extending a copy of his identity card to the Health Marshal as proof of his family background. "Then you can kindly explain to my uncle that you said as such before a member of his family, that you obstructed in the course of a lawful investigation and that you wasted precious departmental resources!" Stefan flipped out his mobile phone and began dialling.

"What are you doing?" asked Gustaf worriedly, the colour visibly draining from his face.

"Calling the Commissioner to advise him of your misconduct in the field."

The Marshal frantically vaulted over the dead body and clasped Stefan's phone hand.

"There's no need for that, no need at all, no, no, no," assured the nervous Gustaf. "Detective Kovac can have the scene. It's no trouble. There's no need to call the Commissioner. We'll leave now. We'll let you be."

"Good," replied Stefan, putting away his phone. The Marshal and his accompanying White Coats departed the scene. "And Marshal!" he called after him. "Next time I see you, you had better be shoulder to shoulder with the White Coats at the picket lines. Understand?"

"Of course, Herr Varga! Of course!" acquiesced Gustaf with two servile bows of the head. Stefan turned to Vaclav.

"The scene is all yours, detective."

"Great, now this is my problem," answered Vaclav wryly.

Part III: Malevolence

There is no asset more precious to us on this earth than human life. We must never allow this great asset to be endangered. No man, woman, or child should live in fear that their life be taken from them. We shall protect them against all perils.

Director Burgenstein's 'Life is Precious' Speech at the Sons of Insurance Convention

"The cuts were made with frenzied slashes," informed Ratko as he examined the body more closely. "They weren't intended to kill the victim. None of the cuts are precise. None except this one." He indicated towards the throat. "The neck was opened almost surgically, and it was carried out after the other cuts were inflicted. Whoever made this cut knew exactly what they were doing. They probably did it before."

"Two different attackers maybe?" suggested Stefan. "One nutcase to gore the body and some cold-blooded psychopath to finish the job?"

"Or just the one," chimed in Vaclav. "The person might have lashed out in anger, realised the gravity of what they had done and then saw they had no choice but to give them a swift death."

"The question then lies as to why they lashed out in anger," said Stefan, peering down more intently into the grotesqueness of the lifeless corpse.

"He was a claims adjuster," rationalised Ratko almost humorously. "What more explanation do you need?" Stefan chuckled. Vaclav held his silence.

"We're going to need his files," said the Detective. "Talk to his colleagues, friends, family. Find out what claim he was looking at, who he was investigating."

"You know," said Ratko. "There is a CCTV camera on this alleyway. If we have the case now, I can get one of our IT guys to access the footage. Might save you some footwork if we can just get an I.D on the perp."

"You don't say," said Vaclav with biting sarcasm. "Get the tech boys working on that ASAP. If there's footage of the attack, then we can get the vaccine number of the perpetrator. We'll have them apprehended before the sun goes down tonight." He turned to Stefan. "Boychik, can you go and get the insurance files anyway. We'll need them for evidence."

"Eh, won't I need a badge or an I.D card or something?" queried the young Varga shakily.

"Your surname will do the trick," returned Vaclav. "Works like a charm every time I'll bet."

"Yeah ok, but I've no training. I'm not a detective. I've no clue what I'm supposed to be doing."

"You've done research for school projects before, right? It's like that except you can carry a gun."

"Wait, what?"

"Detective!" hollered a voice from outside the tent. Everyone spun about and a mutton-head Blue Shirt came through the tent entrance.

"What is it?" asked Vaclav.

"Word just got in," expounded the grunt. "There's another body."

"Tell them Hygiene Security can have it. I have my hands full with this one."

"It's exactly like this one." Vaclav almost froze on the spot with those words.

"Where?" he asked.

The officer looked at the note they had scrawled across the palm of their hand.

"56 Immunity Street."

"Ok…Fuck…tell them I'm on my way. Ratko, bag the body and meet us over there. Come on boychik, you chose a heck of a day to go on the job."

"What about the insurance files?" queried Varga.

"I'll drop you off at the insurance building on the way," advised Vaclav as he hurried him out of the forensics tent and back to the car.

"You think it might be the same killer?" asked Stefan as they hopped into the vehicle. Vaclav gave no answer. He had none to give. This was the busiest day he'd had in years and he had no idea what was going on. Two murders in one day? That was more than he'd ever signed up for. He had a bad feeling in his gut as he turned the ignition and exited Isolation Avenue. The drive to the Metropole Building was a silent brooding one which the preoccupied Vaclav barely recalled even undertaking. White knuckling the steering wheel, he almost missed the turn and abruptly parked the car up on the curb as he saw the building passing out of his purview.

"Right," he said to Stefan. "Good luck." The boy clambered out of his seat and was about to close the car door when Vaclav called after him. "Give me a call when you're done here, and I'll pick you up. Try not to ruffle too many feathers!" Before Stefan could make a reply to that he'd shut the door and driven away.

His fears that worse things might be waiting for him on Immunity Street were confirmed by the sickly shade of white clasping the face of the young police officer waiting for him. As far as Vaclav could tell the man had already smoked five cigarettes during his wait and he was starting on his sixth now. A watery redness was clearly visible in his eyes as Vaclav approached him.

"Detective Kovac," greeted the officer, nervously stamping out the cigarette. "Sergeant Novak at your service."

"You found the body?" enquired Vaclav wearily.

"Landlord," answered Novak. "Hadn't heard from the tenant in weeks. He went in to check on her and…" Novak wiped his brow and began fumbling towards the cigarette pack again. "Go up to the first floor. You'll find her on the second door to the left."

Vaclav nodded. He wasn't going to impress on the shell-shocked sergeant to give him a tour of the scene. He pressed on into the house and subconsciously braced himself as he ascended the creaking stairs to the crime scene. He inhaled deeply and then brushed the bedroom door open. His mind went numb at the sight.

The corpse lay not sprawled out on the bed or mangled like a string-less puppet on the floor. She was hanging upside down from the ceiling. Holes had been drilled into both her ankles so a wire could be weaved through her feet. From there, she had been hauled up like the prized quarry of a hunt. Her hands had been hacked clean off, leaving two bloody stumps swaying above the floorboards alongside her dangling strands of hair. Slashes had been inflicted to her throat, stomach and thighs just like the unfortunate insurance man on Isolation Avenue. Her mouth was stuffed with a kitchen towel to stop her from screaming as the life was torn out of her.

"Give me one of those," he urged Sergeant Novak as he emerged from the house. The officer swiftly handed the cigarette pack to him and offered his lighter.

"*Fuck,*" swore Vaclav, rubbing his eyes in a useless attempt to wipe the horror from his memory. "Fuck, fuck, fuck."

"She was gagged," muttered Sergeant Novak as he took another drag of his cigarette. He looked over at Vaclav with tears nearly welling in his eyes. "*She was alive,*" he said. "She was alive when the holes were drilled into her, when she was hung from the ceiling by her own ankles. I asked around before you came and eh…no one in the neighbourhood heard anything…no one heard her scream."

Vaclav hadn't taken much heed of their surroundings. Immunity Street was a typically Ward Four neighbourhood: rows of terraced houses glued to one another. It was a sleepy little place with barely any road or foot traffic.

And yet, '*no one heard her scream*'.

"This isn't a self-murder. No fucking way…What…what kind of person could do a thing like that?" asked Novak, expecting a rock-solid explanation from the 'expert' detective. "To deliberately…take someone else's life away from them. No chance, no fluke of nature, no luck of the draw. Just a decision by another person to take your life from you, and to…" Novak wiped his eyes before continuing. "…and to use your life against you…to *torture* you in your own home. What kind of monster could do that detective?"

Vaclav gave no answer. He himself truthfully didn't even want it. He stamped out the cigarette and exhaled the last puff of fumes.

"You have the details on her?" he asked in a matter of fact way. The sergeant plucked the notebook from his breast pocket and flipped it open.

"Vaccine number was VN 7412777. Birth name was Lidija Ivanevic. She was a supervisor at Hospital Administration down on Inoculation Way."

"You know if there was any links to an insurance claim?"

"Maybe. Maybe not. I didn't do a sweep of her belongings. Why do you ask?"

"Might be the same perpetrator is all."

"There's another body? You mean to say there's someone on a…" Novak lowered his voice to a whisper. "…on a killing spree?"

"Possibly. Whoever it is they didn't think it through very well. We have CCTV footage from the other crime scene. We'll have them behind bars before the sun goes down today."

"And ready to be euthanised I damn well hope. You don't get away with this shit…nobody does, not in this day and age…life is precious you know. Everyone knows that."

"Not *everyone* apparently," corrected Vaclav eerily.

Part IV: Perseverance

We are engaged in a mortal struggle for the survival of our very species. We must fight on against all odds and all obstacles. No matter the cost we must never falter! Never slacken! Never tire! This virus will not be the end of us!

Vaccination rallying cry of Professor Rakosi

"Never leave me alone with insurance people again!" cursed Stefan as he climbed back into the passenger seat carrying a box full of files. "Good god, what tedious creatures they are! They've all lost their heads over these street protests! Premium this! Premium that! Give me a mutilated body any day!"

Vaclav was too tired to humour the youth's petty troubles. He'd spent the rest of the afternoon going through the home of Lidija Ivanevic looking for anything at all that might link her to Oleg Krivokuca. Hours of thrashing through paperwork had produced nothing but disappointment. He could afford such disappointment though. Once they had the CCTV footage, it would be a matter of hours before they had the perpetrator behind bars. Once that happened, the blank spaces would all be naturally filled in and the jigsaw fitted together.

"Well? Was it the same as the other body?" asked Stefan as he shut the car door.

"Worse. Much, much, worse," tersely replied Vaclav, unwilling to elaborate. "What did you find out?"

"A number of things," said Stefan as he fingered over the folders resting on his lap. "These are the files on all his current claims right here."

"Anything on Lidija Ivanevic?"

"I only took a quick glance so I'm not sure. I did speak to a few of his colleagues though. They said he'd been acting strangely for the past few weeks."

"Strange how?"

"Like as if he was afraid of something. Like someone was following him. They told me he'd taken up a Virus Claim caused by someone trespassing

Quarantine Lines." Stefan leafed through the papers and plucked out a profile document. "It started with this girl, Katja Černý. She was a school dropout from Ward Two. Somehow, she ended up here in Ward Four, pissed off some old lady who coincidentally contracted the common cold not long afterwards. The little old lady then made a claim. Our guy Oleg tried to investigate with a medical team but was unable to track the girl down."

"Did he ever find her?"

"Nope. She's completely MIA. Vanished into thin air."

"What? That's impossible. Nobody can get off the grid. Everyone leaves some kind of paper trail. At worst, she would have been homeless and even then the sanitation teams would have picked her up."

"That's what the insurance guys told me. Oleg was trying to find her, but he kept running into dead ends. They said he spent more and more time in Wards One and Two as the investigation went on. They said that was when the paranoia started with him." Stefan fingered through the files again and handed a clump of papers over to Vaclav. "He was looking up other kids who'd crossed the Quarantine Lines. He claimed there was some kind of secret network that all these kids were operating through and I think he hoped that if he found even just one of these kids then he might find Katja."

"Did his colleagues say what his findings were on any of these?" queried Vaclav as he looked over the profile mugshots of these young runaways. As he flicked through them he couldn't help but notice that a great many of them had the same punkish rebellious look which his daughter Justyna had.

"The same as Katja. They're all MIA. He didn't find any of them."

Vaclav froze and considered that last piece of information. He pensively nodded his head back and forth and then threw an eye over his watch.

"Ratko told me he'd have the CCTV footage by about six," he said. "You have the address for Katja's parents, right?" Stefan nodded. "Okay, I think we'll take a little drive down to Ward Two and see what's going on. We should get back to the station in good time to get an ID on our perp then."

"Sure thing. You're the boss."

"Yes, I am," confirmed Vaclav with a smirk as he started up the machine again.

Green light after green light graced their passage through the financial sector. As they knifed across the junctions, they caught fleeting glimpses of the ongoing demonstrations and the White Coats deployed to contain them. Moment by moment the gathering choir of upheaval gradually faded away entirely as they drew closer to the looming Quarantine Wall of Ward Three. At the Containment Gates, a Health Marshal scanned the vehicle registration and waved them past into the outer districts of the city.

As surely as the city transformed when going from Ward Four into Ward Five so too it changed when entering Ward Three. There was a definite air of mediocrity to these streets. The convenience stores were sparser. The houses neither old and grand nor fresh and modern. Both people and place felt like the afterthoughts of someone's grand design for the city. Unlike in the higher wards where people confidently walked the streets as though they owned them, there was a desperate air of restless anxiety about these people as they drove past them. They glanced at Vaclav and Stefan with a degree of both envy and longing in their eyes. They prayed and craved for the comforts of the higher wards and yet simultaneously they feared to fall lower down the rungs of the vaccine ladder. In sum, they never quite knew if they were born to be kings or paupers.

Of all the city wards, Vaclav found this one to be the most unbearable at all. As snobbish as the subjects of the 'Forbidden City' were, at least they knew they were the ruling class. The urban dwellers of this dreary habitat never knew who they were.

"At the second crime scene," he said, deliberately taking his attention away from the miserable specimens on the sidewalk ogling him and his car. "None of the furniture was out of place. Nothing was broken. Nothing in the house was moved. Do you know what that means boychik?"

"Nothing coming to mind I'm afraid," answered Stefan.

"It means there was no struggle," explained Vaclav. "The victim went down without a fight."

"So they must have known their attacker then," elaborated Stefan. "They obviously let them into the house on friendly terms and didn't expect to be attacked."

"Yes," conceded Vaclav. "Or…they didn't know each other. In which case, the attacker must have overwhelmed them very quickly."

"But that would mean…"

"That they've done this before. Many, many, times."

Vaclav heard Stefan audibly gulp at that.

"I hope you're wrong."

"Me too boychik. Me too."

Before they knew it, they had passed through the gates to Ward Two and once again the cityscape took a dramatic turn as they entered the outer rim of the city. Vaclav had always considered Ward Two to be a district with two faces. One was the face it was obliged by the laws of economics to wear; the smiling face of customer care agents and helpline operators. Behind this mask of feigned patience and politeness though was the other face, the real face, of the Ward. The second the phone lines stopped ringing, the workers returned to their hopelessly depressed selves.

The Commission had forbidden the sale and consumption of alcohol and tobacco to the lesser vaccinated on the basis that it made them more vulnerable to the viral threat. Yet beneath the rulings on intoxication and festivities, this two-faced race of despairing 'smilers' found sustenance in plenty from the black-market trade in banned goods. From sundown, they would drink, smoke, fuck, and dance their misery away before rising at sunup to smear the compulsory smile back on their faces again.

These people knew who they were. They could just never show it. And that, in Vaclav's opinion, made them the most tragic of all the Ward nations.

"Take a right here," instructed Stefan as he read the GPS. "And. yep here we are. Containment Park Avenue. Katja's home was number 65."

"Okay, let's go knocking so," said Vaclav, pulling the car up by the pavement. The two of them exited the vehicle and almost automatically scanned the area. It was a horse-shoe neighbourhood with an island of grass in the middle. The houses were of a uniform grey concrete. A clutch of hooded men stood loitering next to a broken-down garden wall. Vaclav couldn't help but notice that one of the houses was completely dilapidated, its doors and windows knocked out like teeth. On the decaying walls of the abandoned house, three simple words had been graffitied in red spray paint:

Beware The Night

Stefan gestured over to the little gang of malingering hoodies.

"Should we head over and see what they're up to?" asked the young Varga. Vaclav made no reply. He slowly took his eyes away from the graffiti sign, looked at the gang, and then looked back at Stefan. "Oh sorry I forgot. Not our problem, right?"

"Good, you're learning," said Vaclav, pointing to the house for number 65. "Let's give the bell a ring, shall we?" Stefan nodded without a word and followed in behind him. Vaclav gave the electric button a press. A dull ring could be heard reverberating through the house. No one came to answer. He rang it again. And again.

Halfway through the fourth ring, he heard someone stomping down the stairs. The front door was yanked open to reveal a dishevelled middle-aged woman standing there in a bathrobe with a cigarette caught between her fingers. Her greying hair streaked with highlights of blonde was an unbrushed mess. Fading eyeliner from the night before bled over her baggy eyelids. Her fingernails were painted a gaudy gold and pink. She gave Vaclav and Stefan a look over and then a defensive aura gripped her haggard features.

"The fuck are you?" she said without hesitation.

"City police," replied Vaclav, smoothly displaying his badge for her to observe. "I'm Detective Kovac and this is eh…" Vaclav's tongue caught in his mouth as he struggled to find a way of introducing Stefan in a professional manner. "…eh my partner, Agent Varga. And you must be Agata Černý? Katja's mother? Yes?"

Agata at once scrunched up her face in discomfort at those words.

"The fuck do you shitheads want? Are you looking for money like that insurance cocksucker? Is that it?"

"That insurance cocksucker is dead madam," informed Stefan with a prickliness Vaclav hadn't expected of him. Agata too seemed a little taken off guard to hear such language come out of the young man. "We're following up on some leads. We know he was investigating your daughter's disappearance before he passed."

"That's right," she confirmed, taking another drag of her cigarette. "No favours it did me or anyone else. She's dead. Long fucking dead."

"What makes you say that?" queried Vaclav. "No one ever found a body for her."

"I know what I know," she answered with bared teeth. "Some nerve you fuckers have to come to my door asking questions. You give a shit about my daughter only now because some trim cunt-licker in his suit and tie got offed in the night. You fuckers leave us here to rot and say I'm in the wrong for letting my daughter go to find a better living on the far side of the wall!"

"We're not here accusing you of anything," assured Stefan. "We're just following up on some leads and looking for the murdering fuck that got—"

"Yeah! Yeah! You're fucking following! Not chasing! The fucker's moved on and you're trailing behind!" shouted Agata.

"What? Who are you talking about?" asked Vaclav in a bid to make sense of her fresh accusations. She pointed with her cigarette to all the houses on the street around them.

"All these houses once had kids running around in them," she said, a quiet tear welling in her eye. "Till they ran away! They ran away to your shiny city and vanished without a word. I tried to look. We all did. But all we ever get is: No vaccine, no pass! Some paedo fuckhead is out there grabbing our children and you're too busy with your god damn shitless virus to do anything about it!"

With that, she flicked her cigarette to the floor, stomped it out with her bare foot, and then slammed the door in their face. Vaclav and Stefan stood there in stunned paralysis for a moment. Vaclav noticed the ominous hooded gang had now hopped off their garden wall and were eying them up.

"I think that's enough foul language for one day," said the detective in the calmest voice he could muster. "Even for me...Let's get out of here."

"Beware the night detective! Beware the night!" howled one of the hooded figures over to them as they got back in the car. "Come in the night to get you! Come to take you away!" Vaclav paid no mind to them and simply hopped back into his vehicle and drove away.

"Do you mind me asking where you learned to talk like that boychik?" asked Vaclav out of curiosity.

"If anyone talks to you like that in the countryside, then you rise to the challenge. You fight fire with fire," explained Stefan innocuously. "Evidently it did not help in our endeavours."

"No, not particularly," concurred Vaclav, still trying to process exactly what he'd just experienced.

"What do you think happened to that abandoned house?" asked Stefan in his young overly curious way.

"Right now, I don't really care. Not my problem."

"And what if it is?"

"Then it can wait till tomorrow. Been one problem too many for one day."

"So back to the station then, yeah?"

"Yep, back to watch the tape and wrap this up before things gets any weirder."

"I hear that."

The streets were bereft of life upon their return to Ward Four. The crowds had been dispersed. Sanitation teams were cleaning up the mess the protest had left behind. On the vacant streets, their vehicle speared onwards alone. The grey sunlight was dipping into the horizon as they pulled up outside the station. Ratko was waiting for them with a tablet in hand. The artsy forensics man seemed unsure of himself as Vaclav and Stefan approached him, as though he were wearing the wrong pair of shoes almost.

"You have the footage?" asked Vaclav. Ratko spun the tablet in his fingers and handed it to the detective.

"Right here, ready to go," assured Ratko. "Just press play." Vaclav pressed the lopsided white triangle in the middle of the screen and let the clip run. He and Stefan watched the footage run its course while Ratko stood there shuffling on the spot.

On the screen, they could see Oleg Krivokuca walk into view. As expected, the surveillance video had labelled his vaccine number onto him, hovering above his head like a digital halo. The insurance man walked past the alleyway and then came running back. A blurry shape panned across the screen after him too fast for either Stefan or Vaclav to get a proper look. Within a matter of seconds, then they saw Oleg being dragged into the alley by the blurred shape before he was systematically butchered to pieces. Above the blurred silhouette there was no number, just the words *'unknown error'* between two brackets.

Silence filled the space between the three of them as the replay button sprung up on the screen. Vaclav handed the tablet over to the speechless Stefan and focused his attention on Ratko.

"What was that? Didn't you get the guys to scrub the footage or something?"

"We tried," whispered Ratko with a quiver of fear in his voice. Vaclav buried his head in his hands. "Nothing worked."

"But…but this isn't possible," protested Stefan as he re-watched the footage.

"I was expecting to come back here to paste a number into a search bar Ratko," fumed Vaclav aloud. "Instead of a vaccine number I get…I get whatever the fuck this is! How the fuck is there no vaccine number over the attacker? And why the hell can't I even see their face? It's like they're blocked."

"The system doesn't recognise them," explained Ratko.

"Then there must be something wrong with the camera on that alley."

"The cameras never lie detective," asserted Ratko forcefully. "I checked the footage afterwards. Vaccine numbers showed up on everyone else that came into view. Including you and me."

"Then how on earth did this happen? *Everyone* has a vaccine number. *Everyone* is on the system."

"Apparently not everyone," butted in Stefan. Vaclav almost turned on his heel to tell the boy to shut up but Ratko beat him to it.

"There's only one explanation detective. Whoever our attacker is, they've never been vaccinated. Otherwise they would have showed up on the system. The cameras don't recognise unvaccinated persons. To put it neatly: if you're not vaccinated then you're not on the system. And if you're not on the system, then technically you don't exist at all."

"But again, that's impossible. Everyone is vaccinated!"

"Not on the North Side," reminded Stefan. "Their streets don't even show up on your GPS. Why would their people show up on the cameras here?"

"The kid is right Vaclav," confirmed Ratko. "The most likely culprit is a saboteur sent across the river by the crazies on the North Side."

"Agata said that it was a paedophile kidnapping the children," recalled Stefan. "Don't the Refusers believe that a secret cabal of paedophiles runs the world and is behind the vaccine? Maybe they sent this covert agent over here to prove a point."

"Ugghhhh," groaned Vaclav, not wanting to hear any of this.

"I hate to say it Vaclav, but your little partner could be right," said Ratko. "It's the only explanation."

"And how the hell do we catch this 'saboteur' hmm? It'll be like catching smoke without a vaccine number to track them," countered Vaclav.

"I guess you'll just have to do some actual police work," said Ratko. "Once you have something more tangible, I'd recommend taking it to Barodnik's boys at External Hygiene Security—"

"No!" slammed Stefan. Vaclav rolled his eyes to the heavens "This is a police case. We'll follow it through to the end. Right Vaclav?"

"Yeah," sighed Vaclav resignedly. "In the morning though…after coffee. My head hurts enough from today."

"Let me know what you want to do with this tomorrow so," said Ratko who was about to leave Vaclav and Stefan on their own when the detective stopped him.

"As a matter of fact," said Vaclav. "If you could get the guys tomorrow to go through the records of unsolved missing persons, that would be great. You know, categorise and label them."

"Sure," accepted Ratko. Stefan looked at Vaclav questioningly.

"Just a hunch I'm getting," he explained before the boy could ask. "I'll meet you here same time tomorrow." Vaclav started walking for the exit.

"What are *we* going to do tomorrow?"

"I'll sleep on it and let you know."

Part V: Patience

It is only with a strong hand that the people can be protected from themselves.

Advice of Doctor Barodnik to President Dvorak (last elected head of state)

The next morning was as grey as the one before. Vaclav winced in agitation as he saw the time on the clock. He'd overslept. Worse still, he could hear Veronika downstairs gossiping with one of her so-called friends. He rolled out of bed, sent Stefan a text to let him know he'd be late, and dressed himself in a rush. He hurried down the stairs and barrelled into the kitchen where Veronika and her guest were sipping coffee at the table together.

"How interesting!" he heard Veronika exclaim mid-sentence. "My daughter Justyna will be back shortly and I'd just love for her to meet you." Vaclav tried to lunge out to grab a banana for the road before a word could be uttered but to no avail.

"Why, good morning, darling," said Veronika with that entitled plastic smile of hers. "You slept like the dead! I wondered if you'd ever wake up. This is my new friend, Angelika. Remember I told you about her the other night after you came in from work. She's new to our book club and involved in goodness knows how many charities."

Vaclav cast a quick look over their guest at the table. Angelika was about as close a clone to Veronika as he'd ever seen. The same lustrous blonde hair. The same perfectly manicured face. The same fake expressions of emotion. The same brands of clothing. If it had been permissible to do so, he would have rolled his eyes to the heavens.

One Veronika was bad enough.

"How do you do?" she greeted courteously in a voice almost identical to Veronika's.

"Hi," he responded tersely. "I have to go. See you later."

"Ta ta!" went the farewell and Vaclav was not entirely sure which of them had said it, a fact which made him run for the door all the quicker.

Stefan was waiting for him at the station with the coffees in hand.

"Get in and give me my coffee!" hollered Vaclav as he pulled up in front of the boy.

"So," said Stefan after buckling his seatbelt. "What's the plan?" Vaclav raised a finger to silence the young Varga while he finished his gulp of coffee. Upon the completion of the ritual, he vigorously shook his head.

"Ok," he said with a sigh. "Now I'm awake. Talk away."

"What's the plan?" repeated Stefan. Vaclav started driving down the road. "Where are we going?"

"A place where the snakes all go and the sun don't shine."

"Is that a joke or is it a place we're going to see—"

"We're going to Disinfection Hill," interjected Vaclav, instantly silencing the boy.

"That's where all the unvaccinated people are locked up, isn't it?" said Stefan a little nervously.

"I did some research on it last night—hence my late start today. If what you and Ratko say is true and there's a saboteur on the loose, then the best place to start would be someone who knows how to get a saboteur across the river without us knowing."

"So, who's at Disinfection Hill that would know anything about this?"

"Marius Zielenski. He was a big deal back in the day, long before your time. He used to be with the Refusers on the North Side and was a human trafficker. He helped unvaccinated people get across to the other side. Then he had some kind of ideological falling out with Citizen R—you know, the lunatic-in-chief over there—and wound up getting arrested by the White Coats over here. He's the only person on this side of the river who would know how to pull off an operation like this."

"Okay," said Stefan quietly. "So, let me get this straight. We're going to the very edge of the city, to a high security facility, to consult with a nutty anti-lockdown human trafficker for an ongoing case."

"Pretty much so yeah."

"Okay…cool…cool."

Once again, they neatly skirted around the massing crowds of protestors—clearly undaunted by the reprisals of the previous day. Unlike the previous day, however, the demonstrations did not stop once they departed Ward Four. Walls of human beings were blocking roads all around Ward Three too and Vaclav had to make a number of detours to steer clear of the mustering storm. Only in Ward Two did they leave the crowds behind them.

From there, they passed into the most dismal of all the city wards. Ward One was the abode of the bin collectors, the deliverymen, the builders, and manual labourers more generally. It was a ward of company warehouses enclosed within snares of barbed wire. Lacking in just about everything else, the people here were in just enough luck to be classed as 'essential workers' so their wages could afford the lowest tier of vaccine.

"Look," pointed Stefan as they passed a bleak eye-sore of a housing estate. Vaclav shifted his attention off the road momentarily to take a peek. The entire side of a house was daubed in the words:

Beware the Night

"It's everywhere here," added Stefan as he shuffled around scanning the ruinous scenery. "There it is again! And again!" He eased himself back into his seat. "It must have started here."

"It would make sense," said Vaclav. "Start killing and kidnapping people in a place that no one ever notices and nobody really wants to notice. I don't think the White Coats or anyone else ever even come down this way."

"But not anymore. We're here."

"Yep we're here," Vaclav scrunched up his face and tightly clenched the steering wheel. "Do you have any idea boychik what a can of worms we've just opened? Do you have any idea how many years of negligence by the White Coats this case might uncover? How bad this could be for the credibility of the Commission?"

"What are you saying?"

"What I'm saying boychik, is that we've *really* let the genie out of the bottle on this. That woman was pissed with us yesterday for a reason. People out here get the vaccine, so they don't get sick. That's about all the attention they get. Consider for a moment if we were to blow this open and show them *exactly* just how negligent the government has been of them. How happy do you think your uncle is going to be when all these dirt-poor scumbags join the protests too?"

"But, you yourself have been part of it. You and your 'not my problem' attitude. How many lives could have been saved if you'd intervened earlier?"

"Yes well, I didn't have you before now did I?"

"All the same, you could have protested on principle. Besides, you said yourself you're not the biggest admirer of the Commission. You said you wouldn't shed a tear if the whole thing came crashing down."

"Principles are a luxury boychik. And generally, they don't put food on the table. It's all well and good in your bedtime stories. In the real world, there are serious consequences for…for doing what's right…That's something we might both be learning very shortly if we keep up with this case. Are you ready to accept that? Are you prepared to face the shitstorm when it hits?"

"If there was no shitstorm detective, then none of this would be worth doing. So, yeah, let's see this through to the end. No matter the cost."

"Alright…alright," tentatively accepted Vaclav. "We'll keep following the bread-crumb trail to Hell."

No further conversations were had on the journey. After another half an hour on the road, they took a turn onto the old motorway where they looped around the abandoned airport and came face to face with the towering security fortress of Disinfection Hill.

The monetization of the vaccine had created a new hierarchy within society based on a person's financial means of acquiring the sacred needle to inoculate them. Ward One however was not the bottom of that hierarchy. The bottom was right here at the dreaded Hill where all those unable to pay for even the V1 were kept in a permanent state of quarantine. The Commission had locked them up here on the basis that were they to roam free in society they would pose a threat both to themselves and others. Here in their cells, their 'frail' and 'fragile' unvaccinated bodies would be safe from the ravages of the virus. At least, that was what the Commission liked to say. In truth, Vaclav knew that the people here were considered the lowest of the low of humanity.

"Mad Marius? You want to meet Mad Marius?" double-checked the clerk at the reception when they landed in requesting an audience.

"Yep," said Vaclav. "At your earliest convenience, if you don't mind."

"Okay, your funeral boys," the bureaucrat said, grabbing two clipboards with forms attached. "You'll need to sign these."

"What are these?" asked Stefan as Vaclav snatched up a pen to sign the paperwork.

"The Hill is not liable for the contracting of any pathogen during our time with Mr Zielenski," explained Vaclav. Stefan looked uncertainly from the paperwork to Vaclav, unsure if he should sign or not. "It's insurance. Just sign it and let's get this over with."

At that, Stefan put his name to paper and they were escorted to an interrogation room by a White Coat.

"Please stay behind the Perspex glass at all times," advised their handler. "Do not make any physical contact with the patient. Do not exchange materials of any kind with the patient. Failure to do so will result in your sterilisation." The White Coat opened the steel door to the cold tiled room fitted with two chairs for them. "Wait here please. Your interviewee will be with you shortly."

Vaclav gave no thanks to the White Coat and plonked himself down on one of the rickety metal seats. An identical room stood facing them on the other side of a wall made entirely of Perspex glass. How exactly one could ever not be behind the Perspex glass to exchange materials with or touch the patient, completely escaped Vaclav. The handler's words were probably the echo of an earlier age, repeated to the present day as part of their ritual.

"Is the glass really necessary?" asked Stefan who was gawking at the gigantic screen of protection in bewilderment. "We're vaccinated and they'll have a mask on him."

"Not Zielenski," replied Vaclav.

"What?"

"He refuses to wear a mask. So much so he hacked off his ears, his nose and part of his chin. That way no one can ever put a mask on him."

"Are you serious?"

"You heard the guy at the lobby. They call him 'Mad Marius' here."

"Sweet Jesus."

"Also, this will most likely be the first piece of human contact the man has had in heavens knows how long…so he's probably going to be a proper nutjob when he walks in."

"Okay," muttered Stefan who then paused for a moment to let the information settle in on him. He sat down next to Vaclav and inhaled deeply. "Okay," he repeated.

Of a sudden, the door on the opposing side of the Perspex glass shuddered open. Two guards clad from head to toe in PPE awkwardly shuffled in with leashes in hand. Between the two of them was Mad Marius, a black bag over his head and a straitjacket encasing his body. Dragging him by the leashes around his neck they tugged him over to a seat opposite Vaclav and Stefan. Once seated they undid the straps of the strait jacket, loosened the leash around his neck and pulled the bag off his head.

Both Vaclav and Stefan were compelled to blink at the sight of him. The anti-mask measures he had taken were just the half of it. There were layers upon layers of scars all over his face. The lids of his left eye had clearly been shorn off with a scissors. His left hand had been amputated and the little finger was missing from his right hand. Burns and abrasions were all over his forearms. His unhinged grin was red-raw with his mutilated gums and missing teeth. A scraggly grey beard the colour of slushed snow hung from his hacked-up face. His head was entirely bald though not by the whim of nature for one could clearly see the scars and burns where he had slashed and scorched his curls away.

The two guards exited the room and thereupon then they were left alone with this self-harm maniac.

"Why so many?" gawped an awestruck Stefan before either Marius or Vaclav could make introductions. The young Varga was utterly transfixed by the hideousness of Marius' ragged body "So many scars." Marius giggled like a little girl at the young man's question.

"Hehehe," he sniggered. He pointed to his ears and chin and nose. "These I did to keep the muzzle off me."

"And everything else?"

"For kicks," spat Marius. "For my self-love and for the love of others." He held up the stump of his left arm. "This even got me into one of your sacred hospitals. They let me in, and I had a fondle and a cuddle with your nurses and all their curvy hips." Marius begun to swing his shoulders and hips to mimic a seductive dance and then started licking the air with his fat tongue to intimidate the boy. Stefan's face began to redden involuntarily "Hahahaha," he laughed. "You like curvy nurses, kid?"

"Mr Zielenski," boomed Vaclav to get the inmate's attention.

"DE-TEC-TIVE!" boomed Marius in answer, spirals of madness slithering in his eyes. "What a big voice you have! May I say too what big beautiful eyes you have! Maybe later on you and I can have a cuddle and a fondle eh? Poor Marius needs some gentle loving! Hehehehe."

"My name is Detective Kovac and this is my partner Agent Varga," continued Vaclav undaunted. "We're here on official business with regards to an ongoing murder investigation. We believe you may have some expertise that could provide some useful insights on the case."

Marius shook his smiling head and giggled away.

"You people never cease to surprise old Marius. Expertise for experts. You going to set me free now eh? Make me one of your essential experts in your perfect beautiful world? That your angle detective?"

"You're not going anywhere Mr Zielenski."

"Then what's in this for me, hmmm? Why should I help you?"

"You'd be saving lives," said Stefan. Vaclav could have slapped the boy there and then if he'd had the nerve to do so. Marius instantly burst into roars of laughter.

"Hahahaha! Who do you think I am boychik? You people never cease to surprise! All this time cooped up in here and not a thing has changed eh? You're still the same old addicts of salvation! Wanting me to join your cult of immortals! Boychik so long as you're alive you're a prison in your meat suit! When I'm dead I'll be free! You give me euthanasia and then we'll be talking real business hahahaha!"

"I'm afraid the Commission banned the practice of euthanasia some time ago Mr Zielenski," blandly informed Vaclav. "All life is precious, as they say."

"All life is a prison detective."

"Maybe so. But I could make your prison a little easier maybe? I was thinking you might appreciate some new reading material. The latest academic literature?"

Marius rolled his head about on his shoulders and chewed the offer over and he visibly began to calm down in front of them.

"Alright, keep talking," he agreed before pointing at Vaclav and looking over at Stefan. "See how this man does his homework on me boychik. See how he knows my puppet desires. Learn a little eh? Hahaha…Now! What puzzle has you puzzled, detective?" Both Vaclav and Stefan let out a sigh of relief. Stefan began to go through the case files while Vaclav relayed the facts to Marius.

"We've come to believe that a saboteur has been sent across the river by Citizen R to commit a series of murders in this city. If this is true, how would the Refusers do this?"

"The only man's the Ferry Man."

"The Ferry Man?"

"Only way across the Borava. Give him a coin for your trouble and he'll take you over the edge and back." Vaclav exhaled tiredly at that. He began to wonder exactly how far deranged this man actually was if his answer was some illusive mythological figure.

"I think things may have changed a little since you were in the smuggling business," he replied as politely as he could without betraying his misgivings. "There's no river traffic anymore. Is there any other way someone could cross the Borava?"

"There's no river without the Ferry Man. There's always a Ferry Man detective. And the Ferry Man's the only man."

"Right ok, well do you know if this is something your former comrades on the North Side would try and execute? Was there ever anyone you spoke to on the North Side that talked about sending a covert agent over here to—"

"That's all anyone ever talks about over there!" butted in Marius with renewed excitement. "Citizen R and his flock are more paranoid than Chairman Mao! They talk about covert agents all the time! You understand?"

"Yes, thank you, we know this. But did anyone ever talk about sending an agent over here?"

"All they wanted was to be left alone. They didn't want nothing to do with this upside-down world you made. Last thing they'd want to do is come here, let alone send someone that would get your silk panties in a knot and make you retaliate. Citizen R and his flock are keepers of the peace! Bunch of swine-shit cowards! They're just like you, truth be told! They're trapped in the prison of this life and afraid of being free."

"Was there anyone who specialised in assassination?" pressed on Vaclav with his questions, trying his best not to get distracted by the man's tiresome philosophical statements. "Kidnapping? Mutilation?"

"Everybody and nobody detective. Your own parents kidnapped you from nonexistence and birthed you into this world did they not? We're all assassins of our own freedom! We all mutilate this earth with the poison of our minds! Hahahaha!"

Stefan leaned over to Vaclav and whispered to him while Marius kept on howling with laughter.

"Are you sure you want to continue with this? This guy is fucking nuts."

"Show him the pictures," advised Vaclav who then returned his attention to Marius. "Mr Zielenski, my colleague is going to show you some photographs from the crime scenes. Could you please let us know if this appears familiar with anything you've seen?"

"I've seen everything and nothing detective," replied Marius in his vague riddling way while Stefan pressed the photos up to the Perspex glass. Marius cupped his half-chin in his hand while he looked over the images of the two corpses. Of a sudden, his eyebrows became raised and a quiet laugh of genuine excitement came tumbling out of his laugh. "Hohohohoho," he crowed as he got out of his chair and stood closer to the glass for a better look at the photos.

"What is it?"

"I know these slashes. I know the dance of this cutter. I *know* them."

"Where? Where do you know them from?" asked Vaclav with sudden urgency. Marius cocked his beaming head and tittered his involuntary giggle.

"Where? Where? Where? Where? You people! You people! You say you're as clean as the gold and the green, but I can see here detective clear as day you people have got dirt under your nails hahaha! Real deep under your nails too!"

"*Where* did they come from?" reiterated Vaclav impatiently.

"Can't you hear me detective? Can't you see what I'm saying? The dirt came from under the nails of yours truly! She's not from over the river. She from *inside* your walls hahahaha!"

"What? That's not possible," rejected Vaclav as he tried to make sense of the strands of truth slipping through the cracks. "The only other place where an unvaccinated person could come from is here. And nobody gets out of here. You yourself know that."

"Oh I do detective, I do. But that wasn't always so now, was it?" countered Marius whose eyes then glanced back over the pictures. "Ohh, you've got a real avenging Angel of Death on your hands here…" Marius got down on his knees and raised up his scarred arms. "It's the Ghost of Christmas past come to haunt you hahahahha!"

"What do you mean it wasn't always so?" Marius retracted his arms and held them close to his ragged beard as if he were clutching a coveted talisman. He sunk down onto his hunkers, his knees screeching off the Perspex.

"The hotel, detective," he hissed. "Before the Hill, there was the hotel."

"The hotel was burned down fifteen years ago."

"Hmm truly. The man covered in paper next door lit himself on fire and brought the whole place down. Seventeen of us were left all dead and crispy and wrapped in the black folds of the reaper."

"So, wait hang on. Are you suggesting that the killer came from the hotel? Once again, that's not possible Mr Zielenski. I am aware that you could come and go as you pleased back then but everyone was accounted for after the fire. All the survivors, yourself included, ended up here." Marius abruptly hopped to his feet like a frog.

"All accounted for, *really*? All your sweet precious beautiful paperwork went up in smoke with the hotel, detective. The only thing you and your people had on us was the number. You counted a hundred and forty-three survivors and seventeen corpses, and you asked no more. You didn't ask any further because you didn't give two shits about us filthy half-humans…But, you see, I know who was *really* there. I know who *should* have been there. And I know who *shouldn't* have been there."

"You're saying there was a mix-up with the bodies?"

"In black and white I am. She was gone that night. She got away and never came back to us."

"You're certain you recognise—"

"Course I'm certain! Course I am! I never lie!"

"Do you have a name for this woman? Could you describe her?" Marius shook his head again.

"I don't recall your labels detective. I don't recall your meat suits. I'll forget you the moment you walk out this door! I only see your souls, detective. I see your soul in your eyes. I see it in your actions and reactions." He tapped the glass where the photograph was. "I see it in *this*. No two people bite the same. This is *her* bite, detective. And she's been on the prowl for a long, long, time. I'll bet you've passed her on the street. I'll bet you've even shared a lift with her. Ohh she's a chameleon detective. Invisible to your eyes. Hides within the trends of the flock as they might say hehehe."

"Yes, we're aware of her ability to elude capture. I—"

"She's getting closer and closer to you detective!" interrupted Marius. "From this Hell Hill to your Heaven Hill she hunts. You just wait now and she'll be sitting pretty on your precious Castle Hill drinking schnapps with the doctors hahahahaha."

"Okay, thank you Mr Zielenski, you've been very helpful," thanked Vaclav as professionally as he possibly could. He gestured to Stefan. "Let's get out of here." The young man nodded without a word and gathered up their things. As they reached for the door Marius called out after them both.

"Just remember!" he hollered after them. The two of them stopped and looked at his leering devilish face behind the Perspex glass. His voice was lowered to the pitch of an unnameable horror and he hissed to them:

"There's a devil on your streets detective...There's a devil on your streets... ha. ha...ha...ha...ha..."

Part VI: (In)Justice

There will always be those who are deserving and those who are undeserving of our treatment. Generosity has its limits, my little friend.

Private correspondence of Doctor Slovenko to Doctor Varga

"With all due respect, can we really trust a deranged maniac like that as a credible source?" questioned Stefan as they left Disinfection Hill. "You said yourself, the seventeen bodies were completely cremated after the fire at the hotel so there's no way of confirming his story."

"This is true," conceded Vaclav. "But we'll pursue it for the time being until we have evidence to the contrary. If nothing else, it gives us a theory to work off. Say what you will about him as a crackpot, his story does make sense when you think about it. The Commission was a lot looser back then with unvaccinated patients. It's not impossible that someone slipped through the cracks. And there would be no lack of motive for them killing a claims adjuster and a hospital administrator. The humiliation, the discrimination, the alienation, they would have gone through is inconceivable to the two of us. It would be enough to make an axe-wielding psychopath out of anyone."

"Alright but I still think this is a faulty road to go down. I mean he also said the killer was a woman. How many paedophile serial killers are women do you think? Not very many I'll wager. Doesn't seem very likely."

"Stranger things have happened." Vaclav's phone began to beep. "Could you get that for me and see what the message is?" Stefan plucked the phone from its resting place by the gearbox.

"There's an emergency meeting of the Commission for you to attend," informed Stefan as he scrolled over the message.

"Does it say what time?"

"About half an hour?"

"Ok, I should be able to cut across the city in time provided there's no traffic hold ups. Could be tight though and you'll need to come along with—"

"Oh, you have a video call coming in," said Stefan as the phone began to ring.

"Answer it." Stefan pressed the green button and the two of them were confronted with Ratko's face. "Ratko, what do you have for me?"

"I just wanted to let you know about the checks you asked me to do on missing persons in the city."

"Okay."

"We're barely halfway through the archive and we're already at a hundred and seventy unsolved missing persons."

"What? You serious?"

"Yep."

"What's the demographic of people?"

"Mostly kids from ages fourteen to twenty from the lower city wards. All of them were Quarantine Wall jumpers."

"And the timeframe? How far did you go back?"

"Oldest case was fifteen years ago. A fifteen-year-old called Sergei Tóth was on a night out with his friends who said he went home with an undescribed 'woman' and he was never seen again."

"What ward was that in?"

"On the edge of Ward One. We're not through all the records yet but from what I can see here Vaclav, there's a clear correlation between the timeframe and the wards. The further back you go the more missing persons in Ward One. The cases have been getting closer and closer to us over the years. At its current rate, there'll be vanishings in Ward Five by this summer."

"Okay, thanks for the update Ratko." Vaclav reached across Stefan to close the call.

"Just one other thing Vaclav," interjected the forensics man. "We got the report in on the two victims."

"Oh, and?"

"There's blood missing from both Lidija Ivanevic and Oleg Krivokuca." Both Vaclav and Stefan frowned at one another in confusion at that.

"Well obviously, they died from blood loss—"

"No. I mean there was blood *missing* from both scenes. The killer *took* it. All the main cuts on both victims were made to arteries where there would be a healthy blood flow. If they just wanted to kill the victims, then they would have cut just the throat or just the wrists. But all of them? The killer was trying to *drain* them. We also haven't located Lidija Ivanevic's hands. We can only assume the perpetrator kept them as trophies."

"So it's the same killer for both then. Yes?"

"More than likely. I have some of the guys doing interviews with friends and family. I'll let you know if anything comes up."

"Okay, thanks Ratko. Keep us posted." With that, Vaclav nodded to Stefan to close the call. The young Varga did so with tense fingers and then stomped the car floor irritably.

"Fuck it anyway," he cursed. "That crazy fucker was right."

"Hate to say it boychik but looks like it."

"You need to bring this to the Commission," urged Stefan. "You need to let them know."

"Are you serious? Did you not hear me earlier? There's fifteen *years* of missing persons! Fifteen years of negligence by the health authorities. Fifteen years of them not giving sufficient funds and training to the police department. They're in the middle of an emergency meeting over these stupid street protests. Do you really think they will want to hear any of this? This is the last thing they want to know about."

"So what then? You're going to keep it under wraps and not tell anyone? Perpetuate the pattern of inattention, the not '*my problem not my job*' attitude?"

"Stop it."

"No. People are being murdered here. They're being hunted down, cut to pieces, and harvested for God knows what fucked up reasons. You're a police officer for crying out loud! You're supposed to protect everyone from sick bastards like this! And instead you're going to return to cruising the city as your own personal tour guide? You heard Ratko, there'll be disappearances in Ward Five in a matter of months. And when the trouble starts there, who do you think the Commission will blame? Because I can guarantee it won't be my uncle and his White Coats."

"That's enough!" bellowed Vaclav to silence the youth. Stefan visibly shrunk back in his seat. "Sorry…I just need time to think. I need to think it out what I'm going to do." Stefan held his hands up in surrender.

"All I'm saying," sighed Stefan. "Is that you're worth more to everyone doing what you're doing right now: a real police detective. You're no use to anyone cruising the city to kill time, least of all yourself."

"Thanks," begrudgingly accepted Vaclav. "Now…shut the fuck up boychik and let me think."

In truth, there was no need to think about it. The Genie had been let out of the bottle from the instant he had taken over the crime scene from Gustaf Schnell. It was too late to go back to the way things were before. He *had* to follow it through to the end now. It was *his* problem to resolve. More than any sense of duty though, he knew that deep down he also *wanted* to solve the case. For the first time ever, he felt as though there was a purpose to his job, that there was substance and meaning to his profession and to his life as a whole. He was no longer just a man with a job title and a badge. Hour by hour he had started to ease himself into the role of the watchful protector, a lone knight tasked with fending the city from the hungers of a dark and restless monster.

He knew what had to be done.

After skirting around the growing sprawl of unrest that gripped whole swathes of the dying city, they eventually reached their destination. By the time they arrived, the City Castle was alive with frantic activity. Droves of panicked civil servants were running back and forth across the courtyard with handfuls of paperwork in hand.

"We're a little late," noted Stefan, pointing to the clock on the dashboard.

"They were always late for me," replied Vaclav. "They can afford to wait for once." Stefan chuckled a little at that and the two of them exited the vehicle. "Stay in the lobby and keep to yourself," he instructed the young Varga. "If you overhear anything of interest, let me know."

"No problem."

No sooner had Vaclav left Stefan behind him in the lobby than he could hear the thundering of voices echoing from the conference room. The doctors had actually started on time for once. As he neared the room, the voices became progressively louder and angrier till finally he opened the door and the full raw power of the argument washed over him. So wrapped up with their verbal battle were they that no one even noticed him enter the room.

Vaclav had never seen them like this before. The dull methodical rhythm of their typical meetings had been utterly blasted away. The smug and conceited Varga was now a nervous shivering wreck. Burgenstein had wasted away with stress so thoroughly that his flesh was almost entirely translucent over his skull. The blubber on the gross face of Rakosi had soured to an ill grey colour, a potent odour of sweat steaming off him. Barodnik had his head down in shame, one hand gripping the arm of his chair, the other grasping a handkerchief to wipe both mucus and tears alike from his face. Towering all over of them, risen from his seat with cane in hand, was a fuming roaring Slovenko, his aged face turned to a fiery rubicund red.

"We intend to deploy the sanitiser cannons to clear the streets tomorrow Doctor," uselessly promised the trembling Varga. Slovenko slammed his cane on the table. The Commissioners jumped with fright.

"Tomorrow! Tomorrow! There will be *no* tomorrow little Varga!" howled Slovenko pointing out the window to the city below. "The wolves are at the gates and your White Coats have proven themselves less than useless! You have *failed!* Failed! Failed! Failed! In two days, you have managed to turn a spark into an inferno! There are demonstrations out in Hrisko city and down south in Kolomsaw province! We are losing the country thanks to you!"

Slovenko's voice cracked into a cough and he snatched up his inhaler off the table to regain his breath.

"With respect Herr Slovenko," gulped Burgenstein, the saliva visible to the naked eye as it rolled down his throat. "All is not lost yet. It is true that we have underestimated the situation and that we have inadvertently kicked the hornet's nest. But we can regroup and buy some time to muster our strength if we make some concessions to them, accede to even a few of their—"

"To concede to them would be to concede to Death itself!" hammered Slovenko, his eyes brimming with wrath again. "If we give them an inch, we are finished! One inch to them and we'll be back to the Age of the Wilderness when planes filled the skies and men roamed the globe as they pleased! Like animals! One inch to them and the virus will return! One inch to them and we're all dead! Your soft hand will give us nothing but misery! And I will not have it! I will not follow in the footsteps of Erich Honecker and his Berlin Wall! Our Quarantine Walls must stand for another hundred years and not budge one inch!"

"The vaccine premiums are rocketing!" advised Burgenstein more forcefully than before. "If the rioting continues, then the rates will rise out of control and not even the people in Ward Five will be able to afford it. If we do not act quickly, then we will be heading towards financial—"

"We will be kneeling at the feet of the Primitives on the North Side!" abruptly advised Barodnik, shutting up his skeletal counterpart on the opposite side of the room. "Word has reached us that the Refusers are planning an offensive across the river to take advantage of our misfortune. We must fire on them first to deter them from—"

"And add petrol to the fire?" exploded Slovenko angrily. "Have I surrounded myself with fools? You call yourself doctors! Do none of you have a shred of common sense! I should have condemned you all to my operating table and sold your vital organs to the black-market witch doctors of China! Just as I did the dithering talkers of old! The blood of future generations will be on your hands gentlemen!"

An uncomfortable silence filled the room, a tangible feeling of inadequacy and shame oozing off the Commissioners. Slovenko sat in his chair, clasping his rugged wrinkling head.

"We have tried to convince them of the science," lamented Slovenko quietly to himself. "We have tried telling them we will take care of them. We have tried to return them to the safety of their homes. And yet these apes grow angrier and angrier. They won't listen to reason out there. They don't even care about their lives. The lives we gave them in our...our magnificent hospitals...our cathedrals of medicine...We brought them into this world...we helped keep them in this world...and this is how they treat us? They don't want to be our patients...The people of this country have lost their way...It's all lost."

The Commissioners bowed their heads in shame in imitation of their leader.

"If I may," piped in Vaclav, taking the opportunity to make his case.

"No, you may not," rejected the watery-eyed Varga.

"Oh, what does it matter," overruled the despairing Slovenko. "Soon everything will lie in ruins anyway. Let the policeman talk. What harm can he do now?"

"Thank you. Doctor," formally responded Vaclav before clearing his throat. He rose from his seat to address the whole Commission. Each and all of them gazed across at him with an eerie sense of doom in their eyes. Truly this must be the end of times if the police detective dares to speak.

"It has come to the attention of my department," he began a little shakily. "That...there is a...skilled and professional...*Murderer*...on the loose in this city." No one moved a muscle. He had their full attention by use of the tabooed word. "As a matter of fact, I believe this…murderer…has been on the loose for quite some time. Fifteen years in all."

"Fifteen years?" muttered Slovenko with a frown. "That can't be right. How could anyone have eluded us for that long?"

"We have evidence indicating that they are one of the unvaccinated," explained Vaclav, jumping to elaborate further before one of the Commissioners could concoct an explanation to promote their own department. "While we first believed they might have slipped across the river from the North Side as a saboteur, the evidence now suggests that they are an escapee from an old quarantine facility on the outer rim of the city. Hundreds of unsolved missing person cases—which, due to lack of both funds and manpower, we were never able to pursue—show a pattern of killings that have been spreading all the way from Ward One into the city. I would like to emphasise gentlemen, that this is based only on the records we have access to. Scores if not hundreds of potential homicide cases were classed as health code violations over the years and never fully investigated."

"From what we know so far, the killer primarily specialises in hunting young people who are in violation of Quarantine Lines. The two victims we have direct access to, gave evidence of vampirism, cannibalism, and sadomasochism…I believe, gentlemen, that what I have uncovered is only the tip of the iceberg. It is predicted moreover, that, being invisible and virtually undetectable to our surveillance systems, the killer will be operating right here in Ward Five by this summer at the very latest."

Vaclav sat back down. No one said a word for what felt like five minutes easily.

Slovenko then pointed across at him and threw his eye over his fellow Commissioners.

"This, gentlemen," he said. "This is the genius we need." Vaclav was not quite sure if he heard the Surgeon-General correctly. "*This* is the solution to our problems. Thank you, Detective, for bringing this to our attention."

"Beg pardon sir?"

"You've saved us," explained Slovenko with a half-chuckle. Vaclav looked around the room. Everyone else seemed as confused as he was. A new energy suddenly overcame the old doctor. "We must inform the people of this threat; the invisible killer in our midst. Brilliant!"

"Herr Doctor?" piped up a confused Burgenstein. "What are you suggesting?"

"Don't you see it gentlemen? Didn't you hear the man? There's a killer out there. A killer with the blood of hundreds of people on their hands. As guardians of human life, we cannot simply stand by and let this killing spree go on. We must first inform the country, and then..." Slovenko trailed off for a second, the cogs of his mind clearly running faster than he could give voice to them.

"And then?" questioned Rakosi.

"And then...we bring about a *lockdown.*" The eyes of every Commissioner lit up with excitement at once. "How else can we keep our dear fragile, helpless, patients safe? Patients are trying to breach Quarantine lines and are being killed as a consequence. We must save the patients from themselves."

"Yes," agreed Barodnik resoundingly, all the other Commissioners nodding their heads in unison. Slovenko turned directly to Vaclav.

"What are you? A liaison officer?" he asked.

"Yes, Doctor," confirmed Vaclav.

"You are promoted to the rank of Commissioner," conferred Slovenko without second hesitation. Vaclav felt he almost needed to pinch himself to confirm he wasn't dreaming. "Money, manpower, expert advice, labs, technical support, you name it, you'll have it. As of this moment the city police will be invested with half the duties and responsibilities of the Department of Internal Hygiene Security." Varga's mouth gaped open in protest, but Slovenko cut him off before anything could be said. "The same department I might add that not only failed to quell the current insurrection but, as Commissioner Kovac has so bravely revealed, was also responsible for the gross negligence and incompetence that allowed this new threat to fester right under our very noses!"

"My eh...my thanks doctor," responded Vaclav, not knowing exactly how to react.

"You have the gratitude of the Commission and of this city," said Slovenko, inclining his head in a show of unprecedented respect to him. Across the room, Vaclav could see it was Varga who was now nearly brick red with indignation and fury. Before any argument could be made over the new realignment of power however, the doors suddenly swung open and Stefan marched in. Vaclav and the others were about to say something when the youth whispered into his ear. The detective listened and nodded attentively, no one dared interrupt the exchange.

"I'm afraid you must excuse me gentlemen," said Vaclav as he rose from his seat. "It appears that our killer has struck again." He turned to Burgenstein. "The boy you sponsored with the vaccine donation."

"Emil Bauer, yes?" confirmed the living skeleton.

"He's dead?" asked Slovenko disbelievingly. Vaclav nodded. "Why that's wonderful! Make sure you have plenty of photographers there at the scene with you. That will really scare the wits out of these miscreants on the street when they see that! A good terror campaign on all media outlets will set things straight. I know it!"

"A wise decision Doctor!" agreed Rakosi and Burgenstein together.

"Indeed!" concurred Barodnik. "We must have some schnapps and vodka to celebrate!"

"Another fine idea!" laughed Slovenko.

Vaclav did not wait to hear anymore. He was a Commissioner now. He didn't need to explain his leaving. He just strode out with Stefan at his side and returned to the trusted interior of his car.

"He fits the victim profile," said Stefan as they got behind the wheel and took off. "He's a young adolescent crossing Quarantine lines."

"He's a high-profile victim too," noted Vaclav. "The kid just got tonnes of coverage on the news a few days ago. If she was looking for people's attention, then she just struck gold. People are going to be running scared shitless once the Commission starts its ad campaign."

"You told them?"

"Yep. They're happy as pigs in swine shit now, gave me half your uncle's workload and made me a Commissioner." Stefan boisterously slapped him on the shoulder.

"Congratulations!"

"I'd hold off on that yet. God only knows what problems will be in my purview now. I'll have to move to 'perfect-land' Ward Five. At least, the wife will be happy about that."

"Don't even think about that man. Now's not the time. There is after all a …eh…a dead child waiting for us."

"Yes. You're right. Did Ratko give any other details about Bauer other than he was found outside his new school on Nurse's Street?"

"Only that his parents said he hadn't come home last night. No record of him passing through the gates back to Ward Three either and he wasn't there for morning class. The body was discovered in the playground when the kids were let out on an early lunch break. Obviously, she must have taken him, killed him, and then brought him back to the school for everyone to see."

"Okay," acknowledged Vaclav. "She wants our attention. She has it."

The streets were littered with debris from consecutive days of social unrest. In the background, they could still hear the rumble of scuffles and the shrieks of shouting demonstrators. From the windows and balconies of high-rise apartments, residents hung out banners in a show of solidarity with the protestors reading: *"End to Hospital Politics," "Sterilise the Doctors," "We are not sick,"* and *"We are not helpless."*

Of a sudden they turned a corner however and they were greeted with an altogether different city. School children were huddling together on the pavement bawling their eyes out. One schoolgirl surrounded by her friends was screaming without stop, her hands clasped over her head as she wrenched tufts of hair out of her scalp. Parents were running down the sidewalk with frenetic abandon looking for their children. Teachers were standing by, covering their mouths and eyes in a useless bid to contain their own dismay.

"I think we might be here," said Stefan in a declaration of the obvious.

"Thank you, Sherlock," joked Vaclav. The two of them smirked thinly as their eyes soaked up the scenes of distress around them. Vaclav felt his heart beat a little harder within his chest. He looked at Stefan and was reminded in that instant that he was still so young and inexperienced. He saw the trepidation in him. "You sure you want to do this? You really want to come with me and see a dead little boy?" he asked.

"For sure," answered Stefan with inflated confidence. "The more I see, the easier it will get."

"Don't be so sure of that boychik," warned Vaclav as he parked the car. "Let's go." As they made their approach to the forensics tent, Vaclav spotted Sergeant Novak standing at attention next to the gates of the school. The sergeant was smoking heavily again, but this time he was down on his knees, his eyes unblinking as though he'd been told his own child had been savaged by wild dogs. If Vaclav had had any doubts that this was going to be bad, that sight alone put them to rest. This, he knew, was going to be very bad.

Ratko was waiting for them outside the tent. His face was a sickly pale. His hands were trembling involuntarily. His eyelids were blinking incessantly.

"Vaclav!" he greeted with an air of urgency, running over to them.

"Ratko," retorted Vaclav lowly, gesturing towards the forensics tent. "What's waiting for us in there?"

"There's something else," said the forensics man in a flustered manner that did not become his normally casual personality. Stefan, as though transfixed by the sight of the tent, continued walking forward and left Ratko and Vaclav behind while he entered the tent alone. "Some new details came out about Lidija Ivanevic. One of her close friends told us she was going solo on a personal crusade to help runaway kids."

"Just like Oleg Krivokuca," said Vaclav to himself, keeping an eye on Stefan as he vanished into the forensics tent. He anxiously threaded forward to the tent, eager to not leave Stefan there too long on his own. Ratko backed up. "Anything else?"

"Only that she was putting all her energies into saving a girl called Jane Kelvin."

"Jane Kelvin?" said Vaclav with a frown, the words tasting strange in his mouth. He'd heard that name somewhere before.

"I know, such a western name, right?" said Ratko. "Anyway, I just thought you should know before—" Stefan came stumbling out of the tent almost head over heels. He collapsed onto all fours and vomited on the ground. "Before you see what's in there," finished Ratko fearfully.

Vaclav inhaled deeply and then brushed past Ratko. He let one of the Blue Shirts help Stefan off the ground. As he approached the tent, he heard a teacher break rank from her silent colleagues and wail aloud for everyone to hear.

"He was such a nice boyyyyy!" she wept, her voice distorting into stutters and stammers under the weight of her tears. Her colleagues crowed around her and tried to escort her away from the children. "Such a nice b-b-b-boy! W-w-w-hy h-h-him? Such a nice nice b-b-boy."

Vaclav stepped into the tent.

No one else was there. Like a sacred religious shrine, it could only be visited by one person at a time. For what lay inside the tent was not so much a sight for the eyes as it was an existential experience of the inhuman.

What he saw done to the little boy's body was outside the bounds of human understanding. It was so indescribably monstrous he couldn't even think. His mind was incapable of processing it. He wished in that moment he were blind. Every instinct within him wanted to howl in denial at the heavens above. What had been done to Emil Bauer was so hideous that it presented an unnameable horror to the human eye, one that devoured the very senses into darkness. This was not so much a murder scene as it was a nightmare in the flesh.

He stared and stared into the stillness of the abyss before him.

Then he saw *it*.

Chiselled into the boy's exposed flesh were three guiltless little words.

"*Ta ta detective.*"

Vaclav's heart turned to dust. He felt his very being sink into the bottomless pit. He turned and sprinted out of the tent. Ratko and Stefan called after him, but they may as well have been in another galaxy. He pushed people out of the way indiscriminately, launched himself into the driving seat and sped away as fast as the engine would carry him.

"No, no, no, no," he chanted to himself mindlessly as he rocketed through the traffic lights and nearly killed two pedestrians. "No, no, no, no, no, please not her," he intoned as a form of prayer, hoping somehow that his words would bend reality.

The car screeched around the corner and slammed into another car. Windows shattered around him and he knocked his head off the steering wheel. After a slight blur of vision, he kicked the car door open and clambered out. The other driver had gotten out of their car and was screaming curses at him. Vaclav just ran.

"Hey! Hey come back here!" the driver yelled after him. "I hope you have insurance!"

He barely heard any of it. He just kept running and running till he reached the house. He fumbled for his keys and realised he'd left them in the ignition of the car. With three desperate kicks, he booted the front door off his hinges and came barrelling into the front hall of his home.

"*Too late,*" taunted the words written in blood across the corridor wall upstairs.

Veronika and Justyna were hung upside down from the bannisters, gags stuffed into their mouths. Their throats and wrists were slit open and drizzling blood on the tarnished floorboards. Their hair and hands dangled in the air like the branches of a weeping willow. An iron bar had been drilled through their ankles to keep them from plummeting to the floor below.

On Justyna's hand, he saw a personalised silver bracelet. On the bracelet the name 'Jane Kelvin' was inscribed.

Vaclav fell to his knees.

"She was here," he gasped to himself, the vague and fleeting memory of his morning introduction to the so-called Angelika flashing before him. *"She was here...she was here..."* He looked up at his butchered wife and daughter.

"No one heard them scream," he whimpered quietly before more quietly whispering *"I...I didn't hear them scream."*

The blurry memory of Angelika, like the blurred image caught on the CCTV footage, flashed before his eyes. And then he heard the recalled voice of the Shadow speak in farewell to him one last time:

"Ta ta."

The Young Spring Protests failed to bring about any meaningful change.
The city remains in lockdown.
The Commission remains in power.
Commissioner Detective Kovac suffered a nervous breakdown shortly after these events. He was forced to resign from his post and currently resides in a mental institution undergoing therapy.
Despite the efforts of Kovac's successor, Detective Stefan Varga, the origins and whereabouts of the serial killer, popularly known as 'the Shadow', remain unknown.
None of the missing persons have been found.

Chapter II: The Dissenter

Part I: Defiance

Vaccination is Annihilation!

Rallying social media status of Citizen R

Sheets of frail rain breezed across the peer. Rusting steamers wept iron tears into the passing river. The Borava swelled and bristled beneath the wintry shower, its depths dark and impenetrable beneath the shadows of grey buildings crouched beneath grieving skies.

Amidst the wreckage of this dying place, a teardrop from the heavens splattered across Amelia's face and her eyes shot open into consciousness to find her feet dangling puppet-like above the undulating river water.

Her face scrunched up in irritation at the realisation she'd fallen asleep here, again.

People seldom came down to the river here, a fact which made it so easy to just drift off into sleep and the misty dream-world beyond. This was the one place in the city she could take a breath from the claustrophobia of family life. Moreover, here at least, on the very edge of the world, the air was that little bit cleaner and that little bit fresher. For just across the river, lay V-land—the land of the brainwashed and the delusional where the covenant of scientists and their Frankenstein vaccine reigned.

It was said to be unwise to even linger here on the edge so long. The Enemy was rumoured to wield a vaccine ray-gun that could be fired across the river. If unfortunate enough to be struck, your cell structure would supposedly be reorganised for your prompt assimilation into the System of the World Octopus. There was some exhilaration in that fact to be sure, to be so close to the edge and to risk the Evil Eye of the Enemy.

Mostly though, Amelia simply utilised this sanctuary as the one spot she could read in peace. That fact alone made it all the more irksome that she had dosed off into the dreamy pastures beyond again. She hated dreaming. *Hated* it. She never felt in control when she dreamed. She could cut her hair, she cut dress in different clothes, change her language, improve her knowledge. But she could never stop herself from dreaming. The oneiric journey was too subjective, too erratic, too esoteric, and too laced with so-called hidden meanings. The High Council had an open fascination with uncovering such 'hidden meanings' and that fact alone made her hate dreaming even more.

She valued clarity, rationality, empiricism, and consistency, when it came to approaching life. Something which dream analysis sorely lacked in. Above all else, Amelia prized the truth, only the truth, and nothing but the truth. No arbitrary distortions or distractions. Just good clean facts based on hard evidence. The fewer mysteries in the world, the better. Hence why she preferred to read a good decent book than drift into somnolescent vision.

This latest book was from the history shelf; 'Stalingrad' by Anthony Beevor. The week before she had leafed through the scientific works of James Lovelock. The Exchange was hit and miss when it came to books though she could hardly complain. Any and all of them were forbidden works. They were relics and vestiges of a bygone age, manuscripts that by some fluke had escaped the cleansing flames of the Great Awakening. With the ongoing blockade, it was impossible to even photocopy one of these gold-dust scraps of paper.

She needed to finish this one soon. There was a long line of people waiting to get their hands on it afterwards. It needed to be returned to the Exchange and secretly passed down to the next eager reader. She had devoted the entire afternoon to completing the book yet already the faded sun was retreating, and the chilled rain was starting to splatter across the browned pages. Rather than risk damaging the precious manuscript, she grudgingly chose to give up and head home. She would have to leave this one unfinished. Perhaps another day in the future she would find out if Hitler's Sixth Army beat the Russians at Stalingrad.

Back in her schooldays, history had been a clean straight line from start to finish. Everything outside of that straight line was considered unimportant and distracting. She and everyone else had been taught a simple narrative: in Ancient Babylon, wealthy merchants had formed a villainous Cabal and from that moment onwards had ruled the world behind a veil of illusions and lies. Having almost lost their grip on the world during the Great Bronze Age Collapse, the

Cabal had sought to attain immortality. This they believed could be achieved through the essence of youth. And so, year by year the Cabal had turned into an international paedophile ring bent on kidnapping and devouring the essence of children. In a final bid for total world domination, the secret Cabal had terrorised the world with a so-called pandemic. The truth however—as everyone knew now—was that it was a manufactured event; a 'Plandemic' to reset the world where they could wipe out the adult population and leave the children of the world orphaned and helpless to their lecherous desires.

But, as became clear to everyone with a morsel of intelligence, there was no virus, there was no disease. Anyone who supposedly died of the virus had in fact been murdered by the puppet doctors who claimed to be trying to 'stop the spread'. In the Cabal's rush for final victory, the brainwashed masses of humanity finally became aware of their servitude and rose in revolt before the Great Reset could be completed. In a courageous act of defiance against the slave masters, a single anonymous internet figure known as Citizen R chose to lead the rebellion against them. Under his direction, the freedom fighters pushed back the Great Enemy and established a new society. Though they failed to liberate the whole world, one piece at least lay in the hands of freedom and here on the banks of the Borava a new world would be constructed.

From this city would sprout the wings of global revolution.

For Citizen R had promised it so.

As the Enemy was driven back across the river, Citizen R and his anonymous High Council of Cyber Czars had declared the old world to be nothing more than an illusion, a dream concocted by the Puppeteers to keep the human race subservient to their will. Every shred of it was a specially manufactured nonsense, a delusion intended to keep people from realising their true selves. None of it could be allowed to survive. A blank sheet for Year Zero was required. It all had to be destroyed. And so, the Council launched a campaign against what they called the Four Fakes:

1. Fake Elections
2. Fake News
3. Fake Science
4. Fake History

Amelia remembered her parents showing photographs to her of that time. At Whistle-blower Football Stadium, the huge bonfires had swallowed every lie the Puppeteers had ever told. Where books and paintings were scorched to ribbons so too were the Puppet Preachers—the academics, the journalists, the philosophers, the writers, the politicians, the doctors, the scientists.

All liars.

All puppets.

All loyal pawns of the vile Puppeteer Paedophiles.

All deserving of the flames.

Every year the purge was re-enacted in a celebratory festival with dancing and singing. Amelia remembered going to the annual gatherings as a child. Those were such happy, simple, times. As she grew older though she recalled more clearly how the Red Coats ran out of books and traitors to burn and so resorted more and more to blank sheets of paper and scarecrows as symbolic gestures to the glories of the past. Finally, with the international blockade placing such a strain on resources, there was nothing left to burn. And so, just like everything else in this tired dying wreck of a city, the celebrations had fizzled out.

As she strolled homewards through Martyr's Park, she could faintly hear the propaganda speakers behind her blasting out Judy Garland singing *'Somewhere over the Rainbow'* to try and entice the zombies to defect. In this unvaccinated Shangri La, Amelia walked upon overgrown footpaths flanked by crumpling meadows of dead grass. To her left and to her right she was faced by two memorials dedicated to the days of the Great Awakening. To her left was the Liberation statue depicting brave men and women cast in bronze. They stood there in heroic poise, the masks issued to them by the Great Enemy being torn apart in their strong muscular hands or being set afire with cigarette lighters. On the plaque beneath them, the epithet read:

"Dedicated to the men and women of the Free the Voice Campaign. Never Forget: Only Slaves Wear Masks."

On the right meanwhile was the much simpler dedication to the parental mission of the High Council. It portrayed a ring of school children holding hands as they danced in a circle. On the plaque beneath their feet, the inscription read:

"Save the Children."

Both structures had turned green with rust. Even on a good day now it was hard to discern the writing on them. If this was what a few decades of neglect and decay could do, she wondered what a few centuries would do. Would the people of the future even grasp why such metallic fossilised shrines were made?

Towering up over this grim scene were the temples and monuments of this rotting civilisation. Eclipsing the greying sunlight of the dusk, the apartment blocks stood dark and forlorn. The fresh layer of vibrant red paint given to them after the Awakening had long since peeled away under the relentless hand of time. They stood raw and bare and grey. And within the walls of these oversized concrete totem poles, the citizens of this decrepit place lived out their lives. Even from the park, she could distinguish the bare-chested scumbags smoking their joints and shooting up on heroine on the tiny garden balconies.

On the garbage littered streets below, the packs of Red Coats roamed in their pick-up trucks, shotguns and meat cleavers in hand. Named as such for the bright red boiler suits they wore, in a time long since gone they were an elite guard of toughened revolutionaries dedicated to the freedom of mankind. The Red Coats of today however were as pitiful as the broken society they defended. Their leaders were old men who drank and smoked too much. Their recruits were uneducated half-wits with nothing better to do. When Amelia was a girl, everyone had wanted to be a Red Coat when they grew up. Nowadays, nobody with any morsel of sense would want to associate themselves with such human dung. Lacking obvious targets to persecute and lacking the initiative to hunt down any remaining deviants, the Reds spent their days just driving around the city and taking selfies for their Platform accounts.

As Amelia walked within the crushing shadows of these living towers, she saw a lone street vendor with his cart of canned fruits. The vendor was a stocky middle-aged man with a balding hairline. He stood there patiently with a cigar in his mouth, his hands grasping the hips of his cart. Amidst the plastic bags tumbleweeding down the road behind him and the soggy mounds of cardboard on either side of him, he was a sight for sore eyes. Planted in amongst his stacks of preserved peaches and strawberries was a sign which read: *"Death to the Puppeteers! Liberate the World! Long Live Citizen R!"*

Amelia could not help but smirk at it. The vendor no doubt had little interest, let alone comprehension, of the words he so freely advertised with his canned goods. If he only ever looked around him, he would know exactly what so-called 'liberation' from the World Octopus looked like. Did he really want Citizen R to live forever like the peaches inside his tin cans? Hardly. It was just for show. Yet removing the sign would just attract unwanted attention. By doing so, he might actually give the Red Coats something to do. *Truth* be told, the vendor just wanted to get through the day like everyone else and go home without a fuss. He didn't care if the Puppeteers of the Cabal still ruled the world beyond the Borava River.

He never had.

He just had the misfortune of living on this side of the River when the Millennium Bridge was blown up to keep the hated doctors out.

Amelia held onto that thought as she came upon the door to her own apartment block. She navigated her way through the carpet of shattered beer bottles and bloodied heroine syringes thrown from the balconies above and shouldered her way through the door. The phosphorescent lights flickered like withering candles above her head in the dim lobby. She stepped into the elevator, grabbed the shutters and locked herself in. With the required four presses of the faulty button, she was on her skyward way home.

To her annoyance, the lift stopped at the second floor and an old lady joined her. Shoulder to shoulder in the cramped compartment with the hunchbacked and worn-faced old woman, the ascent continued.

"I heard a joke today," the old woman said, paying no heed to Amelia and speaking as if to herself alone. "A man commits suicide by walking into oncoming traffic. His bones are shattered, and his organs are splattered across the pavement. A concerned citizen comes running over and asks why he did it. They ask if it was because of a family crisis? The lack of jobs? The inflation? The blockade? The narcotics? In his last breath the man says it was for none of those reasons. He tells them he had nothing better to do and out of sheer boredom he'd done it by accident. He says he'd actually like to live."

It took a moment for Amelia to realise that was the punchline. Of all the reasons to kill yourself in this life, only a fool would do it by accident and still want to live. She chuckled lightly just to complement the old woman's guffaws. The lift then shuddered to a halt.

"Well, this is me," said Amelia and she made her swift exit into the faintly lit corridor. As the lift continued on its upward journey, Amelia exhaled in despair. This was what it had come to; so many were committing suicide that jokes were being made about it. "Why would anyone want to live in this shithole country," she bemoaned to herself, and she made her way down the hallway to the family apartment. She turned the key in the lock and was already able to taste, smell and even breathe the potent blooms of mould which plastered the apartment walls. Before Amelia could even take her coat off, she heard her mother's voice.

"Dishes," the matriarch instructed tersely, pointing to the sink full of unwashed delph.

Amelia's mother, Maria, and her father, Vlad, were slumped together in a lethargic heap on the sofa, both of them glued to their phones. Amelia knew her mother had once been a beautiful woman with long braids of golden hair with a sweet and tender smile. Her father she also knew to have been a strong handsome man once upon a time. Somewhere along the way, those two people had steadily faded away. Maria had a pair of permanent brownish-black bags drooping beneath her eyelids. Her hair now had a dry straw-like quality to it. Her once radiant skin was now nearly as grey as the apartment walls. Her father's muscles had sagged into fat. A pop belly full of vodka and horse-burgers ballooned outward from his body like a giant tumour. Both Vlad and Maria were dressed in the unwashed tracksuits they always wore, day in, day out.

. She wondered sometimes if there was even any point in them being alive anymore.

"Where were you?" queried Maria, not swerving her attention from her phone for one second.

Amelia plunged her hands into the sink and began scrubbing.

"Out," curtly replied Amelia without further explanation.

"Out where? You weren't sleepwalking into neighbours' houses again, were you?" queried Maria with feigned concern. Amelia rolled her eyes up to heavens. Not since her childhood days had she embarrassed herself with one of her infamous sleepwalks. To her clueless mother though, yester-decade may as well have been yesterday.

"Looking at the microchipped Zombies across the river again, were we?" suggested her father more accusatively.

Amelia still gave no answer. They didn't deserve one as far as she was concerned. The less she gave them the better. At any rate, they would only interrupt her if she spoke further. Theirs was the louder voice in this household. Her silence managed all the same though to steer her father's attention away from his phone.

"I told you before it's not safe there," he continued irritably. "The pervert doctors on the South Side probably had their telescopes out to have a letch at you."

"The buildings on the South Side look nicer," justified Amelia quietly, her nerves cringing as she braced for the predictable reaction.

"Nicer? That's exactly what they want you to think. It's all a delusion! They're trying to lure you over there with their lavish lifestyle so they can vaccinate you and put strings on you! They want to make a lying Pinocchio out of you! Only *real* people can dream you know! Have you ever known a zombie to dream? They want to make Pinocchio's out of us all! I'll not have it. I'll not have the Svoboda family stringed up as playthings for the puppeteers! Not in my house!"

"Someone's commenting," notified Maria to her husband and he swiftly returned his attention to his phone with frantic alacrity. Maria turned to her slaving daughter. "Where's your phone Amelia?" she asked a little worriedly. "The astrologers have declared the stars are aligned for a vote to be held tonight. We'll be deciding on Czar Kowalski's lizard theory becoming the official ethos of the movement."

"Pah! It'll never pass," coughed Vlad. "The cretins over in Block C will never get the votes. Half the user profiles over there are gone dormant anyway! Its good old Czar Kovalenko all the way!"

Amelia paid little attention to the political ramblings of her parents. Rather than live in the dying material world, they had devoted themselves to the virtual matrix known as the Platform constructed by the High Council. In this secondary world, their avatars were engaged in never-ending ideological debates. The days of politicians and parliamentary assemblies were memories of the decadent past. There were no elections in this world. Elected leaders, according to Citizen R, were not the representatives of the people but the representatives of the Cabal and the contested elections they ran in were but rubberstamp formalities to validate their position before the brainwashed masses.

But no longer!

In this world, democracy existed in its truest form. Debates were no longer hosted by parliaments infested by the vermin politicians but were hosted by the whole of society within the virtual secondary world in which all users had a voice. To avoid total anarchy the users were organised into factions through which to channel their voices. Each of these factions then was headed by a Cyber

Czar who acted as the people's direct representative on Citizen R's High Council.

Amelia found the whole process utterly exhausting. This was partially because her parents were so thoroughly engrossed by it. Night and day, they committed their energies to the Platform, craving the adrenaline rush of making their voices heard by thousands of other users. For all the so-called virtues of this technological direct democracy compared to its corrupt predecessor run by the puppets in suits and ties, Amelia could not help but notice that it seemed to get very little done. The few times she had logged in, she had noticed that the vast majority of users were just like her: quiet onlookers to the verbal battles of loudmouthed maniacs...like her parents. For all its inclusivity, precious few people actually cared to partake in it anymore. So fed up were the users of Block C that whole sections had gone dark. The debates never addressed anything of substance like public transport, infrastructure, agriculture, taxation, and certainly not the tabooed area of healthcare.

Instead, they just spiralled deeper and deeper into obscure arguments about the destiny of mankind and the nature of the Puppeteers.

In effect, it was next to useless. She had long ago lost faith in the capacity of the Platform to provide a better life for her and her friends. Was it too much to ask to live comfortably? Apparently so according to her parents' generation. Comfort was the means of seduction used by the Enemy. The most she might ever aspire to in this life were she to engage with the Platform discussions, was the reputable Platform status of "Esteemed Troller" like her parents before her.

"Come on Amelia! Finish those dishes!" insisted Maria urgently. "Get your phone and join us for the debate! We need as many voices as we can get!"

"I don't know where my phone is," quietly said Amelia behind grated teeth.

"Don't be stupid! Get your phone and—"

"I'm not voting!" she snapped suddenly, almost breaking one of the dishes as she faced off with her parents. Maria and Vlad both looked at her wild-eyed. They were about to say something when a knock came at the door. The family standoff was frozen for a second and then another knock tolled on the door. Maria got up to her feet and waddled across the apartment to answer the door.

"Ah Governor Friedrichs," she greeted with genuine surprise and a bow of courtesy.

"Please, please, to old friends it's just Conrad," said the Governor with artificial modesty. "May I enter?"

"Of course, of course," agreed Maria like a servile peasant girl. Vlad cast aside his phone and jumped to his feet with hand outstretched to receive their guest. Of a sudden, Amelia's parents had transformed from sedentary statues into beings of living flesh and bone, eager to both serve and impress their visitor. "Please come in, come in. It's not every day we get a Tower Governor!"

"Thank you! Thank you!" said the Governor and he came marching into the tiny apartment.

Conrad Friedrichs was a little older than Amelia. He was one of the many 'orphans' of the Plandemic and had become a poster child of the Awakening—one of the children everyone was so desperate to 'save'. Using this profile, he was able to boost himself into the upper crust of the ruling caste and attain the rank of Tower Governor. Amelia did have to admit that he was rather handsome to look at. He was tall, lean, blue-eyed, and blonde. That perfect appearance however was no doubt the product of constant attention by his many followers and sycophants. At any rate, it was practically buried beneath the rather ludicrous uniform which befitted his rank and station. Draped around his shoulders was a leather cape dyed in crimson red, the tails of which were held up by two attendants to make sure it never trailed behind him. Beneath this he was wearing a bright red cassock, like that worn by a cardinal, and a set of red gloves to warm his hands.

All in all, he had the appearance more of a sorcerer than a 'governor'. Amidst the dreary greyness of the apartment block though, Amelia could not deny that the stark redness certainly caught the eye.

"To what do we owe this great pleasure?" asked Vlad as he pulled out a chair for Friedrichs. Maria hurriedly rushed to the kitchen to fetch some glasses and a bottle of vodka for their esteemed guest. The Governor dismissed his two attendants to a corner and with a whirl of his leather cape, he planted himself down at the coffee table to address his resident serfs. Amelia turned her back on their guest and kept scrubbing the dishes. If there was nothing to be gained by speaking to her fanatical parents, then there was less still to be had from engaging with this agent of the system.

They would only talk over her anyway.

"Can a man not make conversation with his troops?" he chuckled. Amelia's parents mirrored his guffaws as he pulled off his gloves finger by finger. He thereat adopted a more serious tone. "I just came down to make sure all was in order for tonight's vote. You pair are after all the most reliable of voters in our dear Block B. If everything goes to plan, I will be sure to put in a good word for you with Kovalenko himself."

"Everything is quite in order Herr Governor," assured Maria as she waddled over with tray in hand to the table. "Kowalski and his lizards! Where is his head gone? The Puppeteers are evil we know, but lizards? The man is gone delusional. I heard he's even written a book on it; the Lizard Tales or something or other. He's gone mad. Plain mad!"

"Well it's funny you mention it," noted Friedrichs. "The push for Lizardism came not from Kowalski but from his Governor on Block C. To be honest, I'd say Kowalski is just using it to boost his position on the Council. At any rate, with so many users from C Block gone dormant, it will likely come to nothing and you my friends will be the ones to reap the rewards. At the very least, there will be 200 bio-slots in store for you. The loudest voice wins as they say!" Maria and Vlad both nodded and grinned to each other.

Amelia's shoulders automatically tensed with discomfort at her parent's greedy reaction. Ever since the Plandemic, the depraved bankers of old had been done away with and a new cashless, technological, digital currency had been born into being. The R-Mark was a bio-currency encrypted into a person's DNA. Stipends of the R-Mark were awarded to users of the Platform in accordance with their status—hence, the more followers and the more attention one attracted, the more money one would receive. Where exactly this money came from, Amelia had not the faintest idea. All she knew was that because she shared DNA with her parents, she could not afford to ditch them. At least, not until she made a name for herself on the Platform and could attract followers in her own right, something she had little to no intention of ever doing as a matter of principle.

"We will not disappoint," proclaimed Maria. "And we of course appreciate that our efforts do not go unnoticed. But it is very strange that this lizard business started with a tower block governor." Friedrichs nodded.

"I know. The man must have been doing some archival work on the early years of the movement. It's quite some time since this whole lizard thing saw the light of day."

"I was thinking exactly that," agreed Vlad with wholehearted enthusiasm, slapping the table with the flat of his hand. "Not since before the Plandemic if I rightly recall. Why the surge Conrad? Why are they promoting this whole 'reptilian' agenda? It's completely out of date."

"Beats me," chuckled Friedrichs as he sipped his vodka. "Truly it does. It's come out of nowhere. It is an interesting take on things though I must say. Are you familiar with their argument? They're saying that not only are the Puppeteers all lizards hiding inside person suits but that the 'vaccine' itself is in fact the venom milked from their fangs. That explains why all the vaccinated people on the South Side are so submissive and servile—they've been drugged with the reptile toxin. But they go further still! They claim that the Puppeteers have an elite squad of lizard-assassins who have chameleon qualities. According to the beliefs of the lizardists, it was these chameleon-assassins who, being able to shape-shift and avoid our detection, murdered all the innocents during the Plandemic and then covered it up by claiming it was the fault of a 'virus'. It's quite a well-thought-out narrative I must say."

"Yes, yes, but such nonsense!" refuted Maria with fanatical earnestness.

"Yes, I mean they're practically re-writing history over there! Its' borderline fantasy!" chimed in Vlad. "The world was being governed by paedophiles! Not lizards! I'm not sure if I told you before young Conrad, but back in the day when the Plandemic was kicking off I had a friend who knew a man whose sister was the girlfriend of a man who was friends with a public servant who worked for President Dvorak, and he said that the government was planning for every adult in the country to die. So there! Straight from the horse's mouth! They were paving the way for the Cabal to seize our children! That's a fact. End of story. There were no lizards involved!"

"I know, I know, their claims are quite far-fetched I must say," concurred Friedrichs with another gulp of alcohol. "But, as you all well know, nothing will come of it. It's nothing more than the ravings of a fool trying to attract some attention to himself. He's not nearly as dangerous as that Pawel Ziga." Vlad and Maria both shook their heads in vigorous revulsion at the utterance of that name. Amelia scrubbed the dishes a little more intensely as she braced for her parents' predictable rant.

"Such treachery, such treachery," disapproved Maria. "For a former ambassador of the Council to lose his way like that!"

"He'll have us grovelling on our hands and feet before the Puppeteers if he and his cretins ever had their way," supported Vlad. "I've said it before, and I'll say it again Conrad. It does not matter what mask the Enemy wears. *The Enemy—*" Vlad thumped the table with his fist. "*Is.*" Another thump. "*The Enemy.*" A final slam of the fist was delivered to ram the point home. Conrad nodded in agreement and then cocked his head a little uncomfortably as he considered the subject.

"They *are* gaining ground," he had to concede. "A lot of people my age especially, are flocking to his ranks. They find the narratives of the High Council to be…lacking…somehow."

"So I've heard!" exclaimed Maria. "They're scrolling back over the lies of the past. Agnieska down the hall told me her young ones are discussing the so-called 'crimes' of Hitler. Why do they even care about that garbage the Puppeteers used to spoon-feed us with?" Friedrichs shook his head and sighed at those words. Amelia scrubbed the dishes harder still in a vain attempt to filter out the conversation.

"Such misguided curiosity," bewailed Conrad. "If they ever read the *real* history, they would know that Hitler was in fact a hero fighting against the Puppeteers. You could say in fact that he was our only chance."

"Until now!" erupted Vlad of a sudden. Friedrichs slammed his hand down on the table in elation.

"Until now!" he echoed in wondrous agreement with a wave of his finger. "Quite right! Until now! I could not have put it better myself!"

"Long live Citizen R!" hailed Maria.

"Long live Citizen R!" toasted Vlad and Conrad with a toast of their vodka glasses.

"Whenever shall he return?" asked Maria a little anxiously of Conrad, evidently thinking he might have an answer for her on the missing leader of the High Council. "I am so sick and tired of looking across the Borava at those paedophile doctors on the other side. It's about time we took the fight to them and brought the whole Cabal crashing down! I can barely stand the thought of all those child brothels serving the perverts over there. When will he return and save us all?"

"God only knows dear Maria," said Conrad. "He does not disclose his location to us on his search for the weapon that will defeat the Cabal for good. So far as we know though, he is currently on a hunt for the Holy Grail."

"*The* Grail!" exclaimed both Maria and Vlad aloud. Amelia's shoulders tensed a little tighter still and she cleaned all the harder still.

"The very one," confirmed the Governor with confidence before his voice trailed off a little "His quest to seek out the Ark of the Covenant came to little I'm afraid." His voice then perked up with renewed excitement. "But! Once he has the Grail, the Cabal's 'science and medicine' will be shown to be no more than a superstition and the true healing power will be in our hands! When he returns, we shall be unstoppable! The Council's stewardship will be at an end and Citizen R will lead us to glory!"

"And we shall succeed where Hitler failed!" cried Maria aloud in rapturous jubilation.

"ENOUGH!" roared Amelia as she flung a plate against the wall out of raw frustration. A shock of silence filled the room. She could feel the stare of everyone's eyes on her. She spun around on her heels and faced down the Tower Governor. She knew she shouldn't. But she didn't care anymore. She couldn't take it any longer.

"Excuse me?" said a dumfounded Friedrichs.

"This is such utter swine-shit!" slammed Amelia without hesitation. "Are you even listening to yourself? Do you even have the faintest notion of who Hitler was? For all we know he might have persecuted our very own ancestors! But instead of getting your facts straight, you spew out this total rubbish and there's not a shred of evidence for any of it!"

Both Maria and Vlad were now looking upon their esteemed guest with a sudden fearfulness, not for Amelia's sake, but for *their own,* fear that they might be associated with her deviant behaviour. Their faces were turning red with embarrassment.

"And what evidence is there for what *you* are claiming, young Amelia?" retorted Conrad coolly as he assessed her up and down. "Where else could you have found such lies than in one of the evil libraries of Pawel Ziga's Exchange? The clue is in the word my dear; they're called 'lie-braries' for a reason. They're full of lies. There's not a shred of evidence for anything you've said."

"There's no evidence, because you and your vandal Red Coats ransacked everything!" fired back Amelia. "Everything and anything you could get your hands on you plundered and burned like barbarians! And for what? There is no Cabal! There is no international paedophile ring! There never was! It's a fantasy! There's no evidence for it! Not a single piece! That's why you destroyed it all; because if there's no evidence for anything else, then there's no way of disproving your nonsense! If everything is a lie, then your lie must be the truth!"

"I will tell you now that it was *our* sacred truth which saved this city, girl," countered Conrad with narrowed eyes. "If it were not for Citizen R, you and I would both have been chained up in a children's brothel pleasuring the needs of the degenerate doctors. The People know who to place their faith in."

"The people? The people rot and suffer here because of you and your breed! Hundreds beyond count take their own lives because they cannot bear the world *you* built! The only people who believe in this madness are fanatics like you who exploit the gullibility of brainless bootlickers like my parents who pledge themselves to a nameless leader they have never even laid eyes on!"

"Amelia!" shrieked Maria bitterly.

"No!" slammed Amelia back at her mother. She started towards Conrad and grabbed him by the collar of his cape. "Out with you! You and your lies have no place here! Out! Out!" The Tower Governor was so shocked by her conduct that he was paralysed with disbelief. Within a matter of seconds, she was opening the door and flinging him down on the mouldy corridor carpet, his attendants trying their best to help him up in a hurry. "Go fuck yourself!" she shouted in a final damning curse.

Just then she looked up and saw all the corridor doors were open. All the neighbours were looking at her. They all had their phones out and were filming the whole thing. She slammed the door in their face and instantly knew that it would soon go viral on the Platform.

Everyone would know.

The Red Coats would come for her.

Both her parents were mortified. Maria was on the brink of tears. Vlad was red and fuming, steam almost smoking out of his ears.

"What was that?" he bellowed at her. "That was the Tower Governor! Who the fuck do you think you are!"

"I'm a dissenter Dad!" barked Amelia without any hesitation. His face visibly paled as she said those words. It was too late to turn back now. She might as well come clean with them. "I'm one of Pawel Ziga's followers and I don't believe in anything the Council says."

"You…You ungrateful child," muttered Maria in horrified astonishment. "All this…This is *all* for you my child—"

"Yes! Yes! I know! 'Save the fucking children!' I'm not a child anymore for fuck sake! And I see now that the only thing I've ever needed saving from was this fucking…this fucking place! This *hole* we've dug ourselves into! You saved me from a vaccine, great, well done you! But you can't save me from this place! Or from the High Council!"

"Don't you say another word against them," warned Vlad crossly.

"Oh, come on! Can't you see? Can't you see the hypocrisy? They claim they're fighting against a secret cabal and yet, somehow, it's *them* that are anonymous. We don't even know their real names! They claim that they're fighting against a planetary paedophile ring and yet it's *them* who are so obsessed with children all the time. What are *they* saving the children for? They claim that every religion, every philosophy and every school of thought that ever existed were bent on the conquest of the world and the submission of all humanity to one dogma. Yet when someone opposes *their* beliefs, they call it a lie and a delusion! They claim to be fighting for freedom and yet no one is free to speak against *them*! They claim that we'll all be microchipped if we were vaccinated by the Doctors. And yet we all have *their* DNA encoded money in our veins that's doing God only knows what to us! Can't you see it? Can't you see that *they* are the Cabal? Can't you see that we're in Hell?"

"Enough!" growled Vlad, punching his fist into the mouldy wall. He glared at his daughter with wolfish eyes. "You weren't there," he snarled at her. "You didn't see the bodies stacked up on top of each other in the streets. You weren't there when the world fell apart. If you believe these blasphemies, then you truly know nothing. The Council saved us. And they continue to save us. The Enemy is right there across the River! Ready to send their agents across here to make it happen all over again!"

"The Plandemic is *over* Dad! There are no agents trying to kill us! It's over! Not in ten years has one single person even displayed symptoms of the poison the assassins used to use! It's over! It's a convenient lie you've been living in! The *truth* that you refuse to see is that this place is fucked! People are out there dying from fucking hopelessness! Not from the so-called Enemy! It's *you* that knows nothing! Who the fuck are the two of you to talk anyway? A taxi driver and a shopkeeper! Neither of you know anything about anything! If you had any real intelligence, you'd know that it's all bullshit! That it's all a lie! But you can never admit that! Because if you do, it would mean admitting to yourselves that you were too gullible and stupid to know fact from fucking fiction!"

"THAT'S IT!" suddenly screamed Maria with her hands raised to the air. "I've heard enough of your lies and your insults! You're out of here Amelia! You're gone! Get out of this house before your father boots you out! As of this moment you're cut off from us! I'm not transferring one more cent of my hard-earned Marks to you. You don't want to be saved by us? Fine! Fine! Go out and fucking starve on the streets like a dog! Get out! Get the fuck out!"

Amelia grabbed her coat. She was about to open the door when the thought struck her to snatch up her bag with the Exchange's book in it. She dared not leave it here for the Red Coats to find.

With the prized pages safely in hand, she slammed the door behind her and left the Svoboda household behind. She brushed past the lift. The last thing she wanted was to be trapped in a suspended cage. She went for the stairwell instead and raced down the steps to vent her rage.

She punched the front door of the building open and of a sudden she was out onto the street, her shoes crunching on broken syringes. The yellowish glow of the streetlights barely illuminated the empty spaces of Infancy Road before her. Her chest at began to lightly heave in bated trepidation as she scanned the area for Red Coats. No one was around though.

Not yet.

She was about to get on the move when out of the corner of her eye, a black shape came plummeting down from the heavens. The sound of a bloody splash and a brittle snap echoed in her ears. She looked across the road to Block C.

Someone had jumped off their balcony.

Instinctively, she sprinted across to see if they were still alive. To her amazement, the fall had not killed them. They lay there as broken and splintered as the syringes and beer bottles around them, their arms and legs in a contorted mess of spiking bones. Blood was gushing out from their mangled limbs. So disfigured were they that Amelia could not even distinguish if they were male or female. Yet still she saw that their eyes swivelled and blinked in their sockets, their mouth was opening and closing for breath. They were still alive.

She got down on her hunkers to inspect the living corpse to see if there was anything at all she could do for this latest soul claimed by the Suicide God.

"*Run,*" croaked the corpse with a struggle. She gazed into the person's pulped up face. "*Run,*" they repeated with genuine fear in their bulging eyes. *How could they still be afraid?* she thought to herself. *They were already on death's doorstep.* Then they said something that made no sense at all to her.

"*The...Black Dragon,*" they rasped. "*...She's coming...*"

Part II: Dissidence

In a world of Lies, it is our task to unveil the Truth. Where we cannot unveil it, we must construct our own Truth. And it is within our very own Truth that we must live.

Pawel Ziga, Section 3, Paragraph 4, of 'A Critique of the Great Awakening'

Amelia walked through the dark and vacant space that had once been the site of the Innocence Square Carnival. Between the disintegrating horses of the carousel, she strode with a deliberation towards the one remaining spark of light on the edge of this forgotten place. The store was at the base of a derelict post office. A middle-aged woman, lounged across the till, secretly reading a book to kill the time. As Amelia came into view, she stirred from her reading and faced her first customer in hours.

"Oyster or beetroot?" asked the bespectacled woman, her hazel eyes peering out over her crescent-shaped glasses.

"What I'd really like is a green pepper," replied Amelia calmly. The grey-haired shopkeeper kept her stone-cold composure.

"I'm sorry," she said with deafening monotony. "We only have oyster or beetroot flavours to offer. Which will it be?"

"I'd like to make a deposit," retorted Amelia as though it were the most logical answer in the world. "I have a great deal to give and nowhere to deposit it." The woman nodded to confirm the completion of the secret code and pulled a lever behind the till. The shelf of canned oysters and beetroot swung aside to the left and revealed a stairway leading deep into the belly of the earth. "Thanks, Ludmila."

"Always a pleasure," responded Ludmila wryly as she returned to her book.

"Actually," said Amelia just before she vanished down the secret stairway. "Could I just check something with you? Could I try and buy one of the beetroot cans?"

"Sure," said Ludmila without a thought and she pulled out a tablet. Amelia pressed the face of her thumb against the screen. Her name and Platform profile picture automatically came up with all her personal details followed by a notification in red stating *Purchase denied. R-Mark balance too low.* Amelia retracted her thumb and Ludmila put away the tablet. "Looks like you're all out of pennies, dear," said Ludmila. "You'd better get your voice heard on the Platform or at least follow someone important if you want to make ends meet."

"Thanks, just wanted to check," said Amelia and with that she descended the stairway, her mother's threat to cut her off now fully confirmed in her mind. The doorway automatically closed behind her and once again she was alone.

There was no going back now.

Amelia had given barely any thought to where she would go after her parents turfed her out. The answer seemed obvious to her. Fearful of the coming Red Coats, she had wasted little time diving for the shadows once the last ember of life had abandoned the splintered suicide victim. With the Reds on her heels, she had had little time to contemplate the last eerie words spluttered at her by the dying human vessel. Only one thing had mattered: getting off the grid. There were only two ways of doing that. One was to try and cross the Borava River for the land of vaccinated zombies. An option tantamount to suicide. The other was to descend into the Underground, into the roots of the city, into the hidden world of the dissenters.

Amelia had made the journey into the deep many times. This, after all, was where the Exchange was. But every other time she had made the journey with the intention of returning to the surface. No longer a mere tourist or visitor, she now entered as an exile in search of refuge.

After skipping down three flights of stairs, she was confronted with a short corridor that made a sharp turn to the left at its end. Sitting idly by, holding the fort as always at the corner, was her friend Sophia. Not unlike Ludmila, Sophia too was killing time with reading. Sophia was of an age with Amelia. She had short dyed purple hair with matching purple contact lenses clasping her eyes. Her bare arms were awash with tattoos and her petit face was decorated with piercings.

"Hey!" she said with delight, closing her book and getting up off her seat. Amelia did not return the greeting but simply embraced her friend. "Since when are you a hugger?" asked a surprised Sophia.

"I've left home," explained Amelia as she pulled away. Sophia raised her eyebrows in surprise. "I'm cut off. There's not a cent to my name."

"Fuck," said Sophia with genuine astonishment. "That's harsh. Even I'm not cut off and my parents hate my rebel guts. Come think of it I don't think I know anyone who's gotten unplugged entirely. That's crazy!"

"As you can appreciate then, I need some temporary lodgings and I'd rather not sign on as a civil slave."

"Of course! Of course! I wouldn't wish that on anyone. Let's get you down to the Room. We'll find a couch for you to kip on and get one of the tech boys to hack a bio-vault for some pocket money for you."

Without further ado, they continued on their venture into the subterranean world. After turning three corridors, they were faced with a fire exit door. The walls were trembling with sonic vibrations. Sophia slammed down the green handle and of a sudden they were weaving their way through a packed crowd of drugged up revellers. Epileptic green and red lights flashed across the swarm of delirious faces as the ear-splitting grunge metal of the outlawed band, *'Plastic Souls of the Galaxy'*, blared from the booming speakers.

The Underground was home to all those who had no place in the world of Citizen R. As the High Council had deemed all popular music composed after 1950 to be a manipulative tool of the Cabal, such festivities as this could only ever be enjoyed deep beneath the earth. Down here amidst the tunnels and the pipes of the dark, the artists, the intellectuals, and the activists all made their nests.

Amelia felt the weight of wandering eyes fall upon her as she passed through this subterranean Sabbath. As always though, most people were too caught up in the hype of the music to pay much heed to the passing pair of dissenters. After squeezing through several clumps of moshing punks, they reached the secret door on the other side of the dance floor. Once again, they were within the narrow confines of the corridor realm. Up and down three flights of rickety metal stairs they passed and then at last they were faced with an inconspicuous white door one might have mistaken for a cupboard. Sophia gave three special knocks and the door opened. With that, they had arrived at journey's end. The Room lay before them.

The lair of the dissenters was a hybrid space, a cross between a living room, an office, a library, and an art studio. At one end of the Room, a cluster of desks hosted antique computers with access to the World Wide Web of old—or the Planetary Paedophile Platform as the Council had renamed it (relabelling the old URL of WWW with PPP). At the other end was the Exchange itself with a set of bookshelves crammed against the wall, it's caretaker, known to everyone as Professor Michal, constantly reordering the leafy volumes. Finally, in the centre of the Room there was a circle of second-hand couches and armchairs. A portrait of Pawel Ziga hung from each of the walls so that there was no direction anyone could turn without seeing him. On the wall overlooking the library section was inscribed the dissenter's eternal oath of servitude to the greater good of all humanity, reading:

"Service is our Purpose."

Professor Michal aside, the Room was sparsely populated. One fellow dissident was on the computers, his focus so acutely directed upon the screens that Amelia could not identify him. Two others were lounging on the couches. While the Room served as the safe zone from which the dissenters planned their operations and stored their political and cultural writings, few if any of them actually lived down here. The vast majority, like Amelia herself until now, resided in plain sight, their true identities and motives kept hidden. Ziga had insisted on a strict policy of anonymity for all his followers. If two dissenters were to meet in person outside the Underground, they were to pass each other by as though they were strangers. Only when the Council was at its weakest would the veil of anonymity be thrown off and their true identities revealed. Until then, complete and total secrecy was paramount.

"You know where everything is," said Sophia. "I should get back to the lookout post in case anyone else needs a guide. I'll leave you to it."

"See you around," retorted Amelia.

"A lot more than before I hope," said Sophia with an uncontainable smile as she departed the Room.

Amelia made her way over to the Exchange and plucked 'Stalingrad' out of her bag. Michal narrowed his eyes as he saw her approaching his library, clearly interested to see what book she was returning. Michal was a tall lanky middle-aged man with a neatly trimmed beard and a set of rectangular reading glasses.

Though everyone called him 'Professor', in truth he had never been anything more than a research assistant. The title of academic prestige had been awarded to him purely on account of him being the most educated member of the dissident movement, and quite possibly the most educated person still living on the North Side of the Borava.

"Enjoy?" he asked curtly as the book was surrendered to him.

"Didn't finish in time," answered Amelia while Michal started scanning the shelf to see where the book fitted. "Maybe another time though now that I'll be living here."

"Ah, so you join the ranks of us mole-rats down here," retorted Michal in his downbeat fatalistic way. "You'll become quite acquainted with the tunnels soon enough. You won't need Sophia to come and fetch you anymore."

"Did you ever need someone to guide you through?" asked Amelia out of genuine interest.

"Me? Good grief no! I've been here too long for that!"

"Of course, sorry, I forgot you've been here since before Ziga's time even. Since it all started."

"Well not quite the start," corrected Michal with finger raised like a tutor to her. "I wasn't here when Marius Zielenski ran the show. He was the first real dissenter you know. I'm glad I wasn't around then. Not something I'd like to have had on my conscience. He used to go around encouraging children to self-harm and commit suicide. Quite a wild character he was. I think he got exiled to Zombieland across the river in the end."

"Evidently his interpretation of 'Save the Children' did not sit very well with the High Council."

"Manifestly so," declared Michal as he slotted 'Stalingrad' in next to Jonathan Steinberg's biography of Bismarck. "At any rate, the world is well rid of him and his ilk. There were a few followers of his left when I arrived, but they all drifted away or got caught by the Reds. We've moved on to more hopeful days since then." Michal grabbed a stack of books off a stool. "Now, unless you need a book off me, I'd best get back to work."

"Work? You do realise it's the middle of the night."

"It's *always* night-time down here Amelia," said Michal as he started scaling up a short stepladder with books in hand. "The sun might as well be dead and gone. It makes no difference to us mole-rats. You'll get the hang of it in a few years."

Amelia did not particularly like the sound of that. She was too numb though to voice any discomfort. Too much had happened in the last few hours for her to care right now. This was only temporary, she told herself.

She let the resident librarian get back to his sleepless endeavours and joined the two dissenters on the couches. One she recognised as Velvel Varga. A man of middling stature and greying hair, he bore a face chiselled down by years of disappointment. Peering out from behind his crumbling facade however were the most striking set of bright green eyes. Unique among the dissenters, Varga had family on the other side of the River and was in routine contact with one of them who was said to be in the higher echelons of government. Given these family connections it was never safe at all for him to leave the Underground. Like Michal, he was a permanent resident here.

The second dissenter Amelia did not know. He was sallow skinned with black hair and soft brown eyes. As she sat herself down next to him, he looked up from his book and held out his hand to her.

"Ahmed Hussein," he introduced himself.

"Amelia Svoboda," returned Amelia as she accepted his hand. "I haven't seen you here before."

"Nor I you," he said. "Are you new?"

"No, and I take it you're not either."

"No."

"There are more dissenters than both of you think," interjected Velvel without glancing up from his book. "You both used to come here at different hours. Now, you'll be here at the same hours all the time just like me." He pointed to Amelia. "She threw a Tower Governor out of her apartment, look up the video." He then pointed to Ahmed. "He forgot to salute a Red Coat sergeant. There's a funny GIF of it on the Platform. Look it up if you care." Ahmed and Amelia both gave each other a voiceless salute of respect.

"So we're both new exiles then," chuckled Amelia. Ahmed laughed.

"Nothing new to me I'm afraid," he said. "I've been an exile all along."

"Really? How so?"

"Oh I'm Syrian originally. My parents moved the family here before the Plandemic and decided to stay on this God forsaken side of the river when the vaccines became mandatory." His voice then took on a more sarcastic tone. "According to them, the Prophet Mohammed would have disapproved of it so here we are in 'Blessed Shithole City'. But on the bright side, we can still practice Islam, so it's all ok."

"But," said Amelia thinking it over in her head. "Religion is banned here too. Just like it is on the South Side."

"Not in H Block," sighed Ahmed tiresomely. "The tower governor and Czar Kaczynski have a soft spot for niche religious beliefs. Living to the left of us were the evangelical Christians who thought the vaccine would turn us all into homosexuals, and to the right of us were the Hindus who thought the vaccine had cow's meat in it. And that was just our immediate neighbours!"

"And what did your parents' think was in it?"

"Pork and vodka," he said dryly. He gestured to the book he was reading. "Having done my homework on immunology and vaccines, I think I can say with confidence that their theory lacks some evidence."

"You want to be a doctor?"

"When things change for good, then yes," answered Ahmed with that honesty only found among dissenters. "There's more behind every cough and sniffle than 'an agent of the Cabal spiked my drink!'. The world is more complicated than that. I'd like to know every bit of it and use it to help people. Not that my parents would ever listen to the truth."

"In time, perhaps they will," consoled Amelia hopefully. "When Ziga brings the whole Council crashing down, they'll have no choice but to accept the Truth."

"Yes, when the sky falls on our heads," scornfully snapped Velvel. Ahmed and Amelia both looked at each other in confusion at the veteran dissenter's remark.

"Beg pardon?" Velvel put aside his book and straightened himself in his armchair.

"Do either of you have any idea how long Michal and I have been down here?" he started. Neither Ahmed nor Amelia were given time to guess. "I haven't seen daylight in years. In all that time, I've seen plenty of leaders come and go. Ziga is just the latest in a long line of promisers who talk a big talk but have no bite. Mark my words, he'll disappoint just like the last dissident leader before him and the one before that. So, don't you two get any ideas about this being temporary? Once you're down here, you're here to stay."

"But don't you have relations across the river?" countered Ahmed. "Aren't you in contact with them? Don't the doctors want to liberate this place? Once we get rid of the Council then the blockade can be lifted." Velvel sighed wearily with a look on his face clearly indicating that he'd had this conversation many times before.

"Yes, it is true. I am in contact with my cousins on the South Side. I've been in contact with them for some time and yet, *somehow*, I'm still living down here in the Underground. Has it never occurred to you, that the international community imposed the blockade on us, *not* because Citizen R was trying to undermine them, but because they regard *us* as a hazardous leper colony? We're *all* unvaccinated you see. They don't want anything to do with us. They don't want any society here to thrive. They want to make life here unbearable so that eventually the whole place falls to pieces and they can just move in and clean it all up. That's why they won't give dissenters like us any help. We're calling for reforms like changes to taxation, food production, consistent legal procedures blah blah blah, but we've never disagreed with the Council's position on vaccines. If we ever did, and called for vaccination, then we'd lose any chance of winning the people's support. And so, we've only ever said we wanted to improve society here as it is, not uproot it or destroy it. A prosperous paradise of unvaccinated citizens won't look good for the zombies across the river. They can't allow it. And so…they sit and wait and slowly strangle us."

"But if that's true," noted Amelia. "Then it clearly isn't working. The blockade's being going on for almost fifteen years now and the Council is still in charge."

"Yep, they never quite took into account how much misery people will put up with," he concluded as he slouched back in his seat. "The more we resist…the longer this miserable reality will be perpetuated."

"That isn't true. If it was then, why even bother with this?" asked Amelia almost accusatively of him. "Why are you still with us? If our cause is all for nothing, then why even call yourself a dissenter?"

"Because," he said. "There's nothing else to do to pass the time. Better this than be put under routine torture by the Red Coats."

Amelia slumped into herself. She felt as though a stone was weighing down her heart. She looked about the Room, at Michal, Ahmed, and Velvel.

This was it.

This was the choice she had made. She would never see the sun again. She was here forever. An exile for the rest of her days pouring her energies into a hopeless, futile, movement. Could that be the undeniable truth? The truth she would have to live with?

She sincerely hoped not.

"Oh, don't look so glum," said Velvel almost mockingly to her. "Be honest, did you ever really care about the movement? You're here because you found a community of people just like you. Your *'real'* family, am I right? You're here because you and all your friends are anonymous and it's a big secret that makes your life so much more exciting. The whole *'I'm here to do good'* line is just the excuse you tell yourself to justify your presence here. *Our* truth behind *our* lie is this: you think that you can do better than Citizen R and the High Council. If only *you* were the dictator, then everything would be fine. We'd all be swimming in lemonade! And you're so impatient to realise it that you dismissed the idea of climbing up through the ranks of the Red Coats and Tower Governors and came instead to us with the ambition to overthrow the Council and claim it all for yourself."

"You don't know that!" protested Amelia, insulted by his sweeping presumptions about her. "You don't know anything about me. I am committed, body and soul, to the pursuit of the truth and the construction of a society built thereon. It's those who seek political power, fame, and prestige. *They're* the ones that live within lies. I am a dissenter. And I choose to live within the truth and nothing but the truth."

"But that in itself is a lie zaychik," reiterated Varga. "*We* are as bad as the people we seek to overthrow. That's the terrible truth about Ziga. He was going nowhere as the Council's Global Ambassador. *But*, make him into a revolutionary leader and suddenly everyone knows his name! He's a serious contender now! It's the *truth* behind all the leaders before him. It's the *truth* that resides in us all. We're *all* selfish power-hungry dictators-in-waiting. The *truth* is, every revolutionary relishes the thought of being king someday. And you're no different." He gestured to the meagre surroundings of the Room and then looked back at her. "You got what you wanted zaychik. How does it feel?"

"Guys!" suddenly barked a voice from behind one of the computer screens.

"Don't tell me; you've finally discovered Wikipedia," taunted Velvel.

"No! No! Come here! Everyone! You *need* to see this," insisted the dissenter. At his beckoning, everyone in the Room stopped whatever they were doing and huddled around his computer screen. As she joined the throng, Amelia recognised the dissenter in question to be Danior. Barely out of his teens, he was an enthusiast for all things technological and was seldom seen without a screen in his purview. Given his talents, Ziga had entrusted the young man with the movement's digital and cyber operations along with the effective task of bank robber for hacking into the Council's vaults of R-Marks to provide the likes of Velvel and Michal, and now Amelia herself, with some pocket money.

"Well, what is it?" inquired Michal as he scrubbed the lenses of his glasses with the rim of his jumper. Danior pointed to his screen.

"Ziga just sent me this," he explained, clicking into a document which revealed pages and pages of writing. "It's a Manifesto," he clarified as he scrolled through it. "He wants me to publish it on the Platform tonight."

"What?" exclaimed Velvel.

"You heard me. He wants me to publish it on the Council's system. He wants all our sleeper agents to rally around it on the Platform and to go public with the movement."

"No more anonymity," gasped Ahmed.

"No more hiding," whispered a disbelieving Velvet "We're taking them head on…The time has finally come."

"Is the man insane?" questioned Michal rhetorically. "No one's done that. No one's tried to engage with the system like that."

"Until now," corrected Amelia who then turned to the open-mouthed Velvel who could barely believe his eyes. "I'm sorry, what were you saying about our cause being hopeless and never getting anywhere?"

Part III: Resistance

Know it now, and know it always, the words of our mighty Struggle
against the murderous Demons of the Cabal:
Rage! Revolt! And Revive!
Rage! Revolt! And Revive!

Czar Kovalenko's livestream sermon on the meaning of R

Within a few hours of the announcement, the Room had transformed from a tranquil living space into a hub of activity as dissenters from across the city flocked in. Sophia and other tunnel guides ran tirelessly back and forth escorting people to the secret subterranean headquarters. Danior's eyes were ceaselessly scanning the computer monitors for activity within the digital sphere. Michal was running about his library searching for political essays written by his fellow dissenters. Velvel meanwhile, had completely cast aside his disillusioned cynical self and was in the thick of the ongoing conversations about how the operation would be executed.

With so many people and so much commotion crammed into one space, Amelia's voice had gradually become lost in the throng. Amidst so many other loud and passionate speakers, it did not take long, as usual, for her to get drowned out. As the discussions dragged on, tiredness began to set in on her. It was all a little much to stomach in the course of a single day. She retired to a dusty corner of the library and curled up by one of the desks. Not long after taking up there she was joined by Ahmed.

"Feeling useless too?" she asked sleepily.

"It's all very exciting," he conceded drowsily. "Real change in our time and all. But I'm more a doctor than a revolutionary."

"So you're a rebel by circumstance, not by calling then, yes?" Ahmed laughed warmly at that.

"Exactly so," he confirmed. "I've only ever wanted to help people. But if I can only help them by changing society first, then a revolutionary I am." He leaned back in his seat and closed his eyes, his head hanging backwards as he relaxed.

"We've gone live!" came the cry of Danior from the other end of the Room. "The Manifesto is on the platform! We have clicks coming in! We have their attention!" A jubilant cheer went up from among the dissenters. Tired as she was, an involuntary smile of delight escaped Amelia.

"Whose attention do we have?" asked Velvel with urgent seriousness.

"The only people who matter," answered Danior almost giddily. "They're all users that haven't posted or commented on anything in years. We have the attention of the disenfranchised citizens."

"Any discussion on it yet?" queried the veteran dissenter both nervously and impatiently.

"Let me take a peek on the comment section. We have one here from an Ursula Gottwald of Block D, hasn't been active on the Platform in five years. She says 'About time someone said it as it is. Enough is enough! How many more suicides will it take to get their attention?'"

Velvel at once let out a laugh of triumph and Amelia could hear him punching the air.

"We did it! We really did it! We struck the motherload!" he yelled to the cheers of all his comrades. "Danior! Send out the message that we're taking to the streets!"

"I should really get clearance from Ziga before I—"

"Don't argue with me boychik!" hammered Velvel commandingly. "Just do it! If we wait on Ziga for everything we'll lose our chance! We need to seize the moment! Now! We've all put our names to the Manifesto by backing it online! They know who we are! We've nothing left to lose by confronting them on the streets!"

"Let's take the city back!" roared somebody and a wave of hurrahs rippled through the room.

That was the last that Amelia heard before she dosed off into the embrace of sleep.

"*I dreamed a dream,*" her silent inner voice whispered. In the murky oneiric realm of dreams, her mind wandered freely. She became conscious of her dreaming and for the first time ever she chose not to resist it but to accept it. For this was the dream she'd wished to dream for so very long. She saw the streets of the city jampacked with fellow brothers and sisters, dissenters all, answering the call to insurrection. She felt the rumble and reverberation of explosions tremble through the broken concrete. She saw Red Coats being overwhelmed and taken prisoner. People were singing and dancing with glee. The copper statues of the Czars guarding the outside of the Apartment blocks were being torn down. She saw her parents helplessly looking on in abject horror from their balcony.

That made her feel good.

Wild ecstasy pulsed through her now as she looked upon this triumphant scene. For the first time in her life, she allowed herself to indulge in the art of divination and dared to interpret her dream. She cared to do so only because there was but one simple interpretation to take from it all:

This would come to pass.

But within the massing sea of rapturous faces, something she saw in her dream was not quite right. Alone amongst the crowds of strangers was the dark shrouded silhouette of a woman glaring across at her. Faceless, eyeless and lightless she was. Yet more disturbing to Amelia than her view of this anonymous being was the lacerating gaze which the woman cast right back at her. A malice beyond comprehension radiated out from the silhouette and at once the scenes of joyous celebration began to blend with the balefulness of this malign figure. Scores of her singing and dancing comrades, began to gravitate towards the dark spectre, the happiness peeling from their eyes as they were drawn into the aura of the void. No longer victors revelling in the possibilities of the liberated future, they now became eternal slaves of this unknowable darkness, condemned to its infinite will to consume all in its path.

"Sing me a nightmare..." demanded the shadow in a voice dripping with the ravenous lust of a razorblade. *"And I'll feast on the last of your dreams."*

A tremor of dread shuddered through Amelia's psyche. None of this was part of *her* dream she realised. A terrifying thought shivered through her conscience that she was not even dreaming this dark silhouetted woman, but that instead, they were *inside* the dream by *their own hand.*

Just as Amelia's brain came to this disturbing conclusion, she was ripped away from the revelries and faced with her unfortunate suicide victim that had thrown himself off C Block. Those twitching bulged-out eyeballs zoomed out at her and she saw once again the terror beyond terror pulsing within them.

"*Run,*" their voice insisted to her.

"Oi!" hollered an external voice and she was abruptly snapped awake gasping and panting for breath. Velvel was right in front of her. "What are you two sleepy-heads still doing here?" Amelia glanced to her left to see Ahmed groggily scanning through another medical journal.

"I just got back from that armour job, I needed some rest mate," explained Ahmed reasonably.

"Just getting some sleep," explained Amelia a little annoyed by the intrusion.

"Some sleep? Do you have any idea what's going on?" exclaimed Velvel, clearly not appreciating her tone with him. There and then Amelia noticed that the Room had returned to its former quietude. The flocks of dissenters had gone. It was just Michal in his library and Danior with his computers again. Velvel was wearing a flak jacket and had a pistol holstered by his hip.

"Sorry, just a lot to adjust to," reasoned Amelia. "My parents did just kick me out of the house earlier today and then I saw—"

"Today? That was two days ago zaychik!" revealed the exasperated Velvel. Amelia had to make a forceful blink to absorb that information. She couldn't possibly have been asleep that long. Could she? Perceptions of time were different down here. But even so. Two days? That didn't seem right. "It's all-out war up there! There's revolution on the streets! They've killed some of us and we've killed some of them! E block is entirely on fire. There's Red Coats starting sweeps of the Underground!"

"Oh," innocently responded Ahmed as he cleared his vision. Velvel rolled his eyes to the heavens and turned to Michal who was still stacking shelves.

"How did you not notice them?" he asked of the Professor.

"Easy to overlook them," calmly said the academic. "There's been so many people coming in and out over the last few days." He turned confusedly to Amelia. "There was a woman here talking to you though. Ivana, I think her name was. Long golden hair, had a kind of funky artist look to her."

"What?" responded Amelia involuntarily, swiftly searching her memory to find a match for that description to no avail. "I was asleep this whole time! I didn't speak to anyone! I've never even met anyone like that!"

"Well, someone was definitely speaking to you," assured Michal with crystal certainty in his voice. "There's been a lot of people in and out as I said but I've definitely never seen her before. She did leave in a hurry after speaking to you, so I thought maybe you had recruited her and that she'd come to take orders from you." Velvel was about to reprimand them all when the shock of an explosion shivered through the ceiling. Everyone held still for a moment and instinctively peered upwards. As the shockwave faded, they all returned their focus to the discussion at hand.

"Never mind," concluded Velvel now in a hurry, returning his attention to Amelia and Ahmed. "There's an old stash of machetes from Zielenski's days down under Orphans' Quay where the tunnels meet the river. Make yourselves useful and go fetch them. We need them."

"I don't know the way," objected Amelia as Velvel purposefully marched away.

"Then fetch Sophia," he advised as he strode out of view. "Or get lost until you find what you're looking for." Amelia tried to clear the grit from her eyes and slumped back in her seat.

"I'd get going if I were you," advised Michal. "He's on a short fuse at the moment and he'll want to see you gone when he comes back." Amelia took a good long yawn as she nodded in acknowledgement and then both she and Ahmed staggered to their feet. Amelia was trying to get her head around the situation and the job she had been tasked with when Sophia welcomed in a whole crew of battered dissenters with riot shields and iron batons in hand.

"Sophia!" called out Amelia as the bone-tired combatants collapsed upon the couches. "A little help please!"

"Of course, anything for a pal," agreed Sophia with forced amiability as she wiped her sweaty brow, her purple hair now laced with the dust of pulverised bricks. "Where do you need to go?"

"Velvel said something about a stash of knives left by Zielenski under Orphans' Quay."

"Okay, I know the place," said Sophia weighing the location in her head. "Shit!"

"What?"

"The Red Coats raided a speakeasy on Unchained Avenue and are now occupying the tunnels there. We'll need to go up and back down again."

"You mean up to the surface?" asked Ahmed a little nervously.

"None other," confirmed Sophia as she exhaled deeply. She pointed to a set of handheld torches in the corner. "Grab one each. There's no lights under Orphans' Quay." Amelia was not sure how she felt about that, but she gathered that Ahmed felt as queasy as she did, for they both jumped for the torches without hesitation. Once adequately equipped they made their departure from the safety of the Room.

The corridors shivered and quivered. The withered electric lights flickered and blinked. People limped by, clasping cuts and abrasions weeping blood. Clumps of living bodies were cluttered together at the bottom of the metal stairwell, bawling and growling with pain.

"So, Velvel wants us to finally take Zielenski's stash," said Sophia, evidently trying to distract Amelia and Ahmed from the scenes around them. "No one's been down that way in a long long time."

"You do know the way though, right?" asked Ahmed worriedly.

"Oh yeah," assured Sophia. "Memorised the Underground maps a long time ago. And I have been there before too as well. Though it was a long time ago, back when my auntie was one of Zielenski's devotees."

"He was the first dissenter, wasn't he?" said Amelia.

"Ehh yeah as far as I know he was, Michal would be the one to ask about those kinds of things. Pretty eccentric character it must be said, even my auntie called him 'Manic Marius'. Apparently, he slit open the underside of his penis so that he could menstruate, ejaculate and urinate all at the same time."

"Fuck off!" instantly yelped Amelia in shock. Sophia laughed at her reaction.

"Allah would not be pleased," said Ahmed, himself shuddering all over in revulsion at the thought of it.

"I doubt somehow that Allah would be alone in that judgement," giggled Sophia.

"Did you really have to put that image in our heads?" asked Amelia as she tried to shake the image off.

"It distracted you didn't it?" replied Sophia.

"Please don't tell me it's true."

"Just something I heard. Could be total swine-shit, but then again, it is Manic Marius we're talking about so who knows. He was one seriously fucked up individual."

"Thank god he's not leading us."

"I hear that!" concurred Ahmed.

In a flash, they went through a door and were back on the deafening dance floor where moshing crowds were still banging their heads to the rock anthems of *Plastic Souls of the Galaxy*. Squeezing between herds of dancers and struggling to see anything under the epileptic lights, they eventually made their way to the other side. From there, they proceeded to the familiar stairway which led up to the corner shop.

"Now, whatever you do," advised Sophia before she pulled the lever for the secret door to open. "Just remember to keep your head down."

"How far do we have to run?" asked Amelia, her heart now thumping as she heard the rumbling chorus of the raging battle up above her.

"Just follow me," instructed Sophia.

The lever was pulled, the secret passage opened. They sprinted up the steps into the store and of a sudden they were on a different planet. It was early morning, or early evening, by the look of the twisted red sky. Ludmila, the gatekeeper, was hiding under the till with a hammer in one hand and a bloodied screwdriver in another. Beyond the front desk, complete anarchy reigned. Dead bodies littered the abandoned carnival. Some lunatic had switched on the power for the carousel and the half-rusted horses had come back to life with decapitated corpses riding them round and round and round. Specially trained dissident Street Fighters darted back and forth with Molotov cocktails and knives in hand, their faces concealed by balaclavas. Red Coats ran amok shooting and stabbing at everything not dressed in red. Like their anarchist forefathers of old they wore Guy Fawkes masks and clown paint. One of their pick-up trucks rolled past with a megaphone attached to the roof. Standing on the back was a Red Shaman. His boiler suit was unzipped down to his waist to bare his chest tattooed with swastikas and neo-pagan runes. Upon his head, he wore a 16th century Turkish turban helmet he'd most likely pillaged from a museum many years ago.

"Delusions!" he roared through the megaphone for the whole city to hear, his arms outstretched like a messiah as the tune of *'Somewhere over the Rainbow'* was blared out in the background. "Delusions of the World Octopus! The tentacles will strangle us all! The undead are among us! Zealots of the paedophile demon-king! Kill the Zombies my brothers! Kill them all! Save humanity!"

"Let's go!" shouted Sophia and without a second thought they all somehow worked up the courage to make a dash through the mayhem.

"Fuck! Fuck! Fuck! Fuck!" Amelia chanted to herself as shotguns boomed and ricocheted all round her. She turned a corner and found a clown-faced Red Coat butchering someone with a fireman's axe. The clown spun about and set his gaze upon her. A heartbeat was skipped as he raised his axe to her. A dissenter ran past, pointed a revolver, and shot the clown's brains out at point-blank range.

Seconds later the street fighter got blown away in a shot gun blast and a cloud of red mist showered over the transfixed Amelia.

In that split-second of paralysis as the blood-dust settled around her, Amelia spotted a girl sitting cross-legged amidst the dead and the dying. A crown of white roses was nestled around her head, her long blonde hair reaching down to her waist. She wore baggy turquoise trousers and a woollen purple tunic. A pair of blue-tinted shades hid her eyes. *Ivana,* thought Amelia. This *had to be* the girl Michal was talking about. She matched the description exactly. Contently meditating amongst the tattered wrecks of human bodies, Ivana cast a smile that was too long and too intent for Amelia to feel comfortable with.

"She sees you," whispered Ivana in a croaking voice that squelched out from behind her leering grin. Before Amelia could even compute those words, she felt a grab at her wrist.

"Come on! Come on!" howled Sophia, tugging the petrified Amelia along and in a nanosecond she was back in the middle of this murderous festival. She fleetingly looked back at the enigmatic Ivana but she was nowhere to be seen. She had vanished into thin air. The unsolved mystery was swiftly banished from her mind as a machete came flying right past her head.

"I left Syria for this?" screamed Ahmed to himself as he frantically tried to keep up, his hands clasping his ears.

"Shut up and fucking run!" barked Sophia back at him as they exited the carnival and sprinted across the road where bullets were whirring by like wasps. Sophia abruptly halted and held her arm out to stop the others from running in front of her. "Back! Back! Back!" she insisted. Of a sudden, a pair of Red Coats on motorbikes revved by pulling a small wagon behind them with a Red Commander in the back. A bear-skinned hat on his head, a bottle of champagne in his left hand and a submachine gun in the other, the commander suddenly got up off his arse, took a slug of his drink, and then opened fire as his carriage entered the fray.

"Just like the good old days!" he drunkenly cackled as his bullets raked across the face of an apartment block, letting loose a whirl of frightened screams from the residents within.

"Just like the good old days!" echoed another old-timer amongst the Red Coats.

"Let's go!" bellowed Sophia once the wagon had passed and they made a run for it across the road. She pointed ahead to a small concrete cabin lying in the courtyard between two apartment blocks. "Make for the door!" she directed.

No sooner had the words left her than they caught the attention of another gruesome adversary. Clad in a long duster coat and a medieval plague mask, he came upon them riding a black stallion and in his free hand he wielded a flame thrower. The horse brayed and wailed in horror; its eyes frozen open in distress as tongues of fire came streaming from its master's hand.

"Go! Go! Go!" yelled Sophia frantically as the rider tried to chase them down, howling with devilish laughter and shooting gusts of flame into the air. Amelia's heart began to pound to the beat of the hooves. She heard the mounted pyromaniac take aim with his dread instrument, holding it above the ears of his terror-stricken steed.

"Run little piggies! Run! Run!" cackled the mounted pyromancer.

Any moment now, any moment.

Just as incineration beckoned, a Molotov cocktail came spinning down from an apartment balcony and crashed upon the rider, swallowing him and his stallion in spectacular conflagration. The horse reared up with its mane afire, its master emitting a death-wail from his beak-faced mask as he was roasted to cinders. Sophia pulled open the door of the concrete cabin and Amelia and Ahmed rushed in. The gas cannister strapped to the rider's back then exploded and a blaze of yellow fanned outwards. All three of them jumped for the door and slammed it shut before they too were gobbled up in the fiery snare.

Darkness devoured them and nought but their ceaseless panting was to be heard.

A torchlight was switched on to reveal a stairway leading back down into the Underground.

Without a word, their descent to Zielenski's lair began in earnest.

Part IV: Resilience

Beware children! Beware!
For it is known that Chameleons walk among us.
But among the Chameleons…There be Dragons.

Czar Kowalski's 'Lizard Tales of the Plandemic', page 67

"What the hell was that?" exclaimed Amelia when the shivers of shock finally ran their course. In the pitch black, their three shafts of torchlight lunged outwards into the unknown of the deep. Slow methodical drops of water dripped from the cracked ceiling. The patter of rat claws scurrying through the shafts and pipes of the underworld echoed all around them.

"What?" countered Sophia confusedly.

"I thought the movement was taking to the streets. Where were the crowds? Where's Ziga?"

"Where've you been? That's all old news."

"I was asleep for the last while," said Amelia with a touch of embarrassment. "A few days apparently."

"What? I thought I saw you when we were pulling the statues down, no?" countered a confused Sophia.

"No," asserted Amelia more forcefully than usual. "I definitely was not there for that."

"Must have been someone else," reasoned Sophia. "That's the only explanation because clearly you were out cold for all the good stuff. The peaceful protest went to shit once bullets started flying. Ziga is gone missing, either he's hiding, or he's been arrested, nobody knows. We had the upper hand on the fuckers for a while, but they've drafted in reinforcements from the countryside who are made of tougher stuff than the bored shitless idiots we're used to."

"So that's when everything went to Hell," concluded Amelia.

"I don't know, kinda fun, don't you think?" giggled Sophia in her usual sarcastic playfulness. "Just like the good old days when we used to get chased for playing *Spice Girls* music outdoors."

"Fuck off," exhaled Amelia, barely in the mood to talk let alone in the mood to jest and joke.

Their escape from the inferno of violence had been made through what had once been an access point for *'authorised personnel only'* as the faded sign had read. After descending the small flight of steps, they had traversed a snaking corridor of bone-dry concrete. At its natural end, they were faced with a hole in the floor with a ladder leading down into the abyss. As they hopped off the final rung, they found themselves in what looked like an old boiler room. Under pipes and over wires they weaved their way to a metal door which led to yet another godless concrete hallway. To both their right and their left it stretched out into the impenetrable blackness.

"Which way?" asked Ahmed as he worriedly shone his torch from side to side.

"This way," confidently declared Sophia who started marching to the right.

"You're certain?" asked Amelia, anxious to keep up with her guide. "You said yourself you haven't been down here in years."

"If I'm wrong, then we'll just retrace our footsteps," reassured Sophia in a blasé tone.

"I just hope we don't get lost," expressed Ahmed, his torchlight fixating on the rats scuttling around him.

"We won't! That's why you have me!" guffawed Sophia whose light revealed a doorway before them with the standard workman's authorisation sign on it. "Ah yes, I remember this." With a swift kick of her jackboot, she smacked the door open in a wide arc that slapped it against the wall, sending a rattling echo reverberating through the halls of the dark. Their torchlights began to reflect off a glass surface. As they approached closer, they found themselves threading no longer on concrete but on tiled floors. All three of them spun around in stupefaction to soak up their new surroundings.

"I feel like I've discovered a pharaoh's tomb," gaped Amelia as her torchlight revealed stylishly dressed mannequins hiding behind a pane of glass. A huge red band was plastered across the window read: *"Lockdown sale! Everything must go!"* Ahmed's torch meanwhile revealed a dried-up fountain crested in dust. "What is this place? Is this what the High Council mean when they talk about hives of materialism?"

"They call it a shopping centre I think," clarified Ahmed, not taking his eyes away for a moment from his latest discovery.

"Something like that," added Sophia as she surveyed the abandoned retail stores with equal wonderment. "The upper floors lead back to the surface, but they're sealed off. It was used as a hospital of some kind during the peak of the Plandemic."

"Then what are we doing here?" asked Ahmed who was utterly captivated by the mummified inventory of a dark and grimy bookshop which had a hastily applied sticker on the glass door reading: *"We've moved to Ward Four South Side. Find us at 67 Immunity Street."*

"There's an old subway station here about a floor beneath us," explained Sophia.

"We should take some of this with us," said Amelia who had now joined Ahmed to ogle the contents of the bookshop. "This stuff is priceless."

"Yeah when we don't have Red Coats chasing us with pitchforks and we're all still alive to enjoy it then yeah, maybe," rebuked Sophia with a degree of sternness. "We need to keep moving. There'll be another time for sightseeing."

At their guide's insistence, Ahmed and Amelia relented in their childish curiosity and continued with the downward trek. After ambling down a frozen escalator to the next level, they found themselves in the company of ticket machines and outdated timetables. They threat went down another flight of stairs till their feet landed upon a train platform littered with plastic cans and damp cardboard. Signage calling for social distance to be maintained and for masks to be worn were still dutifully standing at their posts to warn passengers that had long since come and gone. Up above them the rusting metal rafters dripped with river water. As they shed their light upon the train tracks, they found only the stillness of accumulated black water staring back up at them.

"It's flooded," noted Amelia in dismay.

"No shit," said Sophia. "I'm surprised it's not worse after all these years. Someone must have been working the pumps to keep the Borava from just pouring in."

"Does this go to the South Side?" asked Ahmed enthusiastically as he started wandering down the platform.

"It used to," said Sophia curtly. "A long time ago."

"So where to now?" queried Amelia as she cast her torchlight over an ancient hand sanitiser.

"Towards the river," answered Sophia. "There's a ledge we can walk along. Hopefully it still runs above the waterline. Zielenski drove a train carriage down there for his base and that's where we'll find the stash."

Amelia and Ahmed voiced no concerns or questions. They simply followed Sophia's lead and they walked further and further and *further* down into the dark. The ledge was wide enough for them to advance at a comfortable walking pace but too narrow for them to do so in any more than single file. Looming parallel to them at all times were the black flood waters.

Silent as the grave, the gutter-water lingered by their footsteps, purring a slow and shuddering reminder of its presence with every drip and drop of liquid it consumed from the world above.

They came about a bend in the tunnel and their torches lit up the silvery flesh of a lone train carriage steadily sinking into the flood waters. As it came closer into view, they saw a single red handprint imposed upon one of the windows. From its glass tomb, the red hand seemed to stretch out to them. The three of them paused for a moment, utterly captivated by this last echoing mark of a poor soul's grasp for salvation, forever frozen in time down here in the belly of the earth, forever reaching for the help that would never come.

"Let's get this over with," quickly uttered Amelia, shaking the haunted hand from her mind. "This place gives me the creeps."

"There's no such thing as ghosts," retorted Sophia with inflated authority in her voice. "But, best not linger. We're right under the Borava River." Amelia hadn't considered that fact. This could only mean that they were in fact outside the jurisdiction of the High Council. For the first time ever, she was standing in a place not ruled by them. Yet neither was she on the South Side. *They were in between worlds.*

One of the carriage doors had been pried open and they made their quick entry into the abandoned headquarters of Zielenski's dissident movement. Nothing at all remained within.

The carriage had been clearly stripped clean of its valuables long ago. Each of them began scanning with their torchlights for the stash of weapons, looking under and behind the seats and checking the overhead bins.

"I think I found it!" called Ahmed and the two girls came racing down the carriage to him. From under a seat, he presented an orange duffle bag. "It feels a little light," he warned. Sophia frowned and snatched the bag away from him. She unzipped it and her eyes narrowed in puzzlement.

Empty.

"This can't be it," she said. "It must be another bag."

"Then why does it say, 'Knife Bag' on it?" asked Amelia rather innocently as she shone her torch at the painted writing on the side of the bag.

"Well because…well because…" Sophia's words trailed off as she searched for an explanation. But there could only be one answer. The two of them looked at one another with simultaneous horror as it occurred to them; *someone else had already been here.*

"Who could have taken them?" gasped Amelia.

"The maps mustn't have been updated," rationalised Sophia in a fluster. "Someone must have taken them and never told Michal."

"Dissenters never keep secrets from one another," said Amelia. "Remember? No lies!"

"Of course I fucking remember!" snapped Sophia as she scrunched the empty bag up her fist.

"This is useless! I'm out of here!" inexplicably bellowed Ahmed, bottled-up trepidation venting through his lips. He shoved past Amelia and perplexingly darted for the door. All of a sudden, their prior confusion about the stash of knives evaporated into thin air.

"Hey! Where are you going?" shouted Sophia after him as she helped Amelia to her feet.

"I'm going to the South Side!" he yelled at the top of his lungs, his words rippling over the static black water and bouncing off the walls. "And you should come with me! We're getting slaughtered up there! It's over!"

"Ahmed you can't go there!" called Amelia after him. "The tunnel's flooded! The way is shut!"

"We're halfway there!" he screeched back, and Amelia knew by the desperation in his voice that something must have snapped in him. "I can swim it! Whoever took the knives must have done it before! If they can do it then so can we!" He now began sprinting down the narrow ledge into the deep unknown.

"Are you fucking kidding me! The knives could have been taken years ago when the waters were lower! You'll drown before you even reach the doctors!" bellowed Sophia, speed-walking after him as she and Amelia tried to keep their balance on the precarious ledge of concrete. Unable to maintain the perilous balancing act, Sophia halted and summoned up the fiery corner her being which Amelia knew only too well. "Ahmed!" she screamed as loud and as authoritatively as she possibly could.

Sure enough, he stopped running and turned to face them. In the glare of the torchlight, Amelia could see the nervous tears welling in his eyes, his chest heaving up and down.

"I'm not going back," he panted, taking on a quieter tone of voice albeit with the shade of anxiety still there. "We're going to die up there. You saw it. Stash or no stash, we can't win. This is the only way out. At least, we stand a chance on the other side of—"

"Ahmed, we *have to* go back," insisted Sophia without compromise. "If you go down that tunnel, you *will* die. The battery on your torch won't last long enough and it's not waterproof."

"I have to go. I have to," he wheezed, almost choking on his own breath. He then straightened himself and gazed right back at them with his full attention. "I just," he whimpered. "I just want to help people. I can't take anymore useless suffering…I…I just want everything to be ok for once."

With silent and unwelcomed impunity, a hand, black as the night snaked over Ahmed's shoulder as he finished what he had to say. In a blink, it grasped him by the throat. A strangled scream escaped him, like the squeal of a televised voice cut short by a power outage. Before either Amelia or Sophia could even cry out, he had vanished backwards into the undulating maws of the unknown, his torch clattering with a slimy splash into the vacuous waters below.

"What the fuck?" breathed a wild-eyed Amelia, blinking thrice as if to confirm to herself that her eyes weren't playing tricks. "What the fuck just happened?" Sophia could not even muster the words to express her shock, she just stared and stared into the thundering void of the deep as though she expected an answer from it. "Ahmed?" called out Amelia, her heartbeat quickening to a gallop and then to a rapid drumbeat as the sight of the black hand replayed over and over in her mind. *Someone was down here.*

Of a sudden, she heard the tip of a blade scraping off concrete and approaching footsteps to match it. In that moment, Amelia once again saw the suicide victim in her mind's eye.

"*Run*," they implored to her.

"We need to go," she said quietly. Sophia was too dumbfounded to hear her. "We need to go *now*!" she insisted, grabbing her by the arm, the footsteps drawing closer and closer. "WE NEED TO FUCKING RUN!" she yelled, and Sophia was finally uprooted from her state of shock. They turned and bolted back up the tunnel, the beating of their shoes thundering throughout the veins of the blackness.

"Fuck! Fuck! Fuck!" repeated Sophia over and over again, their dual rays of torchlight bobbing up and down as they sprinted in mindless panic. Amelia momentarily realised that they had abandoned Ahmed without a second thought. That single instant of guilt distracted her enough to make a fatal misstep. She let out an uncontrollable shriek and was about to regain her balance when Sophia crashed into her from behind. In a flinch of the unthinkable, they both lost their bearings and fell sideways into the dead waters beneath.

A shock of cold rushed over Amelia's body as the water swarmed around her. Rats scattered around them in all directions. Dank and stagnant liquid fountained up her nostrils. Gooseflesh prickled across her body in a flame of total discomfort. Second by second the dark closed in as the life was crushed out of her fragile torch. As the deep blackness gathered round, she began fumbling around blindly. Beneath her she felt the expected rocky crests of miry gravel and metal tracks. Yet her fingers also passed over smoother, cleaner, more *organic* matter. Within seconds, she understood that she was pawing the skeletons of forgotten souls. That dread reality drove her rocketing upwards for breath.

To her relief she found that Sophia's torch had been dropped on the ledge and was still working. She waded over and reached for the ledge. As she dragged her soaking body out of the water it occurred to her that Sophia was nowhere to be seen. In that moment of selflessness though, she once again lost her bearings and failed to notice a shadow eclipsing the torchlight. Down on her hands and knees, Amelia gazed through her dripping fringe at the pitch-black figure towering over her. An invisible hand snatched her by the throat and swung her against the wall of the tunnel. In the iron choke, Amelia's legs dangled like a doll's above the ground. Though she could not see their face, she knew their eyes were boring into her, studying her with what she guessed to be some kind of predatorial fascination.

In that last instant when she thought the killer blow to be nigh, Sophia came screeching out of the water. Without any hesitation, the phantom let Amelia clatter to the ground, and turned on Sophia. Amelia heard a blade biting into human meat and an automatic yelp went out. Wet cloth and skin began to graze against the merciless concrete and Amelia knew at once that her friend was being dragged away. She mustered all her strength and lunged for Sophia's hand.

"Don't leave me! Don't leave me!" bawled Sophia, her purple eyeliner bleeding down her face. Amelia held on as tight as she could but with both their hands so wet and the monster's pull so ravenous, her fingers began to slip.

"I've got you! I've got you!" lied Amelia to her friend as she held on with both her hands. The devilish dark hand emerged from the abyss once more and clasped Sophia's head, the fingers clawing down over her eyes.

"Don't leave! Don't leaaaaahhhhhhhhh!" cried Sophia as her face was ripped backwards with a short powerful wrench that yanked her out of Amelia's grasp and sucked her into the nothingness of the deep.

Amelia lay on her stomach, hopelessly searching the blackness for any sign of life. She seized the torch and pointlessly shone it into the bottomless pit.

But there was nothing.

Only a deafening silence.

Part V: Endurance

Only Faith can save you from the oblivion the Puppeteers have calculated for you!
Faith will save you where Reason will only abandon you!

Czar Kaczynski's New Year Speech to the residents of H block

"This can't be happening, this can't be happening," mumbled Amelia to herself, hoping, against all her dissident principles, that by chanting a lie long enough it might become true. "This can't be happening. This can't be happening. Why me? Why *not* me?"

Guideless and friendless, Amelia wandered through the lightless halls of the Underground. She retraced her steps as best she could, but her grief and shock blinded any sense of direction she had. The sight of Sophia and Ahmed being devoured into the dark, coupled with the unfathomable miracle of her own survival, clung to her mind too potently for her to concentrate on anything else. *None of it made sense*. But there had to be an answer. There *had* to be. Around half-remembered corners and through half-forgotten doors, she eventually found herself amongst the pipes and wires of the boiler room again but could not recall the exact route Sophia had brought them in by.

Her shoes still squelching like sponges, she left a painfully obvious trail of wet footprints behind her as she searched in vain for a way back to the surface. In her impatience, she chose to pass through a door at random and another after that. Thereat she was faced with a metal ladder which brought her up to an empty chamber. For a moment, she feared she might have reached a dead-end but then she noticed a gaping hole in the wall behind her. From the freshly broken shards of concrete, she could tell that this opening had not been intended by the architects who built this place. Someone had taken a jackhammer to it relatively recently. Unwilling to go back, she tentatively edged her way into the gap on her hands and knees, brushing the broken lumps of concrete aside to clear her path.

Upon reaching the end of this little shaft, she got up to her feet and at once she sensed an unwelcome coldness drape its wings around her, an iciness haunted with the screams of strangers. An inner revulsion for this intangible horror, invisible to her mortal eyes, brewed within her. She *knew* that she should go back. She *knew* there was nothing good here. But that was not the dissenter way. There was no hard evidence, no undeniable truth, telling her to go back. A feeling was just a feeling. Her insurmountable curiosity soon overcame her trepidation, and she shone her ray of torchlight into the darkness.

Right before her she saw the letter 'C' painted upon the wall.

She was in C Block. This was the basement of the apartment tower! All she had to do was clamber up the stairwell and she'd be out of the Underground! Fortune favours the bold!

She rushed forward without thinking. In an instant, she felt something snap and rattle beneath her feet. She stopped dead in her tracks and, slowly, shined a light down on the floor. Within a heartbeat, her free hand was cupped across her mouth to dam the scream vomiting up from the bowels of her soul.

Skulls.

Hundreds upon hundreds of them, fleshless eyeless faces all massed together into heaps of unliving. Clattered all around like the scatterings of broken toys were the rib cages and bones clothed in tattered shrouds. Up on the wall overlooking the hole she had crept through a horse's skull had been mounted with human bones fanning out from it like wings. Beneath this grotesque work of art, the painted words of warning read:

"Lair of the Dragon."

Every atom of Amelia's body pulsed with a primal fear that compelled her to flee for her life. Without a thought she darted across the macabre basement for the safety of the elevator. With rampant urgency, she thumped her fist against the elevator buttons, pressing any and all of them. She didn't care what floor she landed on; anything was better than this. Thankfully the cables were still operational and her body almost visible relaxed as the metal cage began to lift her up out of this secret graveyard.

"Fuck…fuck…fuck," she quietly murmured to herself uncontrollably, still unable to process the feast of death she had laid eyes on. Her hands were shaking of their own volition, cold sweat was running over her face still damp with stagnant water.

The elevator jerked to a halt and the doors opened. She was on the sixth floor. Though she could have easily pressed the button to take her down to the ground floor, the idea of going back down into the dark did not sit well with her. She'd rather make her descent by the stairwell. She stepped over the threshold and into the corridor beyond. The doors automatically shut behind her and the elevator returned to its cavernous dwelling.

Like her own apartment block, the corridor lights were flickering and buzzing. There was that same odour of rot and mould in the air. That same greyness. As she observed her new surroundings however, Amelia soon saw that something was dreadfully amiss with this corridor. Namely: all the apartment doors were either wide open or slightly ajar. Once more, her natural curiosity compelled her to investigate. It was a mystery too blatant to leave unsolved.

She pushed open the closest door and stepped into the apartment. Not a single blink of the eye was made from that moment onwards. The instant she laid a hand on the door, she tasted not the scent of mould as she instinctively expected, but the residue of violation, of lamentation, and of desecration. The home was silent now, but the screams were still in the walls, like stains that can never be cleaned. The four erstwhile residents, two adults and their teenage son and daughter, were hanging upside down from the ceiling with meat hooks through their ankles. They dangled there, as cold and stiff like meat slabs in an abattoir. Their throats and wrists had been slit open and pools of dried brown blood lay beneath them. The man was missing an arm. The woman was missing her head. The boy's entire belly had been scooped out. The girl's face had been peeled away like the skin of an apple.

Numb with disbelief, Amelia staggered backwards out of the apartment. She barged in on the next flat to find the same monstrosity repeated. She then went to the next one and the next one after that again to discover the pattern of savagery rhyming with itself, over and over again. So stupefied was she that she felt that she could keep on beholding scene after scene of this visceral butchery. She needed to know. She needed to know what was being done to Ahmed and Sophia. She could not let her conscience walk free of this. It would be morally unforgivable to leave the manner of their fate to the speculations of her imagination. *This* was the hard, undeniable truth.

But then, she came to the *last* apartment.

Unlike all the others, there were no bodies swaying from the ceiling. While there had been agony swirling in the walls of all the others, here it was magnified manifold, as though buzzing like a beehive. The room comprised of one visible victim, a young man a little older than Amelia herself perhaps. He was seated upon a chair in front of a television, his body bound to it by chains. His left hand was cuffed behind his back. His right hand meanwhile was free and was grasping a Swiss knife.

When Amelia had beheld the faces of the dead before, there had always been a tranquil sereneness to them, as though they had simply relaxed into an unawakenable sleep. Whether they had died peacefully or violently, that was the look which a corpse always had. *But not this one.*

The man's face was taut and rigid with raw emotions. His mouth was frozen open in a rictus of howling pain. It was as if his agony had followed him into the afterlife. Somewhere out there in the netherworld, he was still bawling and begging for mercy. *The horror of his life was haunting his death.* A stab wound lay where his left eye had once been and the Swiss knife in his right hand was firmly drilled into his other eye. It was then that Amelia's attention was drawn to the television screen from which a whole cacophony of maddening noises was emanating. She came around the room and bared witness to the hellish vision put on a repeating loop for this nameless victim.

The screen presented the victim sitting in the same chair but with a blindfold ringed around his head. All around him, his family were at the mercy of their uninvited guest, a blurry unidentifiable silhouette upon the screen. A little girl of about ten was sprawled out on the kitchen table, her limbs cuffed to the legs of the table. Amelia looked on as the shadow moved towards the little girl and began its demonic work upon her. The act of malice which followed was so despicable, so irrevocably terrible, that, not unlike some incalculable phenomenon of the cosmos not yet understood by scientists, it completely surpassed human comprehension. Amelia's brain physically began to pulse and squirm within her skull at the mere sight of it. The only thing her mind could process were the wails and cries of the parents, uselessly begging the shadow to kill them in the place of their daughter, for that was the sole piece of humanity to behold in this nameless act of savageness.

"No! God! God! No!" she eventually bellowed to herself in denial and she pulled herself away from the seductive grip of the television. Had she dared to look upon it any longer she might very well have snatched the dead man's knife and stabbed out her own eyes. That small clip of footage she had seen, let alone the entire tape, was enough to make anyone pray for suicide.

How long? She wondered helplessly. *How long was the entire tape? How long did it take for him to kill himself? How many times did he watch the scene repeat itself?*

She came practically crawling out of the apartment feeling ready to faint at any moment. She had never imagined, let alone thought it possible, that so much wickedness could exist. How could a human being be capable of cruelty and inhumanity of such a magnitude? Surely not. Surely no one could be so. so so *evil*. She did not like to use that word. It was too arbitrary and unscientific for her taste. It wreaked of the demagogic vocabulary of the High Council.

But there was no other word for what she had seen.

A fire-exit door opened to the left of her and a tower governor came tottering through. Unlike the handsome Governor Friedrichs, this man had gone grey before his years. His leather cape trailed behind him in tatters. He glanced down at Amelia and then slumped down in a heap, his head lolling about drunkenly.

"You looked," he said quietly, his gaze directed at nothing in particular.

"What…what…what is this?" asked Amelia, taking the first opportunity now afforded to her to get some answers and find out exactly what was going on. He raised his head and looked across at her with past trauma oozing out of him.

"The Black Dragon," he said in a slow methodical way. "She comes in the night. Down in the dark, that's where she's from. She came from nothing…and *is* nothing."

"The hell are you saying?" The governor shook his head in despair.

"She doesn't show up on anything. On every camera and every screen. She's just a black shadow. No fingerprints, no traces. She's a ghost. A chameleon."

"That's impossible. No one can just—"

"Oh! *But she can!* And it is possible! *It is*! She's not from here! She came from the South. She doesn't exist on the system so nothing recognises her. She's a non-person! That's why she's nothing."

"Why…why haven't you done something? You're tower governor for crying out loud!"

"You think I didn't try zaychik? I cried from the top of the mountain that we were under attack. I told the Czar that an agent had come across the river and was murdering people. But they just patted me on the back and congratulated me. No one believed me. Not really. I…*We*…we cried wolf too long about covert agents of the Cabal. Now look at where we are! So many people commit suicide that no one notices a few people missing. So many people don't care about the Platform that hardly anyone bats an eye at so many users gone quiet on this block. That's why I pushed the whole lizard thing…it's the only way to get people's attention…the only way to raise the alarm on…on…the Black Dragon. *And it's the only rational explanation.* She's *draining* them, and *eating* them. Do you think a human being could do what she does? You may think the lizard theory is crazy or fake or whatever but…but if enough people read about it on the platform, they might just start to believe it…And once enough people believe in it…it'll be true. And once it's true they'll have to do something about it."

An explosive brainwave blasted through Amelia's mind as she absorbed those words. It all began to make sense now. Disturbing thoughts began to manifest as she grasped the full scope of this disaster. She considered exactly how many users from C Block had gone dormant. She then thought back to the suicide victim she had seen the night she left her parents. How many others had taken their lives to save themselves from the Black Dragon? *All of them*? Had things really gotten so bad that a lizard theory was the only way for people in the city to comprehend a disaster like this?

"Everyone needs to know what's going on here at C Block," she said as she got off the floor. The tower governor just chuckled.

"C Block," he laughed. "More like 'Coffin Block' or 'Coffin Tower'. Maybe even 'Chameleon Tower'. It'll all be hers soon…She's moving up the floors. One by one killing us off and eating us." Amelia heard the electric 'ding' of the elevator arriving. She saw the doors part and an eerie shadow was cast upon the floor of the corridor. Almost immediately she felt the fear welling up inside her again. She made an instinctive run for the stairwell while the Governor continued to ramble on and on and on. As the fire-door swung back and forth behind her, she heard his final words between the pendulum swipes of the door.

"We should burn it all down," he waffled to himself. "Not a stone should be left—" Swing. "No! Not you! I—" Swing. "I didn't. I didn't say anything to—" A final swing of the door and his beseeching voice was hacked off.

Part VI: Eminence

It is our solemn Duty to serve the Greater Good and to usher in a New Age. No matter the cost.

Pawel Ziga, Concluding Remarks of 'A Critique of the Great Awakening'

"Viva le Varga! Viva le Varga! Viva le Varga!" reverberated the victory chants throughout the tunnel world. Dissidents with captured assault rifles and shotguns paraded their way to the Room, singing and roaring their victory cry, their faces bright and hopeful in the dark of the Underground. "Viva le Varga! Viva le Varga!" they intoned with religious fanaticism.

"Excuse me, I need to get to the Room," said Amelia as diplomatically as she could, trying to squeeze her way through the packs of celebrating revolutionaries. "I need to speak to Velvel! I need to speak with him!" she shouted to one of the lieutenants above the din and the crammed mass of fighters parted enough to let her snake through to the Room.

When she entered, she found Danior at his computer and Michal at his books as usual. Velvel was there in the living space with a handful of street warriors toasting one another with champagne glasses. All the portraits of Ziga she noticed had been replaced with portraits of Velvel. She strutted over straight as an arrow to the newly crowned dissident leader.

"Did you see it?" she asked impatiently, interrupting his prior conversation without consideration. "Did you see my post on the Platform? About the killings?"

"Oh, you," he said a little uncertainly, his head clearly still invested in his discussion with his comrades. "Where's Sophia? Did you get the bag?"

"Forget the bag!" she dismissed frantically. "The bag was empty. Did you see my post? The post I published on the Platform about Block C? The one with the pictures of the dead bodies?"

"What on earth are you talking about?" he asked, his face now scrunching up in confusion while his comrades lightly laughed at the miscommunication. "Where have you been? Don't you know the day is ours? We beat them back! We've retaken the tunnels they occupied. We're on the advance now. We have them on the backfoot!"

"Victory today means nothing!" slammed Amelia emotionally. "There's a monster on the loose in the city!" He frowned at her and chuckled a little, clearly wondering if she was joking or gone mad. "Danior!" she shouted across the Room in desperation. "Log in to the Platform. You'll find my post there. I published it about half an hour ago from the ground floor of C Block."

"What's going on here? Where's Sophia?"

"Sophia is dead!"

"What! How? When?"

"Just look at the fucking post!"

"Alright! Alright! Easy!" he cried with hands raised to try and calm her down while he shimmied across to Danior's computer desk. He peered over the teenager's shoulder and let his eyes scan the screen. Michal came over too and joined them. "The fuck is this?" he gaped as he scrolled over the photographs Amelia had snapped of the lower floors of C Block.

"Mass murder," she explained. "Committed by some kind of foreign agent who can avoid detection. They've been butchering people right under the Council's nose."

"Good God," said Michal as he looked upon the gory imagery. "So, this is why C Block is so quiet."

"Exactly," confirmed Amelia. "The tower governor tried to warn the Council, but nobody listened to him." She paused for a moment as she gathered her words for what needed to be said next. "Put the word out for all dissenters to share my post. This is gross incompetence and negligence on the part of the Council. It will completely destroy their legitimacy even among their most loyal supporters. They've told us for so many years that they were keeping us safe from secret agents of the Cabal, and yet when one actually turns up, they do nothing. This is our chance to rip them to shreds for good."

"No," defied Velvel with self-interested calculation written across his face.

"No? What do you mean, no?"

"I mean 'no'. We're not putting our names to your post."

"What! You can't be serious? This is a golden opportunity to—"

"No!" he shouted crossly at her. "This is *your* opportunity."

"What are you talking about?"

"You want leadership of the movement. You want to take the limelight. You want to be St. George slaying the dragon so everyone will shout your name. You want to be the hero. Well I won't have it! I won't let your selfishness and your ambition eclipse our movement! We have them on the ropes already! We don't need this alternate narrative."

"Velvel, listen to me very closely," persisted Amelia. "We *cannot* keep this information secret. We *cannot* shove it under the rug the way the Council does with everything. We stand for the *Truth!* If we don't then we're no longer dissenters! We're as bad as the Council!"

"Don't be naive! I told you already what the *real* Truth was about our movement! I told you as much that we're as bad as the Council! So don't talk to me about the noble crusade for truth and science and all its ideals! That's for the idiots we want to convert and convince! That's just what we need everyone to think we are!"

"A *true* dissenter never lies," declared Amelia, tears on the cusp of welling in her eyes. She glanced over at the dissenter words on the library wall to reassure herself: '**Service is our Purpose**'. She repeated the motto to herself in her mind and returned her attention to Velvel. "I owe it not only to myself, but to Sophia, to Ahmed, and to everyone in this whole rotting city, to tell the *Truth*. And the Truth is simple: there's a monster out there! And she's coming for all of us!"

"We are trying to stage a revolution here woman!" bellowed Velvel, now growing impatient with her. "And you're starting to sound like one of the Reds, with your talk of 'covert agents'! I'm starting to wonder if it's the propaganda getting to you or if this was your plan all along!"

"That's swine-shit and you know it!"

"We are *not* here to solve murder cases! Today we smashed the Red Coats! Tomorrow the city will be ours!"

"There'll be no one left to take the city if we don't act now!" forewarned Amelia.

In that instant, the lights abruptly went out and darkness swallowed the Room. A chorus of confused voices went up as people adjusted their eyes to the blackness.

"Someone's cut the power," said Danior as he pointlessly tapped at his keyboard.

"Get some glowsticks!" ordered Velvel commandingly. The sound of fumbling hands rummaging through bags and pockets filled the small space. A verse of shakes and cracks went up and a dozen green glowing sticks illuminated the room.

"What do you reckon? Rats again?" hypothesized Michal as he raised a glowstick up to the electric cables that ringed the Room.

"Most likely," agreed Danior.

"*She sees you,*" rasped a devilish voice in the dark. Amelia instinctively spun around to uncover the source of the voice.

"Ivana?" she said. "Is that you?"

A scream, shrill and sharp as a needle, howled out in the blackness. Amelia didn't think twice. She bolted for the door. *The Dragon was here.* She pushed someone over and sent them crashing to the floor. She didn't care.

"Hey! Where are you going?" cried Velvel after her. "We're not done here!"

Amelia barely heard him. She just ran as fast as her wearied legs would allow. She fearfully looked back down the corridors, the wilting lights blinking erratically. Through the flickering she glimpsed the silhouette in pursuit of her. That prompted her to sprint all the faster and in a frenetic fluster she barrelled through the fire door into the dance arena where—somehow—the *Plastic Souls of the Galaxy* were *still* playing, and their willing audience were—somehow—*still* rocking on.

Almost blinded by the demonic pulses of epileptic light, she crashed and hurtled through the rockers. Her heart close to eruption, her lungs on the brink of breathlessness, she struggled onwards and forwards. Hopeful that her pursuer might have gotten lost in the mosh pit, she glanced backwards over her shoulder. To her relief she saw no sign of the faceless silhouette but as the epileptic flashes intensified, she thought her eyes deceived her. She saw *Ahmed* walk among the crowds. No sooner had he appeared though than he disappeared. As the next, almost instantaneous, blast of epileptic light returned she saw *Sophia* standing where Ahmed had before. In the next flash, it was some stranger.

Amelia's heart sank into a bottomless pit and the blood drained from her face. She started running again. She looked back and back again to see Sophia and Ahmed coming after her. As she neared the exit, she saw the flashing white faces morph and mould together. Deformed and hideous, rows of teeth doubled up on one another, eyes came screaming out of cheekbones, maddening noises neither human nor animal tumbled out of their misshapen maws.

"*Don't leave me Amelia! Don't leave me!*" yowled the haunted voice of Sophia after her.

"*I just want to help! Just want to help!*" persisted Ahmed.

"*Heeellllp me! Hellllllpppp mee!*" roared the haunting voice of a stranger. "*TRrrrappped inside! Cannnn't essscape!*"

Amelia burst through the fire door and bolted down the corridor, adrenaline pumping through her like her life depended on it. Yet no matter how fast she ran, the deranged melody of twisted screams and laughs came dancing after her.

"*Please don't leave!*" came Sophia's voice howling up the corridor, the voice more mocking than terrified now. "*Don't leave! Don't leave! We had so much fun together!*

Hahahahahahahaha!"

"There's no such thing as monsters, there's no such thing," Amelia mindlessly repeated to herself as she ran between the wavering shafts of electric light. "There's no such thing as ghosts, there's no such thing, there's no such thing. There's no evidence. There has to be an answer. There has to be a reason. There has to be. There has to be. What the fuck! What the fuck!"

She turned the last corner, ran on all fours up the secret stairway to the corner shop, and rushed headfirst into the wall of blinding daylight which awaited her. So dazed was she by the sunlight that she nearly fell backwards down the stairs. Fear of the coming Black Dragon alone forced her to keep her balance. Shielding her unadjusted eyeballs, she fumbled forward across the now silent carnival—Judy Garland having finally been switched off.

When at last her vision returned to a degree of normalcy, she found the carnival as deserted as ever, populated only with the corpses of the dead. The carousel was now a completely burnt-out wreck, petroleum fumes still billowing from the melted horses. Gazing through the wafts of smoke, she thought she glimpsed some human movement. As she came around the blackened ruin of the carousel, she discovered a squadron of Red Coats and a convoy of armoured vehicles stationed by the roadside. So captivated by the threat of the Black Dragon had Amelia been that she had almost completely forgotten about the menace of the Red Coats. She walked straight out into the open for them to see, not considering they might gun her down just for the fun of it.

"That's her!" exclaimed a familiar voice and Amelia saw Governor Friedrichs come about the corner of a truck. "That's the bitch who threw me out!" She had completely forgotten about the mortal sin she'd committed against him. She looked over the heavily armed Red Coats and knew at once she was screwed. At least, she *knew* what they would do to her. Anything frankly was better than the *unknown* machinations of the Black Dragon. She made no attempt to escape.

"Thank you, Herr Governor, that will be all," dismissed a voice which seemed too courteous and well-mannered to belong to a Red Coat. Amelia then spotted a man standing apart from the Red Coats. His hair was slicked back with oil. Not unlike Friedrichs, he had the cut of a movie star though he was a good bit older, belonging more to her parents' generation. Draped around his shoulders was a grey cloak with red eagle wings sprawled across it. Beneath it he wore a dark leather raiment, combat trousers, and an authoritarian pair of knee-high boots. Under one arm he had a gas mask and under the other he had a Kalashnikov.

"You'll deal with her accordingly I trust," persisted an embittered Friedrichs. "Dissident scum!"

"That will do Herr Governor," assured the commander. "We will take care of the matter from here. Please return to your Tower Block and tend to your flock." Friedrichs gave the commander a withering look for the patronising tone he'd taken with them. But there was nothing he could do. He scowled at Amelia and then he scuttled off out of view.

"Amelia Svoboda!" called out the commander to her in the same refined aristocratic tone. "You have saved us a great deal of our time and energy by presenting yourself so willingly. I am Captain Ulrich von Sauken. Would you be so kind as to accompany me? My superiors are very eager to speak with you…about a great many important things." Amelia hesitated for a moment, not knowing how to respond exactly. The Captain pressed home his point. "Let me rephrase that mein kleine Liebchen. Would you be so kind as to accompany me of *your own accord*? My men and I are very grateful for having located you so swiftly. We would be more grateful still if you did not make us give chase."

Amelia looked over the assembly of armed men deployed before her. These were neither the standard brainless Red Coats she was accustomed to nor the trigger-happy country hicks who had stormed the city. These were Red Troopers, elite soldiers tasked with special missions by the High Council. They were all hard veterans, men who'd killed police officers and soldiers during the Great Awakening. Gas masks encompassed their heads and scarlet armour plates encased their bodies. Automatic weapons rested comfortably in their hands and Japanese katana swords lay in wait by their hips. They were the Council's most capable soldiers. Not even the tower governors dared fuck with them.

And yet, here they were, the best of the best, the vanguard of the vanguard, on a mission to arrest a single dissident girl for pushing Governor Friedrichs over.

It didn't add up.

Motivated by both an urge to unpuzzle this puzzle and fear of what they might do should she resist them, Amelia surrendered to the Captain and his men without a word. Before she knew it, she was sitting inside the windowless truck. Captain von Sauken sat himself down opposite her with a flick of his cloak. As the vehicle carted them away, her hands and shoulders once again began to throb uncontrollably as the aftershock of her prior pursuit through the tunnels caught up with her.

"So," said the Captain, his lucid voice now suddenly imbedded with an intangible remoteness. "You're a dissenter, eh?" Amelia was still too shell-shocked to say anything. He just smirked at her silence, his eyes analysing every piece of her. "I too was a dissident once," he confessed aloofly. "A man called Zielenski was my teacher. He and I were...spirit brothers, you might say. We walked among the people...but he delved too deep and too dark. I on the other hand, reached for the skies and I saw the face of God. I saw the truth."

"What Truth?" asked Amelia, now cursed by her curiosity to inquire into the Captain's mysteriousness. Von Sauken unrolled the sleeve of his right arm and presented a tattoo displaying the characters "-O."

"That *I,* and not he, was *chosen,*" he elaborated with a grin that burned too intensely for comfort. He pointed to his tattoo. "O negative universal donor they called me. By my...*Essence*...I can save any human life. I have in my veins the very serum of life. I contain within me a shard of the Great Spirit. The blood of the Angelic Ones flows within me. We are *higher* creatures amidst a sea of monkeys who fear us and hate us." A fire of violent delight then lit up in the Captain's eyes.

"When the Hour of the Plague was at hand, I went to Rome. I saw the bodies all littered across the Vatican and I saw the Dead Pope on his Dead Throne...and I knew in that instant that he had been a monkey pope all along. I understood all the world leaders to be of the Baboon Brood and that the Cabal had led mankind astray...back into the jungle. They *fear* our *potency*...and so planned to diminish us through interbreeding with the lesser breeds. Where they cannot seduce us...they seek to poison us with the monkey vaccine. But they have failed again...for when the Horde tried to cross the border into our Promised City on the Borava...I pulled the trigger on the anti-aircraft gun and watched their mortal bodies fly apart like red paper...and I knew in that moment I was upholding the intentions of the Great Spirit...that I was chosen. Our heavenly blood shall long outlast them into...Eternity. The Monkey Doctors may salivate with scientific lust at the powers of my magic blood. But they may never cross the river into our Most Holy City."

"Why are you telling me this?" questioned a completely puzzled Amelia, not knowing what to make of these pseudo-historical-scientific ravings. An almost clownish smile, *which did not appear to originate from him,* unravelled further still across his movie star face.

"Oh, I see the Angelic spark within you, mein Liebchen," he answered with esoteric certainty. "All your life you have strayed from the true path and lived a dream of lies your false friends have called 'Dissidence'. Do not fear this, for I too was once misguided. For now, the Council calls you home. I can see you have beheld the eyes of the *Great Demon*. That false idol which Zielenski worships. *Soon you will know your true self.* For you have seen those of my kin who came not from above...*but from below."* Those last words clung to Amelia's conscience. Did this Captain of the Red Troopers know about the Black Dragon? Had he known all along? Did he know through Zielenski? How far back did this go?

Her questions were never answered, the truck pulled to a halt and the back doors were opened with two Red Troopers beckoning her on. As she hopped out of the back though, Captain von Sauken called after her.

"*Beware the Night*, mein Liebchen," he warned more seriously. "Beware the Night. When in darkness the sun is drowned...*then Heaven will be upside down.*"

No time was afforded for her to ruminate on those cryptic words of farewell. The Red Troopers escorted her through a loading depot and on into the cavernous halls of a 19th century mansion, complete with suits of medieval armour, stuffed animals, and grand pianos. In the foyer of this grandiose home, a silvery haired woman dressed in a bland grey suit of tweed stood waiting. She looked over Amelia and then turned to the Red Troopers.

"This is the one?" she asked in the disinterested tone of a bureaucrat. The Troopers nodded. "Take her to the Little Room."

"What is this place?" asked Amelia as she struggled to sponge up her increasingly surreal surroundings. "Where on earth am I?"

"Outside the city," tersely answered the Trooper to her right from under his gas mask.

"This was once the estate of Graf von Mansfeld," elaborated the one to her left.

"Now it is the residence of the High Council," completed the one to the right. They came to a stop outside a dark oaken door with a plaque plainly reading "*The Little Room*" on it. The Trooper turned the handle and nudged it open. A tiny chamber was revealed inside with red and white tiles on the floor, pitch-black wallpaper plastering the walls, and a single chair occupying the entire space. The Trooper extended his hand into the room. "Sit," he instructed.

"Under the chair you'll find a VR headset," said the other as she seated herself in the lonely chair. She groped under the legs of the seat and grasped the set of goggles. "Put it on. They will be waiting for you."

"Who?"

The Troopers did not answer her. They merely closed the door and left her in the claustrophobic enclosure. She did not put the headset on immediately. She had to pause for a moment. Barely half an hour ago she had been running for her life through the corridors of the Underground. Now she was in the very lair of the High Council itself. She clasped her fist and pinched the arms of the chair just to remind herself it was all real. She definitely was not dreaming. With that final piece of self-assurance, she slid the headset down over her eyes.

Stretching out before her was a long dining table fitted with green lamps. Seated at the table were hooded figures clad in red robes. Their faces were concealed by masks in the shapes of wild animals. At the other end of the table was an empty throne with the letter R hovering over it like a halo. *This was the High Council,* she realised.

"*A national disgrace and a travesty,*" read aloud one of the hooded men with a raven mask. "*These are the atrocities taking place on Block C that the High Council doesn't want you to know about. A saboteur from the South Side is butchering our children and the Council can't even try to protect them. Where will the hypocrisy and inefficiency end? Hashtag murder victims, hashtag down with the council, hashtag Ziga forever, hashtag dissident movement.*" The raven faced man then looked over at Amelia. "Powerful words Miss Svoboda. A pity your blasphemous comrades did not rally to your hashtag on the Platform."

"They have other priorities," said Amelia shakily.

"Oh, we know," assured the raven.

"Your cavemen friends are hell bent on turfing us out and letting the zombie horde breach this city," accused a goat-faced Czar.

"They think they have the upper hand," confessed Amelia letting her nerves get the better of her.

"For now," said a wolf-faced Czar. "But whether they prevail or not, that remains to be seen."

"We seldom leave anything to chance though," piped up the Raven. "We are nothing, if not creatures of certainty. Guaranteed, reliable, outcomes are our currency." The photographs Amelia had taken from C Block suddenly appeared above the table in hologram form. "This is solid gold Miss Svoboda. Solid gold."

"Beg pardon?" confusedly questioned Amelia, still trying to guess which Cyber Czar was hiding underneath each mask.

"Your exposé," clarified the Wolf. "We like it. And we'd like to buy it."

"What? What's going on here? I don't…I don't understand—"

"The Plandemic is over Miss Svoboda," said the Goat frankly. "You know it. I know it. Everyone does. And every time we pump the propaganda out, people believe in it a little less. But *this,* this could really put things back on track. Nothing brings people running back to tried and tested beliefs and values like a shot of fear to the system."

"We'd like to pump some resources into your story," proposed the Raven. "Really sensationalise it to get as much attention as possible. Citizen R is willing to put his own seal of approval on it. People will be scared shitless and in so doing they'll be prodded into pogrom-mode. They'll run riot trying to root out the killer from their community. Neighbours will turn on neighbours. Families will consume themselves. It'll be total anarchy."

"But in the end," finished the Goat. "It'll take on such momentum that it'll sap the energy out of the dissident campaign and revitalise the spirit of our movement."

"You're asking me to betray my comrades, my friends, every principle I've ever believed in," protested Amelia, utterly dumbfounded at what was being proposed to her.

"If your so-called 'friends' cared so much about this 'Black Dragon', then why are you here speaking to us and not to them?" countered the Raven. "Your friends might overthrow us. They might. But it's still too early to call. You can wait if you like. But the more you wait, the more people will die by *her* hand. At least with us, there's a plan. It's called Plan Hysterium."

"Hysterium?"

"A fungus that feeds off the dead," explained the Raven. "For we too shall be reborn from this death and decay you have presented to us."

"And that includes you too," added the Wolf. "We are willing to give you a generous package in exchange for your cooperation."

"Why not just kill me and take the story?" asked Amelia, very well knowing that she might just have sealed her own death warrant.

"We considered this, but we've run the numbers and the Plan would yield greater results if the new narrative was fed to the public from a member of the dissenter movement," expounded the Goat. "You'd be the bright young face of the regime. You'll be on every billboard and every advert. You'll be our Joan of Arc, our Virgin Mary, whatever analogy you want!"

Amelia weighed the proposition in her head. This felt too great a betrayal of the dissident movement. All her adult life she had been dead certain about her life-purpose of destroying the Council and building a new government based on the values of transparency, mutual reciprocation, equality, and rationality. But then she recalled how Velvel had hijacked her beloved dissident movement. How he had responded to her warnings about the Black Dragon. How he had treated her as a fundamental threat to his budding cult of personality. If the uprising succeeded and a new regime under Velvel Varga was established, would it really be any better than the High Council? Would it, as Varga himself had said, just be the same regime under a new lick of paint? And if so, would it even take action against the Black Dragon?

"*Service is our Purpose,*" the dissenter motto rang out in her head. *This* was the best way to serve the greater good. *This* was the most certain, the most clear-cut, logical, and rational, way to tackle this problem.

"Well, what will it be?" pressed the Wolf.

"I accept," she agreed. "But with one condition: in exchange for my cooperation the High Council will incorporate a more rational, scientific, and objective approach to its policies and propaganda. One based on empirical analysis and—"

She never finished her counterproposal to the Council. The Cyber Czars were too busy trying to contain their belly laughter.

"No, no, no, no," guffawed the Raven. "We couldn't do that in a million years. I'm afraid that hearsay, paranoia, subjectivity, and rumours are far too entrenched in the values of the regime. It's simply not possible."

"What else did you think the letter R stood for if not for rumour?" asked the Wolf, still laughing.

"R for Rumour!" they all hurrahed at once.

"The package we provide you with is quite generous," assured the Goat. "You will be afforded a luxury state penthouse on the top floor of Block A with a scenic view of the southern riviere. This is complete with an extensive library and an inhouse swimming pool and gym. We are also prepared to grant you the privilege of being unplugged from the R Mark."

"Unplugged? What…what do you mean by that?"

"Well you see, only ordinary citizens have the R Mark bio-currency," enlightened the Raven. "To you it may be cash, but to us it's a recording device to monitor everyone's comings and goings. It digitises human behaviour, emotions, fears, joys, desires, the list goes on. We upload it all to our server and then sell it all off as psychological-prediction-products, or PPP for short, to big corporations around the world who make use of it to refine their advertising campaigns, i.e. to manipulate customers into buying more of their goods and services. This whole society, this city you've called your home, is what we like to call a 'behaviour farm'. It's why we promote so many extreme views on the Platform. The more extreme the stimulation, the more pronounced the reactions we can record, and as a result, the more PPP we can sell on the commercial market."

"But since you'll be one of us now," said the Wolf. "You won't be counted amongst the 'Sheeple' anymore. No strings attached!"

"So…hang on! I was right all along?" gaped Amelia for both their benefit and her own. "*You guys are the real puppeteers!* You've been secretly manipulating everyone and everything!"

"Guilty as charged!" joked the Raven with hands up to frame himself in jest.

"It's what we do best!" chimed in the Goat.

"Ironic isn't it?" laughed the Wolf. "The people here have more strings on them than anyone else in the world! Their 'freedom' is a complete lie! Makes me misty every time I think about it!"

"So, what'll it be?" asked the Raven more seriously, returning to the question at hand. "Will you join us? Or will you remain one of the cows we milk? We need an answer now. This is the only chance you'll ever get."

Amelia inhaled deeply. There was too much information to comb through and absorb. But in the end, there could only be one answer.

"Let's find this bitch," she accepted.

Part VII: (Un)Reliance

But this is the question one must ask oneself:
Who checks the fact-checkers? This is the question.

First recorded social media post of Citizen R

The penthouse was beyond wonderful. A million miles from the mouldy spaces of her parent's apartment for sure. Air conditioning. Central heating. Hot water. Soundproof walls. Electricity without blackouts. Not to mention the extensive collection of books stacked within her own private library. Out from the glass balcony she could see the Borava snaking across the landscape in both directions.

If ever one might call a place heaven on earth, this was as close as it might get for Amelia.

After indulging in a sumptuous dinner, she prepared her evening with enthused delight. As the sun creeped downwards behind the western horizon, she snatched Dante's Inferno from the literature section of her library. She laid it down on the couch and skipped off to the bathroom to enjoy the cleansing waters of a hot shower. Once she was clean and spotless, she could relax in full and enjoy the words of Dante.

The stink of the gutter water from the subway tunnel was blasted off her skin in a sheer gust of godly water. Not until now had she ever thought she might enjoy a shower so much. After towelling herself down, she picked up a bathrobe and ambled back to the warm embrace of her lounge. Before tucking into Dante though, she chose to treat herself again and pour a glass of wine for her pleasure.

As she stood there pouring the glass of wine at the marble kitchen counter, she became aware suddenly that Dante's Inferno was resting on the far side of the counter. Could there be two copies in the penthouse? Surely not. She picked it up and examined it.

"Not where I left you," she said to the book, her attention moving back towards the couch where she had left it. She popped her head around the corner for a better look.

"Settling in, are we?" said the woman stretched out across one of the divans. Amelia nearly dropped her glass of wine.

"*Ivana?*" exclaimed Amelia as she looked this mysterious hippy-lady over.

"None other," answered Ivana, peering over her blue-tinted shades, her crown of white roses twirling around her finger.

"How did you get—"

"That is absolutely irrelevant," interjected Ivana with such self-confidence that it startled Amelia somewhat. "Nice quarters," she complimented as Amelia sat down on the couch opposite her.

"Who are you? I feel like we've met but we keep missing each other."

"Or keep overlooking one another," she said with a seductive smile. Amelia had no clue what was meant by that. "I was an astrologer, if you really must know. I searched the stars for answers to our questions. But there's only so much weather forecasting and cosmic matchmaking for lonely teenagers you can do before boredom sets in. And the School had no use for my, shall we say, unconventional approach. So, I left."

"Unconventional how?"

"Astrology is devoted to predicting the future. But I say, there is no future to predict. There is no light at the tunnel's end. I'm an oneiromancer now."

"A what?"

"An oneiromancer. I divine the universe through the swirls of the dreamscape."

"Right...I see," noted Amelia uneasily, not knowing how exactly to manage this weird and uninvited guest. "And who...who are you with? Michal told me you were in the Room. Are you with the Dissidents? Or...are you with the Council? How else could you have gotten in here I suppose."

"I'm just like you," she said coldly. "I too *was* a rebel. But then I found my true calling and I now serve a greater power."

"The Council? Are you with that Captain? What's his name? Ulrich von Sauken! That's it! Are you in league with him?" Ivana gave a thin smile to Amelia's guesses.

"I serve a greater power still."

"Who?"

"*The Great Demon,*" she said in a slow and hellish pace that made Amelia's skin crawl. Something wasn't right about this. Something was really, *really*, wrong. She began to think the unthinkable.

"What do you want with me?" she asked cautiously, her nerves tensing up. "Why are you here?" Ivana sat up straight on the divan and looked across the divide into Amelia's eyes.

"I just thought you might care for a visitor in your new home," said Ivana as if she was the most normal human being on earth. "I can see you're not comfortable so I will get to my point and then I shall leave."

"Please do. And take your astrology and dream-reading with you when you do." Ivana betrayed no reaction at all to Amelia's insult to her profession.

"I have come to tell you the truth," she said. "And to satisfy your inherent curiosity. *Once and for all.* Now that your home is so close to the heavens, it would be cruel would it not, for there still to be secrets kept from you?" Amelia tentatively nodded, her craving for knowledge now surpassing her distaste for this intruder. "But first I must ask. Do you want to know what I have to tell you? Do you really wish to know the truth? The whole truth? And nothing but the truth?"

"Without a doubt," retorted Amelia without a single doubt in her dissident soul. "The fewer mysteries and secrets in the world, the better. Spit it out and be done with it."

"Then before I do, would you agree with me that it is impossible for a human being to *unlearn* something? That it is possible for us *only* to learn more and never less? For us to become more and more enlightened but *never* to become more ignorant?"

"Why yes," agreed Amelia, again without second thoughts about her convictions on such things. "That is the natural condition of humanity. How else do we progress if not by learning?" A wicked grin slithered across Ivana's face.

"Then here it is," said Ivana with infantile fascination. "You are a wonder my dear. You have *the sight.*"

"The what? The fuck are you talking about?"

"You have the dream vision."

"Yes, I do have dreams. What does it—"

"You misunderstand me my dear…You have the *dream vision.* Your eyes can see the world through the dream-eye."

"The hell are you saying to me woman?"

"You're in a *waking dream.* You are both awake and dreaming at the same time. I can see it in you."

"What! That's ridiculous! I'm clearly awake and speaking to you!"

"This is true. But you are *also* viewing me through the dream-eye. Not everything you see is real."

"Fuck off! You're talking swine-shit! That's impossible!"

"Do you remember the statues being pulled down? The joyful crowds celebrating the uprising?"

"Ehhh...yes. But that was a dream. I wasn't there. And how...how could you know that?"

"Really?" Ivana reached into her pocket and presented a phone. She swiped the lock away and held up the screen for viewing. Amelia could physically feel the mathematical calculations which composed her reality melt apart in her brain as she gazed upon the photograph. Both she and Sophia were front and centre of the image, arms around one another with big warm friendly smiles on their faces as a statue of Czar Kaczynski was pulled down to cheering onlookers. "I took this photograph of the two of you. You and I went back to the Room and I left you there."

"No, no, no, no," denied Amelia. "What the fuck! You're fucking with me! I wasn't there. That was in my dream! I wasn't there! Not in person!"

"You sleepwalk, don't you?" Amelia gave no answer, her silence speaking more than any words could. "I thought so," affirmed Ivana who now looked upon her with renewed fascination. "I'm amazed you haven't noticed. All those *inconsistencies* and sudden gaps in time and you just casually accepted it as part of your reality. How fascinating! How truly innocent! What a wondrous contradiction you are!"

Amelia's mind hastily flicked back over her memories and she remembered the weird sightings of Sophia and Ahmed within the epileptic strobe lights. But of a sudden then, a dreadsome thought occurred to her: What if those things she had seen were *not* dreamed? What if that was all *real*?

"Why are you fucking with me like this?" sniffled Amelia, upset at how incapable she was of controlling her emotions in that moment. "Why me?"

"Some are chosen for necessity," said Ivana calmly. "For survival. You understand. But penniless beggars like you...I torment for the lolz, as your late parents would say."

"What? No!" defied a wild-eyed Amelia. "My parents aren't dead! They're on the Platform. I think I've heard enough of your lies! Get out of here! Get out! You're pulling my leg now!"

"Am I now? *Or are you?*" That fateful question was enough to shatter Amelia completely. Ivana lustfully leered at her despair. "Did you never notice that old Maria and Vlad never changed their clothes? The same tracksuit, day after day. Come on, did it never seem strange? They're on the Platform, this is true. But so is everyone. And nobody dies on the Platform. Don't you know the digitised human soul is condemned to eternity?"

"No, no, this can't be true! It can't be!" insisted Amelia, refusing to believe any of it as she clasped her head in her hands. "What the fuck? What the actual fuck!"

"You were leeching off the bio-slots of the dead—like a fungus. Do you know that? You were living off their dead bio-currency and *lying* to everyone, even to *yourself.* Governor Friedrichs tried to help you, tried to explain you'd be cut off, but you wouldn't hear *the Truth*...You must have been walking around the apartment, replaying the tapes of old conversations with them in your head. Dancing through your dreamscape like Mary Poppins!"

"Shut up! Just tell me! Tell me what's real! Please God I need to know! I need to know what's real! Tell me! Even just tell me how long I've been seeing the world like this! I need to know! I need to know black from white and right from wrong and fact from fiction!"

"Do you now? Would you really like to know if you dreamed your friend's death? Or did you dream trying to save her? Would you like to know if you abandoned her from the first sign of trouble and left her to die?"

"Just fucking tell me!" screeched Amelia, tears streaming down her cheeks in runnels. "Please tell me! Please! Is she alive or dead? I need to know! Is the Black Dragon real? Are you the Black Dragon? Please! Please! Pl-pl-please." A perverted giggle wriggled out of Ivana's lips.

"*No,*" she said in a distorted voice that crushed Amelia's very sense of self. Every atom of her began to combust in that moment. Her head began to reel. She felt like her eyes were about to explode under the pressure. *She was trapped.* Her whole life was a delusion! Everything was a lie! Was she herself even alive? Or was that a lie too? But Ivana gave no answers to reassure her of anything. The oneiromancer just laughed. And laughed. And laughed. This was not a waking-dream, she realised. But a *waking-nightmare.*

"What a wretched creature you are," mockingly crowed Ivana.

"What's real?" pleaded Amelia, her vision of the world now blurring with tears. "Tell me dammit! Tell me!" Ivana lurched across the gap between them and slapped her across the face.

"Was that real?" taunted Ivana in a deep and manly voice. *"Or is it just your deepest darkest anxieties and fears speaking through me all at once? God only knows!"*

"What the fuck!" gasped Amelia, scattering backwards in horror.

"Isn't this fun Amelia?" Ivana said then in Sophia's voice, removing her shades to reveal her friend's purpled contact lenses.

"Shut up! Shut up! Stop it! Stop!"

"I'm only trying to help," the oneiromancer said in Ahmed's voice. Laughs and jeers of a hundred tongues came galloping out of Ivana's maws. Through the haze of tears, Amelia saw Ivana's face morph and reform itself, adopting multiple attributes of manifold persons all at once in a hellish mosaic of souls clambering for breath.

"It's *you*," snarled Amelia. "You're the Black Dragon."

"I am nothing...and I am everything." With those simple words, Ivana's face returned to its former shape and a wicked smirk curled up in the corner of her mouth. A coldness tightened around Amelia's chest and within a heartbeat she sensed the unconsented grip of a stranger's hand on her shoulder. Inch by inch she turned her head to glance at it. Oily black with grime and soot it was. That was enough to send a dagger of despair shuddering through her.

She dared not look into the faceless abyss of the Dragon.

"Oh to be caught between two worlds," hissed Ivana as though she was reading a children's fairy tale. *"Can't fall down into sleep and can't wake up into life. No escape for you my dear...none but one."*

"Just do it," pleaded Amelia miserably, resigning to her ineluctable fate. "Just get it over with. KILL ME! KILL ME!"

"Oh no, don't say that," retorted Ivana with a tone befitting a concerned mother all of a sudden. "Don't even think that my dear." Her voice then writhed into the tongue of the baleful. *"You'll be the one to do it."*

"What? No! Please do it! Please just end it! Why are you doing this? Why me?"

"Why for the lolz my dear. For the lolz," answered Ivana with sadistic impunity.

"Self-torture makes the human animal so very very tender," spoke the dark spectre of the Black Dragon in a voice so devoid of human empathy it would break even the surest soul down to a screech. *"Flee me, fight me, kill me. it will not save you…none of it can erase your curse of knowledge…you need only ask yourself the question you already know: How long? How long can you live this life? Trapped between fact and fiction? Between truth and lies? Between reality and unreality? Your addiction to enlightenment has cost you your sanity. The thirst for knowledge can only lead to one indisputable and undeniable ending. Self-eradication."*

"Self-eradication!" echoed Ivana with shrieking ghoulish glee.

Amelia's whole body went numb in that moment. She felt a darkness, an inner darkness, rise up within her and suck every fibre of her being into it. Ivana got up off her seat. The Black Dragon gripped her shoulder all the firmer. Together then, the two intruders spoke to her.

"I told you what would happen," they both said in one voice. Amelia rubbed her thumbs.

"You sang me a nightmare."

She raised up her hands.

"And now."

She made sure her thumbs were pointing directly towards her eyes.

"I'll feast on the last of your dreams…"

Varga's Rising came to nothing.

The High Council remains in power.

A renewed wave of frenzied violence overshadowed the dissident movement.

Five thousand people were killed in the Hysterium Purge.

Amelia Svoboda, aka Cyber Czarina Kaganovich, was made a Martyr of the Truth.

Her delusional ravings were interpreted as the fingerprints of the Great Spirit guiding humanity to victory over the Cabal.

A shrine is now devoted to her in Martyr's Park.

No one can confirm if the Black Dragon was killed in the Hysterium Purge.

The Black Dragon's identity remains a mystery.

Chapter III: The Predator

Part I: Prejudice

Annihilation is Liberation!

Marius Zielenski's lecture to North Side school children of Block D

The office was stale and sterile. A cage of grey walls decorated with greying certificates and faded photographs. Stiff stacks of paper rested on unremarkable shelves. A clock on the wall methodically ticked itself into boredom. The computer lethargically ran the same old meaningless numbers. Gazing into its digital mirror of knowledge, the inquisitive clerical creature searched for his answers and solutions.

Johanna fidgeted with her fingers to keep herself awake. These sessions with her Vaccine Case Worker were tedious enough to make even a plank of wood appear interesting. Perhaps one of the few benisons of the mandatory surgical mask was that she could conceal her irrepressible yawns from him. There were a dozen better ways of spending her time but, alas, she had no choice in the matter. She *had* to be here with this pen-pushing bureaucrat.

Of a sudden, a notification buzzed on Julius' phone. He took the device from his pocket. Checked the notice with a swipe and then left the gadget on his desk between himself and Johanna. No sooner had it landed on the smooth wooden surface than it began to bleat its warning siren.

"Beep! Beep! Beep!" it wailed in short piercing shrieks. "Beep! Beep! Beep!"

Julius, a rigid little man with a square haircut to go with his square-shaped head, square jaw, square shoulders, and square spectacles, paid no mind to the incessant racket reverberating from his phone. He just sat there and scrolled through his digital paperwork. Johanna squirmed uncomfortably in her seat as the beeping continued and intensified.

"Do you mind turning it off?" she requested reasonably, feeling a headache coming on as the alarm persisted to chisel at her eardrums. Julius looked across at her as if she'd asked him to masturbate in front of her. "You know why it's ringing. You can turn it on again when I'm gone."

"No can do," he said with that bland dialect typical of his white-collar species. "Commission Regulations. Rules *are* rules."

"Come on, even just put it back in your pocket so it doesn't detect me? I'm asking nicely." He looked over at her with subtle disgust quivering in his eyes.

"I was not aware that someone of your disposition was permitted to ask in any other way," he mocked smugly. Johanna exhaled beneath her mask and clenched her fingers together, trying her best to alleviate the audible irritation without giving this desk-chained cockroach any satisfaction. "You really find it that annoying eh?"

"It's driving me up the wall!" snapped Johanna, trying to convey her agitation through her eyes since the mask concealed any other meaningful part of her face. Julius shrugged and pulled the phone back towards himself, the alarm fading off the farther away it was taken.

"Maybe you should have gotten a vaccine then," he said with dry derisiveness that made Johanna's blood boil with rage.

"For the love of—" she nearly bellowed before he rudely cut her short.

"I've finished assessing your file," he asserted plainly, as though this were only the start of their conversation. Johanna calmed herself somewhat and tried to relax her tensed up body so she could negotiate with a clear head.

"And? What's the verdict? How do you propose I get out of my 'disposition'?"

"Get a vaccine. It's that simple. Just pay for a dose and get yourself inoculated."

"Right," said Johanna, feeling her muscles clench with impatience again. "And how exactly am I supposed to do that with no income? I don't have the Pandemic Welfare payment anymore."

"Because the Pandemic is over," justified Julius in his typical condescending tone. "It's time to go back to work. Get a job. Earn your living like everyone else. The Commission isn't running a soup kitchen for beggars you know!"

"Once again, how am I supposed to do that? The Reinther Fitness Gym still can't open because of the Health Code. Is there any sign of the Commission loosening the rules on gyms so I can open up and—"

"Absolutely not. Gyms as you know are not essential services. As you should be aware, the gym environment is the perfect breeding ground for a pathogen to spread."

"Yes, but the Pandemic is over so why keep us closed? Why are we closed when Frenkel's Takeaway is allowed to open? Since when was junk food more essential than physical exercise?"

"I do not make the rules Miss Reinther. If you wish to take this further, then I can log a complaint on your behalf and someone from the Castle will contact you in five business days."

"No, no, no. Don't do that. Don't waste anymore of my time please. I just want to get my life back on track and open up my family's business."

"Well, even if gyms were allowed to open, you still would not be able to receive customers because you don't have a vaccine."

"Then what am I supposed to do?"

"Get a vaccine."

"How? My business is closed. I don't have any welfare. How am I going to make ends meet here?"

"Get a different job obviously! Re-skill, re-educate, re-focus."

"Don't hit me with that propaganda swine-shit! Besides, I've already tried and nowhere will hire me because I need a vaccine. I can't even get work as a cleaner. So, what am I supposed to do here?"

"Get a vaccine."

"I know! How?"

"You do have savings inherited from your late parents after their untimely demise—"

"No, no, no!" rejected Johanna with a wave of the hand to make her position clearer. "I've been through this with you already. My little brother is in hospital with a brain tumour and we need that money for his treatment." Julius looked over the file again and raised an eyebrow.

"It says here that Klaus is your stepbrother."

"What's that supposed to mean? Why the hell would that make any difference anyway? I'm not going to ditch him for my own sake just because we don't share blood. He's a thirteen-year-old boy for crying out loud and I'm all he's got left…and *he's* all I have left too."

"You have no other family that could provide some financial alleviation to you?"

"My father's family all died in the Pandemic. My mother's side of the family all took off on the last flight out of here before the airport was shut down. My stepfather's siblings defected to the North Side and are probably all dead by now. So, no. There's no one who can bail me out. We've been through this already. Is there no charity scheme for people like me? A vaccine donation?"

"Like I said. This isn't a soup kitchen. If you want to live here, you need to pay your way. You need to *earn* your living." Johanna was about to make a rash response to that, but Julius beat her to it again. "If you have a problem with that policy, then you can take it up with the Metropole Insurance Company."

"Like they'd ever listen to me," sighed Johanna. "Do *you* even listen to me? You're supposed to help me but all you ever do is say the same old lines every time. I think you run the numbers in front of me just so you can waste my time, *time* that I might otherwise spend with my brother."

"Stepbrother."

"Oh for fuck sake!" snapped Johanna, unable to control herself any longer. "What about a loan?" she suggested in a last fling of the dice. "Could I get a bank loan to pay for the vaccine and get me started again?"

"You need a vaccine to get a loan."

"What? When did that come in?"

"Does it really matter? You won't be able to get a loan. All I can tell you Miss Reinther is what I've already told you: *get vaccinated.*"

"That does it!" she shouted, jumping to her feet and making her way for the door. "I'm out of here! Don't expect me to walk back in here again!"

"Our sessions are compulsory Miss Reinther!" reminded Julius as she stormed out. "Those are the rules! Dire consequences are in store for those who do not abide by the rules!"

She was in too much of a fluster to hear him. She stomped through the waiting room, her every step setting off a fresh wave of beeping phone alarms amongst Julius' equally robotic colleagues. She flung open the glass door of the building and was at once bathed in the bleaching glow of summer sunlight. The warmth of the sun however could not banish this living nightmare. No sooner had she exited the premises than she incited the phones of several pedestrians to start ringing. As she reached the inside of her car, she removed her mask and let out a deep breath in a hollow attempt to soothe herself. Within seconds, she was hammering at the steering wheel with her fists just to give even a fraction of expression to her anger.

A young couple in their colourful summer clothes ambled by as they licked their ice creams. They pointed and giggled at her unconstrained temper.

"Why don't you take a video?" shouted Johanna from behind the windscreen. "Make it last forever!" The two lovebirds barely even heard her. They only seemed to notice that the show was over, and they continued with their easy-going day, snickering about the crazy lady in her car.

Johanna planted her face into the palms of her hands, hoping somehow that when she looked up at the world again it would all be different, and everything would be fine. But *nothing* was fine. Everything was slipping away from her. She had no control over her life anymore seemingly. Powers vast and unreachable were making all the decisions.

"What am I going to do?" she asked herself as she lay back in the driving seat. "What…the fuck…am I going to do?" She *had* to do something. The odds being stacked her was no excuse she knew. She couldn't just stand by and let it all fall to pieces. She had to act. Take back control. Rebuild and restore what was lost. When she was a girl, her first father, Oskar, had always told her to *'never give in'*, to *'never give up'*, and to *'never lose hope'*, not while one breath remained to be cast. Those words had pulsed through her veins during every fight, every argument, every sweat-drenching workout. All her life she had stubbornly pushed through the pain, no matter how excruciating, and burst through to reap the rewards. That was the irrefutable law of survival. She would fight until the bitter end.

No matter the cost.

She just needed to know which battle to fight. She needed a win. Just one win. Enough to give her an inch to stand on.

But both time and options were fast running out for her she knew. She hadn't known about the new rule on bank loans. She wondered what other escape routes were on the cusp of being sealed off. The more doors the Commission shut on her, the harder it would be to fight back. Another couple of weeks, a month or two at most, and she would be barred from visiting Klaus at the hospital. It was only a matter of time she knew. But she *couldn't* let that happen. She needed to get her house in order before it was too late. The alternative was too terrible for her even to consider.

She racked her brains for a stratagem, a plan, anything at all to get her out of this hole.

Then it struck her.

Angelika! If anyone could advise her on what to do it was her old school friend who now worked as a secretary for Doctor Barodnik. She should have contacted her old pal ages ago. Why hadn't she thought of it sooner?

Within seconds of the solution presenting itself, she was confronted with the grim reminder of reality; the exact reason why she hadn't already reached out to Angelika. She didn't have a Friend Licence, i.e. no right to socialise. As an unvaccinated patient, Johanna was deprived of the right to a Contact Bubble. She was meant to be isolated from everyone, kept quarantined and contained from the world lest she give rise to a new deadly epidemic. Her very existence was a public liability.

Yet again, another door to salvation that had been locked and bolted on her.

The risks of breaking the Commission's Health Code however were now becoming overshadowed by the risk of losing everything she owned and loved.

Sometimes, in order to obey the rules, one had to bend the rules—ever so slightly.

She looked at the clock and saw it was coming to about noon. Angelika would be on her lunch now. And on a sunny day like this, she knew exactly where her old school friend would be. Johanna turned the ignition and set off into the city.

The sunlight glimmered and gleamed upon the rippling flow of the Borava as she drove down the quays. Up ahead she spied the tall towering tombstone of the Millennium Bridge—the city's vain attempt at the turn of the century to imitate the Brooklyn Bridge of America, intended by its architects to symbolise the city's gateway to a bright and prosperous future for the new century. Now, it stood there, gaunt, abandoned, and broken—two arms of steel and concrete reaching across to one another, never to be reunited.

Every time she laid eyes upon its bleak ruin she was reminded of her parents' fate. They, and so many others, had attempted to cross to the northern bank in search of a new green country where they could reopen their businesses and live without the restrictions imposed by the Commission. She had been looking after Klaus at the time and was meant to follow after them once they had set up shop.

But that had never come to pass. She remembered the live stream footage of the exodus, the thousands of migrants compacted onto the bridge, the thin line of men dressed in Red on the Northern Bank. There then came the man in a long cape who, completely unprovoked, decided to open fire on the crowd with an anti-aircraft gun. Screams had risen up and then the footage had ended with blood and brains splattering the camera lens.

She never saw her parents again. Dying as they had in no-man's land and considered as traitors and non-persons to both sides, their bodies were never recovered. They lay either up on the bridge as skeletons picked upon by the crows, or down in the silty bed of the Borava.

Johanna took a right turn back into the city centre, away from the memories of the past, and drove straight as a ruler for her destination. She parked her car by the sidewalk and hopped out. The lunch hour was starting, and the hive of workers were starting to congregate towards their convenient cafes and delis. She speed-walked down the pavement, trying her best not to alert any mobile phones of passers-by. She crossed the junction and entered the public green space known as 'Lovers' Park'.

The park's name had taken on a special significance when the pandemic had ended. The so-called 'Summer of Love' which followed the end of lockdown had seen the green expanse become a paradise for new aspiring couples. The Commission had promoted it as such with billboards dotted around the park depicting happy, smiling, couples with babies in their arms. Next to these doting images ran the Commission's instructive slogan:

"Life is Precious:
Reproduce, Repopulate, Recontribute."

Even today, Johanna could still spy many pairings enjoying the green lawns while they basked in the golden sunlight. None of this though translated into anything other than forbidden fruit being dangled out of her reach. A luxury someone like her could never have.

If she did not have a Friend Licence without a vaccine, then she certainly did not have a Relationship Licence allowing her to engage in carnal pursuits—her unvaccinated body was deemed too hazardous for that. And so, the Summer of Love had passed her by. Her peers had told her again and again that there was '*still time*' to find someone. She had even told herself those words. If she was just patient enough, then she too might be held in the arms of another. She too might one day hold a child in her arms. Perhaps there still was time for her. Once she had her vaccine and got back up on her feet, she might then find someone and lay claim to the future that was rightfully hers.

Indeed, on a sunny day like this, one might well believe the Summer of Love to be still alive and kicking.

There's still time, she told herself silently as she enviously eyed the pairs of lovers frolicking, gossiping, and tittering with one another.

Yet even as she passed through the gates of the park, she could see the workers taking down the plaque of 'Lovers' Park' and replacing it with the more medically correct 'Hygiene Park'. Time as ever it would seem, was against her.

To try and blend in with the crowd, she had taken the risk of not wearing her mandatory face covering. Yet even without the mask and even by staying out of range of the phone alert radars, she still felt out of place. People she could tell were looking at her in strange suspecting ways, unable to figure out why she seemed so alien to their conformist eyes. They were *all* looking at her. She felt like a stranger, an imposter, *in her own home city.*

Every passing day though the city she had called home seemed to be slipping away.

These streets had long since ceased to feel anything like home.

Home was in the past.

Her discomfort created a greater urgency to her search for Angelika. She looked from left to right from one sprawling patch of green to the next. She passed through the tidy groves of birch trees and circled around the centrepiece fountain. Only at the park's edge, did she finally locate her old friend.

She was sitting on the grass and dressed in the blouse and pencil skirt typical of the secretarial profession. Angelika had always been pretty as a picture. Had she so desired, she could have pursued a career as a model. Her auburn hair was kept lush and tidy to perfection. She had a set of seductive hazel eyes, though on this sunny occasion, they were tucked behind a set of blue-tinted sunglasses.

Johanna found herself approaching her friend with caution, as if she was a hunter stalking a deer. Eventually though she had to just throw her fears of rejection to the wind and make her presence known. She put on a brave friendly smile and went in.

"Johanna! Oh my God!" exclaimed Angelika with genuine surprise, getting up off the grass with a half-eaten sandwich in hand. "I thought that was you!

How are you? It's been so long!" Johanna suddenly found Angelika giving her a hug. It had been so terribly long since anyone had wrapped their arms around her that she barely knew how to react. She froze on the spot for a split second before reciprocating the gesture, her nostrils absorbing the rich aroma of perfumes which Angelika no doubt daily treated herself with. Peering over Angelika's shoulder, Johanna spied her friend's phone on the left on the grass starting to buzz.

"Could you turn your phone off?" whispered Johanna carefully. "I need. I need help."

Angelika slowly broke away from their embrace and looked at her. The look she gave was pregnant first with confusion, then shock, and finally with a palpable level of concern. She nodded without a word and backed away to her picnic spot, picked up her phone and switched it off. Johanna took a breath of relief.

Her friend was still her friend.

"What's going on Jo?" asked Angelika worriedly as the two of them sat down on the grass together. Johanna paused for a second before speaking. "What do you need help with?"

"I'm. I'm in trouble Angie," admitted Johanna, a tear almost welling in her as the weight of her lonesome burden was lifted. "I eh. I don't have a vaccine and um. things are getting tight. I can't open the gym and I can't get a job anywhere."

"Shit," exhaled Angelika.

"I need to open the gym Angie. I need to get the business up and running. How am I going to do that? How do I get a vaccine with no money? I would have gotten it ages ago only the pandemic payment was barely paying the bills and I couldn't get it. I...I..."

"Ok well, you may not like this Jo, but you need to forget about the gym," advised Angelika, her tone serious, but not condescending the way Julius was. "It's never going to open. Believe me Jo, I work for the Commission, and I know how they think. They'll never allow it."

"That gym is my livelihood Angie," sobbed Johanna. "My parents spent so much time and money on it. I owe it to them to get it back up and running. Besides, I'm a fitness instructor. What else am I supposed to do?"

"Adapt," said Angelika curtly. "You need to let go of it. If you don't, you'll go broke and you'll lose the gym anyway. My advice to you would be to sell it and use the money to get a vaccine."

"And then what? How do I make a living after that?"

"Use the vaccine to become a personal instructor for people. It's what everyone else in that business is doing. I have one. I think even Barodnik has one believe it or not. The business your parents built up from the ground is an anchor around your neck and if you don't cut it loose, you're going to drown…Do you understand?" Angelika leaned in a little closer and lowered her voice. "The Commission have a new initiative to 'clean up' the city. They want everyone completely vaccinated by this time next year. If you don't get vaccinated now, you're fucked."

"What do you mean? What are they planning?"

"I don't know. All I know is that it won't be good for people like you. Sanitation teams are already being organised to mop up the streets of homeless people. They're making it illegal to not have a house. So, if you don't get sorted and you run out of money…"

"Right," acknowledged Johanna with a nod of the head. "Message received."

"Angelika!" came a shrill female voice hollering across the grassy sprawl. Angelika and Johanna turned to see a newcomer approaching them. Johanna could not help but notice the forthcoming person was a little too close to be shouting a name across the park, as if they had been trying to conceal their presence from the two old friends before ambushing them.

"Ah Veronika!" answered Angelika with a big warm smile. Veronika came hobbling over in high heels and a fine white dress that matched her finely treated blonde hair that fell around her shoulders in a curtain of gold. This living doll held out her elegant hand to Angelika, presenting an engagement ring upon her finger fitted with dazzling diamonds.

"Vaclav proposed!" yelped Veronika with girlish excitement. "We're a perfect match! I'm going to be Missus Kovac!"

"Oh my god! That's fantastic!" congratulated Angelika with alacrity, hopping to her feet to hug her arms around her new friend.

"Congratulations," said Johanna, more quietly to this stranger while Angelika ogled the ring and continued to shower her friend with words of felicitation. Behind the ecstasy of her delighted smile, Veronika's eyes kept peering back to Johanna with uncomfortable nervousness.

"Oh, how rude of me, Veronika this is my old friend Johanna," introduced Angelika. "Johanna this is my neighbour Veronika."

"We live on the same avenue," said Veronika with a smug cockiness that was so obviously intended to make Johanna feel insignificant. "We go to the same book club, go to the same parties."

"Go to the same hairdresser!" added Angelika to which Veronika let out a plastic guffaw of laughter.

"We're practically sisters!" chuckled Veronika, her hand clasping Angelika's shoulder in an overt display of territorialism. Johanna smiled thinly at it all, feeling she had nothing to contribute to this. "So, what were you guys discussing?"

"Oh, you know, just catching up," explained Angelika hastily to which Veronika nodded coldly without a word.

"Well, I'd best be getting on the road," said Johanna, desperate to make an exit from this awkward encounter. As she stood up, she heard the phone in Veronika's purse start to ring. Instantaneously she felt the disgusted glare of Veronika's eyes on her. A shade of embarrassment at once came upon Angelika. "Good catch up," she said to Angelika before turning to Veronika. "Nice to meet you."

"Yes," said Veronika with false courtesy in her voice.

"See you around," said Angelika awkwardly.

Johanna turned heel and began her return journey through the park. Her 'friend' and Veronika were talking about her before she was even out of earshot.

"Where do you suppose she gets her hair done?" asked Veronika rhetorically, opening a flood of sniggering from the two of them.

"Oh god I don't even know," cachinnated Angelika, brushing off the subject. "It's so matted! She probably has lice and all!"

So much for 'old friend', thought Johanna to herself, walking away a little faster now to put the two crowing gossipers behind her.

"Look at her," said a young man very openly, pointing Johanna out to his circle of friends, all of whom turned to gawk at her. The lunch hour was in full swing now and the density of lunching workers had increased manifold, making it virtually impossible for Johanna not to set off at least a faint buzz of phone alarms. Even with just a few phones being alerted to her condition though, it did not take long for the wave of revulsion to permeate throughout the whole hive.

"Vile," one woman remarked at her with unconcealed disdain.

"Idiot girl," heckled an anonymous voice from among the rabble.

"Disgusting," spat a man who walked by her.

A half-eaten apple came somersaulting from an unknown hand and splattered at Johanna's feet. She heard a ripple of laughter. She didn't dare turn and search for the culprit.

"Just keep walking," said Johanna to herself. "Just keep walking. Just keep walking." She fleetingly glanced to her right and saw a boy of seven years almost having a panic attack at the mere sight of her, as though she were a wasp bent on stinging him. The boy's mother shielded him and whispered soothingly into his ear while throwing dagger eyes back at Johanna.

"What's wrong with her?" asked a young girl of her parents in that loud unfiltered voice which all children have.

"She's wrong in the head dear," answered the girl's father, subtly herding the girl and his other children away from Johanna. A glance of parental scorn was cast at Johanna and he told his children: "She's sick. We need to stay away from her, so we don't get sick too."

"You should be put down!" howled a teenager with impunity at her, much to the amusement of his juvenile buddies. "My dad's a vet! He can tranquilise you first!" All around her the heckles and hackles of the hive heaved and howled, the phones buzzing and shuddering all the more with every step she took. She took a breath of relief as she saw the gates of the park up ahead of her. Her walk of shame was almost at its end. She trooped past the welcome sign to the park and noted its full transformation from 'Lovers' Park' to 'Hygiene Park'.

The universal Summer of Love was truly over.

The exclusive Autumn Rot had begun.

Time was up.

Part II: Penance

Your search for Salvation will be the root of your Damnation.

Marius Zielenski, opening paragraph of 'In the Shadow of the Great Demon', page 1

"It's almost over, it's almost over," she silently mouthed to herself behind her mask as she returned to her vehicle from the park. "It'll all be over soon, everything will be ok, everything will be ok."

With every sinew of her being, she focused on the task ahead of her and put the ugly walk of shame through Hygiene Park to the back of her mind. It was all too easy to get caught up in past grievances and grudges. She couldn't afford a grudge right now. She had to escape. And she had a plan to do so. That was all that mattered right now.

Her parents had poured their very souls into building the gym. She herself had enjoyed so many good memories there. But nostalgia would not, and could not, pay the bills. If the family business had to be sacrificed in order to secure the future, then so be it. Dumb pride and sentiment had forestalled such a pragmatic reshuffling of assets until now. Such sentiments now might be the death of both her and Klaus. *It had to go.*

Once the place was sold, she could get her life in order. Clean up her room. Get a fresh hairdo. Buy a new outfit. Ensure Klaus got the best treatment. Become an upstanding member of the community. Get a regular job with standard working hours. Go to dinner parties and summer barbecues. Host her own dinner parties and summer barbecues. Gossip with the neighbours. Gossip with friends about her neighbours. Find a loving partner. Settle down. Raise children. Grow old in peace. And live happily ever after—just like the perfect smiling families up on the Commission's billboards.

For the first time since the Pandemic, it was all within her reach.

She just needed to squeeze through this bottleneck.

As these thoughts ran through Johanna's mind, she kept her head down and averted eye contact with her fellow pedestrians. With no need to conceal her identity anymore, the mandatory mask was clenching her face again. Thankfully these walking commuters were too committed to arriving at their destination on time to give her any trouble. Her efforts to avoid eye contact with them were equally matched by their own efforts. They acted as though she were invisible, as though she didn't really exist. *That was how they wanted it.* They would prefer not to see her at all. Just like they preferred not to see the homeless tramps they strutted past every day. And so, she walked alone amongst the wilfully blind masses.

Yet reminders of her existence were never in short supply to these complicit perambulators. With every step Johanna took, a wave of clicking locks rang out from the cars parked adjacent to the pavement. Just as the phones could sense her presence to raise the alarm, so the private vehicles of the city would automatically lock themselves upon her coming. The message they gave was clear: *to be unvaccinated was to be untrustworthy.*

When Johanna returned to her own car, she found two White Coats standing guard next to it. Her heartbeat skipped a little. This couldn't be good. Hopefully they were just idling there but most likely they had scanned the car registration and discovered she wasn't vaccinated. She took out her keys and was on the cusp of getting into the driving seat, they blocked her passage.

"Excuse me miss," started one of them. "Do you have a licence for this?"

"A licence? Of course," replied Johanna, hoping that a layer of confidence would conceal her uneasiness. She presented her driving licence to the White Coats.

"You misunderstand," said the White Coat after a brief inspection of the document. "I wasn't asking for a driving licence. I was asking if you had a Car Licence. Could you please provide documentation proving you are licenced to *own* a private vehicle?"

"What?" exclaimed Johanna, her heart sinking ineluctably into the pit of her guts. She hadn't heard about this latest ruling by the Commission either. "You can't be serious?"

"Health Code miss," justified the second White Coat with icy impunity from behind his latex balaclava. "We can't have people driving wherever they like. That's how pathogens spread."

"Do you have a Car Licence?" asked the first White Coat again. Though Johanna could not see his face, she knew that there was a smug smirk hiding behind his latex balaclava. The bastard knew she didn't have it and he was asking her anyway.

"No, I don't," she confessed with a heavy heart. "How do I go about getting one?"

"You need a vaccine," said the second White Coat. "Are you inoculated?"

"Do you know what that means?" added the first White Coat condescendingly.

"Yes, I know what it means and no I'm not vaccinated. But I will be shortly once I—"

"Then I'm afraid we will have to confiscate the vehicle," declared the second White Coat.

"You can't do that! That's my private property!"

"Oh yes we can. Whether you own it or not is irrelevant. If you were an unlicensed gun owner, we wouldn't let you keep a privately-owned gun now, would we? It's simply too dangerous to leave such items in your possession."

Johanna was about to raise her voice. She managed to restrain herself just in time. Fighting with these fuckers would only give her more grief. No one would stand up for her she knew. The complicit bystanders would just turn a blind eye to her as they always did and let the White Coats have their way with her.

"So, what am I supposed to do then?" she asked as calmly and politely as possible. "How am I supposed to get home?"

"Take the bus like any other humble patient," curtly answered the first White Coat who then extended his gloved hand to her. "Your keys." Johanna unclipped the key from the keyring and planted the metal implement into the White Coat's sterile grasp. "Thank you for your cooperation."

Johanna walked away from the scene without a word and looked for the closest bus stop. Her nerves and emotions were on edge, but she tried to suppress it all. It was just a hiccup. It could have happened any day. It just happened to be today.

This changed nothing.

She was still on her way out.

At the bus stop, she shared the bench with herself alone. All her fellow prospective passengers chose to stand apart from her by a good two metres. Once the bus arrived, she was condemned to wait until the very end to hop aboard and to sit at the very front on her own. More passengers filed through the doors and filled up the empty space between the seats. Despite the seat right next to her being unoccupied, no one dared sit next to Johanna. They preferred to remain standing on their tired feet rather than risk association with a filthy diseased animal like her. People dared not even speak around her. They upheld a barren silence in her presence, fearing that she might insert herself into their private conversations and infect them all. The moment she got up for her stop she could hear the sighs of relief behind her. As she started walking down the pavement, she cast a quick glance back at the bus to find the two seats now occupied by two happy chattering passengers.

"Just a little longer," she told herself as she entered her neighbourhood only to discover a fresh layer of graffiti over the face of the family home, labelling her and Klaus as '**Virus Whores**'. "Just a little longer," she repeated, trying to shut the image out of her head.

As she closed the front door behind her, she unhooked the mask from her face and breathed in slowly. Here at least, within her four walls she was safe from their judgements. Here within this small holding pen she could be herself. The house was her refuge. It had long ceased to be anything but that. There was more loneliness than homeliness beneath this roof now.

Yet traces remained. Ghosts of a happier time were entombed in the walls. On the door frame of the kitchen, she could still see the markers her mother had made to measure the height of both her and Klaus as children. On the shelf, she saw the photograph of her father Oskar. Next to him lay a more recent family photograph taken at Christmas of her mother, Anna, her stepfather Anton, and then herself and Klaus.

That was all she had left of them now.

Within those tiny, inanimate, photo frames were the places she had called 'home'.

"Soon," she said aloud, hoping the spoken word would somehow usher her hopes into being. "It'll be home again."

Right now though, she merely wanted this hellish disappointment of a day to be over. She put her headphones on, changed into a tracksuit, and ventilated her anger into a muscle-splitting workout.

She had to keep fit.

Had to keep in shape.

Had to keep sharp.

It was essential to her day. To her routine. To her very sense of order. All through the Pandemic it had kept her sane. The ache in her muscles reminded her that she carried the fire of life within her, that she was still alive and kicking and fighting. If ever that struggle stopped, it would be the day they buried her six feet under.

With the fitness ritual completed, she showered down, replenished her calories with a bite to eat, and sought out the comfort of her bedroom. In the morning, she would make some calls and put the gym up for sale. Everything would fall into place from there.

Johanna awoke the next morning to a hammering at the door. She groaned into consciousness, her fumbling brain trying to make sense of the racket.

"Metropole Insurance Company! Open up!" thundered a voice from the front door.

"What the fuck?" swore Johanna as she rolled off her mattress and haphazardly made herself decent. As the insistent tolling continued, she stomped her way down the stairs and opened the door without thinking. A shaft of blinding morning sunlight blasted over her. A man of small build and stature in a suit and tie stood there waiting for her with a plastic visor shielding his face. A mop of brown mousy hair crawled downward from his scalp. His teeth were crooked and yellowed. His eyes had a yellowish feline quality with a certain predatorial hunger lingering within them. A squad of White Coats stood guard behind him. "Hello," grumbled Johanna, still clearing the grit from her glued-together eyes.

"Agent Mattias Bathory," said the man with formal precision as he held up a badge to her face. "You are Johanna Reinther. Yes?"

"Yes," confirmed Johanna.

"Please get your mask Miss Reinther and accompany me to the transport vehicle," demanded the insurance man with confident authority.

"I'm sorry," Johanna vigorously shook her head to wake herself up. "What. what is this about? What's going on? I don't understand what—"

"A virus claim has been made against you Miss Reinther," explained Agent Bathory, his voice devoid of empathy. "You are required by Section Five, Paragraph Six, of the Health Code to cooperate with the Metropole Insurance Company."

"And if I don't?" she inquired tentatively.

"Failure to do so may affect any current vaccine applications or future insurance claims made in your name. Rules are rules."

Johanna stood there frozen for a moment or two. She didn't quite know how to process any of this. She looked over the dozen White Coats with truncheons at the ready. She then gazed across the small convoy of service vehicles parked outside her house. Her attention then switched to her neighbours. They were standing there in their pyjamas and house coats, sipping at their coffee mugs, looking back at her with a veil of shameless satisfaction.

She had to go with them, she realised. She *had* to cooperate. Best to get it over with. To resist would be more grief than she needed.

She fetched her mask and her keys and stepped out of the doorway. Agent Bathory took a step backwards as she approached. He gestured to one of the White Coats.

"Please hand your keys to the officer," directed the Agent. "The premises will need to be taken into custody while your case is being processed." Johanna nodded nervously and hesitantly dropped her keys into the hands of the faceless white spectre. Bathory then gave the nod of approval for half the White Coats to enter the house while the other half surrounded Johanna and shackled her wrists in a set of handcuffs.

Before she knew it, she was sitting inside the cramped compartment of a Medical Transport Vehicle, White Coats sitting all around her as though she were some psychopathic convict. A quiet panic wriggled in the back of her brain, but she fought it all she could. She assured herself this was all just part of the process and she had to go along with it.

Everything was going to be fine.

As the van pulled to a halt, she was escorted into a facility that resembled something between a police station and an office building. She was taken to a room, seated on a metal chair and handcuffed to a table. Agent Bathory came strutting in with a stack of documents under his arm and he plonked himself down on the other side of the table. Johanna sat there vacant-minded while the insurance man leafed through his papers and took a sip of water to clear his throat.

"Unvaccinated, yes?" he asked needlessly. Johanna knew well enough from dealing with penpushers by now to just nod in confirmation. Bathory ticked a box on one of his papers and then kept scanning through them.

"What is this about?" asked Johanna out of turn, unable to stomach the gap in knowledge any further. Bathory fleetingly glanced at her and then returned to his documents. She gulped back her nerves and tried to stop her legs from shaking. "I haven't done anything," she mumbled.

"No?" he said with eyebrows raised, his attention still fixed on his papers. "Then why are you here?"

"A claim was made against me."

"Correct."

"But I deny it. It's not possible. I know I'm unvaccinated, but I wear a mask and maintain social distance at all times…I'm…I'm getting my money together to buy a vaccine soon in any case."

"Soon," echoed Bathory. "But not now."

"Well I need the money first to—"

"You were wearing a mask at all times yesterday, yes?"

"Yes."

"Your case worker, Julius Zuboff, reported that you stormed out of your session with him yesterday. Correct?"

"Yes, what does—"

"So, you were angry then. Yes?"

"Yes."

"So, what did you do then? Where did you go? You chose to do something about your anger, yes?"

"Yes."

"Yes, what? What did you do?"

"I…I…I went to get advice on how to get a vaccine?"

"Where?"

"Lovers' Park."

"You would do well to call it by its medically correct name. You mean Hygiene Park, yes?"

"What? Oh, eh yes."

"And you met someone there to get advice, yes?"

"Yes."

Bathory opened up a binder folder filled with what appeared to be computer screenshots.

"These are witness statements from patients at Hygiene Park between twelve and one p.m. yesterday. All of them, without exception, state that you were not wearing a mask." Johanna felt her face go cold and bloodless. "Several witnesses also claim that not only did you not maintain social distance with your acquaintance but that you embraced them." Bathory looked directly into Johanna's eyes with cold and unfeeling mathematical cogs turning in his head. "You said you wore a mask at all times. You said you maintained social distance. You *lied* to me and to this investigation. That is non-disclosure Miss Reinther, a single shade shy of non-cooperation."

"I…I'm sorry. I forgot," she stuttered anxiously.

"Did you also forget the panic and bewilderment you caused among your fellow patients?"

"Please understand, I just needed to—" Johanna tried to reason before she was cut off again.

"You don't have a Friend Licence, do you Miss Reinther?" Johanna dared not speak. "No. Of course you don't. Then why were you in Hygiene Park? To engage in unsafe socialising? That's what it looks like! Don't you think?" Once again, Johanna said nothing. Bathory slammed the table with a suddenness that made her jump out of her skin. "Life is precious Miss Reinther!" he shouted angrily. "Life is precious! And yet people like *you* flaunt it every day! You think you can do as you please! You think you can go where you please and meet who you please! That is simply not the case! We have a duty of care to safeguard the lives of every man, woman, and child! We have a duty to reduce the risk, to curtail danger, to blunt the edges, to tame all hazards and to extinguish all fires! And yet selfish goons like *you* think your needs and desires eclipse that duty of care!"

"Do I not have a duty to safeguard my own health and wellbeing?" countered Johanna, her patience starting to wear thin with the Insurance Man's sermon. Her words only served to enrage the grotty bureaucrat even further.

"You have no duty!" he bellowed through his crooked teeth. "It is to *us* that your care is entrusted! Not you! You are an entrepreneur! A fitness merchant! A winged-creature of the wilderness that spreads disease and pestilence and misery wherever your greedy desires dictate! You know nothing of life and death! And that is made all the more manifest by yesterday's events! You selfish child-endangering bitch!"

"Alright enough with the fucking antics!" snapped Johanna impatiently. "I've nothing against doctors or vaccines or public health or little kids! I'm not Typhoid fucking Mary! Just tell me who's making a fucking claim against me and let me get on with my life!" Bathory, red-faced with rage by her interruption, looked down at his paperwork and then glared across at her again.

"If you really must know," he said coolly, his feline eyes frothing with wroth. "The claim is being made by Veronika Svoboda."

"Angelika's neighbour?" frowned Johanna, trying to grasp her memory of the snobbish woman she'd met the day before. "That cow made a claim against me? For what? Making her sneeze?"

"That 'cow' is an upstanding member of our community whose caution and vigilance will no doubt save many lives with this swift and prompt reporting! It will do your conscience good to know that she, the finest, healthiest, specimen of a woman ever to walk this city, is now bed-ridden with the flu on account of you!"

"But I don't have the flu!" protested Johanna. "This is ridiculous!"

"This is the Law of Hygiene Miss Reinther! Woe to those who fail to abide by it!"

"Just skip to the important bit! What does this bitch want in damages?"

"On account of your unvaccinated condition, you have no Vaccine Insurance Policy. As a result, you will pay the damages directly. Through the cooperation of your caseworker we have gained access to your financial records."

"Yes! And?"

"All assets in your name will be transferred to Miss Svoboda."

"What!"

"This includes your current residence, the illegal vehicle confiscated yesterday from you, and the premises of Reinther Fitness Gym, along with any savings currently in your account."

"What the fuck! She has a fucking cold! Not leprosy! You've got to be joking!"

"Our underwriters calculate that unvaccinated persons are five times more likely to be carriers of deadly diseases. The numbers never lie. This is no joking matter Miss Reinther. And you are in no position to diagnose the severity of the pathogen you have infected Miss Svoboda with. You know nothing of medicine! Nothing of even the pollutants within your own infected body!"

"Fuck off!" roared Johanna with reckless abandon. "You can't do this! This is fucking illegal! This will not fucking stand! It will not! I want my lawyer now!"

"You have no vaccine Miss Reinther," calmly declared Bathory, clear as day on his face that he was enjoying every bit of this. "You have no insurance. You have no licences. You have no right to anything. The evidence provided by your caseworker, by your own neighbours, and by the public at large, all points to you as a dangerous individual who is incapable of following the rules. Rules, Miss Reinther, that are in place to keep everyone safe. It is clear to my medical colleagues that you are a danger not only to the public, but also to yourself. We cannot allow you to continue on your rampage."

"Rampage? We'll see about rampage when you see what I have to say about this in court!"

"You continue to misunderstand. There won't be a court case. There won't be any mediation or negotiation. There is no law of torts here. I am *telling* you what is going to happen. You are an *old* woman who still thinks in terms of laws and courts and rights. There are no laws, there are no courts, there are no human rights. The Metropole Insurance Company is on the Commission. We and the Doctors and Pharmacists have the *only* right. What we say *is* the law. We are judge, jury, and executioner. Your fate has already been decreed. The paperwork is all sealed, stamped, and approved. You have approximately twenty-four hours to vacate your residence. All assets will be officially transferred to Miss Svoboda at a minute past midnight tomorrow."

"Wait, hang on a second, hang on..." retorted Johanna as she struggled to pick the important pieces from Bathory's little rant. "You already decided? But I only met her yesterday? How have you—"

"We are not talkers Miss Reinther," proudly declared Bathory. "We do not waste time with matters of Life and Death importance. When life is in danger, we do not dawdle and squabble. We act swiftly and decisively!"

"And where am I supposed to live? Hmmm? Where am I supposed to go? Beg for coins on the side of the streets? What about Klaus? He's in hospital! Does he fall under your duty of fucking care?"

"Of course, he does," answered Bathory as though it were the most obvious answer in the world. "Life is precious. He will continue to be cared for regardless of your financial situation. It is *you* who are the Angel of Death, Miss Reinther, not us. We are only interested in taking care of people."

"And taking away their life-savings and turfing them out of their family homes," added Johanna bitterly. "You parasite vampires! You fuckers! You set me up!"

"As to you Miss Reinther," continued Bathory, clearly deaf to her last insults, having heard them all before. "You will also be taken care of. I can assure you, you will not be left without a roof over your head. You need have no fear of homelessness since condemning you to such a fate would only make you all the more unhygienic and dangerous to the community."

"So, what then? Where am I going to live?"

"There is a hotel out by the old airport where unvaccinated specimens such as yourself are being housed by the Commission. From there, I'm sure you can start rebuilding your sizeable little family fortune."

"Rebuild? With what exactly?" lambasted Johanna, her face burning with red anger. She stopped herself before saying anything else. This was how they wanted to see her: an angry, irrational, inchoate woman throwing reckless insults about. She took a deep breath and tried her best to take back control of her life. After a brief pause to catch her breath, she spoke in a lower tone to Bathory. "Every day," she snarled lowly. "Every day I try so damn hard to please you people. I try every day to climb the ladder you want me to climb but no matter what I do you just keep pulling the ladder up further and further and there's nothing, *nothing,* I can do about it. I just want to live my life like you but, for some reason I can't grasp, you fucking animals are hellbent on burying me down under. And while you bury me under, you keep telling me I have as fair a chance as everyone else. That I have the same potential to be a millionaire as you do. Now you tell me, how the fuck do I achieve anything without a vaccine I can't even pay for?"

"Find a job!" answered the Insurance Man with automated quickness. "Make yourself useful! Re-educate, re-skill, re-habilitate! Earn and make a living! Contribute to the health and wellbeing of the city like any other normal patient! Must I really spit out to you? Or are you so possessed with such entrepreneurial greed that you can never contribute to the greater good?"

Johanna was condemned to a condition of wordless mindlessness thereafter. There was nothing left for her to say here that could help her situation. Nothing at all. She'd heard it all before.

The next few hours whirred by before her as she beheld her ruin. It would have been so easy to give up in that moment. To accept defeat and let them have the better of her. But, contrary to their accusations against her, she could never allow herself to be so selfish. She needed to think about Klaus. She needed to be strong for him. She needed to take care of him. For his sake, she really did need to get back on her feet and make a living. She needed to make sure his hospital bills were paid. And if that meant doing things by the book and repeating their stupid mantras about 're-educating' and serving the 'greater good', then so be it. She would follow it to the letter and accept their every belch and fart as pure gospel.

The neighbours whom for many years her parents had trusted, relied upon, and conversed with, were practically celebrating her eviction when she returned to the family home to collect as many of her belongings as she could. Veronika Svoboda was there too to oversee the whole process. Johanna could not help but notice that there was not a single symptom of illness on display from Veronika's body. The blonde socialite was as radiant and manicured to perfection as a barbie doll while she waltzed among Johanna's neighbours receiving their thanks and blessings.

"It's about time," they openly said to Veronika, their words reaching through the front windows to Johanna's ears. "I don't know why we didn't do it ourselves sooner. She was bringing our house prices down and all. I felt uncomfortable even having friends over in case she decided to invite herself. This is a nice neighbourhood, for nice families. We're all newly-weds with children on the way, and we don't want her type around here. Someone like her will never have children anyway. Who'd want to marry her in the first place? We don't want some creepy weirdo hanging around while our kids play on the street. It's in everyone's interests really that she be booted out. She's a bad influence."

"Oh, don't get me started," she heard Veronika chime in with a flick of her advert-perfect hair. "My own brother, Vlad, actually turned down the vaccine. I'm just glad he had the decency to exile himself to the North Side. I can say with experience that the family gatherings are all the better without him. I'm only too glad to help weeding this one out of your lovely community. Things will be safer here now."

"All thanks to you!" toasted the neighbours altogether.

Johanna couldn't take any more than that. She zipped up the two suitcases of belongings in front of her and stormed out of the house without so much as a silent goodbye to this house which had raised and nurtured her. She left in such an unspeakable rage in fact that she even left the sacred photographs of her family behind.

As she walked out onto the drive, two White Coats filed in behind her and escorted her to their vehicle. Just before she got in, she did something she had not done in a very long time: she raised her head. With that one simple movement, she glared straight into the eyes of Veronika and all her neighbours. Her neighbours all started shuffling awkwardly on their feet, as if they knew they'd been caught red-handed. A plastic accommodating smile was cut across Veronika's face so that she feigned some kind of angelic innocence.

No words were exchanged. Johanna had no intention of giving them the satisfaction. She just glared at them and ground her teeth. A White Coat nudged her to move along and with that she clambered into the vehicle and left the neighbourhood behind.

She looked out the back-window. The place that was 'home' sank away into the distance and then, in a flash, disappeared behind a corner. Forever.

Part III: Silence

There is an unimaginable Darkness waiting for You at the End of the Tunnel.

Marius Zielenski, chap. 3 of 'In the Shadow of the Great Demon', page 406

There's always hope, she told herself as two White Coats escorted her into the hotel, her father's voice coursing through her head: *Never give up. Never give in. Never lose hope.*

She had no friends. No family. No connections. No licences. No rights. No home. No vaccine.

But none of that was any excuse. She *had* to try. Just like her workouts, she had to fight through the pain. Fight on and on and on till there was no fighting left to be done. So long as she drew breath, she would never surrender, never let them get the better of her. It would be an up-cliff battle. But no matter. There was *still* hope.

There just had to be.

Her new hotel 'home' lay on the very fringe of the city. The outer rim of the premises was fortified with a towering barbed wire fence which divided it on one side from the city and on the other from the ghostly Pandemic Cemetery beyond which stretched almost to the horizon. Unlike any hotel she'd ever known, it was almost entirely devoid of staff. The only sign of life in the lobby was the typical annoying music one might hear in an elevator. No tourists had been here in a long, long, time.

"You are free to leave any time," one of the White Coats advised her as they escorted her through the dusty reception. "You may live your life as you did before. But you must always return. You can *never* check out." Johanna rolled her eyes at the White Coat's clichéd utterance. Behind his balaclava she was sure he was thoroughly pleased with his 'clever' reference.

The White Coats took her to an elevator and commanded it with a push of a finger to raise them up to the fifth floor. As the electronic doors shuttered apart,

Johanna was confronted with a bleak windowless corridor. Dimly lit beneath dying light bulbs, the dark hall stretched out into a maw of total blackness, grimy wallpaper sliming off the walls to reveal a toxic Prussian blue plaster lingering beneath.

What was more alien than anything else to Johanna's eyes however were the doors to each of the rooms; each and all of them was fitted with a see-through porch constructed from Perspex glass. These porches then were fitted with glass doors with red LED lights glistening from a box resting on the upper frame.

"For your own safety," instructed one of the White Coats as they marched down the hallway with her. "Only one unvaccinated resident at a time may use the corridor. This prevents the possibility of transmission between residents. If the corridor is occupied, the light will shine red and you will have to wait in the Perspex compartment. Only when they have returned to their room or entered the elevator, will the light turn green and the outer door on your Perspex compartment will then be unlocked."

"Great," thought Johanna to herself as the White Coats left her outside her new 'home'. "Another nuisance to drive me nuts." The glass door opened with a klaxon buzz before her and locked behind her once she had entered. As she closed the original wooden door to the room behind her, she surveyed her new 'sanctuary'. The room was a self-sufficient little capsule for her, its true purpose quite clearly to deprive her of any reason to leave. No need to go the laundrette, a washing machine was installed. No need to go to a restaurant, a cooker, sink, and microwave were installed. No need to go to the theatre or the cinema, a television set was there for her use. No need to go jogging, there was a treadmill right in front of the television.

She let her bags slump off her shoulders and ambled towards the window. She had a clear view of the entire city. Looming up out of the horizon she could see Castle Hill. She could see the broken arms of the Millennium Bridge and the downstream bend in the Borava River. She could even see the fires burning and the fountaining explosions amongst the gloomy tower blocks of the North Side.

None of this compared though with the digital billboards right in front of the hotel. The ad depicted spacious white kitchens occupied by happily married couples cooking together while their happily contented sons and daughters played and laughed around them. The advert delivered a whole psalm of meaningless consumerist jargon. The final headline however did hit home for

Johanna. As a matter of fact, she could have sworn it was directed at her personally. It simply read:

"The Future You Deserve."

That spurred her into action. She needed to dig herself out of here and help Klaus. She whipped open her phone and started scrolling through recruitment websites. Anything, anything at all, would suffice. All she needed was a little something to get her on her feet again.

As usual though, even the most meagre menial warehouse job noted the requirement of a vaccine. Even jobs centred on remote working demanded all applicants to be vaccinated. She'd embarked on the search so many times before that she knew it to be a futile enterprise. But she *had* to at least try, for Klaus' sake if not her own, even if it was useless.

HR Administrator, Customer Care Agent, Residential Assistant for medical summer camp, warehouse operative. On and on, the job list went. Each one of them perfectly within her reach.

And yet not.

Vaccination required, they all said one after another. Whether on the initial summary of the job or later on at the tiresome application form, eventually the vaccination requirement always popped up.

But she couldn't give up. She kept looking and looking and looking. When the sun dipped behind the horizon and the streetlights lit up the outside world, she still kept scrolling and scrolling. But it was useless.

The door was shut to her.

There was no escape.

That was the hard truth.

But still her father's voice persisted: *never give in, never give up, never lose hope. There's always hope.* She had to keep fighting. She needed to see Klaus. But how? How the fuck was she going to climb out of this deepening grave?

That was the wrong attitude she knew. Only losers and homeless tramps thought like that. Defeatism could only beget defeat. Only a winning attitude could deliver victory. She had to keep going.

In the end, an alliance of hunger and tiredness drove her away from her mind-shredding hunt. The hotel room was bereft of food and it was too late to do any shopping. Her hunger could wait till the morning. She put aside her phone and fell asleep on an empty stomach.

She awoke the next day with a fresh plan of action. Last night had been a disaster it was true. But there was no reason to believe today would be too. She just needed to pull herself together. She started by putting her new dominion in order. She unpacked her bags, folded and stored her clothes in the wardrobe, gave a new resting place to all her personal items. This was nothing like home and she had no intention of staying here for long. But a tidy room made for a better environment than an untidy one. This was something she could take control of. Start with small steps and make bigger steps with time. That was the key to success. The key to saving herself and Klaus.

She put on the most decent set of clothes she had. Standing in front of the mirror she practiced her smile to emulate the happy grins of those individuals on the adverts. With the right attitude and the right approach, she would fit in with everyone else. No one could turn down a nice friendly accommodating smile.

"You can do this," she said aloud to herself. "You can make it."

She zealously bolted out the door ready to take on the world again only to very nearly smash face-first into the outer Perspex porch. Startled and annoyed by its unwelcome presence she reached for the door handle and tried to pull it open to no avail. A thin laugh came tumbling up the corridor.

"Door's locked zaychik," said a twisted little voice. She peered down the hallway and at once was taken aback by the appearance of the passer-by. In sharp contrast to Johanna's bright and upbeat air, this man was truly ragged in both his look and his character. Not only were his clothes ripped and tattered like that of a tramp, but even his face was torn and scarred to the point of grotesquery. His nose, chin, and ears had been cleaved off to give his face a skull-like character. Johanna felt revulsion welling inside her at the very sight of him as he hobbled up the hallway and entered the Perspex porch opposite her own. The moment he closed the door behind him, the light turned green and Johanna's door was unlocked.

"Fuck sake," she cursed to herself as she strode towards the elevator.

"You'll do this again zaychik," taunted her creepy hallmate as she entered the lift. Though she kept her back to him she could feel his leering grin drilling into her. "And again, and again. That light you see at the end of the tunnel, that's nothing but a crazed maniac holding a candle, guiding you deeper and deeper and deeper into the Abyss... *Is the candle still burning zaychik?*"

Those last words prompted her to look back at him with involuntary perplexity. She gazed back up the hallway in confusion at him, her expression voicelessly requesting an explanation. But he gave no reasoning to his statement. The elevator doors began to close, and he just stood there with that deep and distant smile scrawled across his mutilated face. So unusual was the look he gave her that his tortured face stayed with her even after the lift had started its descent.

"Freak," she said to herself in private condemnation. "There's always hope," she intoned in a stamp of confidence for her father's mantra. She sped across the floor of the lobby. As she exited the building, she draped the mandatory mask across her face and within a few minutes she was walking through the city streets she knew so well. It was a bright sunny day again. People were out in their shorts and t-shirts and colourful flowing dresses. With every atom of will power she had left, she fought against her instincts to look down. She smiled as best she could through her mask and acted as though she was a perfectly normal, ordinary, individual, just taking a morning stroll to the supermarket for some groceries.

The right attitude and the right approach could get you anywhere in life. Politeness was the currency of the world. If she just acted the part, then, surely, she could just get back to being normal, could get out of the hotel, and could get Klaus out.

Thankfully, she knew this particular area relatively well and was able to locate a shopping centre swiftly enough. She grabbed a trolley and crossed the threshold.

"Beep-beep-beep," the phones sang aloud almost instantly. People began to scatter around her as she walked by.

"It's ok," she told herself, keeping her smile in place beneath the mask. "Everything is fine. You're not in trouble. Just nod and smile. Just nod and smile." She paid a blind eye to the dirty looks and scowls her fellow customers cast at her. She focused only on the task ahead of her. She was just doing her shopping like anyone else would.

"Excuse me," came an authoritative voice just as she was about to enter a grocery. Johanna spun around to find a security guard standing there. "What are you doing here?"

"Good morning, I'm just—"

"Turn around and get lost," he said before she could explain herself.

"I haven't done anything," protested Johanna as reasonably as she could. "I'm allowed to shop around, aren't I?"

"Not at these hours you're not," countered the guard. "Latest regulations from the Commission say we can only have unvaccinated patients in here between ten p.m. and five a.m."

"What?" exclaimed Johanna, unable to keep the nice reasonable charade up. Her hidden smile returned to the outraged grimace her face knew too well. "That's ridiculous! Everything is closed at those hours! How am I meant to buy anything if the shops are closed?"

"That's your problem not mine. I don't make the rules. I suggest you get your shopping online like everyone else!"

"For crying out loud, I'm bringing my business here! I'm a willing and paying customer!"

"Yes, and you're scaring away every other customer! Now clear off before I call the White Coats!" Johanna refused to budge for a second. She had never been taught to back down so easily. She had made so many concessions and gone along with the rules and restrictions for so long. It was in her nature to show some backbone and stand up for herself. She was a human being. She deserved to be here with everyone else.

But it was useless to fight this one security guard. It would only get her into more trouble. Trouble that she didn't need. Her fists clenched as hard as stones from pent up frustration, she gave a polite nod of the head to the guard and walked away.

"Great, just fucking great," the inner voice said to her. *"Another door closed. Another liberty stripped from your name. Another simple indulgence that you can never enjoy again. So much for being able to leave whenever you want. Should never have gone out the front door!"*

Upon her return to the hotel, she took stock of the security guard's words and ordered all her food and necessities online with the small stipend of social welfare she was now due as a homeless unvaccinated patient. There was no point going outside again. She would just face more rejection, more revulsion, more disappointment. She'd make do with what she had.

As she waited on her supplies to arrive by courier, she once again endeavoured to take back control of her life by committing herself to a workout. Whereas before her exercises had created routine and order, now she found her stress and anger finding expression on the treadmill. She turned the dial up to the maximum speed and began a manic sprint. She ran and ran and ran. She pushed herself and pushed herself till her muscles ached to the point of snapping and her entire body was coated in sweat. Her body was so exhausted that, fit and healthy though she was, she fell off puking her starved insides out.

"Don't stop," her father's voice said to her. *"Keep going. Keep fighting. Never give up. Never lose hope."* She picked herself up off the floor and got back on the treadmill before she had recovered from her previous ordeal. She wore herself out even faster and tripped over herself, falling on her face with a smack. But still she got back up and did it again, and again, and again. She couldn't let them get the better of her. She had to win. Had to. She couldn't be defeated. She had to keep pushing through.

Yet still the restless crushing feeling of futility would not leave her. As she showered down and wiped the sweat and shame away, she unconsciously began banging her head against the wall. She butted the tacky tiles again and again and then resorted to scraping at the walls with her nails, a hot primal growl snarling out of her clenched teeth.

Anger boiled up from within and as she left the shower, she threw a single punch at the wall. Her knuckles hissed with pain, but she didn't care. She punched the wall again and again and again until finally she unleashed a withering volley of punches that left her bleeding and screaming. A pattern of splattered blood spots dotted the wall she had assaulted. Yet still the wall stood before her, completely unaffected by her outpouring of rage.

No matter how hard she fought, nothing would bend to her will.

But there was always hope.

Hour after hour, day after day, she hammered at the walls and ran the treadmill to death. The meagre food deliveries she received, she gorged on like a glutton. Her stomach would fill up so quickly that she felt ill. But hers was not to complain or whine about such feelings. She had to fight on and so she returned to beating the walls and exhausting the treadmill. Where these activities would not satisfy, her restless searching mind compelled her to pace up and down the room in the fashion of a caged animal.

"What am I going to do? What am I going to do? What am I going to do? What am I going to do?" she said to herself again and again and again, running her fingers through her hair and digging her fingernails into her scalp. "What am I going to do? Can't get out but have to get out. Can't get out but have to get out.

Can't get out but have to get out. Can't get out but have to get out. There's always hope. There's always hope. There's always hope."

In the end, she would find herself uselessly scrolling through job adverts again. For hours and hours, she scrolled and scrolled at these unattainable professions and careers, these dreamed-of destinies that she could never have. All it did was make her feel more and more and more inadequate. That feeling propelled her back to sprinting like a maniac on the treadmill and back to smashing the walls.

When too tired to waste herself away anymore, she filled the hours of nothingness browsing through social media. Demoted to a muted 'observer' status where she could neither comment nor share nor message anything to anyone, she glided ghostlike through the newsfeed. She saw the pictures of people her age, all dolled up and smiling as they danced and kissed and sang for the cameras. When she cared to gaze out the window of her room, it was no different. Children all laughing and playing in the sun, friends and families licking up ice creams and having barbecues. She saw men and women her own age with babies and children in her arms. She saw all the partners that could have been hers, walk by and turn about the corner, out of sight and out of range.

"There's always hope, there's always time," her inner voices whispered to her in circles of reassurance. "You can still have it all. *It's the future you deserve.*"

When her social media touring and window-viewing failed to quench the inner gnawing flame, she finally turned to television. She switched on the news to find them reporting on a small schoolboy for some bizarre unexplained reason.

"It's a big day today for Lazar Renzik," said the reporter as two nurses administered an injection to the little boy in the background. "In an act of unprecedented kindness and generosity, the Commission has donated a V3 vaccine to little Lazar here. Lazar will now be able to attend a school for exceptionally gifted children like himself."

"What the fuck!" cried Johanna, her eyes almost springing from their sockets.

"Let it never be said that the Commission neglected the needs of the most vulnerable in our society," finished the reporter.

"You fuckers!" yowled Johanna with unconstrained rage. "Where's my fucking donation? Where's my handout? Motherfuckers!" In that instant she lost all control over herself and she flung a bedside lamp into the hallowed silvery face of the television. So consumed with ire was she that she barely even heard the electric sparks from within the dying device. "What the fuck! What the fuck! What the fuck! WHAT THE FUCK!" she said to herself again and again.

"Never give up," said her father's voice within. *"Never lose hope."*

The very next day, just as she was transitioning from her wall-hammering spree to her confidence-bashing social media tour, a call came in from reception. Someone had come to see her.

She hadn't been in the mood for human company in days. But at this stage, even an unwelcome change to her routine was welcome. With a groan and a sigh, she picked herself up and headed down to the lobby.

A prim and proper woman stood there in a set of heels waiting for her with a briefcase in hand. A few years older than Johanna herself, she had a head of rich black hair that curtained down over her shoulders and an oval shaped face that had been pampered and adjusted to a condition of faultlessness. She ceaselessly sniffed and frowned at her grotty surroundings and kept reaching for a can of deodorant to clear the air.

"There you are," she said as though Johanna were the one inconveniencing her. She promptly shot up a halting hand as Johanna came within talking distance. "That's far enough. Cover your mouth please."

"I'm wearing a mask," countered Johanna.

"Yes, and who know what particles might leak out. Cover it with your hand please."

"What is this about?" asked Johanna tiredly as she now tried to speak through two layers of face covering.

"My name is Lidija Ivanevic. I'm an administrator at Slovenko Hospital."

"Klaus is there! What's happ—"

"He's dead," flatly informed Lidija before any thoughts or worries could formulate in Johanna's brain. No preamble, no forewarning, no soothing words of sympathy. Just a piece of information to be conveyed. Without even realising it Johanna began slumping against the wall of the reception.

"That," she mumbled, shaking her head as she pictured her brother where she'd left him in the cancer ward. "That...can't be right." She looked up at Lidija. The bureaucrat's face was that stiff bland mask which typified her desk-dwelling species. To her, Klaus was no doubt just a number on a spreadsheet among many millions of other numbers. It didn't mean anything to her beyond this trip out from her air-conditioned office. "What...what happened?"

"The level of treatment was scaled back," she answered vacantly, an underlying annoyance at the question written all over her face.

"What? Why?"

"Because you need to pay for it dummy. We're not running a soup kitchen here. You need to pay for healthcare. The bank account paying for his treatment dried up and we had to scale back. Honestly, you people, I don't know where you get your sense of entitlement from!"

"But…but…you say it all the time that 'life is precious'…how could…how could you let him just die?"

"Don't be dense with me! We're not savages! We would never let any patient die. But there is only so much a doctor can do with limited resources."

Were this any other day, Johanna might have fought tooth and nail with Lidija over this. But not today. She'd lost her brother. Her *only* brother. Her *last* piece of family. *She'd lost him.* More to the point, *she had failed him.* She had tried so hard, done everything she possibly could, and it meant absolutely *nothing.* As she contemplated her failure, Lidija opened the case and presented two photographs.

"These were his only belongings," she said. They were the family photographs from the house, the ones Johanna had forgotten in her haste to take with her when she was being evicted.

"How did he have these?" she asked dumbfoundedly.

"A police officer called Vaclav Kovac came by with them," said Lidija as she closed her briefcase for good. "Apparently they were being thrown away at some derelict house and he wanted to do the right thing by giving them to the closest of kin."

"Vaclav Kovac," mouthed Johanna to herself as she took the photographs in her hands. She'd heard that name before somewhere. "Can I see him?" she asked as she sniffled back the automatic tears. "Klaus, I mean. Can I see him? Please?"

"That won't be possible," refused Lidija. "You're unvaccinated. Your place is here. For your own safety and the safety of the public, we could never allow you near—"

"I understand all that," butted in Johanna, much to Lidija's visible irritation. "But can I at least help with the funeral? There won't be family obviously, but he did have school friends and—"

"That won't be possible either."

"Why not?" suddenly shouted Johanna, losing her patience with this human termite.

"Why? Because he's been dead for weeks obviously!"

"He...he...WHAT!" stuttered Johanna, her heart somehow managing to sink even further in horror. "And you're only telling me NOW?"

"Paperwork takes time Miss Reinther," explained Lidija with a 'how dare you' look on her face. "We're not magicians here." Johanna could have killed Lidija for that, but her crushing grief overshadowed her rage.

"Where is his body?" she asked forcefully, her vision starting to blur with tears. "Tell me where his body is? TELL ME DAMMIT!"

"Alright, alright, take it easy," retorted Lidija with a hand of caution raised to her. "Bear with me a second." She then opened her briefcase and started flicking through papers. "Ah yes here's the doctor's report for you." Her fingers gripped a page from a plastic pocket. She cleared her throat and then began to read. "With the approval of Commissioner, Herschel Varga, the cadaver of Klaus Jungmann has been legally claimed by the Department of Anatomy at the Medical Academy. Under the scalpel of our youngest and brightest medical conscripts, the cadaver's head was sawn open, the brains were removed and dissected. The muscles in the cadaver's biceps and forearms were systematically cut open for experimentation. The cadaver's genitals were surgically removed and preserved in formaldehyde so that future students might study the condition of male genitalia in early pubescence. At the end of the Semester, the remaining components of the cadaver were rendered for waste disposal and thereat incinerated, the ashes were emptied into the Borava River."

Johanna's brain went completely numb. She found herself unable to speak. She was barely able to even think. She just stood there, staring at this godless clerical worker in stupefied silence.

She couldn't believe it.

Lidija folded the report and returned it to its rightful place among her documents.

"You butchers," Johanna finally whispered in a low voice. "You vandals."

"*You* call *us* vandals?" returned Lidija with disgust curling in her voice. "*You* are the barbarian here Miss Reinther. Perhaps if you had had the decency to be vaccinated you would understand that. The people you call butchers are the life savers and scientists of the future. Their essential post-mortem analysis will provide vital data for the creation of new drugs and procedures which will save countless lives."

"My brother wasn't an organ donor. You just…*took* him!"

"What difference does that make? Nothing can be forbidden. Nothing can be sacred. Nothing must stand in the way of progress and the salvation of human life. The more secrets that are solved the better. Everything must be transparent and known. You truly are the most selfish of swine-dogs if you cannot understand that! Also, he was your stepbrother, not your brother. Lighten up a little!"

Johanna was too broken and shattered to even respond to that old line. She was barely able to breathe.

"Just leave," she said in a pathetic whimper.

"Gladly," said Lidija as she closed her briefcase and checked her wristwatch, rolled her eyes to the heavens, turned heel and marched out the door, spraying herself religiously with a fragrance of some kind. Johanna was left there with the pictures of her family.

With a sunken heart, she returned to the elevator. Standing within the confines of that mechanical box, she allowed a tear to trickle down her face. As it dripped from her jawline, she let out an ear-splitting scream that filled the whole metallic cage. She felt her vocal cords strain, but she didn't care. She let it all out. Like some vile vomiting bug, she spewed out all her pain, all her anguish, and all her grief. Only when she felt the elevator chugged to a halt did she cease.

She felt nothing anymore.

Absolutely *nothing*.

Though her body marched onwards down the corridor, she felt herself to be a complete stranger to its movements. She belonged about as much in her body as she did to this whole god forsaken fucking world.

When she reached her Perspex porch, she couldn't even enter her bedroom. She fell against the glass and slumped down to the floor.

There was nothing left for her to do. No reason to live even. *She had lost.* She'd lost *everything.* Her father's words of inspiration were gone. All the voices within her, both the good and the ill, were gone.

A thundering silence had swallowed her up.

In that instant though, in her loneliest of loneliness, a voice came from the porch across the hall.

"Is your candle still burning now, zaychik?"

Part IV: Negligence

We are all of us abandoned, damned and forgotten here. This precious planet you call your home is nothing more than a penal colony. We're all living on Planet Gulag.

Marius Zielenski, 'Burn the Planet' speech from surprise appearance at Environmental Rally

"I used to be an office manager you know," said the man two doors down and across the hall from Johanna. Tall and lean he was. He was dressed in a shirt and a pair of slacks, a thin veil of self-respect still about him. In another age, he would have been quite the handsome catch for a lucky lady to land. But now his black hair had grown wild and greasy and a coarse stubbly beard was spiking from his cheeks. His eyes were tired and weary. His once professional outfit was stained with sweat and heavens knew what other fluids. And all around him, the tacky wallpaper was sliming off the poisonous blue walls.

All the porches were occupied. Men and women stood, squatted, and sat, in their transparent little cubicles of isolation. Johanna, her heart shattered and emptied, lay broken upon the corridor floor, her back resting against the squeaky Perspex glass. In her lap, the photographs of her family lay idle, their ossified smiles trying in vain to reach her from the past. She could not bear to look upon them. She also could not bear to look upon the mutilated neighbour straight across from her. He sat there on a stool with a silent eerie smile on his face, not a word escaping him. No one as a matter of fact was passing a glance at him. Right now, she, and everyone else, was capable only of listening. And in this very moment, she was listening to her hallmate, Dusan Stojanovic.

"I knew every inch of that office," Dusan reminisced. "Made it comfortable, safe, functional. I had friends. I had a family. I had a nice house. I made an honest, decent living. Then one day out of nowhere it all just. just disappeared. No more traffic. No more commuting. No more office. No more office, no more office manager. You turn around and suddenly you're told you're not needed anymore. 'Here's your redundancy Stojanovic, best of luck in the future'. It was a shock, no doubt about it. But I thought little more of it than a stumbling block…not a fall. I had good experience, good credentials, good education, good family. It was only a matter of time before I got employed again. But 'no vaccine, no wage'. Redundancy money ran out. Wife divorced me, took my assets and got herself and the kids vaccinated. No pennies left for Dusan." He peered around the corridor. "That's my story," he said. "Who's next?"

"I was a barmaid," said Eleonora von Rosner from right next door to Johanna. Eleonora had long straw-coloured hair. She had an especially angular face and a pair of dark blue eyes. She was dressed in a pair of ripped jeans and a faded concert t-shirt. She was a few years younger than Johanna and had a gentle but anxious voice. "I grew up in Kolomsaw province. Couldn't stand my parents any longer so I quit the countryside, dropped out of school, and came up to the city. I worked here for a couple of years at a bar and then. Well then, the whole world just shut down. The bar owner died of the virus and the place got confiscated by the doctors. I never finished school, so I wasn't qualified for any real future. I couldn't just take up another job. I could have gone home, but I didn't want to admit to myself that I'd failed. So…I stayed, and I waited for things to pick up so I could work again. And. things just never picked up."

Nothing was said for a minute or two. Everyone recognised that same false hope they'd so uselessly clung onto. Eyes were closed and heads were nodded back and forth in acknowledgment of this same fate that had consumed them all.

"They said it would be for just two weeks," said Alexandra Gottwald, next door down from Eleonora and across from Dusan. She was in her early forties perhaps but dressed as though she were in her twenties. Her greying strands of blonde hair were wrapped up in dreadlocks bundled beneath a bandana. Two piercings decorated her lips and a tattoo of a black Chinese dragon was crawling down her right hand. Unlike the tender Eleonora or the despairing Dusan, Alexandra's temperament was one of bitter resentment. She had the air of someone who felt betrayed and cheated by lesser persons. "I shut down my cafe," she said. "And went on the Pandemic welfare payment with all my staff. They all got new jobs. But I clung on because it was my mother's cafe and my grandmother's before that. I had hoped one day to pass it on to a child of my own one day. But to this day…I'm still not even married. But, like you, I thought things would pick up. So, I waited, and I waited. The Pandemic ended, but the

Lockdown didn't. The customers all went home, and they never came back to us."

"Adapt or die, that's what they say, isn't it?" piped up Jakob Tomkin directly across from Eleonora. Jakob was the type of man who by his appearance alone could convey a string of stories. He seemed to be in his forties. But it was hard to say. He wore the tattered black cassock of an Orthodox priest and had a huge silvery beard hanging from his jaws. Yet his face bore no wrinkles and beneath the layer of hoary bristles, one could see fresh brown and black hairs pushing through. His manner of speech moreover was nothing like that of a clergyman. "I thought I had it made. I used to deal in crack, weed, methadone, heroine, you name it. Every Sunday I gave my sermon to the flock, did the ritual, said the words, blah blah blah. No one suspected anything. Perfect cover. Till the fuckers shut down the churches and told me it was unsanitary and unsafe to give mass. I think there's some God-Fearing grannies out there who think of me as some kind of holy martyr standing up for God and tradition. Truth be told, I was just pissed I couldn't distribute the product safely anymore. Not that my supplier cared much. He just moved online and got delivery drivers to do my work. And here I am…a holy beggar."

"All my life," contributed Johanna in a tearful voice, wiping away the sniffles and dried tears from her face before continuing. "I was told that so long as I worked hard, did my homework, earned my way, and pulled my weight, I could do whatever I wanted, have whatever I wanted, and be whoever I wanted to be." Her voice remained mournful, tears still bled down her face, but a despairing hopelessness now slithered into her voice. "But now. now you work hard, you do your homework, you earn your way, you try everything you possibly can to survive, and you *still* get screwed by these…these *cockroaches.* You do as you're told and follow the rules and what do you get? A mask. A mask that tells everyone who you are and what you are. Everyone else out there. They get to be whoever they want and get to do whatever they like. But not us! They've taken our identity from us and covered our faces with those fucking masks!"

"They've deprived us of our humanity," concurred Dusan sombrely, scratching at his unshaven face. "We're yesterday's news. Bars, offices, gyms, churches, cafes. Enterprising opportunists, entrepreneurs, small business owners. They've learned to live without us for too long. The world has moved on and they've left us behind in Lockdown. We're the afterbirth of the past, the discarded surplus of society."

"There's no point in us being here if we can't 'earn a living'," chimed in Eleonora, imitating a clerical worker for the oft quoted line.

"Always thought that was a weird phrase," noted Dusan self-reflectively. "Even before all this. To *earn a living*. Pretty fucked up when you consider it. You can't live unless you 'earn' it. Earning a wage is just a way of justifying your existence. If you can't earn a living, then your whole existence is pointless. I guess that's what we are now. We're just dead weight."

"Then why don't they just get it over with?" asked Jakob rhetorically as he sank down onto his hunkers. "Why don't they just march us off to the gas chambers and be done with us? Why all this boredom? All this endless fucking waiting!"

"Not their style," retorted Alexandra with a spit of disgust, letting the bubbly saliva snail down the face of her Perspex porch. "They want to 'save' us."

"Save us from ourselves," added Eleonora.

"'Life is precious'," quoted Johanna and everyone winced with discomfort.

"So what? We just sit here and wait around to die?" fired Jakob with unsatisfied frustration.

"*Geduld Macht Frei,*" said Eleonora. "That's what they should have on the gates to this place."

"'Patience makes you free'," translated Alexandra with an acerbic smirk. "Sums up this whole locked down world. We're all stuck in death's waiting room."

"A few days ago," said Dusan, straightening himself up and crossing his legs. "An old friend of mine who ended up on the seventh floor of this place, he used to be a taximan, passed away. I met the White Coats as they were taking him away. He'd kicked the bucket apparently."

"Suicide," said Jakob in a statement of the obvious, taking a second thereafter to chew the word over in head. "I might bite that pill too if this goes on much longer."

"That's the thing," proceeded Dusan. "They didn't call it suicide. They told me he'd committed the grievous crime of 'self-murder'."

"Self-murder?" said Alexandra with an audible frown creasing the brow of her face. "The fuck are they calling a spade a hatchet for?"

"Because," explained Dusan before coughing to clear his throat. "Suicide would imply that you were unhappy. You could only be unhappy if something was wrong. And something could only be wrong if there was a flaw in the system. It would mean that death is a better option than life and they can't have that because 'life is precious'. So, instead they make *you* the murderer. *You're the evil one. You're* the one who is wrong. So, you see, no matter what you do, even in death, they have you. Your suicide is further proof that you're an obstacle to progress, that you're an uncivilised creature of the ancient world who thinks in ancient ways."

"Motherfuckers," cursed Jakob with raw spite billowing off him. "It's all swine-shit man. I've been saying since the start that this vaccine is just a big scam. I think it's all a fucking con."

"Maybe you're right," half-agreed Dusan, the weight of experience carrying in his voice. "I suspect it is a question of business in the end. They can't allow us to have a normal life. If you can live a happy life without the vaccine, then why bother wasting all that money on insurance and inoculation fees. They're making an example of us to everyone. They need everyone dependent on them. They don't want independent business owners navigating the market on their own. They want guaranteed certainties, everything locked down and pinned to the ground."

Of a sudden everyone heard the '*ding*' of the elevator toll aloud. All heads turned expectantly as the metal doors shuddered open. Johanna had to blink twice to confirm what she was seeing. Out of the lift came none other than her Vaccine Case Worker, *Julius Zuboff*! More surprising still, it was clear as day he was not here on duty, but as a *resident*. Two suitcases were trailing behind him as a pair of White Coats escorted him down the corridor. The solid certainty which had been such a constant feature of his presence had been replaced by a frantic look of distress. His square glasses were sitting crooked. His square haircut, once as neat as a freshly trimmed lawn, was now growing in every direction. His square jaw had a fresh carpet of stubble on it. His shirt wasn't even tucked into his trousers. A hush filled the hallway as he passed by. Johanna could tell from both her hallmates and from Julius' obvious nervousness that she was not the only one who had had the pleasure of his 'assistance'.

"Holy fuck," exclaimed Eleonora with a grin of delight almost springing from her once Julius had entered his room on Johanna's left. "That guy was my Vaccine Case Worker."

"Me too," said Alexandra as she cracked her knuckles.

"Me too," added Dusan.

"Me too," said Johanna.

"The fuck happened to him you wonder?" piped up Jakob, his eyes glued to Julius' door.

"I guess we'll find out shortly," retorted Dusan. "Only thing is, as we all now know, it takes a couple of days for the spirit to break. We could be waiting a while before he decides to share with—" The office manager's prediction was abruptly cut short as Julius emerged from his room and planted himself against the Perspex glass of his porch.

"You guys!" he called aloud in a voice that was completely out of character for him. "How do we get out of here? You have a plan, right? I gotta get out of here!"

"What's the trouble? Never had an original idea of your own?" snapped back Alexandra.

"There is no plan," curtly informed Dusan.

"Oh come on! Clue me in!" pleaded Julius, his hands visibly shaking with shock. "I know all your files! You're all entrepreneurs and capitalists! You're always trying to find a loophole!"

"Yes, we are," confirmed Johanna coolly, without even turning to look at him. "And being a hall monitor like yourself, *you* should know there is no way out."

"Oh come on! I know I was an ass but we're all in this together now! There has to be a way out of this!"

"What happened to you?" asked Eleonora, changing the subject to the only thing anyone was interested in. "How does a guy like you end up in a place like this with us?" Julius gulped and cleaned the lenses of his glasses with the hem of his shirt.

"I eh...I..." he stuttered, clearly finding his fate a hard fact to admit. "I ran out of clients. *Everyone* out there is vaccinated...and anyone without a vaccine is here. The Commission decided they had no use for my department anymore. So, I was let go. I tried to get a transfer, but everywhere is full up. Tried to get a job somewhere else in the private sector and the same story. By the time I swallowed my pride and applied for a cleaning job, it was too late. I couldn't pay the mortgage, the bills, taxes, insurance, and also pay for the vaccine. Time ran out on me and well. Here I am."

"So, that's it then," said Alexandra. "No one's safe! We're all fucked! Even the Quarantiners get Quarantined in the end!"

"There must be a way out though," persisted Julius, sweat clearly running off his scalp. "A way out of this vicious circle. If we could make a run for the North Side perhaps? Maybe then could we be free."

"The bridge is gone," reminded Johanna, tightening her grip on the photograph of her mother and stepfather.

"She's right," agreed Dusan. "Even if you wanted to defect to those trigger-happy lunatics, how in hell would you ever get across?"

"FERRYMAN IS THE ONLY MAN!" erupted the voice of the mutilated man from out of nowhere. All eyes turned on him. Even Johanna was compelled to look upon his hideousness. "Give the signal at midnight by the river gardens and he'll take you to the edge and back. All he asks is a coin for the trouble."

"A coin? Like old money?" questioned the desperate Julius. The earless man only smirked in reply. Julius at once winced in despair. "Dammit! How would anyone have the money to buy a coin?"

"Hey! How the hell do you know anyway?" asked Jakob accusingly of the silent smiling man. "Who even are you?" The disfigured spectre cast his ragged eyes upon the drug dealer and ravenously shook his head from side to side like a dog emerging from water. Then he smiled a smile so deep and long that it seemed inhuman almost, as if the impulse behind it had not even come from him.

"*Nobody*," he whispered with a childish giggle.

"Everyone is somebody," said Dusan, an eyebrow raised to their strange alien neighbour. "You care to give your name sir? Contribute to our little Neighbourhood of the Damned?"

"Hehehehehe," giggled the man. "Not me little boy. Not me. I'm nobody…and so are you. You're *all* nobodies."

"What? Quit fucking around and just tell us your name for Christ's sake!" snapped Alexandra impatiently. The man eyes were made bright with interest at the little outburst and every impulse in his body seemed to drive him into a lustful ogling focus that made Johanna's skin crawl of its own volition.

"Marius," he said, opening his mouth as wide as possible for the utterance of every syllable. "Marius Zielenski hehehehe…"

"Oh god," gasped Julius, hand raised to his open mouth in shock. "You're Mad Marius."

"What?" asked Jakob not knowing what the bureaucrat was so stunned by.

"Mad Marius," repeated Julius, looking the wild-eyed freak over to confirm this was indeed the individual he was neighbours with. "He used to smuggle people over to the North Side. No one could catch him. Then one day he just surrendered to us out of the blue. They found him chewing another person's gums between his teeth. I can't believe I'm going to say this…but I think we might be saved! If there's anyone who can get us out of here, it's him! He can take us across the Borava! We can escape Quarantine and get our lives back!"

"*Your* life?" said Marius questioningly. "You think your life is *yours*? You think that meatsuit you stand in belongs to you? All because you just woke up into it one day. Hahahahaha! You people are something else. What wild fantasies there are wriggling in your heads!" His unblinking eyes scanned over everyone with the penetration of a laser. "You didn't purchase your life, you didn't rent it out, you didn't pluck it up off the side of the road. You just woke up into it whether you liked it or not. Your body is not *your* body!"

"Wow…you are seriously high," said Jakob with a mix of both humour and concern. "What are you on man?"

"Don't even bother," advised Dusan, ever the paragon of reasonableness. "The guy is clearly crazy. You don't get a name like Mad Marius for nothing. He's just talking swine-shit."

"Denial is a drug all of its own Mr Shirt-and-Tie," replied Marius without even looking at Dusan. "You're living in a lie. Your whole life is nothing but a bad joke, a nightmare you can't wake up out of. And here you are now, a broken toy on the shelf no one wants to play with."

"Shut the fuck up!" suddenly shouted Alexandra. With lightning swiftness that made everyone jump a little, Marius planted himself against the Perspex glass.

"Look at you! A pretty puppet!" he teased tauntingly of Alexandra. "I made you angry little puppet! If I push another button, I can make you cry!" His mouth at once contorted into that of a wailing bawl. "I pull another string I make you dance!" He performed the pirouette of a ballerina. "I threaten your life I make you scared! I crack a joke I make you laugh! I strip off all my clothes and I'll make you wet and gagging for me right here and right now!" A wave of universal disgust flowed over the hallway. Marius then lowered his voice to a calmer tone and got down on his hunkers so he was eye to eye with the freaked-out Alexandra. "You still under the illusion your life *belongs* to you? Hmmm? You think you have any real control over your life? You're a pawn. A puppet with no puppeteer. You're a self-conscious nothing. Your body is a prison cell woman, it's your tomb. Nothing more. Nothing more. *And it doesn't belong to you.*"

A tense stillness fell upon the corridor as those words soaked in. Johanna's mind flashed to the imagined butchery of Klaus' body. She pictured the students not only cutting open the skull and scooping out his brain, but then proceeding to play with it, passing it to each other with bouts of laughter as though it were a volleyball. Was that all her brother was? A collection of meat and bones tied together with veins and nerves? A concoction of biochemistry to be experimented and played with? She shuddered at the thought of it.

"So anyway," continued the anxious Julius, "Could you hook us up with your guy, the Ferryman?"

"Hahahahaha," mockingly crowed Marius, spinning around in his transparent cubicle. "You all want to escape so badly. You all want to get back to the way things were, go back to 'normal', to being the people you were in your first life, paying bills till the day you die and drinking the blood of the lamb with Father Jakob here, eh?" Out of nowhere he switched to the voice of a little girl. *"And the lost little souls were all diagnosed with Denialism and lived miserably ever after.* Good god you people! Don't you know every prison you break out of only leaves you in a bigger prison still? Can't you see that? Don't you know you've been wearing masks since the day you crawled out of the slime? Living within a mythology that you were anything more than a vessel for urges and desires that were never yours to begin with! Can't you see that you're free of it all now? Can't you see that? This world is done with you. Mr Shirt-and-Tie said so, did he not?" Marius pointed accusingly at the now squirming Dusan. "No one expects anything of you anymore boys and girls! Nobody cares about you. Nobody wants anything from you. They don't care what you have to say or what you have to think. Don't you realise that, the here and now is the only time you can do and be whatever you want…*because nobody cares about you."*

"Okay," said Dusan awkwardly, getting to his feet after an eerie quietude held the hallway in its clutches for an unusually long time. "I think that's enough chatter for one day. I'm going home." The rest of the hallway agreed without saying so, a tremor of horror rattling through each of them.

"Just one thing," said Johanna, her attention directed at Marius. Everyone held still for a moment. She knew not why she found it in herself to converse with this mad preacher, but a gaping emptiness from within pressed her onwards to do so. "If our lives aren't our lives, if our bodies don't belong to us, and we've been living a lie all along, then *who* does own our lives?" Marius peered at her over his shoulder, his tattered lips once more cracking apart into a grotesque grin.

"What I'm asking…what I'm really asking is who do you suppose is behind all this? Why do you think we're all going to live 'miserably ever after' for wanting our old lives back?"

"*Oh, you'll see,*" he teased, his speech now twisted and contorted into devilishness. "*Descend into the Deep and the Dark…and you'll see.*"

"See what?" asked Johanna impatiently, everyone else also listening eagerly to hear Marius' final say.

"*The one who lurks within.*"

Part V: Resonance

Is it you who casts your Shadow?
Or is it the Shadow who casts you?

Marius Zielenski, 'The Masked Prophet', from the poetry collection, 'Verses of the Great Demon'

The solitude of the bedrooms had failed to satisfy anyone. Johanna scanned her own room, her gaze moving from the treadmill to the window to the pattern of bloody dents in the punchbag-wall. A few days ago, even a few hours ago, she might have thrown herself back into that old self-destroying routine. But with Klaus dead, there was no point in any of it anymore. There was no point in her even being alive. For the first time in months, moreover, she had enjoyed the company of other human beings who understood her pain. Why suffer in isolation when you can suffer in solidarity?

On top of all that though were the poisonous words of Marius Zielenski. They simply would not leave her conscience alone. She needed to share her ruminations. She needed company. As did everyone else it would seem. Having been denied of it for so long, the primal urge to gather and socialise was too great for any of them to repress. Though it was clear that everyone had it on their minds, nobody dared to discuss Zielenski's hellish ethos. They bottled it in, as if by not speaking it they could quench his undeniable logic. They devoted their attention instead to a welcome distraction.

Bar Zielenski himself who was looking at no one in particular, all other eyes were trained on Jakob. The priestly drug dealer had installed a pull-up bar on the door frame to his room. He hung upside down from it, his arms and head swaying above the carpet. His bushy beard he had tied into a knot, so it didn't fall into his eyes. Everyone looked on in awe as his whole torso began to heave and convulse. A retching belch came howling out of his throat. Saliva drooled from his mouth and the squelch of internal fluids croaked and rasped out of him.

"It all slides down," said Eleonora. "All the blood goes to his head."

"Everything that descends must one day rise again," said Marius as much to himself as everyone else.

"What if it rips open inside him?" asked Julius with terrified curiosity, unable to pull his eyes away from the horrific act.

"He dies," stated Johanna bluntly. The deep stomach belches narrowed to a choking gasp and little by little their quarry came into view. Sliming out of Jakob's mouth, a condom filled with liquid plopped onto the floor. Jakob breathed in deeply and a cheer echoed from all the Perspex porches. He went back into his room with the condom and returned with a plastic bottle now filled with the fluid.

"Vodka anyone?" he asked slugging a gulp of it down to a universal outburst of chuckles. "Leave a cup outside your door and I'll pour you a bit."

"You'd really go that far just to booze up?" asked Julius incredulously as everyone else automatically went in search of a mug.

"Best way to smuggle goods," explained Jakob before coughing. "Used to do a sword swallowing act as a kid. Comes in useful from time to time."

"Where did you even get the vodka? Who sold that to you?" inquired Alexandra after leaving a cup outside her door.

"I still have my connections," said Jakob with a wink. "They may even have mixed something a little extra in with it."

Marius alone did not take up on Jakob's offer of alcohol. After months, if not years of abstinence, the small amount of alcohol made drunks out of them all within mere minutes. Jokes were made, laughs were had, stories were told, sufferings were shared. Hour by hour their tongues began to loosen and cravings for forbidden fruits were expressed. Such talk was impossible to avoid after having their first decent drink in so many years. Beyond the sentimental things like home and family, the conversation very swiftly moved towards the lust for live music, for parties, dancing, and sex, for the very passion and electricity of life. Julius, being only new to the ranks of the damned, was unable to weigh in so much but even he, having been self-repressed for so long in a straitjacket profession, began to loosen his tongue and convey his humanity. The more the discussion wore on though, the more ravenous became their craving, and worse still, the more apparent that it was all beyond their reach.

Almost subconsciously they began to wind the conversation down, none of them wanting to dwell any longer on things that could never be theirs. Just as their voices faded out though, Zielenski began to speak. No one interrupted him. No one questioned him. They just let him talk and allowed his words to crawl into their ears. And somewhere in that delirium of drunkenness and community, time began to writhe and bend.

"In the beginning, there was nothing but the one we know to be the Great Demon," he started, as though telling a children's fairy tale. "The Demon roamed the nothingness and found he was alone. And in his loneliness, he came to see there was no use for him. He was condemned to a state of purposelessness for all Eternity. And so, driven to madness by the nothingness, he tore himself apart in an act of divine suicide. From this moment of self-annihilation was created the Universe. From that single eruption of cosmic deicide, his essence was scattered across the expanse of Outer Space. All planets, stars, and galaxies are born of this moment of destructive metamorphosis. So, you see, the whole Universe is the Great Demon. Everything that ever was and ever will be is a splinter of the Demon. *All* existence, therefore, is riddled with his wickedness. From the poison of his suicidal madness was made the Universe. The history of all the cosmos and all life is the unending cycle of the Demon's suicide and rebirth. Every act of murder and destruction is a manifestation of his suicide. For nothing can live in this world without feasting on another thing."

"When men and women first came to roam the Earth, they alone, amongst all creatures great and small, came to understand the power of the Demon and their place within the Cycle of Death. But the ancients were left affright at this for they saw their own existence to be a futile enterprise, a mere extension of the Demon's horror. They so loved themselves that they could not bear the thought of parting from this life and falling, like all other creatures before them, into the all-devouring and all-consuming jaws of the Demon's suicide. And so, men and women built up walls and curtains to hide the Demon and told lies to keep the truth from their children. They came to call the Great Demon by the name of 'God' and painted over his vile and evil nature with roses and sunshine and butterflies. Children doomed to die are told they will live happily ever after. Friends and family driven to madness by depression and anxiety are made to smile for every photograph. Advertisers working for robber barons depict a sunny world of satisfied smilers gorging themselves into obesity on consumer goods. A comfortable afterlife is promised to all those who do their chores and brush their teeth before bed. And all things that might besmirch or contradict this pretty picture, and thereby unmask the world for what it truly is, are ruthlessly suppressed and shunned into the shadows. And so, the lie is preserved and humanity clings on helplessly, and uselessly, to its puppet bodies, but forever doomed to live in fear of that very Cycle of Death which is the cosmic order of all things."

Johanna fell into a deep and suffocating sleep that night. In her dreams, she saw Klaus lying on the operating table, his stiff corpse glistening with formaldehyde, his brain exposed to the open air as it slumbered within the nest of his skull. Somewhere in there, within the dark of his head, caught up in a strangle of neurological wires, the idea of 'Klaus' as a living being had once existed. But no longer. Now he was just a broken toy. A toy that had been poorly made to begin with and fated to break and shatter one day or another. Johanna, aware that she was dreaming, moved towards the body. She mounted the operating table and saddled the corpse of the dead boy. She clasped his wet moribund brain with her fingers. Grey matter squished within her hands and a hot and pleasurable sensation spread through her. She looked into Klaus' face and saw nothing but an empty husk staring back.

'Why not?' she said to herself, as her hands groped his frigid corpse with impunity, sliding her fingers through his purple lips and sticking her tongue through his gaping surgical scars. "Why not? Klaus won't mind. He's dead. His father won't mind. He's dead too. My parents won't judge. They're gone too. No one can do anything about it. No one is watching! Remember, *nobody cares about you!* You can do whatever you like! Whatever you like! Whatever you like! Hahahahaha! The boy is helpless and there's nothing he can do! Nothing! He can't even squeal! Hahahaha! That's right Klaus isn't it? Isn't it? Can't stop me fucking your empty rotting child limbs! Hahahahaha!"

"You see in all your life," continued Marius with his sermon. "You were raised up on this multi-layered, multi-purpose, interacting, intercultural, intergenerational, falsehood. When famine and pestilence threatened, you ran in terror. When saviours arose, you fell to your knees and thanked them in gratitude. But you see it was all a nightmare. All your life you've been the deluded cheerleader of liars and illusionists. It is the town hero who saves a dumb fool from drowning, the activist who helps the refugees, the aid worker who gives succour to the starving, the doctor who saves the little old lady from cancer, *it is they who are evil.* It is the optimist who makes empty promises. It is they who are bent upon slowing the cycle and perpetuating the agony of life on earth. In their eyes, a human being who lives for a thousand years is a victory even if those thousand years were spent living in the bleakest desolation and poverty. They are infected with the disease of parental concern. They are all disciples of Gilgamesh in search of the elixir of life that will allow us to escape the Demon's suicide and instead live in a state of misery and loneliness for all Eternity till we destroy ourselves in a pent-up explosion of self-hatred, just as the Demon did before us. Life my children is far from precious. Life is the true evil. Scrape beneath the surface, scrape the painted mask away, and you'll see the terrible truth beneath."

Johanna awoke of a sudden from her necrophiliac paedophile dream. A queer feeling had come upon her. She knew she should feel ashamed of what she had fantasised. She knew it was wrong. Yet no ill feeling overcame her. She was still as numb and empty as before. She staggered from her bed to the bathroom and looked herself in the mirror. She did not recognise the woman in that reflecting glass. The reflection seemed so fragile, so frail, so *tender*. She ambled towards the kitchen and picked a knife from the drawer. She then returned to the mirror, pressed the tip of the blade to her shoulder. Pressed harder, and harder, and harder. Then with a wrench she slashed the blade downwards in a hiss of steel and splitting skin. A thin line of red dots appeared and began to weep. A short laugh of exhilaration escaped her. She felt elation in her veins. Wildness throbbing in her eyes.

"The Doctors want to save your life! The tree-huggers want to save the planet! Religionists want to save your soul! Citizen R and his flock of concerned parents want to save the children! Save! Save! Save! The truth rules out though. Anything that needs to be 'saved' is already doomed. Why save anything when you can just take! Take and devour and consume as the Demon does! The Cult of Salvation is only obsessed with saving itself anyway. The Doctors want to save their jobs. The tree-huggers want to save their conscience. The religionists really only want to save their altars. And parents, well now, they are the oldest and most intimate disciples of Gilgamesh. They want to save and nurture their children only because in them they have invested their future and legacy, thereby ensuring their own genetic immortality. And so, when a child is killed or raped by a paedophile it is the future which is raped and murdered, it is the parents' own dream of immortality which is fucked and slaughtered. In killing a child, you kill the parents also."

"Oh yes!" said Johanna aloud, her mind turning in spirals as the emptiness within was undone and a beauty of a new dimension took hold. "Yes. Yes. Yes.

Yes. Again!" She made another cut. "Again! Again! Again! Come out! Come out and play! Hahahahahah!" Angry red streaks clawed about her body like red tiger stripes. Blood dribbled out from the crimson lips she had carved into herself. The pain did not horrify but refreshed her as her necrophile fantasy had. No thunderbolt struck her. No divine power intervened to save her. No parent cried in horror. She was *free*. If the body didn't even belong to her, who cared if she hacked it to pieces? By mutilating it she claimed it as her own! By violating it she exercised control over it! *She* commanded its strings! It gave her *power* over it, power over this puppet life. "Yes! Yes! Yes! Again! Again! Again! More! More! Mutilation is liberation!"

"You are made in their design. You are conditioned to think, act, and behave as your parents do. You are entombed within the organic cells they have imprisoned you within. And you should be grateful for the life they give you! For they feed you and clothe you and *love you*! And love. Love is the highest good of all! Is it not? The one true sign that there is goodness in the world. But love, you see, is nothing more than the relief you feel when you realise you are not abandoned. Love is the fear of neglect. Your Summer of Love was no more than a Summer of Fear, the fear of being alone. For he who is alone is insignificant, and he who is of no significance will not be noticed when he dies. Love you see is thus no more than the unquenchable longing for someone to hold your hand again, for someone to verify that your biological existence has value. Your longing for a partner is merely a longing to be held as you were by your parents. Don't you know that 'partner' is an anagram for 'parent'? They're one and the same thing! All to keep you weak and dependent and suckling on the milk of others!"

Johanna felt herself curling into a foetal position when she crawled back into her bed. The scars she had inflicted gnawed and corroded into her bones. She had gone against every instinct of survival, every principle, which her mother and father and stepfather had taught her. She awoke the next morning feeling unbearably light within herself, the itch of the raw scar begging a rough and vigorous scratch. She desisted against this impulse though. Ghosts from the past yelled the words 'shame' and 'disgrace' at her for what she had committed in both thought and action.

"*What have you done?*" those dead voices of the past screeched at her. "*What have you done Johanna? Don't you want to live forever? Don't you want to live forever!*"

She waddled out to her Perspex porch, looked to her right and found Eleonora with a long gash across her sweet rosy cheek. One by one, Jakob, Dusan, and Alexandra emerged from their respective doors. Johanna did not recall what was said, but each in their turn rolled up sleeves and trouser legs to reveal their own scars. Julius alone remained unscarred. But, when he laid eyes upon his hallmates, he was gripped with the fear of exclusion and the deprivation of human company. Too weak to resist the Will to Conformity, he took a knife to his wrist right in front of them and joined their bloodied ranks.

"We could die from this," laughed Eleonora, as drunk on pain as on Jakob's latest batch of vodka. "But who cares? Life is trash! Hahaha!"

"I died in Hell," declared Alexandra to the hallway, the fire of renewal in her eyes as she looked upon her surroundings in a dazed stupor. "They called it Quarantine."

"For though we are dead," added Dusan, not a shred of his old self left on display, his form and character identical to the rest of the group.

"We are also alive," finished everyone together, lecherous smiles screaming out of them, the dead parental voices of caution melting into nothing. Vindicated and inspired, Johanna skipped back to her room and laid bare her flesh for the bite of steel again. Skin was split and blood was shed. In her hour of carnal self-destruction, she caught sight of the old family photographs, the faces begging her to stop. But she didn't care. Her red fingers painted the helpless photographs in her crimson ichor, stroking them as she had stroked the paralysed flesh of Klaus. With the power of the cosmos roaring within her, she snatched the photographs from their puny frames, cast them into the toilet, and with a punitive pull of the lever flushed them into the oblivion of non-existence.

They were dead, dead forever. As was she.

Johanna Reinther was dead.

Something frightening, both ancient and novel in its character, a thing with no past and no future, was taking her place.

"But you see there is no future. There never was. And so, there is no hope. There is no salvation. We are each of us broken shards of the Great Demon, entombed within puppet bodies of flesh and blood. And when we die, we are recycled to be born again on this Gulag Planet. Nothing you do or don't do will ever matter. The cycle will go on and on with or without your help. Everything you love, everything you build, everything you hate, will turn to dust in the end. There is no consequence to anything. There is no Heaven and there is no Hell.

Hitler does not burn, but walks reborn among the living, no different than your beloved Nelson Mandela. There are no repercussions, just as there are no rewards. There is only the Demon and his Will to Self-Annihilation."

Phone numbers were exchanged, and a group chat was commenced. Each night standing before the shimmering screen of her bathroom mirror, Johanna cut and cut again. She slashed and sliced and diced her body open for the precious flow of '*red oil*' as her hallmates called it. Jubilant laughs howled out of her with every laceration that drew blood. Every pang of pain shot a corresponding rocket of joy through every fibre of her being. She daubed her fingers in her own blood and smeared her face with it, caked her hair in it, making art of her own desecration. With phone camera in hand, then she documented herself with alacrity, sharing it in the group chat to receive the expected outpourings of digital congratulations.

The more they indulged, the deeper they cut, the hungrier their appetite, the more accurate their techniques became. And with every share and update of their work, the more competitive they became. Who could cut the deepest? Who could make the most slashes per minute? Who dared to cut a limb off?

Where the digital would not suffice though, live performances were resorted to. During the day they gathered in their cubicles and, as the walls were stripped of their wallpaper, so they stripped themselves down to their underwear. One after another they hopped, skipped, and spun their way down the length of the hallway displaying their 'galleries' of scars, burns, and carvings, in a ritual they called the 'Dance of the Damned', their hallmates all whooping and cheering to them in carnal delight. They pressed their self-butchered bodies against the Perspex glass for the others to drool over. The purple lips of open scars kissed the glass and slobbering tongues on the other side tried in vain to lick them. A patchwork of scarlet red handprints was left dripping on the porches at the end of each day.

It was to be sure, the very best of times.

"No matter the fantasies of the puritan Coddlers and the prudish Painters, the Great Demon pulses still through every rock, earth, cloud, fibre, shadow, and flesh. All existence is alive with his wickedness. All existence is doomed to follow his path into destruction. And all those who know this are at one with the Universe. All who are at one with his suicidal will shall know the body to be a wretched thing; an undead scaffold of bones stuffed with organs and hormones, bent unto evil and only unto evil. The body lusts and thirsts for purpose as the

Demon does. Your body is attracted and aroused to others for reasons you cannot even comprehend, and for this to be so the body of your sweetheart need only be in the right shape.

The right shape! What horror! Dead or alive, the shape is all that matters! If it were not for the rose-tinted glasses of the Coddlers, we would all ascend into a great planetary orgy of necrophilia with our decomposing kindred! And you know this to be true! For the cartoons and sex dolls and erotic paintings that excite the imagination are no more alive than all the corpses of Auschwitz! *This is the will of the Universe! The hunger of the Demon! Lean into his will to self-destruction and you too shall descend into His embrace. For everything that descends, will one day rise again!"*

The 'feasting' as they called it, intensified in its hunger. One night then, it reached a marvellous crescendo for Johanna. In honour of the Demon's Suicide Cycle, she carved bleeding spirals into her face. As the blood ran down over the bumps and troughs of all the scars that had come before, she looked into the mirror on the wall. An uncontainable cackle suddenly wriggled out of her throat in demonic delight, and yet, she herself had *not willed* it.

On closer inspection, she soon realised her smile in the mirror, *did not match her own*. Her reflected eyes moved a little slower or a little faster than her own. In a blink, she saw herself with eyes toxic and cobalt as the Prussian blue walls of the corridor. Her skin was black and glistening in the lamplight like fresh oil beneath the sun. Another blink and it had all evaporated into thin air. The living corpse of Johanna Reinther was looking back at her again.

Nevertheless, she felt teeth grind within her teeth, felt eyes swivel within her eyes, and felt hands groping within her own hands. A grin incinerated through her body that splashed over her puppet face, and her eyes spun all around in hellish rapture.

"And so, you see my children," finished Zielenski. *"The Great Demon is both among us and within us."*

Part VI: Deliverance

Life, my sweet, scorches the very earth with its irrepressible desires till all is burned to ash. If you have a way of containing the Plague of Human Life, then I would like to hear it.
No comment? No? I thought not.

Marius Zielenski, response to TV reporter at anti-lockdown protest

Time, as ever when in quarantine, lost its meaning. Night and day, yesterday and tomorrow, before and after, were leftover words from another world, another life. Here and now was the only reality. Save for Jakob and his smuggling runs, no one else left the hotel anymore. They barely even looked out the window. The only connection they had with the planet beyond these walls were the food deliveries left down at reception for them. Everything else was just a blur of cuts and slashes and laughs and howls and blood and kisses in the dark.

Johanna lay corpse-like in her Perspex cell, licking her lips at the horrors unfolding around her. Eleonora was flat chested now. The barmaid had been to hospital and back for the butchery she'd inflicted on her breasts. She was no more troubled by this loss than Marius was by the loss of his left hand—which had been surgically amputated after he stabbed it to pieces for reasons beyond anyone's understanding.

Alexandra and Dusan had almost become identical twins with one another—their faces so afire with cuts and rips that they barely even looked human. Barely a patch of clear skin remained. They both sat in a constant state of delirious drunkenness from their blood lust. Jakob was suffering another coughing spasm after regurgitating yet another condom full of contraband. Using a string of barbed wire he'd stolen from the perimeter fence, he had flossed his cheeks apart, thereby widening his mouth to make the regurgitation easier. Every tooth and gum of his mouth was visible to the naked eye when he dared to speak.

Julius, meanwhile, was more Neanderthal than Sapiens now, his long hair and huge beard reaching down to his elbows. Always intent on proving himself to the rest of the gang, he had now become fascinated with fire and had started setting pieces of paper ablaze on his forearm. The very same papers he once would have filed and arranged so carefully, now curled and unravelled in the grasp of his flames.

It was a day like any other.

Somewhere in that endless delirium between pain and death, where no one was either alive or dead and human bodies were but playthings, an alien thought took hold of Johanna. She felt the strangest otherworldly urge to leave this place, to *leave the Hotel*.

Before she knew it, she was standing. Before she could give it any further thought, she was walking zombie-like down the hallway and entering the elevator. Why she was doing this she didn't know. The 'why not' was all that seemed to matter. It had been so long since she'd seen the sky she realised. So long since she'd laid eyes on the outside world. So long in fact that she had forgotten to even take her mask. She wandered through the ghostly lobby, brushed the front door open, and at once stepped back into the present hour of Time.

It was night and it was snowing. Seasons, perhaps even *years*, had gone by her she realised. In amongst the city buildings, she saw flashing colourful lights and pine trees all decked in ornaments.

Christmas.

It was Christmas. And yet the streets were empty. Only the distant rumble of cars from the inner city was audible. Otherwise, everything was dead quiet. Exactly what hour of the night it was, she had not the faintest notion.

With tentative hesitation, she began to meander out into the sleeping city. She was not dressed for the cold, yet she didn't bother going back to her room for a warmer coat or better shoes. She liked the burning sting of frost on her face, liked how it scratched her scars.

After a time, she came to a public park. None other than Lovers' Park—or Hygiene Park to be 'medically correct'. No coupling lovebirds roamed this sweet place anymore. Not a soul traversed this empty island in the sea of concrete and tarmac. The seamlessly pared lawns had the smooth surface of frozen ice-cream. A few trees were wilting under the weight of the snow. Here amidst the innocent falling flakes she idly sat in shivering solitude on a lonesome bench. And most wonderfully of all, she could enjoy it all by herself. No judges, juries, executioners, or crazy peasant mobs would run her out.

But one is seldom alone in any city for very long.

Voices came tumbling out of the dark middle distance and three figures stumbled into view. From their tone of voice, she could tell they were teenage boys. *drunk* teenage boys. They staggered across the plain of snow, kicking up swirls of white dust as they went, clinging onto one another with cans of cider and take-away burgers in their hands.

"You're a disaster, Sergei! You know that?" shouted one of them hoarsely at his friend.

"Boys come on! I don't need to hear it now!" bellowed Sergei, his inebriated voice so ungainly it nearly took him off balance.

"Even Tibor landed Adriana!" goaded Sergei's friend again as he took another swig of his beer can.

"When are you ever gonna get laid?" frankly blubbered another of his friends. Sergei took a step apart from his friends, He was a pimply faced juvenile with a head of curly black hair. He had a strong enough build to him but was clearly riven with uncertainties and doubts. "People are starting to think you're a poof!"

"Fuck off Antek!" blustered Sergei with a swipe of the air which sent a whip of alcohol trailing across the snowy ground. "I'm every bit a man as you and Janos!"

"Oh yeah?" spluttered Janos, alcohol still gurgling at the back of his throat. "Some time you've chosen to prove it! At this time of night? In this part of town? Good luck trying to get a date at this hour!" Janos and Antek both broke into a flurry of laughter that nearly swayed them off their unsteady feet. Sergei stood before them indignantly, his arms folded angrily over his ridiculous reindeer jumper while he struggled to keep his footing. In a fit of embarrassment, then he started looking around the park, anxious that someone might take stock of his humiliation by his peers.

"What about her?" he exclaimed wildly as he noticed Johanna sitting by herself. His friends quit their laughing and followed his gaze.

"Hey! You!" yelled Janos like an idiot to her. "Will you fuck our friend?"

"Make a man out of him!" added Antek to more fits of boisterous laughter.

Johanna Reinther would have walked away. Johanna Reinther might even have asked how old these mere boys were—a few years older than Klaus by the look of them. But Johanna Reinther, along with all her concerns, opinions, fears, and desires, was *dead*. She rose from the bench, extended her hand out to the adolescent and curled her index finger inward, beckoning him on.

The three fools let out a chorus of cheers and laughs of triumph. They began patting Sergei on the back and feeding the last of his beer can into him. The streetlights were too dim for them to discern Johanna's copious wounds. Even if she had been fully illuminated, she wagered they were far too drunk to either notice or care.

"You're in luck boy!" apishly congratulated Antek. "Look at her hair! She's a wild one you've landed!"

"Alright! Show time Sergei!" brutishly encouraged Janos. "Let's se-se-see what you've got!" Sergei looked at his companions a little uncomfortably.

"I'm not doing it *here,*" he protested. "It's too fucking cold!"

"I have a place," offered a forthcoming Johanna, her hand still outstretched to him. "Come with me." Sergei almost instantly began staggering towards her to further heckle from his buddies.

"She's ready and gagging Tóth-man!" slobbered Antek. "She's all wild and crazy! Crazy! You better be careful she doesn't have Pandemic Pussy!"

"Yeah you don't want lockdown crabs Sergei!" jibed Janos. "Don't forget to send pictures of the deed!"

"Hey! You forgot your phone! Sergei! Your phone!" called Antek after him. Johanna hurried her pace. She suddenly realised no alarm was going off. He didn't know *what* she was. She preferred to keep it that way.

"Ahh leave him!" yelled an impatient Janos thankfully. Johanna instantly relaxed. "Let's get out of here! It's fucking freezing! I hear Todor is having a get-together at his! Let's go there!"

"See you in the morning guys!" bade Sergei farewell, the dumb grin of a happy-drunk on him as he walked away arm-in-arm with Johanna.

"How old are you?" she whispered to him as they exited the park.

"Fif-fiftee-no! I'm eighteen! Eighteen! Eighteen!" he stuttered drunkenly. Johanna made no comment on his painfully obvious lie. She didn't care. She hadn't had a man in her bed for an age. It made no difference how old, or how young, he was. He would do.

The hotel security system was designed to constrain unvaccinated persons. Not the vaccinated.

No alarms were rung, and no doors were locked when Johanna arrived with her horny juvenile 'date'. They walked straight through without so much as a 'beep'. Upon her return to the fifth floor, she found, to her surprise, that all her hallmates had returned to their rooms.

Perfect.

No one would know of her little nocturnal pleasure. She would have him all to herself. Maybe after she'd pass him on to Eleonora and Alexandra to play with. But not yet. Tonight, he was hers alone. But, as she shoved the boy into her room and turned to close the door, she glimpsed opposite her the silhouette of Marius Zielenski sitting in the dark of his room, white glowing eyes grinning at her. Neither he nor she said anything of it. She just closed the door and shut him out.

In the pitch black of the room, Sergei pinned her to the bed. He drooled and grunted boar-like over her, doing his best in his intoxicated condition to perform the zoological ritual demanded of him by his dollish body.

"Your skin is so bumpy and scaly," he rudely complained as he held her in his mindless hormonal embrace, his hands groping her body at the whim of his puppet desires. Johanna's hands swept over his back at leisure. His skin was as smooth and pure as whipped cream. She combed her fingers over his body as she would through the fur coat of a prize stag, soaking up the warmth and youth and life in him. The delights of mutilation had left her feeling so light and ghostly, empty and skeletal. And here, was a warm-blooded creature whose fleshy fullness was right within her grasp, desperate to impose himself into her nothingness.

"So smooth, so young, so tender," a dark whisper hissed inside her at his every touch. *"So sweet, so warm, so innocent."*

"And yet not enough," thought Johanna to herself as their bodies merged, their pleasure one and the same.

There was no fire to it. No power. No electricity.

When she feasted upon herself with knives and razors, she had felt all those things. But not with this, the most pleasurable, most biologically essential, of all human experiences which she had craved and envied after for so long.

With their bodies intwined with one another now though, their senses united as one. There was a clear and obvious solution to the disappointment. She took her hand away from him, grabbed the knife on her bedside locker, and plunged it right through his stomach. She held him tight. His skin began to ripple and prickle and convulse and wince.

"*Yes. Yes. Yes. There it is. There it is!*" she chanted inside her head with ravenous abandon. "*Now we are one. Now we are reunited. For as the splinter of the Demon resides in me, so it resides in you. We are all of us shards of the single whole. By mutilating you, I mutilate myself!*"

She stabbed him again. And again. And again, and again with growing vigour and hunger.

"Ahhh," he suddenly began to gasp as the pain cut through his drunken numbness and eclipsed his pleasure. "What the…What the fuck!" A wave of fear and dread flooded through him as he clasped the puncture holes in his body with wild-wide eyes. He began to pull away, but she would not have it. His terror only heightened her pleasure and she held him tighter still. She plunged her hands through the wounds she'd inflicted and *entered* his body. She groped his innards and took slow sensual licks of his weeping blood. He started to howl in horror, but she strangled his voice with a deep and monstrous kiss that swallowed his screams for her digestion.

"*All-consuming and all-devouring,*" the alien voice spoke within her and she plunged herself deeper still inside him, fondling and violating and raping every throbbing organ and vein of his still-living body. She glared into his wide-open puppy eyes and drank up his helplessness. She glanced over his shoulder and looked down upon her own hands running beneath his skin like serpents slithering beneath desert sands.

"Wha-wha-wha…" he mumbled uselessly, words now escaping him. Her hand found his oesophagus and tore up his throat. A final pale squeal belched out of him as the invading hand shot up inside his neck and her fingers appeared right at the back of his mouth.

"Now," she said in lustful triumph. "Don't tell lies. Are you a real man now?" Pushing against the roof of his mouth from within she snapped his jaws open and shut as a ventriloquist would. "I'm a real boy!" she imitated in a cartoon voice, his juvenile eyes bobbing up and down in their sockets with every bounce and jostle of her hands. She gleefully laughed aloud at the sight of her own amusement and kissed his conquered corpse. Though his fingers still twitched and shuddered with the last flickers of the nervous system, his life and limb were all but abandoned. The battery was all used up. He was just another broken toy to be earmarked for the landfill.

She fell down into sleep that night with the taste of his death on her lips, the anguish in his eyes still in her mind, the power of his possession still in her hands.

The bed sheets were wet when she returned to consciousness. As she moved her limbs beneath the covers, she felt liquid lap against her. She stirred her eyes open and there he was next to her, all gored and butchered like the prize of a trophy hunt, his soulless eyes as devoid of life as a stuffed animal at the natural history museum.

"Fuck," she suddenly swore to herself as the gravity of her actions suddenly struck her. "Fuck! Fuck! Fuck!"

She'd murdered someone. She had taken a boy's life, ripped him out of this world and thrown him into the next. How she hadn't stopped herself she knew not. She found it hard to believe herself even being capable of such a thing. They had bound together in an embrace and it had felt no different than cutting herself, that was the only reason she could think of. But that was nowhere even close to an excuse. The law would not care for any excuses! Murder was murder! No two ways about it. It was one thing to agree with Zielenski. Another entirely to act on his crazy ravings! She'd lost the run of herself! She needed to claw back a slice of Johanna Reinther and think about this rationally.

A momentary panic rushed over her with images of imprisonment racing through her brain.

But then she realised, she was *already* imprisoned. What more could they actually do to her? They couldn't give her the death sentence. It would violate the Doctors' precious Health Code. But they'd still come looking for the boy. And while the Doctors might be bound to protect all life, the same might not be said of the patients they ruled over. If word got out that this this dumb *child*...had been seduced and murdered by an unvaccinated whore, they'd likely form a mob and storm the hotel.

She had to get rid of the body. Had to find a way to dump him in the Borava or somehow bury him. She'd need something to cover him with, something to bury him with, something, something, something.

She needed to go into the outside world again. She needed to do a scout of the area, see where she could dump his body. Without further hesitation she ran for the shower, washed the blood off her body in a blast of water, dressed herself and rushed out the door.

"Have a good night zaychik?" asked Marius with an all-knowing look on his face when she entered the hallway. She ignored him and her dazed hallmates and made a run for the elevator. "Just remember," he teased dreamily. "The Looking Glass is a one-way road…"

She hurried through the deserted lobby with place names and potential dumping spots running about her mind. She was so caught up in finding a solution to her conundrum that she didn't pay any attention at all to her surroundings. Then abruptly, out of nowhere, she was woken from her inner conflict.

"Oh my god! Are you ok?" asked a voice. Of a sudden the world came into view. It was daytime. Sunlight was bouncing off sheets of white snow. Christmas carols were chiming in the background. Shoppers were bustling down the street with gift bags stuffed under their arms. The voice had come from a middle-aged woman who had been approaching her on the pavement. Genuine concern was all over her face. A man marched by from behind Johanna, took a brief glance at her, halted and turned back with an identical mask of alarm. "What happened? Do you have a condition? Is there anything I can do?"

The scars. They were looking at her scars. But more to the point, *they cared that she had scars.* Johanna looked at these two fellow citizens in a state of befuddlement. This couldn't be right. People never treated her like this. Why weren't they spitting or cursing at her? What was going on?

"Would you like me to call someone for you?" asked the man, taking out his phone. There and then it clicked for her.

The phones weren't beeping.

They didn't know she was unvaccinated. But how? The phones always-
She cut that thought short. The previous night's events flooded back to her. She recalled licking the boy's blood. She had ingested it. Consumed it. He was inside her. *His vaccine was inside her.* The phones thought she was Sergei! A smile began to form on her face.

"Miss?" pressed the worried woman, snapping Johanna to her senses.

"I'm fine," she assured the two charitable souls. "Just had a … eh …my cat is a real scratcher. A real hell-cat you know? And a bit of a fighter too." She pointed to her scars and laughed it off to them. "I'm just on my way to the beauty salon to fix myself up. Honestly don't worry! Happens every week!"

"Oh, right, okay," said the woman. "Well you take care now."

"And maybe tranquilise that damn cat!" advised the man as she walked away from them.

"And Merry Christmas!" called the woman after her.

"*A Christmas miracle indeed,*" thought Johanna to herself, two White Coats passing her by without so much as a glance for her.

The hours which followed were a complete blur. She waltzed her way through the city, fandangoing down shopping aisles and pirouetting around fashion retailers. She swerved, skidded, slid, and skipped up and down the streets, her hands and legs twisting and turning and kicking and thrusting in a dance of wild exaltation. Sweet tunes played so hard and loud within her head that she might easily have mistaken there to be loudspeakers fitted to the buildings playing her playlist. Her swirls and twirls eventually took her to a nightclub and beneath the neon disco lights and pounding beats of the surround-sound system, she frolicked and danced to her heart's content amongst the masses of the living as though it were 2019 again.

Night had descended by the time she emerged from the club. She ambled back to the Hotel, flakes of knuckle-white snow drizzling down from the sky. Only now on her return journey did she recall why she had left in the first place. She'd have to dispose of poor little Sergei another day. She just hoped he hadn't started decomposing in her room. Then again, the place wreaked of enough blood and decay already. Who would notice?

As these thoughts waved by her, a fire engine came rocketing past her with lights flashing and alarms sounding. It was followed in quick succession by another and another and then by a convoy of ambulances. The flakes drifting to the earth she noticed had turned grey. The smell of smoke was in the air. She noticed then that the convoy of emergency vehicles were turning left towards the Hotel. Her gaze scanned to the skies and at once she beheld the orange glow of fire. Instinct compelled her to rush forward and she sprinted after the convoy of flashing blue lights.

She turned the corner and there it was. The entire building howling with flames. A towering conflagration of yellow, orange, and red fire billowing clouds of black smoke. Long tongues of white water sprayed skywards over the fuming structure. A few choking silhouettes came coughing and stumbling out the front door while platoons of firemen hurried onward into the inferno with axes in hand.

Only then did the scale of the disaster become apparent to her. The Hotel security system meant that only one resident could enter a corridor at a time. That meant, if one person made a run for it, everyone else on the corridor was trapped in their Perspex porch while the fire kept on spreading through the building. Had it not been for her outdoor expedition, she too might have been burned alive with clumps of hot melting plastic sticking to her skin.

"It was the paper-man I tell you! Your pen-licker boy burned it all down! Hahahaha!" exclaimed Marius in stentorian fashion, his manic bellowing audible to the human ear even over the roar of the blaze. "As I said to the green-belly tree huggers, BURN IT ALL! BURN IT ALL DOWN!" She glimpsed two White Coats grab him by the shoulders and dump him in a corner next to the other survivors.

Johanna was about to approach the scene and make herself present like an obedient schoolgirl for roll call. But she stopped herself.

Marius reminded her of the night before. Reminded her of Sergei.

The boy's body would be burnt to a crisp by now. And in her room no less. The CCTV tapes would surely be toast too. Who would ever know, bar Marius, that she had swapped herself with a human carcass? And who, would ever bother to investigate how that body met its end if every fleck of skin and bone was torched to a cinder?

Johanna Reinther, she realised, really was *dead*.

She was *free*.

It truly was a Christmas miracle!

For the first time in years, she had an inch to stand on! She had a win! She had committed an act of evil. And here she was receiving the blessings of the universe it would seem. That could mean only one thing: *The Great Demon was real.*

A sacrifice had been laid upon the altar, and the Great Demon had rewarded her in kind. And if more sacrifices were offered. Then surely, *more* rewards would be in store for her.

She looked up at the happy family billboard that had once tormented her. Drifting embers had floated across and seared the faces off the smiling mother and father, leaving only ashen-black silhouettes in their place. Right next to the burnt-out figures though, the slogan still stood.

"The Future You Deserve."

"Who are you?" spoke the alien voice within her.

"*Nobody,*" she answered confidently.

"*Nobody?*" teased the Demon with devilish playfulness. "*But why, someone who is nobody could be—*"

"*Anybody,*" finished Johanna, a shameless smirk curling at the corner of her mouth. She beheld the towering blaze one last time and caught Marius' eye. The skull-faced messiah did not cry out and call the White Coats on her. He didn't even smile at her as he usually did. He just gave a nod of his head in a voiceless stamp of approval.

Johanna nodded back in thanks to her mentor, turned her back on him, and walked out into the world.

Part VII: Transparence

The Modern Man is consumed with his hunger to uncover the mysteries of the Dark. Drunk on curiosity, one day shall come when he turns the light switch on in Outer Space. And there behold, in perpetual screaming terror, all the unnameable horrors of the Cosmos, swarming and multiplying in their millions around his precious Planet.

Marius Zielenski, 'In the Shadow of the Great Demon', page 1194

"Don't you ever play with your mamma?" asked Johanna.

"My mamma is always too busy," said little Vasily. He was a plump boy with adorable red cheeks and a happy beaming smile cornered with sweet dimples that would make anyone's heart melt. Despite his age, he still had that baby cuteness about him. Even in the dimness of the abandoned office space, the brightness of his face came through clearly.

"And what's your mamma's name," asked Johanna out of curiosity.

"My mamma's name is Lidija…Ivanevic," he said trying to remember the surname. He didn't even look at Johanna while he said it. His attention was too completely absorbed in the playset she had given him to toy with.

"Oh! I think I know her, she's a nice lady."

"Angelika?"

"Yes?"

"I think I need to go home," he said a little worriedly, fear in his face of what his mother might have to say on his lateness.

"But you're having so much fun," countered Johanna. "Besides, you'd only have to do silly stupid homework. And would mamma play with you like this?"

"No," he said with a shake of the head and she gave him another jelly sweet that made him smile all the more. Just as he began to unwrap the sweet, she gently pounced upon him and started tickling his belly. He laughed and recoiled in delight.

"Heehehehehehe who's got your tummy? Who's got your tummy?" she teased as her fingers ran up and down his infantile torso, lightly patting the soft baby fat which still encased his underdeveloped body.

"Hahahaha stop! Stop!" he giggled helplessly as he writhed around on the floor. She growled in playful jest as a wild beast, lifted him up and spun him around over her head to yet more smiles and laughs.

"I've got you! I've got you!" she said before turning his body upside down. He continued to laugh as his arms thrashed around in childish bliss. She grabbed his ankles and tied them together with a piece of cable, then attached it to a hook in the ceiling she'd prepared in advance. Now he hung upside down as Jakob once had in the Hotel. Vasily still tittered without a care, barely noticing the difference until she stepped away to reveal she wasn't holding him any longer. He wriggled a little but could not break free. "Who wants to swing, eh? Who wants to swing?"

"I do! I do!" he said excitedly, and she pushed him back and forth as he hung upside down.

"Weee! Weeee!" she cried with every swing, squeezing yet more little giggles out of him. One could easily mistake him for the happiest boy in the whole wide world in that moment.

"Higher! Higher!" he demanded but she slowed the swinging. "Higher! I said higher! I want to go higher!" She had stopped pushing him altogether.

That was when she belted him across the face with the back of her hand. The unprecedented attack stunned him momentarily, the swipe of her hand clearly visible on his soft nubile cheeks. Uncomprehending shock filled his eyes. Then, only when he understood that something hurtful had happened, did his whole face contort and transform. The rosiness in his cheeks flushed to a fever red. His eyes watered. His nose began to run. His beautiful smile was inversed, and a terrible wailing noise came weeping out of him.

"I-I-I wan-wan-want t-t-t-to g-g-go home!" he bawled, expecting somehow that Johanna would do his bidding. But she only leered back at him and watched his tears fall to the floor. "I WANT MY MAMMA!" he screamed as loud as his tiny lungs would allow. She slapped him again, hard enough this time for her to feel his cheekbone. His crying intensified and she stroked his puppet body as she would the fur of a cat.

"*Nothing is sacred,*" the voices said to her. "*No one is safe. Nothing is beyond violation.*"

"No one is coming," she told him, and a new unfathomable terror slithered inside Vasily's eyes. The boy had never conceived a day might come where a grown-up would treat him so brutally, had never imagined a day where a grown-up would not come and save him from trouble. "No one is going to help you. No one knows you're here. There's no Mamma here. No Pappa. No teacher. No cousin Igor…you're all alone."

She snatched the knife out from her pocket and clasped his hip to steady his swaying body. The blade rose of its own accord in her hand, the Demon snarling into being behind her fading mask of humanity. In that instant, she felt herself step into the shoes of the invisible darkness that had loomed above the boy since the day he'd been born. She flexed her muscles to his weeping song and with godless tyranny slashed down at-

"Miss Solovki! Miss Solovki!" came a knock at the door and Johanna was summoned out of her dream. "Miss Solovki are you alright in there?" Johanna cleared her eyelids and was reacquainted with her surroundings. She was taking a bath in her private quarters—a blood bath to be precise. Scented candles flickered all about her. She straightened herself up in the bathtub, the bloody bathwater forming miniature tidal waves as she adjusted her body.

"Yes! Fine Hanna! Just dosed off in the bath," she answered. "What is it?"

"Eva and I are just going out for a bit," explained Hanna. "We'll be back in an hour or two. Is that ok?"

"Yes, that's quite alright," approved Johanna, giving the two youngsters right of way. "But be back before dark!"

"No worries! See you in a bit!" retorted the two girls together.

A few seconds later and she heard the front door open and close. She was alone with herself again. Alone that is with the Demon.

Fifteen years had passed since she'd last set foot in Hotel Quarantine. Vasily was one of her early kills. The foolish boy had gone walking on his own through Ward One looking for his big cousin. She'd picked him up promising she'd play with him instead. His flesh had made for a delicious roast. More importantly though, he had had the V3 in his veins, a real jackpot! That slaying had allowed her to skip Ward Two entirely and get a job in Ward Three and from there expand her hunting territory further still. She might well have remained there only, after ten years on the go, there was still not a single hint that either the city police or the White Coats had noticed anything amiss. And thus, five years ago she decided to make the jump to the comfortable byways of Ward Four.

To all the world she was now Angelika Solovki; a diligent, hard-working, industrious executive manager at the Metropole Insurance Company—or MIC as she and her colleagues called it. She was a model citizen. So much so that she now even did workshops with college graduates on 'keys to success' and 'attitude for winners'. Every day she had her hair attended to by the best stylists in the business, had her face plastered in the finest creams and lotions, and dressed herself in the most spotless of finery.

But beneath the paint, the scars remained. Like everything known by the name of 'good' or 'beautiful' or 'decent' or 'polite', it was all just a skin-deep illusion, a manufactured nonsense to camouflage the Demon. And every hour of every day, the dumb idiots lapped it up and praised her for her charitable donations, hailed her for her professional achievements, thanked her for attending their events and dinner parties and barbecues. Her meteoric rise from Ward One to Ward Four and the corresponding rise in missing persons never seemed to occur to them. They were simply incapable of believing that a person was anything more than what their label conveyed them to be. They overlooked it all.

Almost the same way they had all overlooked her when she was down and out and alone on the side of the road.

They were, as ever, creatures of selective blindness.

Those whom she chose to hunt were no different. They practically walked right into her open mouth. The younger generations made for especially easy pickings. Generation L they called them—i.e. Generation Lockdown. An entire age-group that had grown up knowing little more than their own home and the mantra that everyone was trying to keep each other safe. Now that the Pandemic was over, they had emerged into the world conditioned to believe that the same logic applied. The world to them was just an extension of the family homes they'd been coddled in. With innocent complacency, they roamed the city, believing themselves to be safe and that everyone around them was also trying to help them 'stay safe'. And yet, parallel to these assumptions was their overwhelming eagerness to break free of the home nest and explore the wider world.

In Johanna's eyes, it made them not so much 'Generation Lockdown' as it did 'Generation Lost'. A whole flock of little lambs that lost their way and wandered into her jaws. On weekends, she cruised the lower wards on the lookout for young things on the down and out. Fed up with school bullies, fed up with teachers, fed up with parents, fed up with being rejected, fed up with the way the world worked. Each and all were ripe for the taking. One by one she seduced them all into her car and smuggled them across Quarantine Lines. If they were teenagers, she took her time with them, played with them as a cat would a mouse, groomed them as if they were her own children, and finished them off in her own good time. With so many teenagers already jumping the Quarantine Walls and mixing with kids from other wards, she could afford to play the long game with them. The younger ones she banished into the next Death Cycle within the day. They were usually more attached to their parents, more likely to try and run back home.

She raped them living and raped them dead. Every drop was drained from their veins. The flesh was pared from their bones. The heart, liver, and buttocks were always removed and roasted. The rest were dissolved in acid. Their skeletons were pulverised down to a fine powder with the use of a sledgehammer and flushed down the toilet along with their dissolved organs. Anything of their flesh she did not eat or drink she consumed in other ways. Their skulls, she had bleached and then painted with wondrous colours in her spare time. Their surplus blood she bathed in. The peels of their skin she used to line the inside of the bath so that she lay not on the ceramic surface of the tub, but on the rubbery texture of uninhabited skin.

Right now, she was bathing in the flesh and blood of the wayward Katja Černý—the teenage runaway from Ward Two. Katja's lifeless lips numbly kissed at Johanna's toes at the foot of the bath. Under the blood-water, Johanna pressed her fingers through the eyeholes of Katja's skull, an exquisite sensation of hot orgasmic pleasure bubbling through her body as she did so. With every stroke and touch she inflicted on Katja's corpse, she could detect the girl's final nanoseconds of terror still lingering. She wondered sometimes how long it took for the person to descend into the next Cosmic Cycle of Suicide. Was it instantaneous upon their death? Or was it a longer, drawn out, process? A trickling of the spirit? Was a fragmented ghost of Katja still there right now, shuddering and screaming without a voice, as Johanna harassed her destitute corpse? Was Katja still yelling for her mother from within Johanna's gut? Or was Johanna only desecrating a collection of calcium and protein that had once toiled under the psychological fallacy of an individual identity?

Either way, she had consumed and devoured Katja, just as she had so many before her. With every life she cannibalised, another missing shard of the Great

Demon was added to her collection. The hands within her hands, the eyes within her eyes, and the teeth within her teeth, grew more real and powerful with every soul she claimed. Every human life she snuffed out of the world was another act of vindication to the Demon's realness. For, how else could she be so rewarded if it were not for her service to him. By her hand had the Cycle been restored. The Universe was back to killing itself without human friction.

After a time, she clambered out of the bathtub, cleaned herself off and pasted over her old scars with hand cream. She rinsed out Katja's skin, folded it up and returned it to the freezer for another occasion. The skull she returned to the cupboard with the others, placing it alphabetically next to that of Kristoff Samberg.

"We're back!" came the voices of Hanna and Eva just as Johanna was locking the 'Feasting Room' behind her.

"We brought a friend," said the ditsy Eva as Johanna came down the stairs to meet them.

"She really wanted to meet you, so, hope you don't mind," explained the more cautious Hanna as their acquaintance shuffled through the doorway.

"This is Justyn—" introduced Eva before being cut off by Hanna.

"Jane Kelvin!" she almost shouted.

"How very western," commented Johanna as she approached the three girls.

"We all have western names in the Underground," explained Jane confidently, her features ebullient as she came face to face with Johanna. "My boyfriend is Henry Ford!" Eva and Hanna laughed nervously at that.

"Ah, so you are with the resistance," deducted Johanna. "The brave rebels trying to bring down Vaccine Rule."

"Plans are afoot," admitted Jane, clearly feeling comfortable enough to say such a thing. "We all have a part to play." Hanna and Eva nodded almost immediately to those words.

"And what, does a young radical like you want with me?" inquired Johanna, a polite and friendly glint in her voice.

"Oh! I just wanted to say that I think the world of you!" flattered Jane. Johanna laughed at that. "I really do Miss Solovki. I know you work with the Insurance Company but that hasn't stopped you from living this double-life. You have a conscience. A moral compass. You've been helping people our age across the Quarantine Walls for years now, giving them a chance for a better life, and I really just want to thank you for that. Even just giving Hanna and Eva housework to do while they get on their feet, it's so generous. You're one of the few people in this world that I can say, from the bottom of my heart, are one of the good ones."

"*If only you knew,*" thought Johanna to herself. "*Oh, how I'd lick the skin from your bones like caramel.*"

"Listen, I know everyone loves you anyway. But I just wanted to say that you *really* are a gem. No one else is doing what you do for our generation."

"Except Lidija Ivanevic," pointed out Eva. "Willard and Walter were staying at hers, weren't they?"

"Oh, that is true," conceded Jane. "But she's only small time I think and probably just an imitation of you Miss Solovki."

"*Lidija Ivanevic? A charitable matron? Well, well. How the mighty fall. Losing that boy of hers must have really spun her wheels backward. Funny how people twist and turn when you deprive them of their dearest possessions.*"

"Well thank you," acknowledged Johanna. "You're very kind. Too kind I might say."

"I just wanted you to know that the work you've done won't be forgotten." assured the radical youngster with religious certainty in her voice. "I promise that you won't be forgotten when things change…and they *will* change."

"Quite the promise to make. I'd certainly hate to be forgotten about!" laughed Johanna in good humour and the three teenagers chuckled along with her. "Anyway, it is getting rather late. Would you care for a lift home Jane?"

"Would I?" beamed Jane to the giggles of Hanna and Eva. "If it's not an inconvenience to you of course?"

"Not at all," reassured Johanna as she fetched her keys and turned to her two resident lambs.

"You get off to bed now you two."

"Yes Miss Solovki," acquiesced Hanna and Eva synonymously with one another.

"We're going to tear it all down," declared Jane, as Johanna drove parallel to one of the many Quarantine Walls of the city. The girl was at ease in her company it was clear, felt no inhibition at all about conveying her revolutionary intentions to her. But then they were all like that. Johanna was the only person in their lives who listened to them. She was their fairy godmother in the flesh.

"We'll pull the walls down and bring an end to the whole Hospital Dictatorship. No more limits, no more constraints, no more restrictions and forbidden behaviour."

"And then what?" asked Johanna out of curiosity.

"Freedom!" said Jane as though it were the most obvious thing in the world. "Freedom to be whatever we want to be! A world free from tyranny and subjugation, free from the domination of science over humanity and of certainty over liberty. Things are so stagnant in the city, don't you think? There's no opportunities for anyone to exploit."

"*If only you knew,*" silently repeated Johanna to herself.

"Just turn right here," instructed Jane as they came to a junction. "I don't know how people have put up with it for so long. It's not natural to have White Coats sticking truncheons at you for just being a human being. If they got their way, we'd be all locked up in cells and only able to talk to our friends through the window."

"*If only you knew.*"

"Just down this lane here," continued Jane. "And I'm the fourth house on the left."

"Immaculate sense of direction you have," complimented Johanna. "And quite the moral compass too I might add." The girl responded to the note of approval with an easily predicted smile. What was not predicted was the hug which Jane gave her. With the scent of Katja's life-fluid still thick in her nostrils, the spontaneous embrace of this juvenile admirer sent a shiver of gooseflesh over Johanna.

"I know we're not supposed to," said Jane as she broke away from Johanna. "But I don't live by their rules anymore. I'll hug and shake hands with whoever I wish. The Pandemic is dead and gone. Nothing should be restricted anymore." She opened the car door and was about to get out when she looked back at Johanna. "I wish someone like you could have been my mother."

There was nothing Johanna could say to that. If there was anything left of her heart, she might well have wept in gratitude at such words. But that wasn't her anymore. She no longer believed in the myth of love. The girl's warmth was no more than to ash in her ears.

Jane climbed out of the vehicle and ran to the front door of her house. Johanna remained there, eyes following the potential prey disappear behind the face of the house. She looked about the neighbourhood and even in the orange streetlight she still recognised it. Walking the pavements and tending the gardens, she saw the shadows of a time long since passed. She saw the faded imprint of a young Johanna Reinther taking an even younger Klaus Jungmann by the hand on his first day of school. All ghosts of a bygone age.

"*So,*" the voice said to her while she kept her eye on the residence, hoping to snatch a glimpse of its new colonists. *"Jane lives in your old family house…Who do you suppose then…is Jane's mother?"* On that note, she turned the ignition and drove away into the dark of the night.

No matter how far she drove however, that old house and that neighbourhood seemed to follow her. She'd sworn to return there one day, sworn to take back everything that was lost. But she'd more than made up for those losses now. Those were yesterday's grievances. The hates and desires of Johanna Reinther had died in a hotel room long ago. She was no longer a puppet to those feelings. That being said, it was a charming neighbourhood, full of nice people with nice V4 juices in their veins. Some other night she might drop by on her rounds. The idea was intriguing, exciting, titillating even to hunt amongst the ghosts of the past. All she needed was an inch to stand on to get the foot in.

And she knew where to find it.

The next day she approached her fellow manager, Theodor Hoffman. He and Johanna alone inhabited the lofty heights of the thirtieth floor of the see-through Metropole Building. Their completely see-through fishbowl offices stood opposite one another. Johanna had watched her counterpart's comings and goings with a keen and eager eye for some time, but only of late did she at last have a use for him. It had taken time, but eventually—like everyone—Johanna had found out what buttons would make his puppet dance. Silly slapstick comedy apparently was the crack in his armour. Theodor was older than her and had a certain silver fox flair to him. A real lady's man she could tell.

"So, what did you do?" asked Theodor, struggling to keep his giddiness in check as she recounted another ridiculous garden party story to him.

"Well, I put the ring down on Martha's chair while everyone was distracted, and she looked like a proper fool!" finished Johanna and Theodor nearly fell out of his chair in hysterics.

A knock came at the glass door to his office, interrupting his laughter. Right on time as expected, a woman stood there. Johanna needed no introductions to know who it was.

"Having fun, are we?" said Veronika, anxious to be part of the joke.

"Oh, Angelika was just telling me a story," explained a red-faced Theodor, getting up off his seat and picking up his keys. "Angelika this is my friend Veronika Kovac." Veronika gracefully held out her hand to Johanna.

"Lovely to meet you," greeted Veronika. "You know, I used to have a friend called Angelika."

"Maybe you will again soon," said Johanna with a suggestive smirk that immediately disarmed the doll-faced Veronika. "How do you know Theodor?"

"Oh!" hooted Veronika with a girlish flick of her golden hair and a sparkle in her eye for Theodor. "We were childhood sweethearts!"

"We go way back," said Theodor almost as a justification and he took Veronika by the arm. "Now we really should get going for lunch."

"Oh, don't fret Ted!" assured Veronika, saying it with such quickness that it was clearly a private saying she had with him. "They'd never dare overturn our reservation."

"See you again sometime," bade Johanna farewell with a shining bright smile.

"Yes! Would love to talk to you actually!" said Veronika with an identically bleached-white smile, the same plastic hollowness on her manicured face. "I've heard all about you! I'm such a big fan! We'd love to have you in our book club!"

"I will make a point of attending someday," promised Johanna. As the clearly adulterous lovebirds descended the thirty floors to the lobby in a glass elevator, she leaned over the railings for a moment and let her eyes haunt their steps. She'd only seen her from across the divide until now. This was the first time she'd actually spoken to *the* Veronika, the first time at least as Angelika Solovki. And apparently, Veronika was none the wiser. The crushing defeat she'd inflicted fifteen years ago on Johanna Reinther had been so complete that she'd even forgotten the face of the vanquished.

All to Johanna's advantage.

"Miss Solovki?" came a voice from reception through her earpiece. "There's someone here to meet you. A Mister…Drazen Bierut. He's a freelance reporter. He says he wants to interview you. Says it's important. I've told him this is a workplace and that he'd need a permit, but he won't leave. Do you want me to call security? I can—"

"No," rejected Johanna, curious to know what a reporter like Bierut wanted with her. An unscheduled interview, without an appointment? It was highly irregular. Something was up. Better to give him a bone to chew on than have him making false speculations about her. "Send him up. I'll meet him in my office."

"Yes Miss Solovki," acquiesced the receptionist.

Drazen Bierut was a man of middling years with an unimpressive physique. He was bald with a greying goatee cupping his chin. He wore a blue trench coat and a pair of thick-rimmed spectacles. He carried an old briefcase under his arm. His face seemed to be scrunched up in a permanent expression of distaste.

"Thank you for seeing me Miss Solovki," he said dryly with a grumpy twang in his voice.

"The pleasure is all mine," retorted Johanna as she gestured for him to take the seat in front of her desk. "It's not every day a tooth-and-nail journalist shows up on your door demanding an interview."

"You've heard of me?" responded Bierut, a little surprised. He took the seat opposite Johanna and rested his briefcase on his knees.

"I have. Don't see much of your reports anymore though I must say. Did the Weekly Jab lay you off?"

"More the other way around. Couldn't take the swine-shit any longer from the Varga bootlickers," he expounded, clearly not afraid to speak his mind on the status quo to her. "Too degrading spewing out the same propaganda every day. I've gone independent now, I have a blog on the internet where I can report on *real* stories."

"Good for you," commended Johanna before steadying herself at her desk and addressing him properly. "So, what story do you have for me today, Mister Bierut?"

"I've been approached by one of your employees in the claims department," he said seriously with a narrowing gaze. He straightened himself up in his seat, took out his tablet, and shot a cutting stare across at Johanna.

"Do tell," invited Johanna, even more eager now to know what he had to say.

"They were investigating the circumstances surrounding a Viral Claim made against an adolescent girl by the name of Katja Černý. Despite all efforts, your employee was somehow unable to track down this Katja Černý. It was as if she suddenly just vanished…into thin air as it were."

"So…you're here to report the misconduct of an employee to me?"

"No."

"No?" snapped Johanna authoritatively, sliding into her managerial character. "The employee in question disclosed sensitive and confidential information to you. If they encountered difficulties in their work, they should have contacted their supervisor, not some renegade journalist!"

"And there it is," commented Bierut wryly. "The cut-throat no-nonsense reality of the Insurance industry. A second ago you were welcoming me in and now…well now I'm practically subhuman for not obeying the rules of the game."

"The rules are the rules! I will need the name of the employee in question, Mister Bierut," insisted Johanna. "It is technically a violation of the Health Code if you refuse to cooperate."

"I will not be doing that Miss Solovki."

"Why not?"

"Because they gave this information to me on the sole condition that they remain anonymous."

Something wasn't right about this, Johanna realised. He wasn't trying to fill in blanks here. He didn't need her expertise. She leaned back in her chair and assessed him coolly.

"Why are you talking to *me* about this, specifically?" she asked icily. "What do you want?"

"The last place Katja Černý was seen," elaborated Bierut, his eyes quivering with accusation. "Was *your* residence Miss Solovki. And no one has seen her leave since then. In addition, your employee also uncovered a series of unexplained disappearances amongst patients the same age as Katja. All of whom, it might be added were last seen by witnesses outside *your* residence. Now do you understand why I am talking to you, specifically?"

Johanna gave no answer at all, not even a nervous gulp. She just sat there and looked at him, silently assessing him.

"What are you implying here exactly?" she asked openly. "What are you trying to say? What do you think is going on here?"

"I don't know yet. But I *do* know that you're involved somehow. I did a spot of research myself and was able to confirm your employee's findings. I still have my contacts on the streets and from what I've heard, it seems that *you*, Miss Solovki, have been living two very different and contradictory lives. While with one hand you extort criminal vaccine premiums out of decent people, with your other you're helping kids jump the Quarantine Walls without paying a penny. Now that tells me, Miss Solovki, that you know this whole insurance health code mumbo-jumbo to be a heap of swine-shit. You've been actively undermining your own work! And on that I can't fault you!"

"I'm a philanthropist at heart Mister Bierut," justified Johanna. "It is the duty of the rich to give back to the poor. I personally provide adolescent children from the lower wards with the opportunities they need to get ahead in life."

"On that, I can commend you," agreed Bierut. "But you see here's the thing. A similar operation is being run by Lidija Ivanevic who, like yourself, seems disillusioned with the whole damned system. But with her operation, I was able to see where her rescued kids have ended up. They've all moved onto better things. But, and Lidija herself told me she had noticed this about your operation, anyone whose appeared at your house just disappears. Not a trace of them. Now, that as you know is *impossible*. Nobody can vanish off the system. *Nobody!* So, for the sake of the child's mother, and for the sake of the claim your god forsaken company is levelling against her, can you tell me where Katja is?"

"She's moved on," answered Johanna with deliberate vagueness.

"Moved on? What the fuck does that mean?"

"Kids come and go Mister Bierut. I don't keep tabs on them once they've left. New ones arrive and I have to take care of them. I prefer not to mollycoddle them. They need to learn to stand up on their own two feet. Just as I did."

"As you did?"

"Yes. Haven't you heard of my—"

"Yes, I have Miss Solovki. Everyone has. We all know you're a model citizen. You're living proof that a person can rise through the Wards, that with enough can-do attitude and elbow grease you can overcome any and every obstacle the world throws at you. But you see here's the other thing, Miss Solovki, that's all completely *impossible* too. Thanks to your scandalous vaccine premiums, you and the Commission have guaranteed that everyone has just enough money to get by and no one has enough to save up for a higher vaccine dose. The poor stay poor and the rich stay rich. You, Miss Solovki, are a black sheep. You're an exception that proves the rule."

"Hold on now! How is any of this relevant to your inquiry?"

"How is it relevant? Because I think you're full of shit Miss Solovki! I think you've fooled everyone into thinking you're some kind of Angel when the truth is that you're a liar and a con artist."

"Quite an accusation to level at me Mister Bierut," calmly responded Johanna without breaking a sweat. "You sure you have some concrete proof to back any of this up?" The reporter barely heard her, he was on the warpath now and nothing could distract him.

"About sixteen years ago I was working for the Metropolitan News," he continued without providing any context as to why he'd jumped to another topic. "Back then, before the fire wall went up on the Borava, I was in contact with families on the North Side who still had loved ones here on our side. They would give me the details and then I'd track their relatives down and help establish a line of communication. One particular north-sider, a man called Franz Jungmann, contacted me about his brother and sister-in-law. They'd tried to make the crossing but got killed in the Exodus Massacre on Millennium Bridge. But there was more! He knew his brother had two children who were now orphaned and all alone on the South Side and he wanted to bring them over. There was his nephew, Klaus, and his step-niece, Johanna. I said I'd look for them but by the time I'd tracked them down, Klaus had died of cancer and the girl had gone up in smoke with the old Quarantine Hotel."

"What is your point? Why are you telling me this tragic little story?"

"Because I *never* forget a face," forcefully declared Bierut, pointing his finger at Johanna. He swiped his tablet screen and showed her a picture of her younger self. "Look familiar hmmm?"

"Oh please! This is getting ridiculous now! It happens all the time that people look the same! It's a coincidence! A fluke of genetics!"

"Is it? I did some more research into you—"

"I'm sure you did."

"There's no record of any Angelika Solovki prior to fifteen years ago. The airports have been shut for twenty years, so you couldn't have flown in from another country. That means you're from here, just like the rest of us. But somehow there's nothing to show you were here prior to fifteen years ago. There's also no record of a 'Solovki' family in this city or a family name even remotely similar to it. The only match of any kind I came across was for Angelika Salakova, a secretary for Commissioner Barodnik, who just so happens to have been a school friend of the aforementioned Johanna and who then died under mysterious circumstances from a gas explosion at her house—*also* fifteen years ago I might add! You appear, out of nowhere, just after the Quarantine Hotel burnt down *fifteen years ago!*"

"This is getting embarrassing," retorted Johanna, trying to brush it off. "You're starting to sound like one of those crackpot conspiracy theorists on the North Side. Connecting dots between things that have no relation to one another. Next, you'll be saying it rains whenever I wash my hair! Are the pyramids also aligned with these events? What are you even accusing me of here?"

"What am I accusing you of? You're clearly a fraud! An identity thief! And most likely a child trafficker too! That's what I'm accusing you of! This whole image of the hard-working executive is a lie! I don't know how you've done it or what you're doing with those missing kids, but I sure as hell know it can't be good. I *know* in my gut it can't." He winced with internal agitation and mournfully gazed out over the cityscape visible through Johanna's enormous window. "This whole city has gone rotten," he lamented, shaking his head. "There's a sickness coming up from within. In the lower wards, they talk about children just disappearing from their beds in the middle of the night. They all go around warning each other to 'Beware the Night'. I don't know what's going on. But I know something is dreadfully, dreadfully, wrong." He paused for a moment and looked back at Johanna with a scowl. "And I feel right now like I'm looking the sickness in the eye. That's the truth of it. You, Miss Solovki, represent everything that is wrong with this world! That's the truth being kept secret behind all the dumb lies everyone chooses to live within."

"Ahhh," exhaled the voice of the devilish one within her. *"He senses us...Feels us. He knows it's all lies. He knows it's all a mask. He knows it's all just a lick of paint covering up the shadows beneath. And he seeks the Truth. But he does not grasp what it is. He does not comprehend us."*

"Truth and lies," casually retorted Johanna. "That's more North Side talk. Are you going to tell me next that the Vaccine is fake? Or perhaps that the Commissioners are all secretly involved in a Satanic paedophile cult?"

"Not everyone on the North Side is a crackpot you know! There are decent people over there. A whole underground movement who strive for the truth just as I do! They want to bring Citizen R and his cronies down, but *you and your breed* would never see that! You only see 'primitives' and 'apes' when you look across the river and colour them all the same! All because it's convenient. Just like it convenient for everyone to see you as this saintly paragon of success! Everyone sees what they want to see! And it's all lies!"

"Okay," said Johanna, starting to tire of the journalist's venting. "What do you actually want from me Mister Bierut? Do you want me to admit to it, is that it? Admit that I'm a liar? A false idol?"

"I want you to come clean!" he demanded. "Tell everyone the truth! Tell everyone who you really are! Tell everyone that the system is rotten and that's why you're helping those kids! And for the love of Christ tell everyone what's become of those kids!" He stood up from his seat and put his tablet back in his briefcase. "If you don't, then I will have no choice but to bring my findings to the police. Once you're in an interrogation room you'll simply have to confess it all. One way or another Miss Solovki the truth is coming out. You have forty-eight hours." Johanna nodded to his proposal and smiled.

"Alright, fair enough then," she said getting up off her seat. "I will think it over."

"I mean it," he reiterated as she opened the door of her office for him. "If you're not back to me in two days, I'll spill the beans."

"Oh, I understand," said Johanna, walking side by side with him towards the elevator, the railing overlooking the thirty-floor drop to the lobby below standing parallel to them. "But tell me, just one thing, Mister Bierut. Why did you come to me with this?"

"Why! You ask that?" he erupted, almost offended by the question. "Any true journalist doesn't shy from holding the powerful to account. We are the fourth estate, Miss Solovki. We keep things in check. People deserve to know the truth about their leaders. Some might say those are bygone values from the old democratic days, that they have no place in a world of confidential calculations made by insurance underwriters that no ordinary person could ever understand, but I stand by the old ways! I'll stand by it to the day I die that people should know the truth! If something is being done in the shadows, people ought to know about it!"

"Yes, I understand all that Mister Bierut. But you appear to have misunderstood my question."

"Oh?" said Bierut with a confused frown.

"Yes. What I really asked was why did you come up here to me personally and tell me all this? Why not just go to the police directly? Why bother confronting me at all like this?"

"Well eh...much as I detest what you stand for, I do believe in the humanity of every individual and I do believe everyone should at least be afforded the agency to confess their sins of their own free will and—"

"You see I find it quite astonishing really," sharply interjected Johanna who had stopped walking, forcing Bierut to halt too and confront her with that dour cynical look again. "That you not only came to me like this but went so far as to impose an ultimatum upon me."

"You consider yourself above ultimatums? Some nerve you have!" fired Bierut, clearly unimpressed with her attitude. She bade no heed to his judgement. It meant nothing.

"What exactly did you think would happen to you, Mister Bierut, when you chose to threaten...*a cannibal child-rapist*?"

He almost laughed at first when she said it. Almost. But then it dawned on him. The stubborn irritableness which had characterised his every response to her earlier began to vaporise. After tolerating so much bullshit from her and so many others over the years, he could tell she wasn't lying. He could tell by the tone of her voice. The cold calmness in her face. The shock of ice in her eyes. His face went from blotches of pinkish red to an ill sheet of white. Words gurgled at the back of his mouth but failed to escape his lips. And a terror now gripped him as he stood barely a foot away from her.

"Wha-what?" he gasped incredulously, a glimmer of hope clearly discernible in him that it wasn't true, that he'd somehow misheard her.

"You wanted the truth, didn't you?" taunted Johanna with an unquenchable smile that brimmed with the horror of murder. "So, what's the matter then? Can't swallow it?"

He blinked wildly with fear behind his spectacles and a sizeable gulp went down his throat. With hurricane speed, Johanna gripped him at the crotch. A squeal came tumbling out of him and he dropped his briefcase. With her free hand, then she clasped his ear, pushed him against the railing, and with the application of a precise amount of force, lifted him up off the floor and sent him plummeting over the edge.

His screams fluttered in passing tatters of sound through the whole building as he fell thirty stories, his limbs flapping about uselessly as he nose-dived to his death. He struck the lobby floor with such force that his body exploded like a glass of water. Whips of his blood and gore splattered outward over the clean white tiles, a shattered leg went flying and struck a bystander in the face.

Anything and everything he ever was or ever might have been was now laid bare for anyone and everyone to see.

"Oh my god! Oh my god!" came the inconsolable screams from downstairs as Johanna idly went through his briefcase and snatched his tablet.

"Fucking hell! What happened?" came the voice of the receptionist through her earpiece.

"He had a heart attack and fell over the railings," calmly explained Johanna as she sat back down at her desk. "A tragic accident. Put it on the website that our thoughts and prayers go to his family."

"Eh…yes. Miss Solovki…yes…oh god," faded off the speechless receptionist as Johanna switched the earpiece off.

"Fuck!" snarled Johanna internally to herself. This wasn't part of the plan. She opened Bierut's tablet and went straight to his emails. Within seconds, she had the name of the treacherous agent from the claims department: Oleg Krivokuca. "Motherfucker!" she screeched between grated teeth.

She'd have to kill him. He knew too much. But then there was also the trouble with Lidija. She posed a threat. The threat of a good example. All her children could be traced, and Johanna's had been vaporised. That couldn't continue. It didn't look good. Bierut most likely spoke in depth to Lidija too. She needed to die. She was long overdue as it was already.

She typed in Lidija's name onto the Kodel Search Engine and swiftly located her insurance policy. With one simple click, she was able to see Lidija's date of birth, her address, her mobile number, her bank details, her vaccine-booster schedule, and the number of years she'd had without a claim. With another click, she had Oleg's policy and found out where his residence was.

Killing good, honest, tax-paying, patients, however, was not in the same league as killing vulnerable runaways. People would notice. Or more to the point, *people with clout,* would notice; vaccinators, landlords, tax collectors, employers. They'd come looking and start asking questions when Lidija and Oleg didn't show up to their next appointment. Their absence would be noted. It would be an infringement of the rules. And the rules had to be obeyed at all times. The rules were the rules. Too many eyebrows would be raised if she just vanished the two of them into thin air.

"You can't get away with it," the voice said to her. *"The breadcrumb trail will lead them to you. Bierut you've silenced, but who did he speak to? Who else*

did the snitch snitch to? The clock is ticking. They'll come looking for you Sooner or later. The game is up. The crack in your person-suit will keep widening till at last you can't conceal the Nobody beneath any further. The Angelika Solovki mask is due for expiration. It is an inevitability."

"Fuck!" she repeated scornfully. Once again, the walls were closing in around her. Escapeways were starting to shut for her. She'd rather die than be quarantined at Disinfection Hill. Never again.

Unlike before, however, she now had an available means of escape: she had a coin for the Ferryman. She could just bail out. Make a run for the North Side like her parents before her and put it all behind. Maybe even link up with her step-uncle, Franz and start over as.

But her thoughts of redemption and renewal were cut down in a flash as the presence of the other invaded her conscience and levelled its terms and conditions on her.

"*The Demon does not run,*" he said to her, eyes of toxic blue flexing in her sockets. "*A predator does not flee its prey. Not when the Cycle is incomplete. There is Karma still to be fulfilled. If leave you must, you will walk away, not run. You will walk because they will be too crushed and terrified to pursue you.*" Her skin flexed and crawled with his darkness. His hands swam over her bones and his teeth scraped at the back of her gums. They were of one body. One mind. One synthesis.

One Will to Self-Annihilate.

"*Damn them all,*" they cursed together in one hideous merging of their voices. "*Damn them! Damn them to the nothingness that awaits them all!*"

To the devil with their coddling and their censorship and their wallpaper! She'd played their fake games long enough! She'd had it with pretending! No more masks of normality! No more concealing the truth! She'd tear it all down! If they wanted the truth, they could have it! Let them taste the forbidden apples of Eden! Forever after they would be left bare and exposed and helpless in the clutches of the Demon! The safety of blissful ignorance would be undone! And they would know that no one, no matter how careful or cautious or healthy, was untouchable! They would know that every assurance of safety was a lie! *No one was safe!*

And though they might uncover it all through their own natural intuition for curiosity, it would be *she* who laid the bread crumb trail for them. *She* who would dictate the terms and conditions of the unveiling. *She* who would be in control. And when they reached the trail's end, they would know this to be true—that they were never in control.

The snitches would die first. But they weren't enough. To truly unveil the Demon, she needed something beyond the reasonability and comprehension of plain revenge. Something that could not simply be explained as a rational response that could then be weaved back into the Coddlers' narrative. She needed a victim whose total annihilation would leave so terrible a mark on their memory that it would stay with them into the afterlife. She scrolled through the email inbox relating to Vaccine Requests—the digital storehouse of sometimes desperate, sometimes plain cheeky, people who were trying to make the case for a higher vaccine dose. She scrolled past all the disrespectful whiners and complainers and halted on one of the charity requests. There it was. The name was Emil Bauer. An intellectually challenged schoolboy from Ward Three.

Magnificent. A prize specimen.

She picked up the phone.

"Director Burgenstein," she greeted on the phone. "It's Angelika here. How are you? Yes, I'm quite alright too. Nasty business with Bierut I know. I have a little suggestion for you to bring to the Commission."

Part VIII: Vengeance

It is the natural order that every question is met with an answer that is it's equal.
This is the tidal gravity of the Cosmos.
In the Orient, they have come to call it by the name of Karma.

Marius Zielenski, 'The Demon through the Eyes of Shiva', Journal of Oriental Studies, Vol. IX, Issue 4

Johanna was waiting in the upstairs bedroom when Lidija got home from work. She took a crowbar to her head before she could even turn her bedroom light on, stunning her enough to gag her mouth and bind her hands and legs together. Like all the ones before her, Lidija never saw it coming. The prey always assumed their home to be their castle and that nothing could ever touch them within those four walls. Nowhere was a sanctuary from the Great Demon though, because everywhere *was* the Great Demon.

"You have a faster turnover of kids than me," said Johanna as she got the wire ready to string the trophy up. A groggy-eyed Lidija stirred from her unconscious state. "I really must thank you for that. Elsewise I would have been waiting around for your house to be empty. Instead I could just stroll right in. I suppose you prefer it that way. With the quicker turnover I mean. Do they keep reminding you of Vasily? Is that why you send them on their way? Do you keep thinking of how old Vasily would be now? Where he could have been? What he might have become?"

Lidija's eyes burst into life. She struggled and writhed on the ground within her bonds. Muffled curses tried to make their way through the kitchen towel stuffed into her mouth.

"Sorry, can't hear you," apologised Johanna jokingly. She loved talking to them like this in their last moments. Reciting a monologue while they lay there muted and voiceless was more satisfying than any physical act of violence. It meant that her words were the last they would hear, she would dominate the narrative of their death, not they. Any ounce of agency or control they ever had to make their voice heard, to have a last say, was deprived from them.

She opened her toolkit and took a hammer and nail out. Lidija began to squirm even more as she saw what her assailant was preparing. "You know he called out for you at the end. 'Mamma! Mamma!' that's what he cried. And nobody came for him. Nobody stopped me. Just like no one will stop me now." She aimed the nail at Lidija's ankle and slammed the hammerhead against it. A crunch of punctured bone and cartridge rang out. Lidija convulsed in agony but no scream escaped her.

"You must have felt so empty all these long years," continued Johanna, sitting herself down on Lidija's stomach to hold her still. "Always searching for your little boy. Must have been tough for you, am I right? Everyone saying that he'd show up someday. That at worst he might have drowned in the Borava or be living with some other family. Must have been torture not knowing. Your imagination must have gone wild wondering how he somehow just vanished. But I'm sure you kept telling yourself, there was no way anyone killed him because 'Life is Precious' right? No one would ever dare lay a hand on him. I mean, he had a vaccine. That would have made him safe, wouldn't it?" She hammered the nail through again and again. Strangled sounds wheezed out of Lidija's mouth. Tears of both physical and emotional anguish came gushing from her eyes.

"Oh, don't be such a cry-baby!" teased Johanna as she weaved the wire through the holes in Lidija's ankles. "This is all just a routine procedure. Part of the nine to five slog. Same shit different day, am I right? Don't worry, I can assure you my papers are all in order for this. I'm just sorry it took so long to get to you. But, in my defence, I was very busy. And quite frankly you just weren't on my priority list. Paperwork takes time, right?" She snatched the opposite end of the wire and wrenched it with all her might. Lidija's puppet body twisted and turned with every tug of the string as Johanna hauled her up and up.

"But anyway, here I am now, fifteen years later with the news about your son," proceeded Johanna as she took up her knife. Lidija was now completely upside down and biting hard on the towel in her mouth to ease the pain. "So, here's the truth of it. I hung him upside down, just like this, I skinned him alive, and I butchered what was left." Lidija's eyes had widened to the point of popping out of their sockets. "I then drank his blood and cooked his flesh. I still use his skull to practice my kissing technique, French style you know? Hahaha. Every atom of his being, every hope you ever had for his future, I digested. He's still inside me now, recycled into the fibres of my hair and skin. *Would you like to know if he's still screaming inside me?*" Lidija's eyes thereat closed tight and she began to sob so hard that her whole body was shuddering with her grief.

"You may be asking yourself right now, why? Why did I do it? But the only question that confronted me at the time, truth be told, was *why not*? There is no Hell. And there is no future. The only thing that matters is here and now. Fifteen years ago, I plundered your son's dolly body. Yet not a day has passed for you has it? You've lived in the shadow of that moment ever since. *My shadow*. And now, the shadow comes to take you too. Right here *in the after*, just as Vasily was *in the before*, of that very same *here and now*!"

Lidija opened her eyes and scrunched up her face in defiance. A muzzled snarl came out of her and she rocked back and forth in a pointless bid to break free.

"Oh, how I've made you dance!" laughed Johanna. "Now let's see what happens when I press this button!" She sunk her knife into Lidija's abdomen. "And this button!" She stabbed her in the chest. "And pull this string!" She stabbed her through her elbow. A spasm of pain rocketed through Lidija and she wriggled wildly. "Hahahahaha! Oh, how you dance!" She skewered her again and again as she pleased. Once she'd had her fun, she got to the business of cutting the strings. She slit open Lidija's arteries and took a handsaw to her wrists, chopping right through her bone till the bound-together hands fell with a thud. With the life draining fast from the bounty, Johanna grabbed a bucket and lined the inside with a plastic bag to collect the prized vaccine blood.

Another successful night on the job!

Bar the hands, which she added to her private trophy collection, she left Lidija's corpse hanging there. She wanted it to be found. Wanted some innocent well-meaning fool to stumble over it and alert the authorities. Once the word was out, she'd sit and watch the puppets play to her tune.

Weeks went by though, and no one raised the alarm on Lidija. Perhaps nobody actually cared after all! Maybe she was in the clear! Nonetheless she held back. As a friend once said, 'patience sets you free'. She sat back, went to book club with Veronika Kovac and her sorority of mannequin house-wives, sipped on Lidija's red oil from her corporate water bottle, masturbated with Lidija's hacked off hands, and amused herself watching Oleg from a distance as he ran around in circles not knowing what to do or who to speak to. Sooner or later though he might crack and spill the beans to the authorities, and she couldn't have that. Not yet. The window of opportunity was closing. If things didn't unfold accordingly, then she'd have to make a pre-emptive strike.

But there was no need for that. The children of the city, once again, walked into her open jaws. The powder keg of frustration finally began to blow. Hanna and Eva came back telling of their repeated confrontations with the White Coats and Jane Kelvin egging them on to keep 'pushing back'. With the Health Code being flagrantly ignored and White Coats being given more trouble than they knew what to do with, the Commission took the bait as expected and gave Emil Bauer his vaccine to show they weren't so bad after all.

Immaculate timing. The Great Demon was on her side!

That very same night that little Emil received his charity injection, she finished Oleg off. She'd tracked his phone signal for weeks and knew exactly where to find him. She came in the dead of the night and broke into his house on Hospital Quay. He was such a nervous wreck that he hadn't even gone to bed. He bolted out the front door like a rabbit and ran and ran. She was stronger, faster, and fitter than he. But letting him take the lead was part of the fun. Every now and then she'd speed up to really terrify him and a new spurt of energy would flow through his veins. Only when she'd had her fun did she move in for the kill.

"I didn't tell anyone!" he yelped in a sweaty wheeze as she pounced on him. "Please! Please! Oh goahhhhhh!"

The next morning, she stood there amongst the concerned citizens of Isolation Avenue. She watched as the forensics tent was raised over the body, looked on as two police detectives, a young one and a middle-aged one, showed up and were predictably told to leave by the White Coats. The two detectives had a short argument, and then, to her own astonishment, went storming back into the forensics tent, and booted out the White Coats! What luck! The police had actually grown a pair and taken over the scene! They'd look into it properly and peel away the entire wallpaper on their own initiative! Better still, she overheard one of the Blue Shirts confirming a new scene at 56 Immunity Street. They'd uncover the two corpses on the one day!

As the two detectives sped away, Johanna got into her own car and drove down to Nurse's Street. She parked outside the school there and just waited and watched for Emil Bauer. She watched him sit alone while he ate his lunch. Some teachers tried to induce the other children to play with the new kid on the block, but he was too awkward and shy. He just sat there, alone with his stunted thoughts. From time to time, Johanna noticed his eyes following a schoolgirl around the playground with innocent longing lurking within him. He parted from the other children when the final bell rang and started his onerous trek home to Ward Three. Johanna cruised by next to him and wound down her window.

"Hey there, kiddie kiddie," she purred softly. "You ok?" He made no answer. Just put his head down, embarrassed by the attention, and kept walking. "You want a lift home? You're that kid from the TV, right? You've got a long walk home, don't you?" Still no response. "Would you like to talk to that girl from school?" *That* induced him to look at her.

"How…how do you," he tried to ask, his voice so slow it seemed like it caused him pain to even speak.

"I know everything," she said with a friendly smile. "I know how you could speak to her. Would you like to know how? I can show you. Come on! I can help you. I'm sure she likes you. And if she doesn't…well then, I can make her like you. I can make everyone like you forever and ever and ever. Everyone can know your name. Come on in. I have jellies. You like jellies, right?" The temptation was too compelling for the little boy and with a naive little click of the door handle, he got off the pavement, closed the car door behind him, and fell right into the chloroform cloth Johanna had waiting for him.

The next morning, she stuck what was left of Emil in the trunk of her car and set out to deposit him back at the school for all the children to see. On her way there, however, she found herself at the same junction she'd been at when she had dropped Jane home. For reasons she could not explain, a gut feeling impelled her to make a wrong turn and take a detour. She just got a good feeling about it.

"Angelika!" exclaimed Veronika as the door opened. "Come in! Come in!"

"Sorry, I know it's early, but I took the morning off and was in the area," explained Johanna as she followed Veronika through the hall into the kitchen.

"Oh, no need to explain, how did you know where I lived? Tea? Coffee?"

"Insurance database is a great way of finding people. And coffee please if that's alright."

"Coffee it is! Oh, it is good to see you! I was wondering actually if you'd like to be part of the Book Club committee. If you're interested of course! It goes without saying that you'd be greatly appreciated."

"I'd love to!"

"Marvellous! Here's your coffee!"

"I'm thinking of starting another charity myself actually. One for children. With all that stuff going on in the streets, I think the youth of today need real guidance."

"I couldn't agree more! It's shocking what's happening out there. What was your idea for the charity?"

"A vaccine scholarship for gifted children. I just got the idea from what they did the other day with Emil Bauer. I think it would be a good incentive for people to work harder and stop all this, well…whining haha!"

"How interesting! My daughter Justyna will be back shortly and I'd just love for her to meet you." Thereupon then a man suddenly emerged through the kitchen door and grabbed a banana from the fruit bowl. Johanna instantly recognised him as the elder detective from the day before. Was this another man Veronika was having on the side? "Why good morning darling. You slept like the dead! I wondered if you'd ever wake up. This is my new friend Angelika. Remember I told you about her the other night after you came in from work. She's new to our book club and involved in goodness knows how many charities."

"How do you do?" greeted Johanna courteously. Veronika's husband looked her over with that disoriented look which men have in the morning time. *If only he knew. If only he knew what she had in the trunk of her car right outside his own house.*

"Hi," he responded tersely before turning to his wife. "I have to go. See you later."

"Ta ta!" bade Johanna farewell before the front door shut.

"That's Vaclav for you," chuckled Veronika. "He's on a case at the moment. Has him all fired up and excited. He was even talking in his sleep about it last night. Something about a serial killer! Can you imagine?"

"How terribly interesting," responded Johanna. She sipped her coffee and thereat noticed the door frame. Thinly etched into the wood yet nonetheless visible beneath the layer of white paint was the name 'Klaus'. Not so far away from the etching, she spied photographs of Vaclav, Veronika, and Justyna—or Jane—altogether at some Christmas gathering. "Do you mind me asking, who is Klaus?" she asked, pointing to the door frame. Veronika turned and rolled her eyes to the heavens.

"Oh that! People always ask. It's from the previous owners. Unvaccinated vandals I'm afraid. Who else would feel the need to make etchings into a doorframe? You know how unhygienic those dirty people used to be! Vaclav and I moved in just before we got married and I had the whole place fumigated, gave it a new lick of paint, a full makeover. I had wanted new frames on the doors too, but Vaclav insisted on keeping them. I think he felt sorry for the previous owners somehow. Thought they were hard done by when in truth they were just, as you put it, whiners. Anyway, just a distant memory now, eh? All in the past! I prefer to ignore it," promptly wrapped up Veronika, clearly a little uncomfortable about the subject. "Would you like a top up for your coffee?"

"No no, this will do. I'd better get back to the office soon," said Johanna.

"Oh, of course. I imagine the insurance world is going crazy with all the riots going on!"

"It is rather busy. Some people are having real freak outs about it. They think their jobs are at stake. But truth be told Veronika, in the insurance industry one doesn't really make a living."

"Oh, how's that?"

"Well we don't make anything. We're not workers. We just take what other people have. We're parasites in suits and ties really. Financial vampires. We feed off people's fear. The fear that they might make mistakes. The fear of living as human beings. So, you see, we don't make a living, *we take a living.*"

"Oh… I suppose I'd never really thought of it that way. But I do know from Theodor that there are benefits the insurance industry gives to the economy. Don't you invest in—"

Johanna clenched the back of Veronika's head and slammed her face off the kitchen counter before she could finish her sentence. And just like that, without warning, without provocation, the Demon was in the driver seat again.

She hadn't intended on doing this. It wasn't part of the plan. But Vaclav. Vaclav. Vaclav. Oh Vaclav! The police detective who was now trying to chase her down, was also Veronika's husband, was also the kind soul who returned the family photographs to the now deceased Johanna Reinther. But both then and now, he was *too late.* She was eight steps ahead of him and he didn't even know it. What a note to leave on! And in *this house* no less! A family tomb for a family home! What better place to finish the cycle! It was too good an opportunity to pass up.

"Understand that this isn't personal Veronika," said Johanna as she stood over her quarry. "It's just business. It's what I do for a living. *I take what others make.*"

"Wha-wha-who...who are..." mumbled Veronika from her busted lip, cogs turning wildly inside her head as she tried to understand why she was under attack like this. Then, whatever way Johanna looked down at her, the penny dropped for Veronika. Finally, she saw what she had refused to see for so long. "*You*...oh my god. Oh my god! How? No! You're dead!"

"I was quite different in my first life," said Johanna as she stood over the concussed Veronika. "And it was quite a while ago. You could be forgiven for that. That is the thing about a nobody. You can never recognise them. Until, of course, it's too late." She delivered a sharp kick to Veronika's jaw and knocked a tooth out, sending it skipping along the sterilised kitchen tiles.

"Wha-what do you want?" choked Veronika, blood leaking down her manicured face. "We have money. I can get it for you. Just don't hurt me. Just don't hurt me. Anything at all. Just tell me what you wan-want."

"Nothing," answered Johanna who then got down on her hunkers, gripped Veronika's left arm and bent it backwards across her knee. "And everything." She applied pressure and snapped the arm at the elbow. Before Veronika could even let out a yell, Johanna was unloading a salvo of punches to her face. Well-hardened from hammering at hotel walls, her fists pummelled Veronika's mannequin facade as though thrashing a cardboard mask. Veronika's face was so thoroughly battered by the time she was finished that she gagged her with a kitchen towel without any trouble at all.

"Veronika!" came an adolescent voice from the front door. Johanna hid herself behind a corner. "Veronika! Where's Dad? Hanna and Eva just got arrested and—" Justyna stopped dead in her tracks as she saw her mother lying battered on the floor. "Oh my god!" she cried, running forward. "What happen—" Johanna spun around the corner and smashed the base of a coffee mug into her forehead. The girl was taken clean off her feet.

Mother and daughter! And Vaclav nowhere to be seen! What luck! No one would stop her!

The universe was smiling on her today! The hour of the Demon was truly at hand!

"What's the matter little Veronika?" taunted Johanna as she strung the two Kovac women up in the front hall. "Aren't you glad you spent your last days paying bills? Aren't you glad you spent your whole life nodding your head and agreeing with other people just so they'd like you? Aren't you glad you didn't marry the man of your childhood dreams and instead hitched with a policeman just to please your peers? Aren't you glad your daughter idolises me and hates you?" She picked up a carving knife and sauntered towards the two Kovac women. "Funny, isn't it? Everybody dies, but barely anyone lives. They live somebody else's life and then come to the end of the line realising it was all a waste. You were never really alive you see. Only a conforming member of an undead herd. And when you die, you'll be replaced by someone who is equally as undead as you. Why look around at your glorious castle? You could spend your whole life making something! Building something! A legacy! A future! And then one day you just realise it was all for nothing because just like that *I* can take it all away from you!"

She raised the knife and in a sweeping arc of psychopathy brought it slicing down into Justyna's vagina. Both mother and daughter instantly began struggling within their bonds, shaking their heads and throwing their shoulders and hips from side to side. But nothing could stop it. Johanna struck again. And again. And again, till she felt the blade scraping on the tail-end of Justyna's spine. Trickles of yelps and screams came whispering through the gagging implements. But no one could hear them. No one could save them.

For all things in need of saving…were already doomed to die.

"You see! Voila!" cried Johanna with a spark of the dramatic. *"There* is the future. A little tweak of violence and just like that! Bang! Gone! Destroyed! All of your plans and dreams turned to ash!" Justyna's bladder opened in that moment and urine came pissing through the open wounds, overtaking the thicker rivers of blood and dripping into the girl's nose and eyes. "Would you look at that?" laughed Johanna while Justyna shuddered from the trickle of her own urine in her nose. Johanna twisted her tongue to mimic an automated voice from an advertisement. "This edition of barbie girl has a urinary function hahahaha!" She combed her fingers through Veronika's golden hair and clasped her by her scalp. With a pull and a tug, she wrenched the mother's head over to her daughter's and smothered their broken faces into one another. "Go on! Kiss! Kiss! Just like my dollies used to! Go on! You know you want to! A doll always does as its master says!"

She let go of them and stood back for a second—to really take in the full view. Justyna was crying uncontrollably. Veronika was trembling and shivering all over, her bruised and busted face suffocated in both her own and her daughter's blood. A pool of red had gathered beneath their heads.

"Right," said Johanna conclusively. "As I said earlier, I do have other things to do today so please excuse the early departure. Afraid I can never mix pleasure with business for too long, so, without further ado." With mechanical, bureaucratic, efficiency she slit both their throats open and let them bleed out. In conjunction with the task at hand, she dipped her fingers into their puddle of blood and painted the words *"Too Late"* up on the wall for Vaclav.

She left the house in her own time and at her own leisure. Not a soul in sight paying any attention to her whatsoever. She was about to get back in the car when a wonderful thought struck her. She opened the trunk of the car, plucked up the pen knife she kept in the back, and made a few 'adjustments' to the horror show of Emil's body.

"There!" she said in triumph. "Perfection! It'll be a hundred years before they sleep soundly in their beds after this! So long! Farewell! Auf wiedersehen! And goodbye!" Down on the patch of infantile skin, her bloody inscription spoke back to her:

Ta ta, detective

Part IX: Reminiscence

As they lived and laughed by day,
So they wept and howled by night.
For, to those joys they once had revelled in,
And those sufferings that had once terrorised them,
They were shackled in perpetuity.

The Ferryman, 'Sonnets from the River Borava', page 16

The city was awash with fright as it plummeted into lockdown. Every screen and billboard flickered with warnings about an 'invisible' and 'nameless' terror. Establishments were closing down. Supermarkets were carnivals of confusion filled with desperate hands groping at loaves of bread and toilet paper. It was 2020 all over again. There was a degree of karma in all this to be sure: after so many years of people wanting Johanna to be locked up, she was now the cause of everyone else being locked up. Johanna smirked at the thought of it as she stood waiting at the dock with her luggage by her side, a coin in her hand.

The terror was at hand, her work was done. The Demon's hunger was satisfied. She could move on now with her life. Get a fresh start and put it all behind her. Just as it was when she had escaped the Hotel, so it was again now. She was a nobody who could be anybody. She could link up with Uncle Franz. Help with his business or perhaps start a business of her own. Endless possibilities yawned before her.

She just needed to cross the river.

He came from upstream. No search light on his vessel. A gentle chug of the engine and no more. His 'ferry' was a small and unassuming steamer with a column of smoke billowing from its chimney. Save for that, it was completely inconspicuous, so much so that had it not been so close to shore it would have evaded the naked eye completely. The dark colour of the hull matched the murkiness of the Borava. And even the chugs of the engine were easily drowned out by the chorus of urban voices on either side of the river.

The Ferryman brought his river ship about by the dock and without any bargain or exchange, Johanna stepped aboard. With that, he brought the steamer around and began the secret voyage across the Borava. Johanna sat herself down. She looked ahead and only ahead to the looming tower blocks of the northern shore.

The man in her company was wearing a long double-breasted coat of dark leather. He had a thick beard of fiery red and a set of clear grey eyes that were faintly illuminated in the pale glow of the city lights of both shores. His skin had a rough and weathered texture. He sat there in a composed and tranquil state by the rudder of his steamer, not a word escaping him till out of nowhere he held out his hand to Johanna.

"Coin," he demanded coarsely. She placed the circle of metal in his outstretched palm and he slotted it into a jar he kept by his side. "Good," he said, his voice as rough as his skin. "No coin, no crossing. A passenger with no coin is no passenger."

"Is that so?" asked Johanna with rhetorical coolness.

"Ask the skulls under the water and you'll know all about it. Toss me a coin or I toss you over. That's how it works."

"Good for you," said Johanna, finding herself automatically disliking him for the self-righteous tone in his voice. He clearly thought himself her equal or, somehow, her superior. "Some amount of blood you must have on your hands then Ferryman."

"No less than you."

"You don't know anything about me," she fired back defensively.

"It's my business to know," he contended. "Have to know who I'm likely to be carrying. And tonight, there's only one person I know of who'd want to bail from Vaccine City. You're the Shadow on the wall. The one who comes in the night. I've known about you for a long time." His voice writhed of a sudden into that of a bard and he recited to her thusly: "*When the Shadow comes to play, everyone runs away. This be our rhyme, foretold before your time.*"

"I'm retired," said Johanna. She had nothing to hide from this riverman. He already knew what she was anyway. There was no point denying it. "That's all behind me now. I'm starting fresh in the North. Going out to pasture. That person you think I was, is dead."

"No one's ever retired," warned the Ferryman. "There's no happy solution to all your woes. Everything that is just is. No way of anyone getting a clean slate. Not really. That's why a man needs a code to live by, a reliable rock to stand on. Elsewise he doesn't live at all."

"And how exactly do you live?" she asked with a bitter taste on her tongue. "Far as I knew, river traffic was shut down years ago. How the fuck are you still on the go?" He took his eyes off their course and gave her a knowing look.

"Someday, maybe, you'll understand how it all works," he answered vaguely. She rolled her eyes in annoyance at him. "You must be one of Zielenski's," he said after another moment of silence. That made her turn towards him. It had been a while since she'd heard that name. "Been a while since I plucked anyone from that dock. Only his kind ever used it. That of course, and that scent of blood and madness you could only get off Mad Marius. You wreak of his touch."

"You know him?" she asked, a thread of respect now in her voice.

"Like my own face," he said. "I knew him in the before and in the after and in the here and in the now. Knew him back when he had the soul of a gentle poet. He was a good man back then, and a good friend."

"That doesn't sound like the Zielenski I know," said Johanna, unable to reconcile her memories with this description.

"It isn't. That was before the Pandemic. Before the madness. Before his revelations."

"What happened?" she asked, at once curious to know of her mentor's obscure origins.

"We went on a road trip," started the Ferryman as he lit a cigarette while he recounted the tale. "The three of us set out in a Ford Mustang and drove across Europe. The ninth wave had just finished. Empty motorways. Empty fields. Empty towns and villages. We went through whole cities where everyone and everything was dead. We listened to music, and tripped out on LSD, looking at all the skulls and bodies through our labyrinthine eyes." He took another drag of his cigarette. "Then on our way home we stopped in this forgotten town. There was one man alive in the whole place. One man. No one else. Marius nicknamed him the 'Omega Man'. We found the rest of the town piled up in a heap next to the Cathedral. But that night, just as lonesome Omega Man went to bed, the whole place came to life. There was music and dancing and laughing and drinking in the streets. The empty square was all full of people. But as we talked to the townsfolk, we found ourselves having conversations we'd already had with the Omega Man. Then we realised they weren't really alive at all. When the Omega Man went to sleep, his spirit had left his body. He had splintered apart a hundred times and possessed all the heaped-up corpses of the dead. They were all fragments of his spirit. Disparate pieces of his self that were being tyrannised by one greater self. He was a puppeteer of the soul, a necromancer, one of the *Malandanti* as the Italians would say."

"That didn't really happen though," rationalised Johanna with deliberate cynicism. "You said yourself you were all tripping out." The Ferryman shrugged.

"Whether it happened or not is unimportant. The experience is all that counted. Do you think you'd be the same if you saw something like that? *That* was when Marius snapped. You don't come back from that the same as you were before." He took another puff of his cigarette and surveyed both sides of the river. "I think we've all been traumatised in our own way by the Pandemic. All gone a little funny in the head. Nobody is the same. Maybe that's why this whole city of ours is so irretrievably fucked. Can you imagine how many ghosts the Pandemic has left behind across the globe? Leaving not just haunted houses, but *haunted cities*. We saw enough dead cities on that trip to know it. I wonder sometimes if any of us are alive at all. Or perhaps it's just us three still alive, watching all you ghosts, killing each other, over and over and over again."

"You could go further," added Johanna. "I'd say we're all on a Ghost Planet. And why stop there? What if the whole Universe out there is haunted? Entire systems and galaxies filled with nothing but dead things and dead memories."

"That was Marius' conclusion," finished the Ferryman, confirming in his mind that she was one of his old friend's pupils. "After the encounter with the necromancer, he was left with the nagging question that perhaps everywhere was like that little town. That we were all dead things, possessed by some sleeping deity having an out-of-body-experience. He came to believe this had been the case, not just since the Pandemic, but since the very inception of everything. All human history was just the story of ghosts driving themselves deeper and deeper into the Circles of Hell."

"Do you believe it too?" asked Johanna, curious to know if he believed in the Great Demon as she did.

"I don't believe, I just know," he answered with a shrug. "I know we're all trapped." He pointed ahead to their destination as they came close to the northern quays. "You may think I'm taking you from A to B. You may think you're starting a new life. You may think the past is dead. But the future, as you should know, is what's really dead…You'll soon find I've just taken you to a different side of the same coin." Johanna got up off her seat and slung her bag over her shoulder as the steamer slowed down and came to a halt. She stepped out onto the rotting edifice of the northern dock. The ship began to pull away. "I'll see you in the after. You'll see," he prophesised serenely.

"Just one thing," she said before he vanished out of earshot. "You said there were three of you on the trip. There was you and Marius. Who was the *third* man?" He chuckled wryly.

"You'll see him for yourself," said the Ferryman as his ship floated backwards into obscurity. "If you find yourself in need of refuge, zaychik, go Underground. Zielenski haunts this place no less than the vaccinated country you came from."

Part X: Virulence

It is with the dashing Sword of Conquest that the Spirit has marched across the Globe, guiding Mankind to its penultimate Manifest Destiny.

Ulrich von Sauken, 'On the Dialectic of the Great Spirit', page 54

"I'm looking for a Franz Jungmann, do you know anyone by that name?" asked Johanna.

"There's no time for questions," Yang dismissed curtly as he escorted her down the corridor, the distant echo of the *'I Love You'* song from Barney the Dinosaur playing faintly in the background. "Just listen to me and everything shall go accordingly for you. You are most fortunate that you were located by the relevant authorities. If you had lingered much longer on the quays, then the tentacles of the World Octopus might well have dragged you back to the South Side."

"Yes," responded Johanna awkwardly, unsure if that last bit was a joke or not. "So, once I'm on the system then can I—"

"Hush!" he hissed. "The rules are that you must listen to me! No questions! The rules are the rules." She was starting to dislike him now, starting to feel an old and familiar frustration from her days with Julius bubble up inside her. Bar his Asian heritage, he reminded her quite a bit of her vaccine case worker. He wore a pair of aviator spectacles and a suit of bright red. His black hair was as precisely cropped as Julius'. By the cut of him, he was about twenty years of age. "You must count yourself fortunate to be here. This is an island of paradise surrounded by a sea of darkness controlled by the lies of the Cabal. You should be grateful that we have let you in at all."

"I am."

"You should be! In the old days we used to open fire on birds that flew across from the South Side! We don't do that anymore. But you can never be too careful! You'll need to be stripped and hosed down once you're registered."

"Why?" asked Johanna, disregarding the rule on questions.

"Why? Because there could be robotic fleas or head lice on you, specially designed to infiltrate our community and spy on our children! We'll have no oglers here! This is a sanctuary from the tyranny of paedophilia! We thank you for your defection from them, of course, but we cannot trust you entirely you understand. After all, where were you twenty years ago when we overthrew the Puppeteers hmmm? Regardless of whether you are a spy or not we cannot ignore that you have been a complicit bystander to the paedophile monstrosities committed by the Cabal. We cannot trust you."

"Then how can I convince you that I'm trustworthy?"

"By not asking any further questions for a start!" he fumed with clenched eyebrows. "People who ask questions are the most suspicious of all! Only strict and uncompromising obedience to the rules can prove to the High Council that you are a reliable and consistent member of our wholesome community." They turned a corner and came to a door. He placed the flat of his thumb down on a scanner which brought up his profile picture and face.

"*Esteemed Wizard, Yang Xu, welcome back,*" came the unliving voice of the computer system as the door opened. They proceeded through the digital gateway and entered an enormous office space fitted with hundreds of desks occupied by servile workers. Up on the walls hung huge television screens, some displaying scoreboards while others presented what appeared to be the news feed of some kind of social media platform.

"This is where you'll be working!" proclaimed Yang, sweeping his arm outward over his horde of workers. "Working to earn our trust! Where you are from the people must obey the dictates of the bureaucrats! Bureaucrats who are clearly in the secret payroll of the Puppeteers! But not here! Here we do not have civil servants! We have *civil slaves*! They are slaves to the will of the people!" He pointed to the televised board. "Behold here the will of the people on the Platform! It shall be your duty to interpret every statement and comment they post and to translate it into policy. If you make five hundred correct translations, then we shall procure you with a lump sum payment of bio-currency and send you on your merry way! Until then we alone will provide bed and board to you. Your cell will be stripped of furnishings, thereby removing any distractions that would otherwise interfere with the re-education sessions you will be undergoing between work shifts. We will also install a tracking device on your person in the unlikely event that you decide to break our trust and run away." He stopped walking and faced her with stern formality. "I understand you may scorn the tracker, having had a vaccine tracker on you for so long, but it is entirely necessary I'm afraid. Especially, when you are doing your mandatory community service. What community service you might be thinking? During your time you will be required to partake in a bimonthly community event wherein a placard will be slung around your neck identifying you as a paedophile sex-offender. School children will then be brought out to pelt you with stones and kick you as they please. Like a pinata! It's terrific fun!"

"But I'm not a paedophile," she protested, only realising after she had said it that she was lying. "I've never hurt a child in my life."

"Yes, yes, I understand you think that. But we can't be too careful. Hence the tracker. We couldn't have you running about loose in our city like the boogiemen across the river!"

"What boogiemen?" she asked, now wondering if they knew about the lockdown on the South Side.

"The child-molesting doctors of course!" explained Yang as though it were the most obvious answer in the world. "Now if you please, this way to my office!"

Johanna looked out across the expanse of desks spread out before her. The vast majority of the civil slaves were migrants and defectors like herself, though they had come from much farther reaches than from across the river. Regardless of their origins though, each and all of them looked equally miserable trawling through pages upon pages of digital shouts, slurs, rants, and insults. They had as much chance of getting out of here as she and her hallmates had at the Quarantine Hotel.

The doors of opportunity were shut to all who walked into this place.

"A lot of immigrants I see," she mentioned as Yang closed the door to his office behind him.

"Yes, many people across the globe seek the freedom we have here," he said with pride. "But we can't just let anyone in. Our democracy would be destroyed if so many strangers suddenly went online on our Platform and began voicing their untrustworthy opinions. Many former citizens end up here too. They ran out of R-marks and couldn't pay their rent. We provide them with bed and board they couldn't afford themselves. It's a perfect system."

"So, it seems," said Johanna as she sat down in front of him. He pushed a pen and paper over to her.

"Now if you would please just fill out your details for our records, I can then send you to the sanitation team for hosing," instructed Yang. "Please fill out every section truthfully. We'll have no lies of the Cabal here!"

Johanna did not read the paperwork put before her. She just thought about what she had been told and what she had seen.

She hadn't come over here to be made a slave of. She had already gone through this swine-shit before. She was here for a fresh start. A clean slate. She hoped to open a new gym with Uncle Franz perhaps or help him with his business. If she put pen to paper, then she would never leave this place.

"You know," she said as amiably as possible. "I actually used to run a business of my own over on the South Side. Is there any chance I could—"

"Business owner! Pah!" interjected Yang, spitting down on his own carpet. "All the more reason for you to be here! It was you merchant dogs that facilitated and aided the work of the Cabal! It was you and your independent greed and desire that distracted the human race from the truth of the Cabal!"

"Okay, okay," she responded with hands raised to try and calm him. "I was also a manager though for an insurance company. Surely those skills could be transferred here to a higher position and—"

"Worse again! Insolent woman!" he thundered, slapping the table in anger. "Mind controllers and liars! You and your globalist network of so-called commerce and finance! All a fabricated cover story so you could breed more servile children to perform fellatio for your Puppeteer Masters! You must atone for your sins! Four community service sessions a month for you! And eight during the summer holidays!"

Johanna fell silent. It had been worth a shot at least. But there were no loopholes here. At least, with Julius the Commission had been in the process of shutting the windows of opportunity to her. Here though, the windows were already shut tight. She had come too late. There was no way out of here once she went into the system.

There would be no fresh start here. Whatever plans she had had of going out to pasture were as null and void as her plans to find a loving partner and settle down with children. There was no point holding onto them. Whatever hope of redemption the North Side had offered, was nothing more than a mirage. She took her eyes away from the paperwork and stared across the desk at Yang Xu.

Dark and shadowy hands began to swim inside her head.

"Please," he insisted, gesturing to the paperwork. "Complete the form."

"No," she said, her heartbeat slowing to a steady pace as she eyed him. That single utterance seemed to hit him like a sledgehammer. His oval eyes widened in disbelief.

"But. but you have to," he fired back. "Those are the rules! And the rules say that—"

"Your rules don't exist," she declared, baleful eyes of Prussian blue sliming behind her pupils.

"How dare you interject me! I am an Esteemed Wizard of the Purified Council of—"

"They exist no more than the imaginary friend you had as a child. You just made it all up to make life a little easier. There are no rules. Only illusions."

"What? What are you talking about?" he roared at her, his face beetroot red with rage. *"The rules are the rules!"* She smiled at his short-fuse temper. He reminded her of an autistic boy she had tortured with mere words to the point of suicide.

"I don't believe in your rules, you're living in a dream world!" she laughed in mockery. In a storm of rage, he swiped all his accessories off his desk. She wondered if Julius would have acted the same if she'd ever refused him. Probably not. Yang would only have been a child when she was negotiating with Julius and apparently had remained a child ever since. It seemed that what 'save the children' *actually* meant was 'preserve and pickle the children'.

"YOU HAVE TO SIGN! YOU HAVE TO SIGN! YOU HAVE TO SIGN!" he yelled at the top of his lungs over and over again, his skin crawling all over with frustration.

"Alright calm down, I'll sign," she acquiesced suddenly, picking up the pen.

"Oh, thank god, thank god," he said panting as he clutched his heaving chest. "That makes me happy. That makes me so happy. Very very happy. You can't do that again though. The rules are really very important. They're very important!"

"I'm sorry I can't fill this out."

"Why not?" he exploded again.

"Well you see here on section one it asks if I've ever been a sex offender, child trafficker, paedophile, or a murderer. And then there's this box here for 'none of the above'. But there's—"

"That's the one you need to tick! 'None of the above'. That's what everyone ticks. It's the right one!"

"No, no. What I was going to say Yang, is there's none for '*all of the above*'."

"What? But why would you..." Yang's words trailed off as he caught a glance at the smile Johanna was casting at him. She rose from her seat with pen still in hand. His face went from red to white in seconds.

"You have no option for *cannibal* or *necrophile* either," she advised further, moving away from the desk, advanced on him in a tide of concentrated genocide. He backed up against the wall of the office, his hands shaking all over, tears welling in his eyes. "And I have to be truthful, don't I? No lies. You said so yourself. *Those are the rules.*"

"No! No!" he yelped, his entire body squirming in discomfort. "You're lying! You're lying!" He closed his eyes and began praying to himself. "It's just a story! Just a story! You said it was a story, Muqin! You said it was just a story! You're not real!" Johanna cupped his cheek in her hand and a wave of shudders rippled over him. He opened his brown eyes to her.

"That's right little Yang," she said in a cartoonishly motherly voice. "That's right. It's all just a story. Your *whole life was just a story*. And this...this is the only part that was ever real." She clasped the side of his head in her free hand and with her other she rammed the point of the pen into his ear. His whole body jumped off the ground and his lips parted into an instantaneous wail. He thrashed about wildly, his arms flailing about and his legs buckling beneath him. Once inside the canal of his ear, she twisted and turned the pen around and drove it deeper into his eardrum. "Look how you dance little Yang!" she cackled. "Look how you dance for Mother Death!"

"AHHHHHHH! P-P-P-PLEEAAAASE! ST-ST-ST-STOPPPPP!" he wailed for mercy while his living corpse went into spasm on the floor.

But she just laughed. And laughed. And laughed.

Tormented to deafness, he lay there shivering, his mouth opening and closing like a goldfish, his eyes wide open with shock. The smile of the Universe brimmed from her face as she leered over him. Her hands slipped into the invisible gloves of the reaper that had loomed above him since the day of his birth as she bent over him and bit down on his throat as hard as possible. With a tear and a pull, she ripped his neck open and swallowed down his 'wizard' blood.

Red oil dripped from her chin as she strode out of the office and marched past the desk slaves. So self-absorbed and miserable were they that not one of them even raised an eyebrow to her. She reached the maximum-security door and pressed her thumb to the scanner.

"Esteemed Wizard, Yang Xu, thank you for your service," chimed the digital voice like clockwork. The door opened before her and as before, so again she walked out into the world.

"Looks like we're back in business," the Demon snarled from within.

Part XI: Decadence

It is in times of peace that opulence takes hold, and a new Age of Heroes is needed more than ever to restore the natural balance.

Ulrich von Sauken, 'On the Dialectic of the Great Spirit', page 241

"Stop that! Stop! Stop!" angrily yelled the handcuffed woman at Johanna. "Take your hands off my daughter! Take your hands off her! Stop doing that! Stop! Stop! Don't you touch her there! Don't you. Don't you. WHAT THE FUCK! WHAT THE FUCK ARE YOU DOING TO HER! IN THE NAME OF-! WHAT THE FUCK! WHAT THE FUCK! WHAT THE FUCK! OH MY GOD! OH MY GOD! OH MY GA-GA-GA-GA-GO-GO-O-OD! NOOOOOOOAHHHHHH!" Johanna pulled away from the infant and let the baby's body roll off her lap with a thud. The butt of the broken wine bottle slipped from Johanna's fingers and clunked to the floor.

The mother sat in a pile of emptiness on the apartment floor, her maternal instinct at last eclipsed by total despair. So overcome with grief was she that words could no longer even be mustered. A potent numbing silence could be seen on the edges of her eyes. Johanna circled her as a shark would its bounty.

"Have you ever considered the horror of photography, dearest Helena?" she asked unconcernedly, as if the two of them were having a chat with a cup of coffee.

Saliva trembled from Helena's lips and tears drooled from her eyes. She sat there in a frozen condition, staring into the cold dead eyes of her infant daughter. Johanna stood up and picked a framed photograph of the young family off the mantlepiece. Encased within the frame was a tired but smiling Helena in bed with the new-born daughter in her arms. Johanna took the photograph out of the frame and sat down on the floor opposite Helena.

"P-p-put that back," demanded the petrified Helena, still not taking her eyes away from her daughter. "PUT IT BACK!" she suddenly screeched before another wave of sobs broke out of her.

"Photographs are taken," said Johanna, beginning her well-memorised monologue. "They're not made. They're *taken*. It's an act of conquest. You kidnap a moment when you take a picture…The moment is kidnapped and entombed…forever. Whatever way you were feeling, whatever false face you had on, whatever way you looked, it's all mummified and ossified for all eternity in that moment. People who are dead and gone from this earth now have snapshots of their existence frozen and encased so that generations to come might gawk and stare at them as they would an animal in a zoo." She glanced at the happy family picture and then showed it back to Helena. "I'm sure you thought your happiness would last forever when you froze this moment." Helena's shoulders began heaving with grief as she dared to look at the mirror-image of her younger happier self. Johanna scrunched the photograph up in her hands and then tore it in half. "Apparently not. Now, your mummified face from the past serves only to mock you with its so-called happiness."

"Why…Why…" trailed off Helena, unable to form a full sentence.

"We've come a long way since the first photographs though, haven't we?" proceeded Johanna. "Motion picture, virtual reality, social media profiles. All designed to freeze reality. Have you ever considered how many dead people lie frozen on Google Maps? Frame by frame you can watch the digitised souls of the dead walk among the living. Trapped! Forever! What horror! And now, thanks to the kind and generous technology offered by our very own High Council, we have digitised bio-currency. Those R-Marks in your veins record every feeling, every emotion, every reaction, every mood that you've ever been in. They've *taken* your entire sensory experience, everything that makes you a person. Some might even say it records the trappings of your soul." She cuddled in closer to Helena, raping the woman's personal space, and whispered to her with timeless malice. "When I drink you dry, I'll swallow this experience. Your digitised soul will be mummified forever in eternal pain. Every day hence from now, you'll be weeping inside me. You'll be in this room watching this happen over, and over, and over again, *forever…*" A fresh wave of shivering trembled over the heart-shattered Helena. "Oh, don't look so glum!" She slapped Helena across her shuddering face. "Stop your crying you miserable sow!" Slapped her again. "Don't you want to live forever? Don't you want to live forever? Don't you want to live forever!"

"Just fucking kill me-e-e-e! Just get it over with! I can't. I can't...I can't," she cried pathetically, shaking her head. "I can't go on. Ivana... please... Ivana...please..."

"Well...there's the truth of it, isn't it? Everlasting life is a nightmare you can never wake up from because, you see, *there is no future*. There is only the here and the now. And *this* is the here and the now you'd live in, *forever*. But here's the thing, here's the thing sweetest Helena. You needn't worry. Not at all. Death will be your salvation. *I* will be your deliverer, your liberator, your saviour. I'll send you on your merry way into the next Cycle. You can let go of all this. Be free of all your appetites for love and fulfilment. Be free of all this pain. Be free of the thousand years of sorrow you'd experience for the rest of your life. But I'll still be taking *my fee*. One does not cross the River Styx for free my dear! A piece of you, of this moment, will live on inside me...with your infant daughter...*forever*. And so, your soul will be torn in half as it transcends into its next life, caught between the spokes of the wheels. *You'll wake up screaming in your next life*. And though you'll have no memory of this, you'll know, *you'll know*, that something dear was *taken* from you. And you'll never know exactly what it is that makes you feel so lost and empty. You'll spend the next cycle, and the one after it, searching for a piece of yourself that can never be yours again."

Helena had nothing more to say. Her head just bowed forward in abject defeat. Silent tears dripped from her eyelashes. Johanna took that as her cue to wrap up. She slit her throat open with a razor blade. With the succulent passion of a lover then, she suckled on the lips of the wound she'd inflicted and guzzled on her blood and tears.

When she had had her fill, she retracted her tongue from of Helena's throat wound and wiped clean her own mouth with the back of her sleeve. She walked out into the corridor and subconsciously counted all the doors she'd already broken through. A man came out of the elevator and saw her approaching. A fear beyond fear ensnared him.

"The Black Dragon," he gasped to himself as he tottered backwards. Johanna kept on advancing as if he wasn't even there, as though she was going to walk right through him. "The Black. Dragon." he uttered in a whisper of existential terror. He turned on his heel and jumped through the window overlooking the street below, sending him plummeting to his death.

Johanna just got in the elevator and pressed the button for the basement. She'd seen it all before. People committing suicide at the mere sight of her was nothing new. Just another day on the job. Without any further thoughts on her bloody enterprise, she returned to the tunnels of the Underground through the gap she'd hammered into the basement wall. From there, she weaved her way under the city, through abandoned sewers and subway stations and into secret speakeasies and art galleries, till finally she returned to Block A.

Night descended on the city as she ascended to her premium apartment on the top floor of the tower block. She took a shower and made herself presentable for fashionable company, applying the same old myriad of lotions and creams to conceal the scars of long ago. An hour later and she was sitting pretty at the foot of a dining table. Ornate plates of the finest china and cutlery of the best silver decorated the table. Three golden chandeliers hung above them. Buckets of champagne were passed about and clumsily emptied into an array of cups, jugs, mugs, and glasses. Front and centre of the table was a dead orangutan, hollowed out and stuffed with fruits and nuts and cheeses for guests to pick at, its ginger hair made sticky with honey to lick at one's leisure.

Sharing this extravagant banquet with her were her fellow socialites and aristocrats, the cream of northern society. To her right was Myklos Nagy, a well-known Platform personality who had thousands of followers and who was dressed in a costume straight from Versailles—one he'd no doubt looted from the wardrobe of an abandoned film set. To Johanna's left then was Myklos' wife Natasha. Like her husband, she too was a prominent 'Platformer' with thousands of gullible believers waiting for her next status update. Johanna thought little of her. She looked like a manufactured whore, the type one might find in a waiting room magazine. Her bosom and lips had all been inflated with Botox and silicon. Her artificial blonde hair looked about as lively as the hairs of the lifeless orangutan on the table.

Down from them was the notable tower governor and Orphan Celebrity, Conrad Friedrichs, dressed in his usual attire of dazzling crimson, and his wife Helga who was a delicate twig of a thing. Not unlike the bionic Natasha sitting next to her, Helga too had an air of the unnatural. By virtue, no doubt, of some hideous hormonal surgery she had undone the process of puberty and restored her girlish looks. The result being that she looked like a flat-chested overgrown schoolgirl. At the head of the table then, directly opposite Johanna, was the only guest which she had not met prior to tonight—Captain Ulrich von Sauken. The leader of the Red Troopers had come at the invitation of Conrad Friedrichs and seemed a little out of place in their lavish company. Johanna could not help but notice the same subtle display of scorn and disapproval that she herself felt at the appearance of these human peacocks.

"Quite a remarkable specimen, isn't he?" boasted the eccentric Myklos of the orangutan centrepiece. "I acquired him off a private zoo owner who'd fallen on hard times and I just knew he'd be perfect for this dinner party! After I strangled and stuffed him with goodies of course! I always did love monkeys as a child!"

"You've outdone yourself Myklos!" shouted the tipsy Natasha, spilling champagne from her coffee mug, a loose bra strap hanging down the side of her left shoulder. She pulled out a phone, snapped a dozen shots of the grotesque piece of macabre art, and then was sucked into the Platform world of posts, comments, and status updates while she shovelled mouthfuls of food through her fishy Botox lips.

"It's a testimony to our age of peace and prosperity," said Helga with a wholesome smile, picking at her food as a little songbird might. "That we might dine so handsomely as we do."

"Long may it last!" shouted Myklos, rising from his seat with drink in hand. "Long live Citizen R!"

"Long live Citizen R!" they all toasted together.

"You must have smuggled this through the international blockade," suggested Johanna as she observed the piece of lobster flesh on her fork, the taste of her last human victims still fresh on her tongue even after many glasses of champagne. Myklos smiled and wagged his finger at her.

"When one has connections Ivana, the blockade is of no concern! Isn't that right Conrad? Eh? Isn't that right?" Conrad grinned boisterously while he cut up his steak.

"What can I say? Exceptions can always be made!" he said confidently. "Especially for the very best of friends and the very best of company!" Everyone laughed and toasted and drank once again. "Fate willing," continued Conrad more seriously as he carved another section of his steak. "The blockade will soon be ended, and exceptions can be made for all citizens." He pointed across at his wife with his fork. "Feast your eyes on my sweet wife my friends. With the help of a wonderful physician, we were able to subvert her aging process, undo the werewolfery of puberty, and restore the wonder of infantile innocence!"

"It has always been a grey area," said Myklos. "Puberty I mean. Teenagers kissing one another. Is it a sign of paedophilia or not? Always puzzled me. We're better off without that kind of uncertainty. The less complications the better."

"Quite right!" agreed Conrad. "Once circumstances are suitable, we can make this available to all citizens. Everyone will be doing it with their sons and daughters! The very possibility of sexual perversion will be banished forever!"

"Tell me Conrad," said Johanna, eager to make the tower governor dance. "Was it a doctor you sought the help of for this…miracle procedure?"

"Good heavens no!" exclaimed a disgusted Helga in her squeaky voice. "I would never let some vile creature of the Cabal lay his hands on me! The man who came to us was an exile, a whistle-blower, an anti-vaccine hero!"

"Quite right my love! Quite right!" drunkenly bellowed Conrad.

"But Conrad, tell me," proceeded Johanna teasingly. "Do you still fuck your wife? Because, if you do and you've made a child out of her, wouldn't that make you a paedo—"

"Absolutely not!" roared a furious Conrad. "I am an Orphan of the Great Awakening. I have devoted my life to the extermination of those wicked creatures."

"There are no paedophiles north of the river," calmly informed von Sauken, laying down his knife and fork and sitting back in his chair. Of a sudden his presence was felt among all the guests and silence fell upon the room. "Not anymore. When we stormed the city council buildings, we got full access to the public records. We knew in a matter of days where every known and suspected sex offender and paedophile in the city was. We tracked them down, rounded them up, and lined them up against a brick wall. Then we all took out our AKs and mowed them down in front of everyone."

"I remember that," quietly added Conrad, looking up to the Captain with big puppy eyes. "You spotted me in the crowd and gave me a handgun. I was just seven, but I knew what I was and what *they* were. I remember how good it felt to pull the trigger and shoot the monster dead in the head." He returned his attention to his dinner plate. "Evil. Pure evil. That's what I saw that day. Thanks to those executions the days where paedophiles and child-molesters ran our world are over. We've nothing to fear."

"I don't know Conrad," said Johanna as she confidently chewed on some meat. "I mean, *I'm a paedophile.* I've raped and butchered children, sometimes right in front of their parents. Sometimes I've even fed pieces of the children to the parents. You sure you don't have anything to fear?"

Silence.

All eyes were frozen on her. Even the phone-addicted Natasha was looking at her in stunned astonishment.

After what felt like several minutes, the palpable tension finally burst open. Conrad exploded into fits of laughter, and everyone followed in his wake…everyone bar Captain von Sauken. "Can you imagine?" guffawed Myklos, clutching his stomach in pain from the extent of his cachinnating.

"A paedophile on this side of the river!" wailed Natasha, tears of laughter trickling down her waxen face.

"Why would they even come here?" asked Conrad rhetorically, slapping the table with the flat of his hand. "To die maybe? To put themselves out of their own misery!"

"That's a good one Ivana," commended Helga trying to break her fit of giggles. "You're a real hoot! We should have you around more often. You're so funny!"

The evening dragged on thereafter for some hours. More servings of exotic food. More drink. More lude and vulgar jokes. More drink still. More laughing. Johanna went around and gave free dream interpretations to them, each and all of them proceeding to post her predictions on their Platform profiles. At the end, the Captain alone remained for her to dream-read.

"I would like a private session with the oneiromancer," he declared coolly. "My dreams are not intended for public knowledge."

"Ooooohhhh," teased Myklos jokingly. "Spooky Sauken! What dirty secrets does the Captain have?" The Captain gave no response to the Platformer's jest. He just cast a knowing look at Conrad and the Tower Governor obeyed at once.

"Come on everyone," said the Governor. "We'll move into the other room and put some music on." That was enough to get chairs scraping on floorboards and bodies tottering across the room to the doorway. Conrad shut the doors behind him and the voice of Gene Wilder singing 'Pure Imagination' began to tumble from a set of speakers.

"You may fool them, Frau Nazinskaya," started the Captain, his eyes regarding her in a distant and ghostly manner. "But you don't fool me." Johanna smirked.

"I don't?"

"No. You don't fool me. *I see you.* I see you well and clear."

"I fool no one," she countered, leaning back in her chair and gazing at him across the now crumpled carcass of the orangutan. "It is *they* who fool themselves. You are merely alone amongst the blind, Captain." He chuckled lightly and wagged his finger.

"How right you are," he said in good humour before cooling down again. "In a world of lies, neither they nor anyone else in this city knows what is real and what is fictional anymore. They live within some blurred misty realm. Picking and choosing only what they wish to see. They look upon this extravaganza of food and think this to be the universal truth. They read the rallying cries of hell-raisers on the Platform and think that victory over the Cabal is nigh. But they do not see the suicides, the heroin addicts, the rust, the rot, the decay. And they do not see *you*... You who are the devil that feeds off this collapsing dream world."

Johanna regarded the smile on his face. It was not he who smiled. But *something else* lurking within him that smiled through his movie star face. He *saw* her, she knew. *He* was the *third man*. The old travelling companion of Zielenski and the Ferryman. And he knew exactly what she was. To deny him was useless. She had left the habit of hiding behind her on the South Side at any rate, but she was sitting before an equal here. And truth was the only currency among equals.

"I'm the devil before you," she freely admitted, the eyes of the Demon twisting in her sockets.

"I thought so," he said, looking her over to confirm his suspicions.

"From the looks you've been giving me all night, I'd say you've known for some time about the *Black Dragon* of C Block," teased Johanna. "Do tell! I always enjoy a good detective story! Tell me how you found me, and I can compare you to the last man who tracked me down! See how you stand up to him!" He chuckled again and then sighed as he recounted the tale in his head before telling it.

"Some years back," he began. "A man tried to assassinate me. He held me responsible for the death of his brother and sister-in-law who perished trying to cross the Millennium Bridge. He said I was no saviour of children for in so firing on the caravan of refugees I had made orphans out of his niece and nephew who lay marooned and forgotten on the South Side." *He's the one,* she realised. *He's the one that killed them. He's the reason for everything!* "The man's name was Franz Jungmann," he continued. "And, as many had before, he failed to slay me.

I took his head before he had the privilege." He rooted through his pockets and tossed a crumpled photograph down the dining table to her. "Look familiar?" She plucked up the photographic tomb and stared at the half-recognisable face in it.

"He had this on him?" she asked casually. The Captain nodded. She rolled her eyes to the heavens. "Fuck sake," she muttered beneath her breath as she eyed the awkward pose of a twenty-something-year-old Johanna Reinther. The girl in the picture was so pitifully weak. So woefully unaware of the sufferings and challenges yet to beset her. She thought she had killed that helpless girl. Had flushed her down the toilet. Had cut her up and mutilated her.

But somehow, *somehow,* she just kept on creeping back to her in frozen snapshots of another life, back to haunt and mock her.

"I thought nothing more of it at the time, other than I had deprived two children of their parents," admitted von Sauken. "But, then about three years ago an alert came in from one of our Civil Slave Centres. An Esteemed Wizard called Yang Xu was found dead in his office with his throat ripped out and his eardrums ruptured. We killed a dozen slaves at random as a precaution, but I knew the killer wasn't amongst them. Whoever it was, had disappeared without a trace. One of the men I executed said it was a woman who had defected from the South Side. A few weeks later I saw a woman walking down the street who was the spitting image of the person in *that* same photograph I found on Herr Jungmann. But, no one of course wanted to hear any of it, because that would mean that the killer had bypassed our security system and had now infiltrated our city without detection. It would mean that a covert agent was in our midst."

"Saboteurs are always talked about here. We curse them for every little difficulty that befalls us in life. But at the end of the day we do so in the safe knowledge that there are no saboteurs and there are no paedophiles…just like there are no goblins or unicorns. They exist only in stories and fairy tales. Monsters from crueller and more savage times that have since come and gone. They are fixtures of the abstract alone. Like the Cabal. People believe in it, but they've never physically seen it, and so the subconscious assumption is that, maybe, it doesn't really exist."

"But you already know all this of course. You've been taking advantage of it for years now. I've stood underneath C Block some nights and listened to the screams. I'm always amazed that no one ever runs to the rescue. No one ever considers that unspeakable acts of terror are taking place because that would be impossible. They write it off as just an especially bad domestic argument or some lunatic losing his mind on mushroom spores. When the tower governor first contacted me and showed me your first victims, they were all gagged at the mouth. But you don't do that anymore. There's no need. You don't silence them because *you know* that no one is going to stop you. And no one is going to stop you because they don't believe you even exist."

"But you do," said Johanna having held her silence so the Captain could tell his tale.

"I have *always* believed in your existence," declared the Captain. "I knew from the first drop of blood that the Great Demon was among us. *That* is who you are. Isn't it? Whoever you are, it isn't the Ivana Nazinskaya label you wear. You're a nobody. That's the truth of it. A ghost in the flesh. Everything and nothing. The Demon."

"Ivana *was* a somebody," confessed Johanna carelessly. "A somebody who was treated as a nobody. I found her squatting in my uncle's empty apartment. She told me she was the discarded follower of the Indian love guru, Harbinder Anand. She'd come here seeking a new Summer of Love and all she got was digital hatred. There was no love for little Ivana. Nobody wanted a hippy girl preaching free sex and love to sweet innocent children. So, nobody cared if she just disappeared and reappeared with a new face…making forecasts for the future."

"Your oneiromancer business is small game," said von Sauken with a touch of admiration. "I'll bet you've made a fortune drinking people's life savings out of their veins. Leaves me wondering how many family fortunes you've swallowed whole to get where you are now?"

"More than either of us can count," she answered truthfully, not entirely sure how many lifetimes' worth of bio-currency she'd gulped down. "Your investigation is all very impressive. But I must ask Captain; you've known about me all this time. You've known what I was doing. You've known that I was most likely a relation of your would-be assassin. You've known that you killed my parents. Why haven't you stopped me? Why haven't you saved your city? Saved yourself even before I turned on you? Why hold off?" Von Sauken looked away from her, embarrassed not so much by the question she had put to him but by something closer to heart beyond her sight.

"This place had so much promise when I came here first," he elaborated in poetic poise. "We were building a New Jerusalem here. A New Eden where mankind could be reborn. Now look at it." He gestured towards the obscene carcass of the orangutan. "Lies laid over lies laid over lies. Contradictions within contradictions. All stifling and suffocating each other. The High Council has failed to deliver. It has strayed from the righteous path. This place is now slowly decomposing. And it is within this decomposition, invisible to the eyes of the masses, that you lurk. If I killed you, no one would even notice. Only when all the complications are burned away, and the bare simple truth is laid clear again. Only when the mob sees you and knows you to be real, can I give battle to you. Only when the monster's presence is revealed can a hero rise to face it."

"And you believe yourself to be this hero? You who cut down hundreds of people with an anti-aircraft gun? You're no less a monster than I."

"We are alike you and I," he conceded. "Two sides of the same coin. As you are a disciple of the Great Demon, so I am a disciple of the Great Spirit. All history has been a war between our two cosmic tribes of Heaven and Hell. Everything that has ever existed has been a war between the thesis and antithesis and their eventual fusion into the synthesis. This is the law of progress we are all bound to and it is the duty of the Great Spirit to guide this war in the right direction. While you may kill for the sake of profit and pleasure, I kill only in the name of Spiritual Evolution."

"Then you are no less deluded than the mindless sheep you scorn. There is no progress. There is no guiding hand. There is no one at the steering wheel. There is only the anarchic Suicide Cycle of the Great Demon."

"Spoken like the true heir of Zielenski. But as the Demon pulses through you, so the Spirit pulses through me. When I killed your parents and all their fellow companions, I heard its voice and I knew I was one of the Great Men of history destined to usher in a new era. And behold! The bridge remains sundered to this day on account of my actions! Our two worlds of north and south remain in unending conflict with one another just as the Demon and Spirit do."

"And so, what? You seek to do battle with me now? Make war upon the Demon and usher in another era?"

"If the Spirit wills it so. But you jump to conclusions too early mein Liebchen. A duel is not my intention. The ultimate goal of the Spirit is synthesis—the fusion of contradictions to bring about a new era. What I am proposing—"

"Careful where you thread Captain," forewarned Johanna. "The last man who gave me a proposition met an unwelcome ending."

"I am no more a man than you are a woman mein Liebchen. We two are one of a tiny cadre of souls on this earth who are truly awake. We are alive. It is the rest of the world that is dead! I saw it in the town of the Omega Man! You have seen it too no doubt in every murder you have committed! The masses are but monkeys and puppets! We few are the rightful rulers of the earth! If we were only to stand together against the masses of the unliving we could bring about a new age of Spirit Kings. A true Golden Age. You and I, Demon and Angel, could form this new synthesis…A New World Order."

"And if I refuse your proposal? What then?" she challenged.

"I publish my conclusions about you on the Platform and let the mob butcher you. I would rather it not come to that. There is opportunity here for both of us mein Liebchen. We can both be free."

"Okay," accepted Johanna pensively. "Keep talking. What's your pitch?" A palpable relief washed over the Captain at her acquiescence. He had bet his whole destiny on this gamble she could tell.

"Good. Good. Then I shall tell you of my plans. I have discovered a catalyst for our synthesis in this very city. A person you might describe as a Spirit Walker. Conrad uncovered her to me earlier today. She is, alas, a member of the treacherous dissenter movement it appears. But we can woo her to our divine will. Day and night, she communes with her dead parents, speaking to them as though they were living. All we need do is move her into position and we can build a new bridge between Life and Death, North and South, Spirit and Demon. It lies within our reach! Together we can rule this earth and raise the dead to escape the relentless march of time and decay! Escape the cycle! The door lies open before us! We need only snatch the opportunity!" At that he calmed down somewhat and gained his breath. Johanna sat there waiting for him to spill the details to her. "Her name," he said. "Is Amelia Svoboda."

"Svoboda," thought Johanna to herself with a malefic smirk. *"That rings a bell."*

Part XII: Violence

Nothing makes the world turn on its axel quite like violence. It is pointed bullets, not pointed speeches, that are the Spiritual Engines of History.

Memoirs of Ulrich Von Sauken, Chap 4, 'Nurturing the Iron Fist', page 105.

An eyeless Amelia slumped forward with her own thumbs firmly planted inside her head. Johanna strode over to the pristine kitchen counter and picked up the glass of wine the girl had prepared for herself. She wandered back to the couch then and put her feet up while Amelia's penniless blood slowly oozed across the floor.

All too easy.

The very next day after the dinner party at Conrad's, the dissenters had, of a sudden taken to the streets calling for reforms and a change of societal management. Amidst the frustrated herd of angry little sheep, von Sauken's 'golden child' Amelia had stood out like a sore thumb to Johanna. The dissenter had been the spitting image of her South Side cousin, Justyna Kovac. There was even a faint resemblance to Veronika. For that reason alone, Johanna could have picked her out of a crowd. She was a magnet for her violent desires.

But there was more.

The girl was *mad!* Stark raving mad! As Johanna had weaved through the crowd, she had observed Amelia engaging in full conversations with her own shadows. Multiple personalities had been scrambling for control of her consciousness at any given moment. At times, she walked and even ran about with her eyes closed. She was not so much a Spirit Walker as she was a sleepwalker. With her circle of dissenter 'friends' all being helpfully anonymous, invading her social circle and winning over the 'trust' of this sleepwalker was a walk in the park for Johanna.

The Captain had wanted the girl alive. He had instructed her to bring Amelia to him. Then acting together as vessels of the Spirit and the Demon he had planned for them to harness her 'power' and interact with the souls of the dead. In so doing, he hoped to undo the Cycle of Death and thereby bring about the end of the established order—somehow.

It was all a little too far-fetched for Johanna. Even if his necromancer scheme was remotely possible, speaking to and raising the dead was the last thing she wanted. The dead were dead. And the Past too, was dead. As there was no future, so too there was no past. There was no progress. No order. No reason to anything. There was only the chaotic lusts and hungers of the Great Demon. Von Sauken was a fool for thinking otherwise. And a greater fool still for believing she would play to his tune at his threat of revealing her activities to the public. Such a grand and scandalous unveiling would strike much greater fear in the cretinous public than in Johanna. She had made no efforts at all to conceal the truth since she had emigrated to the North Side. She no longer valued her life enough to care if a mob came and skewered her with pitchforks. If he wished to declare her existence to the world, so be it.

To have said that to his face at the dinner party though when he made his proposal to her would have spoiled the fun. It was better sport to lead him along and let him indulge in his illusory fantasies of grandeur. Better sport still to terrorise and manipulate the deranged Amelia to the point where she clawed her own psyche in half and killed herself into the next Cycle. Relation or not to the purulent Veronika, Johanna derived the highest satisfaction from hunting and traumatising the hapless girl with such impunity—especially given that Captain von Sauken was under the delusion that his threat of retribution would prevent her from doing such a thing.

Wallowing in her victory, Johanna was still sipping from Amelia's glass of wine when a notification came through on a mobile device. *Amelia's mobile.* Johanna picked it up off the coffee table and clicked on the red flashing notice popping up on the screen. It was from the High Council itself:

"INFILTRATION! SABOTAGE! FAMILIES BUTCHERED! CHILDREN DEFILED! BEHOLD THE WORK OF THE CABAL'S EVIL AGENT LIVING IN OUR MIDST! THE BLACK DRAGON WALKS AMONG US! OPERATION HYSTERIUM NOW IN EFFECT! PERMISSION GRANTED TO USE DEADLY FORCE! ALL

SUSPICIOUS AND SUBVERSIVE BEHAVIOUR MUST BE CRUSHED! #Savethechildren, #AllHailCitizenR"

A single scroll of her thumb and Johanna was met with gory images of the work she'd done on C Block over the previous three years.

She gazed back at Amelia and then took a second look at the penthouse she was standing in. Why else would the dissenter be living in a place like this? Just across the hall from her own apartment no less? The girl had brought her horrors to the Platform, and now the Platform would unleash its horrors on the cities. She peered out the window to the plaza below.

"THE DEVILS ARE INSIDE THE WALLS!" she heard a voice cry aloud in the night sky. Gunshots started to go off. Wails and cries went up. The strum of breaking doors cracked in the air. Curses and accusations were howled and bellowed. Pleas for mercy fell on deaf ears. People were thrown off balconies and out of windows. Mobs of ruffians swarmed around defenceless loners and beat them to a bloody pulp.

"*Cycle's over,*" the inner voice said to her. "*These pigs are back to purging just like the southern sheep got back to locking down. If they fire enough bullets, one of them is bound to find you. Your work is done. They know the Demon is among them. They know their sense of security was a falsehood. Let them marinate in their fear. Time for you to move on. Greener hunting grounds await.*"

She quickly double-checked her pocket. The Ferry coin was there. She'd taken it with her just in case Von Sauken had made good on his threat. She was good to go. She calmly walked over to the kitchen, picked out two knives, left the apartment, walked down the corridor, and with the press of a button summoned the elevator to her. Moment by moment it brought her lower and lower. As it came to its natural rickety halt at the ground floor, she heard the ring of metal mixed with the cries of the maimed and the dying.

"Lying fuck!" she heard a woman scream. "Liar! Catholic scum! I knew you had international connections to the World Octopus! You're the Black Dragon!"

"Franziska please! We've been neighbours for years! I haven't done anythaahhhhhhhhhh!"

The elevator doors opened.

The lobby lights were flickering as they always were.

A vengeful mob of paranoiacs were heckling and hissing while the saggy-faced fifty-year-old woman bashed and battered her defenceless neighbour. They were too absorbed in their vengeance to notice the elevator's arrival. Too busy to see her standing there. Too busy to see the knives in her hands. Too busy to see the smile of Death's Delight blooming across her face. Too busy to take any heed whatsoever of the lust and hunger glowing behind her eyes.

They were the same sheep. The same dumb animals. The same self-obsessed vessels of systemic neglect she knew so well. Creatures of the herd and the flock and the mass and the swarm and the horde.

Only weak animals congregate together.

"What are you looking at?" abruptly questioned the same abusive middle-aged woman. Stimulated by their herd elder, the rest of the human animals now turned to the elevator with accusing eyes.

"I'm watching the Muppet Show!" answered Johanna, her eyes glued open in madness. "And you must be the star of tonight's entertainment, Miss Piggy! Hahahahahahaha!"

"What!" retorted the woman, now taking steps towards her, twisting a baseball bat in her right hand. The others followed behind her as expected. Johanna only giggled a little more. "What did you just call me!"

"I say it as it is, I say it how it stands," said the smiling Johanna, tightening the grip on her knives. "And I'm here to eat you and your little piglets, bone by bone. Just like I'll devour and go doggy-style on the skeletons of your grandchildren hahahahaha!" A man pushed out in front and strode up to Johanna with a crowbar in his hand.

"The fuck are you saying? You think you can talk to my wife like that?" he barked at her, his face red with indignation. "You hippy piece of shit! You dare talk about eating children at a time like this? What kind of psycho are you?" Johanna stepped forward. And forward. And forward. She stood close to him. Automatic discomfort rippled over him and he edged backwards momentarily before standing up to her in manly bravado. "You don't talk like that! Not ever!" he snarled at her. "Not to anybody!"

"No more lies, little boy," she whispered seductively to him, the tip of her nose almost rubbing off his. "No more."

"Step away from my husband you fucking whore!" screeched Franziska at her. Johanna's eyes scanned over the rabble one last time under the on-again off-again flickering lights. She stared directly into the man's dumb simple pitiful eyes.

"Now," she hissed, demonic tongues lapping at the insides of her cheeks. *"Nightmares shall be at Feast among the children!"* She rammed both knives up into his groin, lacerating through his testicles. She slid them out and drove them back in again and again and again. His red anger turned to pale fear. His roar turned to a scream. The crowbar clattered out of his hands. His tense knuckles went limp and numb.

She left him in a shocked and sobbing mess of his own blood and seed on the floor. Others came running through the curling shafts of light with weapons in hand. She weaved and darted and ducked and dived by them, cutting and slicing and tearing through each of them in a roaring dance of unstoppable violence. Under the wilting lights she vanished in and out of existence. Their curses turned to ash in their mouths. Their rage rotted into dread. Their dread then burned into horror. Silenced screams came squealing up from the pit of their guts.

And like the herd animals they were, they took fright and began to run for the exit.

"This little piggie went to the market!" she sang into the face of another victim. She pounced on an overconfident teenage boy amongst them and slit his throat. "This little piggie should have stayed home!" She slid across the floor and slashed across the ankles of an obese lump of a woman. "This little piggie ate too much beef!" She caught sight of Franziska fleeing the scene, her mouth open in terror as she rushed for the exit on all fours. Johanna slammed the knives into the back of her knees and dragged the blades down over her calves. She grabbed her ankles then, wrenched her backwards, screaming and howling, and turned her over.

"Oh my god! Oh my god! Please! Please! I don't want to die!" begged the pathetic creature. Leering down into her eyes, Johanna slid the knife into Franziska's open gob.

"And this little piggie," she finished, her voice mixing with that of the Dark One. *"Well, this little piggie went all the way to Hell! Hahahahaha!"* Johanna punched the blade downwards till it punctured the back of the skull.

"Now they see you," said the voice in the dark of her skull as she rose from the petrified corpse of the hive-creature. *"Now they see what you are. Now they are enlightened."*

She exited the apartment and block and beheld the anarchic purge in all its glory. The whole plaza was a riot of everyone against everyone. Judy Garland's *'Somewhere over the Rainbow'* crowed from giant-sized speakers as families and communities imploded into madness. At the killing of each victim, the perpetrator proclaimed their holy justifications to the night sky, invoking their right to purge them from the earth.

"SHE EXPERIENCED SEXUAL PLEASURE FROM BREASTFEEDING HER BABY! SHE'S THE BLACK DRAGON!" they yelled. "THIS WOMAN SMILED AT MY SON! SHE'S THE BLACK DRAGON! I CAUGHT THIS MAN IN THE GIRLS' BATHROOM WHEN HE WAS FIVE YEARS OLD! HE'S THE BLACK DRAGON! THIS MAN HAD A PRIVATE CONVERSATION WITH MY DAUGHTER! HE'S THE BLACK DRAGON! LONG LIVE CITIZEN R!"

Johanna wound her way through the sea of violence, killing any that dared get in her way. Step by step though she widened the distance between herself and them and as she walked through the overgrown lawns of Martyr's Park, the mass hysteria and violence faded away behind her, the violence being concentrated almost entirely amongst the tower blocks. As she cleared the treeline, the waters of the Borava and the city lights of the vaccinated southern shore beckoned to her.

She was back where she had landed over three years ago.

"Going somewhere?" a familiar voice questioned from behind her. She turned and saw a cloaked figure emerge from the shadows, an AK-47 smoking at the barrel couched in his arms.

"Captain," courteously greeted Johanna, wiping a spot of blood from the corner of her eye. "So nice for you to see me off." Von Sauken stepped into the light to reveal that he too was dripping in the blood of others.

"I'll see you off into the next Cycle!" he growled, raising the gun to her. "You killed her! She was our ticket out of all this rot and decay! And you killed her! I didn't want this! We could have achieved great things together! I gave you the chance to escape with me! But instead, you elected for there to be war between us!" He pulled the trigger. Having died in her mind so many times before, Johanna barely flinched. But all she heard was the click. He looked at his weapon, pulled again. Click. He took the magazine out and reached for another at his waist.

Idiot.

Johanna flung her knives at him one after another. The first pinned him in the shoulder, the second in his left knee cap. He dropped his rifle and fell to the ground snarling from his wounds.

"Seems like the Spirit lost this round," she derided.

"Damn you!" he spat as he tentatively gripped the handle sticking out of his shoulder. "Come on then! If you won't join me then kill me! Finish me off!" Johanna didn't move. She just stood there and looked at him slowly pulling the blade out of his body and letting it clang to the ground. "Come on! Send me to the next Cycle! Let the Spirit be reborn!" Still nothing. "Come on! I'm here! Kill me! It's what you want! Isn't it? I killed your uncle! I killed your parents! I'm the reason your life went to shit! I'm the reason you are what you are! Kill me!"

"No," whispered Johanna, staring down her parents' murderer, lying there bested and defeated before her.

"No?" he spat. "What do you mean no? You've beaten me! Finish it! This is the tidal gravity of the Universe! Do—"

"It's like you said," she interjected him. "*You* destroyed my family. Everything I am today I am because of *you*. Without you, all those children, both north and south, all those families, both north and south, would still be alive and well…Their blood is on *your* hands. All because the Great Spirit told you to open fire on some defenceless refugees. Sounds to me like your Spirit is just another mask of the Demon."

"No!" he protested with anger and worry shivering across his face that she might just be right. "You assign your own sins to me! I am a vessel for Good! The Greater Good! It is you who are the Evil One! You who kill for sport and spite!"

"Haven't you heard? There are no good guys and bad guys Ulrich. The good guys are just bad guys who are very good at lying. We are *all* splinters of the Great Demon. You are not like me, you *are* me."

"NO! Deceiver! I am descended of Angels! That is my truth! And I shall die by it! Now kill me!"

"No," quietly denied Johanna. "You are the greater monster here than I. *That is your truth…*" She turned her back on him and started towards the river. "*Live with it.*"

Part XIII: Convergence

In time you will see that just as all rivers must reach the World Ocean. So all legends, myths, stories, and narratives, must meet together at one undeniable, irrefutable, incontrovertible, incontestable, and indisputable, Truth.

The Ferryman, Meditations of a Riverman, page 108

"Right on schedule," commented the Ferryman as she jumped aboard.

"You were expecting me?" asked Johanna as he pulled his river vessel away from the northern shore.

"Something like that," he said. "A rough estimation of how stupid the northerners are multiplied by your refined capacity for blood lust divided by Ulrich's capacity for vanity and egoism. Comes down to in and around three years."

"That's a fair calculation," conceded Johanna. "I take it that Ulrich was the Third Man?" The Ferryman gave no reply, he only smirked lowly in confirmation. "The fool wanted to raise the dead like that Omega Man you told me about. Said he wanted to end the divide between north and south that he had started in the first place, merge everything together into a new union of his own design."

"He always was the more optimistic of the three of us. Him and his Great Spirit of Manifest Destiny. He likes to think of himself as one of the Great Men of history."

"I got that alright. All because he burned the bridge between north and south."

"He always credits himself with that. But it is funny you know. On the South Side, the Doctors say that they blew the bridge to keep the unvaccinated out. But on the North Side the Cyber Czars say that the bridge was blown to keep the vaccine out."

"So, which is true then? You know both sides. Who did it?"

"I don't know actually. All I know is that it wasn't blown to keep people out. It was destroyed so that they could keep people *in.*"

"I don't follow."

"It's pretty simple really. Each side has its view of the other. Consider how those views might start to fracture if people from either side were coming and going. Pretty difficult don't you think for the Doctors to keep calling the northerners a bunch of 'primitives' when the High Council's internet is better than their own? More difficult still for the High Council to maintain the appeal of material austerity, if people could go and buy whatever they wanted on the South Side."

"Never thought of it like that. Makes sense though why I ended up being drafted as a civil slave the moment I arrived. I guess I'd be right in thinking that northern defectors end up in Disinfection Hill then, yeah? Keep the outsiders isolated. Quarantine the infection of alternative perspective." Once again, the Ferryman said nothing to confirm or dismiss her hypothesis. He just smirked and nodded lightly. He pointed up towards the broken arms of the Millennium Bridge. Bathed in the glow of the city lights from both shores, the eerie ruin hung there as a gloomy monument to the city's division.

"A long long time ago," he said. "Way before the Pandemic. This was all part of the one country. One vast empire. Didn't matter which side of the Borava River you lived on. Most people don't care for that fact. They don't care because it happened before the Pandemic and so obviously it's not relevant to their lives. They'd rather not be told that we're all part of one greater whole. But the truth is, it doesn't matter if you live on the North Pole or the South Pole, you're still on the same old Planet." He looked at Johanna directly. "Ulrich likes to think of everything in terms of positives and negatives, good and evil. But you and I and Zielenski, we know the truth of it. It's all the same thing. We're all bound to one fate, one destiny. If the red button were ever to be pushed and the whole planet was to go kaboom, it wouldn't matter which side of it you were standing on."

Just as his words soaked in on Johanna, the ferry came to a halt next to the same dock which she'd been picked up from three years earlier.

"Thank you," she said with a double meaning for both the lecture and the transport. She stepped off the vessel and turned to him. "Anything I should know that's happened here in the last three years?"

"Lockdown ended a year ago," he said as he pulled away. "I'll see you again in the after."

"See you in the after."

Part XIV: Governance

But you see, my dear Ulrich, the mantras of Citizen R have it all wrong. The Cabal as it is depicted is but another painting of the Painters and Coddlers. The true Cabal, the Rulers of the World, are those who exercise control over the wheels of Life and Death.

Correspondence from Marius Zielenski to Ulrich von Sauken

The room was stale and sterile. A cage of white-washed walls decorated with bone-pale tiles. Stiff chairs rested on unremarkable metal legs. A clock on the wall methodically ticked itself into boredom. Behind the mirroring sheet of glass, she could tell the computers were lethargically running the same old meaningless numbers for the same old clerical creatures of infinite inquisitiveness.

Johanna fidgeted with her fingers to keep herself awake. Her wrists were sore from the handcuffs they'd put on her. There were a dozen better ways of spending her time but alas she had no choice in the matter. She *had* to be here. All because of a simple misstep. One single moment of idle carelessness.

The door opened. A young police detective walked through and took the seat in front of her. He landed a stack of papers on the table in front of her.

"Detective Stefan Varga," he introduced himself as he pressed play on the recording device.

"Nice to make your acquaintance detective," retorted Johanna with a biting grin that bared her teeth to him. He looked across at her. He looked long and hard at her. A palpable smugness was all over his face. But there was also pain. And sorrow. And grief. He interlinked his fingers together and exhaled heavily.

"You were passing through security at the gates of Ward Five," he started.

"That's right. I'm a V5. I was starting my new job."

"You walked through the scanner and nothing showed up."

"The strangest thing."

"So, you walked through again…and again. And still nothing."

"Must have been an error with the software then."

"Except the system never makes mistakes. But the clerk humoured that same excuse you just gave me, and he took a small blood sample from you. Just to confirm that you were a V5 which you obviously were because no alarms were going off."

"Exactly."

"And that's when he called us. Do you know why he called the police? Do you know why you are here…Matilde von Bojna?"

"Not a notion detective. Not a notion." Stefan took a sheet of paper out from his stack of files and turned it towards her. He pointed with his finger to the rows upon rows of faces.

"This is what came up on the system when he tested your blood. Do you know who these people are?"

"I've never met any of these people in my life."

"They're all part of an ongoing investigation into the serial killer known as the Shadow. They're all either dead or missing." He wrenched out a tuft of other papers and flung them across the table in a fan of documents, all of them identical to the first. "There's the rest. There's a whole ream of others that are classed as 'unknown' on our system. So, I'd guess they're unvaccinated persons from the North Side, wouldn't you?"

"As I said," politely replied Johanna as if there was nothing amiss at all. "There must be some terrible mistake here. I'm a good law-abiding citizen."

"*Citizens,*" corrected Varga with a hiss on the 's'. He displayed a photograph before her of some corporate event. He pointed to the woman who was front and centre of the image. "This is Angelika Solovki. Look familiar?" He then showed another picture, a much older one, a mugshot school portrait of a teenage girl. "This is Johanna Reinther. Look familiar?" Johanna only smiled at him. "The system is not at fault. *You are*. We know that the Shadow was eating and drinking her victims. *You* are the Shadow. And we know it's you because we've been chasing your trail of bones for three fucking years."

Johanna only laughed at him.

"What can I say," she said, not caring what happened next. "You got me. Red handed! Literally!" Disgust and revulsion came over Stefan's face.

"Is that all you have to say? This whole city has been living in terror because of *you!* Children are still scared to go to school because of…because of what you did to Emil Bauer! And…my partner is still recovering in a mental institute because of what *you* did to his family! You fucked his life! And all you can do is laugh? You psycho bitch! Do *you* even know how many people are dead because of you? Do you have any idea of how much pain you've caused to the families of your victims? The gaping holes you've torn in their lives?"

"Life is just the absence of death detective."

"Don't fuck with me with your Zielenski-talk! Don't you fucking dare!"

"Or what? What are you going to do to me, exactly detective? You have me here in chains. Going to send me to Disinfection Hill? Send me back to Hell? The Hell you and your people built that went on to build people like me?" Stefan tensed his knuckles and breathed in deeply.

"I know where you come from," he said pointing down to the school photograph of Johanna Reinther. "I know who you were before all this. I know you were put through the meat grinder. And yeah, maybe the system was at fault for what it did to you and others like you. But nothing, *nothing*, that was done to you can possibly excuse what you did. You're a fucking monster. You're evil."

"Am I evil? Or am I just something you can't understand?"

"There's nothing to understand about a child-raping psychopath like you. You're evil. That's it!"

"Is that so? And how did that come about do you suppose?" She gestured with her eyes down to the old photograph of Johanna Reinther. "Do you think the girl in that picture was evil? Do you think I was just predestined from birth to do what I did? If you believe that then one day, it'll be one of your daughters or one of your sons that will follow after me…all by some fluke of bad genes. When you next look at all your children frolicking in the playground, you'll know that one day maybe one of them will grow up to be a paedophile psychopath that'll kill, rape, and eat all those other gorgeous little children."

Stefan gave no reply. He just sat there glaring at her. Though it was she who wore the handcuffs, it was he who was the more restrained. He wanted to kill her right now. Wanted to bludgeon her to death. But he couldn't. And it was so painfully obvious he couldn't. That made her smile.

"Maybe that's easier for you to accept," she continued. "A roll of the dice determines your place on the good and evil spectrum, because if it's not your genes then it'd have to be the environment, right? And if that was true. Well then that would mean that society as a whole, the system, is responsible for me? *You made me.* If I'm a mistake detective, then I'm the system's mistake. And if your perfect system created me once, it'll make me again and again and again. Your entire society is a factory that produces paedophiles and cannibals, detective! You think you've caught me? You'll be doing this again and again and again for the rest of your days."

"Maybe you're right," he said, clenching his fists tight together. "But it changes nothing. This is the end of the line for you. You're finished. For good. You're *not* going to Disinfection Hill. The Commission has decided in light of the evidence we've provided, that you're *not human*. The department of virology has classified you as a 'humanoid virus'. A conscious pathogen. As you may be aware, viruses do not share the basic traits of all other organisms and are technically not alive. As such they absolve themselves of their duty to preserve your life. You'll be sterilised by incineration."

"Well, well," she chuckled. "The rules are the rules until it doesn't suit them, eh? They're all for the loopholes when it suits themselves!"

"You deserve everything that's coming for you," persisted Stefan, the glint of a tear almost in his eye. "There's no hole deep enough to bury you in for the things that you did."

"I did not do anything," she grinned. "None of what you say I did was done by me, but *through* me."

"Quit the damn antics! You're responsible for these deaths and you know it! Lie to yourself all you like but don't you fucking dare lie to me! Don't you dare lie to the memory of those you killed!"

"Judge your own lies detective! You really still believe each individual is responsible for their actions? How old are you exactly? No one thinks like that. There is no soul! There isn't! There is no salvation! The human animal is just a collection of nerves and hormones and proteins. A series of inputs and outputs. Anything I am or anything I do is just a product of those inputs and outputs. Something greater than both you and I determines our actions. There is no responsibility! There is no judgement! There is no Hell! You're living in the past boychik! Living in the past! Hahahaha!"

"We're done," he said and he rose from his seat. "Fuck you!" he shouted into her face. "I hope they burn you slowly!"

"The Demon is watching you detective!" she howled after him as he walked away. "He sees you! He sees you when you're sleeping! He sees you when you're awake! So be good for goodness sake! Hahahahaha! I'll see you in the after detective! I'll see you in the after through the eyes of your children yet to be born! You'll see! Hahahahaha!"

The door shut behind Stefan. The echoes died down. The sterile stillness returned. She'd had her fun and she was alone again with her thoughts. Just as she was in the before. She'd been killed and reborn so many times now that death was a familiar colleague at this stage. She preferred it this way. This was the only way she would have wanted it to end, with them bending their own 'life is precious' mantra. In order to destroy her, they had had to destroy themselves. How many others would they now conveniently torch to death as 'humanoid viruses'?

As she sat there ruminating on her fate, the door swung open again. Two men walked through. One was an elderly doctor in a long white medical coat. The other was in his fifties perhaps, had his head shaved and was dressed in a black turtle-neck jumper. Both of them had their faces clad with enthused and eager smiles.

Something wasn't right about this. They weren't here to take her to the incinerator. They weren't here to rub victory in her face either.

"Who are you?" asked Johanna, not knowing what was going on here. The two men seated themselves down in front of her, each of them glad it seemed to be there with her.

"I am Doctor Slovenko," said the elderly doctor.

"And I'm Jozef Rabinek," said the other, adjusting his nerdy set of glasses ever so slightly. "Though you probably know me better as 'Citizen R'." Johanna's heart skipped a beat there and then.

"You're fucking with me!" was Johanna's automatic response as she looked the two men over. She stalled at Jozef. "Why the hell are you here?"

"I live here," he said in a relaxed and comfortable tone. "You didn't honestly think I'd live over on the North Side did you? That place is a shithole! I work from home here! R stands for remote working in my book!" He delivered a playful punch to Slovenko's shoulder and the Doctor emitted a boisterous little laugh. "Me and old Doc here are best pals! I love this guy!" Johanna sat there in stunned befuddlement for a second. She didn't know what to make of this.

"We're so glad to finally meet you zaychik," said Slovenko more seriously.

"Yeah I mean we've been trying to get a hold of you for ages," chimed in Citizen R. "But even for the two of us you were a hard woman to track!"

"We've been headhunting you for quite some time!" added Slovenko enthusiastically.

"Yes, well, you have me now!" retorted Johanna holding up her handcuffs to them, a little weirded out by their enthusiasm.

"Oh never mind that!" insisted Slovenko who then began to chuckle coarsely. He turned to the grinning Citizen R. "She probably thinks we're here to interrogate her!" Citizen R slapped his knee and laughed with the doctor, as if they were old friends.

"I'm sorry," said an utterly confused Johanna. "I must be missing something here. What is going on exactly? Why are the two of you here with me? Why are you two *together*?"

"Why to hire you of course," answered Slovenko in a soft and caring tone.

"Like we said, we've been headhunting you for ages," said Citizen R.

"We've seen what you can do on both the North and South Side," added Slovenko.

"And it's one hell of a portfolio you have! We're huge fans!"

"You want to *hire* me?" asked Johanna. "For what exactly?"

"For what you do dummy! The whole slasher rapist paedo thing you do!" clarified Citizen R with a big childish smile.

"Are you familiar with the Arctic Tern?" asked Slovenko. Johanna didn't answer. She just stared at him with her mouth half-open. "It spends three months of the year in the Arctic to enjoy the summer there. Then, just as autumn sets in, it starts flying south. After three months of flying south, it reaches the Antarctic. It spends three months enjoying the summer at the South Pole and then flies to the North Pole again. *That* is what you are going to be for us. You'll spend half your time here, killing, raping, and disappearing people. When word of what you're doing gets around, we'll put the place into lockdown."

"Then you'll get the Ferry to the North Side," continued Citizen R, his hands wildly gesticulating as if he were making a pitch for a fun TV show. "And do the exact same thing until people go ape-shit crazy and start killing each other. At which point you'll get the Ferry back across to the south and start the same thing all over again."

"What? Why? Why do you—" exclaimed Johanna, unable to process what was going on here.

"The Pandemic is over," said Slovenko in a frank and formal tone. "You know it, I know it, everyone knows it. Nobody has died of the virus in decades at this point. It has no relevance anymore. There's no need any more for the rule of doctors or conspiracy theorist internet demagogues. You've seen it on both sides of the river. People have had enough. They know we don't belong. They want to move on."

"So why not give it to them?" asked Johanna dumbfoundedly. "Go back to the way things used to be for heaven's sake! Democracy, freedom of speech, the whole thing!" Citizen R and Slovenko just laughed at that suggestion.

"You think we haven't considered it?" Citizen R said. "But no can do I'm afraid. We're too far gone from those days. Even if there was a smooth transition, do you really think they'd let us get away with what we did? There's too much blood on both our hands. Besides, even if we did go back to the way it was, nobody knows how to run a country like that anymore. Compromise? Mediation? Equality? Liberty? Due process? Come on! We all know those things don't mean anything anymore. Bureaucracy used to be a mess of conflicting interests. Public interests, private interests, special interests, corporate interests, et cetera et cetera! Now it's just one interest. Ours. It all flows in one direction now."

"There's only one way we know how to run this place," informed Slovenko. "And that's fear. We need to keep people afraid. So long as the people were more afraid of the virus than they were of us, they'd put up with us. Better the devil you know than the devil you don't as they say. But without the fear of death, there's no need to tolerate us. A population that doesn't fear death is one that won't pay its bills and taxes. That's why *you,* zaychik, are the new Pandemic."

"Or Plandemic," suggested Citizen R jestfully. "Depends on what way you look at it. But in a nutshell, you see what we mean. We need to keep everyone terrified. We want cowards under our roof. We don't want people to be brave or courageous. It would screw everything up. Any brave people that do exist, they already work for us, like Ulrich von Sauken."

"And the Varga family," added Slovenko. "And even them we keep on a tight leash. We want everyone to be dumb, stupid, cowardly, and weak. Dependent and reliant on us to save them from any trouble that befalls them."

"And truth be told," said Citizen R with honesty coursing through him. "And, as you probably already know yourself, the people were already a bunch of dumb, stupid, idiots to begin with. We just want to make sure it stays that way, because, a few truth bombs detonated over them and well, you see what kind of chaos and confusion that can cause! I mean if it wasn't for you, God only knows how things would be with those dissenters running the show!"

"Thanks to you we've been able to keep them docile and scared!" acknowledged Slovenko with genuine gratitude. "If it weren't for you, why, both sides of the Borava would probably be a heap of ruins by now. That's why *we want you!* You complete us! You bring the whole system into a perfectly balanced equilibrium! We'll form a single all-powerful triumvirate! A synthesis of healers, tricksters, and reapers if you will! Now don't worry about Varga or von Sauken! We'll give you a new identity and fake your incineration here. All expenses, including the Ferry fees will be paid for of course. And in addition to all that, you'll have the best of healthcare, the best Wi-Fi, the best of every luxury you could ever wish for! You'll get to do what you love every day and get paid for it!"

"So!" said Citizen R clapping his hands together. "What do you say? Will you accept our offer for the dream job of a lifetime? Will you join us? You've been a wolf among the sheep for long enough, don't you think? Time for you to join the wolves in shepherds' clothing!"

Part XV: (Un)Prescience

Long they spoke and pondered of this New Normal.
And the People they did both Love it and Fear it.
For as they loved the brave Face of this New World.
So, they feared the Teeth it bared to their Old World.
But ever they failed to see it was the Normal they had known all along.

The Ferryman, 'Sonnets from the River Borava', page 47

"So, that's it then," said Johanna as the Ferryman took her back across to the North Side after her 'job interview' with the world rulers. "No more job applications. No more prostituting myself to the highest corporate bidder. It was all a waste of time. All I had to do was just kill enough people and they'd come to me offering the highest job in the land? And here I was thinking the system had it out to get me."

"That's how it works," said the Ferryman, his ghostly eyes shining in the scream of the twilight sky. "Sooner or later, everyone becomes a cog in the great super-machine."

"That's what happened to you," said Johanna. "Isn't it? That's how you're still on the go."

"I take unvaccinated people across to the North Side," he openly confessed. "And, because they're outsiders, they end up as civil slaves. I take some civil slaves then and, because they're unvaccinated, they end up in Disinfection Hill. A simple swap from one oppressor to another. But it serves the interests of the powers that be. Looks good for propaganda that a certain amount of people 'defect' to the other side every now and then. It helps convince everyone that the people on the other side of the river have it worse off."

"And round and round the cycle goes. Tell me, as a fellow cog in the system, what do you do with your infinite income? How do you pass the time? And why do you still insist on coins? Surely you could go cashless!"

The Ferryman smiled in the turquoise light of the evening and picked up his jar of coins. He clawed one out and walked across the deck to an old jukebox and slotted the coin in. The wheels and cogs of this antique machine turned and writhed into life and of a sudden the voice of Paul Robeson singing *Ol Man River* crackled aloud.

"It only takes coins," said the Ferryman before Johanna could ask any questions and he returned to his station at the stern of his vessel.

"So Zielenski was right then," said Johanna more reflectively as the crackly old song rippled over the river waters. "There really is no future. There is only the here and the now. One vast cycle of death regurgitating itself over and over."

"Yep," agreed the Ferryman stoically taking out a cigarette and looking down at her. "But not as you might imagine it. You seem to think there's also no past."

"There isn't," she insisted. "There is no origin to anything. I have no beginning and no ending. I just am."

"Really? And yet from everything I've heard, you've been caught every time on account of that same past. The ghost of Johanna Reinther just keeps on coming back to haunt you. Every time that girl appears in photographs you try to destroy her. You lean in deeper and deeper to the monster you've become. But it's still there. You can't escape your past. Just like the city can't escape it either."

He took a deep drag of his cigarette and puffed the smoke out through his nostrils. "There is no future," he said. "Precisely because there *is* a past. A world that can't escape the nightmare of the past is a world that has no future…We're all on an old videotape, stuck on repeat, looping round and round. Every new chapter we live through, rhymes with the one that came before it…And in that world, nothing can evolve or develop, nothing can truly live and nothing can die. Children can never grow and elders can never die. It all just gets recycled one way or another. And anything bold and novel and radical that does come along just suffocates in the shadow of the past and forms a fresh layer of decay that never fully decomposes."

"Everything that came before the start of the shadow, doesn't mean anything. Anyone who still talks about 'going back to normal' is just kidding themselves. Just nostalgia for the glory days of the Lost World…You can't turn back the clocks. No one can. The ink is already dry. The world that came before is dead and gone. Anyone who tries to resurrect it only finds themselves in the dark of the shadow again…*We all live in the Shadow of the Pandemic.* It is not we who cast the shadow, but the shadow that casts us. And there is no escape from it. Until a darker shadow overtakes it…"

Johanna buried her face in her hands and sighed deeply into herself. She knew he was right. She knew she was living in her own shadow. Wherever she went, whatever she did, it would follow her. Like a bad dream that could never be shaken off. But that wouldn't stop her trying to cover up and destroy it. She was doomed to keep running away from it, to keep embracing the Demon.

She looked back and forth from north to south. She was the virus now. She was the Cabal. And because of that, the Pandemic would continue. As if it had never ended.

"How long?" she asked rhetorically. "It's decades since it all began. Since…since that invisible germ, an organism that has no awareness of its own existence, came along and turned the world upside down! It's come and gone and yet its ghost is still dictating how we live our lives. How long do you think? How long do you think its shadow can stretch?"

The Ferryman looked at the Borava River on whose familiar watery shoulders he cruised.

"A long time ago," he said. "Back when I was a boy, that is, there was an accident upriver. An oil tanker ran aground, and all its cargo leaked out. River went black. You'd stick your fingers into the water, and you'd feel it burning your skin. You could barely breathe it, never mind get any fishing done. So, my father and I, we decided to take our boat downstream, away from the spillage. But lo and behold, we kept on finding the oil shining on the water surface. It got thinner and thinner the farther we went till one day, we came to a spot where there was no sign of it at all."

"And that was the last time we went looking for clear water, because we knew that it had broken down so much that there were particles and atoms of it everywhere. It was in all the fish. All the reeds and the willows and the lilies had soaked it up in their roots. It had permeated through everything. We didn't see it, but we knew, that the pollution had slithered through the whole river, that it went all the way down the Borava…all the way to the point where there was no river at all and there's just the abyss of the sea… *That's how long this Shadow will last.*"

"Yep," said Johanna. "That's what I thought. Just wanted to check."

"Yeah…I know."

The Ferryman took one last puff of his cigarette and flicked it overboard into the Borava. The twilight shrunk beneath the watery river horizon of the Borava. Night descended.

And the Shadow rose again.

End of Tape—Press Play to Watch Again

CPSIA information can be obtained
at www.ICGtesting.com
Printed in the USA
BVHW051448301222
655313BV00009B/1122